shadows ascend

By B.K. Cavaleri

The
VOLTAM
VAGARI
SHEOL
EITHNE

SLOTH
Gluttony
VAGARI
WRATH
HELL
The Well of
Souls
GREED
PRIDE
LUST
ENVY

shadows Ascend

Book Two of Remnant Archives

Trilogy

By B.K. Cavaleri

 Evangeline Press

INTRODUCTION

A hungry power that threatens all existence.
A realm where death is the only way.
A shadow that quivers, a shifter that flickers.
A well of souls they need to brave.

***

Only weeks after the shifter Emon forced her out of her one hundred years of exile, Remnant Ezra Solaire Dark, the last shadow fae, finds herself on a perilous path within the land of the dead. In a world of gods, demons, and spirits, Remnant must determine who to trust as she fights for the fate of her people. Together with her soulmate Emon and their newfound family, she faces higher stakes than ever before—a battle not just for their lives but for their very souls and all those of Faerie. They will stop at nothing to find redemption and save those they love, even traveling to the depths of Hell where sacrifice and death are inevitable.
But Remnant is haunted by her failure to save her people in the past, and with even more on the line, will she be able to conquer not only her enemies but her own fears? – And can Emon save her without losing himself?
May the shadows keep you safe in this second installment of Remnant Archives, Shadows Ascend.

Content & Trigger Warnings

This is a dark fantasy romance with themes of language, violence, sexual assault, mentioning of rape, infantile death, maternal death in pregnancy, loss of parent, and infertility complications. Your mental health is important to me, please read TW thoroughly and I am open for clarifications if needed.

Dedication

For all the times when you wanted to tell death
"fuck you".

SHEOLS PROPHECY

Beware, behave
Darkness takes your life away.
To the city of death
Where love is regret
The end of your soul.
Lives within the Sheol.
Beware, behave
The darkness you will obey.
Beware behave,
Night will lead the way.
An old power rises as the fair one weakens,
Golden becomes the one true beacon,
Blood will run on the darkened moons,
Run child run, I will see you soon.
Beware, Behave
May the shadows keep you safe.

JOURNAL
EXCERPT

Gerald S. Gio,

Former Head Researcher of The National Fertility Institute.

Saturday, December 12th, 2158

I wish the golden one would have killed me or that I could have run faster like he suggested...

I don't even know how I am still alive. Every day I have etched a mark deep into the stone floor. There were 33,935 marks when I finally achieved what she asked of me. I've done the math, I know what that means...I am now over one hundred and thirty three years old, yet I haven't aged a day since I was abducted by that black eyed bastard and delivered to the feet of his silver haired goddess, the Former Queen of Faerie.

I didn't think I had much to live for after I realized I would never be returning home. My wife has most assuredly passed on and likely my children too. There's nothing left for me back on Earth, nor would I want to be reminded of the life stolen from me. There's no place for me anymore...a human scientist turned immortal, everything I once believed unethical and morally wrong skewed into the shades of gray like the cell I rot in.

But after a few decades of numbness, I have been able to rise above my crippling depression. Whether it be from years of building hatred or utter self preservation, I work through the night, in a lab made just for me—for with all her power, she has been unsuccessful in creating new life. One monster after another she creates over and over again. I tell myself this is my form of redemption, my way of finally rectifying a wrong. The golden ones roaring and the dark ones screams, still haunting me as I work, remembering them sends me into an inspired feverish madness, the same one as my silver haired captor.

May whoever reads this understand my deeds and pray for my damned soul. For I have given her exactly what she wanted, a fae child, born from a lab with the specimens saved, before my colleagues and facility were destroyed.

But I did not alter her make-up like my captor wanted me to...no I created a new fae species with the very genetics my captor despises. A tiny beautiful miracle and now it's my turn to protect her. Amazingly, science has a wonderful way of confusing even the most cunning and I weaponized it to perfection, convincing the queen that her new ward needed time to assimilate in a natural environment to fully change. Away from this horrible place—an escape that I will never have.

No, for me only the pits of hell beckon. I look forward to it. Any place is better than here.

PROLOGUE

Remnant

Two Thousand and Forty Years Ago: Post Blood Wars

"Oh my chickadee, what have you done?" My mother's sorrowful tone was like poison in my veins, burning and searing, and the disapproval on her regal face was the bitter aftertaste of that poison.

Standing behind her, in shadows that flickered in and out, my brother Kade's disappointment was more direct—it's sharp sting stealing my breath from my lungs, leaving behind nothing but a sickening ache.

Opening and closing my mouth, I was momentarily lost for words before the anger set in. Gritting my teeth, I raised my chin. "I have done nothing wrong. You said yourself that I needed to come here, the sight *saw* me here. Maybe this was what it was for." My shadows wrapped around me, their darkness soothing the gaping wound of my family's reproach.

I knew what my mother was thinking, I was young, just barely past my centum—fully recognized as an adult fae and no longer a faeling, I was also untried. Except now that I was fresh out of my final stages of training, I was tired of being locked away from the Blood Wars. I wanted to heal this land, banish the haunting ghosts the Blood Wars had created within the souls of all our people, and restore us back to our former glory. But more importantly, I wanted to protect the remaining shreds of my family and court.

Staying in the City of Light allowed that and my oath finalized it.

"You would align yourself with *her*...abandon your own court," Kade spat, his face full of dark anger.

Kade would never understand my decision. He was still a baby in the fae's eyes. My brother loved the City of Night and all of the shadow fae court. He would be an excellent leader to our people one day and I was immensely proud of him, but there was nothing for me in our homeland, nothing that I could add by staying.

Ever since I was born, I had either been admired or feared for the shadows I wielded. My power was isolating just as much as it was revered, and so an outsider I became. It did not take my mother's seer ability to know that this great power, unknown in its origin, was meant for something more, and if using it to protect my family was one way of achieving this then so be it.

Biting back the words I wanted to say, knowing they would not be accepted, I steeled myself against Kade's anger and glared back. *Play the game Rem.* "I have given my oath already and accepted the position as the Queen's War General."

"Your oath—your oath was to our own court!" Kade hissed. He took a threatening step forward but my mother's hand reached out, stopping him, her green ringed sapphire eyes never leaving mine.

I held her gaze. I would not be made to feel less. I knew what I was goddess damn doing.

Pursing her lips she shook her head, her long dark hair falling around her delicate and petite frame, moving like the shadows that rolled off her in the moonlight of the City of Light. "This path you take, it is a dark one."

Bristling and hurt that my mother could not see my true intentions, I snapped. "Your *sight* has been wrong before. You saw that I should have been in Atlantis, to save it, and look how that turned out. I couldn't even save them all, let alone the city, and I barely escaped with my own life doing it. *All because your sight said so.*"

My mother didn't often flinch at biting words, she never showed weakness, and she never ever revealed her sadness even though Kade and I both knew she suffered. Unable to remember the fae she loved but knowing that a huge piece of her soul was somewhere out there, lost.

But this time she did, her face paling and her shadows sucking into her as the breath left her lungs, never exhaling.

Kade snarled, pulling her into his warm embrace and glaring at me through sudden hate filled eyes.

Eyes that spoke of abandonment and betrayal.

How could they not understand?

And just like that, the poison was quick, killing and severing the relationship between me and my remaining family. A sacrifice I was willing to make if it meant they were safe.

"So be it," my mother whispered in the cocoon of my brother's arms, a broken look on her face that I knew would haunt me for years to come. "We will always be here for you and we love you, my little chickadee."

Then they were gone, shifting through the shadows.

I watched silently as the shadows settled, revealing the moonlit glow of the city's splendor, and my hands fisted at my sides. Finally, releasing the words I had refrained from saying.

"I am doing this for you because I love you too," I whispered brokenly into the night.

For my mother was not the same, the shadow court was not the same, and I was one of the few fae left that was not constantly haunted by the ghosts of a war. Being in the crown's favor was the best way to ensure their survival, I was sure of it.

***

"Mother?"

I watched the low sun sparkle over my mother's bronze skin as she stood on the newly built balcony my father and I had constructed for her. Following her gaze eastward, I could see that evening's darkness was spreading across the valley as the day surrendered to the night. There was something so peacefully calm yet foreboding about it tonight. As if the night was here to stay, blanketing us in armor for what would come next.

Queen Skylar of the shifters turned towards me, her light brown hair swept to the side in an intricate braid falling over her exposed shoulder, her stunning caramel eyes softening with happiness, replacing the worry I had seen there moments before.

"Daemon." She held her arms out to me and I took them. I had grown much since the aftermath of the Blood Wars, now a fae in my centum years, I towered over my mother, forcing her to tilt her head high in order to meet my eyes.

"When did my cub become so handsome and so tall I wonder?" She reached up on her tiptoes and swept my hair back from my face.

Grinning cheekily, I took the queen's hand and kissed it softly in greeting. "I have you to thank for that, mother." I gave her a shrewd look. "But all mothers would say that to their sons I believe. Flattery won't change what I just saw no matter how much you attempt to mask it. What ails you? The blood wars are over, our people are happy again, hopeful with the building of Finlandia, and yet I find you standing here as if death is upon our doors."

She sniffed, her brows drawn. "I should rephrase. When did my cub become more like his father?"

I wrinkled my crooked nose. "Now that's just insulting, mother."

"You should be so lucky, fairy boy." My cat retorted.

I growled.

"Whatever that nuisance of a panther is saying to you, ignore it my son," she said, reading my irritation. Sighing, she dropped my hand and turned back to the east. "You must learn to school your thoughts better and shield your anger at your beast Daemon. You both are stuck with each other. The more you learn to tolerate one another the better off you will be, especially as you enter the courts of the fae."

I stepped next to her tilting my head in thought. "You don't like the panther either, why?"

Baring her teeth, she hissed, "Of course I don't. He took my son from me for weeks before you shifted back. A being of his power should have better control."

The beast inside of me growled but he did not speak, staying blessedly quiet.

We were both silent for a moment as the night finally shrouded over us and the three moons lit the valley in a soft glow.

"Why am I so different?" I whispered, watching the shadows ripple as the grasses blew in the soft night wind. Something about them intrigued me...almost called to me.

My mother shook her head, leaning against my shoulder. "I wish I could answer that for you my cub but I cannot. Perhaps it is time we look at this as a blessing. The goddess knew you would need each other one day."

"If only she would come back so that I could ask her. Why would she help us and then abandon us?"

"We are but mere pawns in the hands of the goddess, Daemon, but Faerie would not abandon us in our need. I fear...I fear it is more than that. Something we are missing, something we have forgotten."

I exhaled harshly and looked down to see the worried wrinkles return on her beautiful face. "You don't think it is over with, do you?"

She pursed her lips. "The other courts have relinquished their rule. Faerie crowns a new queen to rule over all...only we stand apart, only we have not bowed to Deirdre Seelie and she is not a fae to be refused nor ignored, Daemon Ash Strider."

I scoffed. "Father would never put our people in unnecessary harm and there is an entire sea that separates us from her reaches. Not to mention Shen's wall."

My mother took a deep breath and stretched her hand out to the approaching glow of a violet wisp. It snuggled into her palm, humming and pulsing with pleasure at her gentle touch. "Never underestimate a fae that has not taken a moment to grieve, my cub. A heart that does not grieve never loved, and if a heart does not love it only has one purpose. Hate." She shook her head. "Deirdre suffered the most out of us all during the blood wars, events that would have brought even your father to his knees and yet...not a single tear has she shed. Instead, she celebrates by attaining power and a crown. A dangerous and dark path to take."

Reaching out, I scooped the wisp from my mothers hand, and released it back into the night. "Love, hate, it matters not, I won't allow any harm to befall us, mother. We will not bow down to her darkness should she walk that path."

She grew quiet then while we watched the wisp disappear into the hills of the valley. When its glow finally twinkled out of sight, she turned towards me, standing on her tiptoes again to kiss my cheek. "I hope you are right Daemon." She whispered softly, then walked away, back into our new home. Pausing, she peered back over me, her caramel eyes softening. "But know this my cub, sometimes—sometimes you can't always stop the darkness from spreading. Like the night...sometimes you just have to submit and unleash it in order to fight against it."

CHAPTER 1

Remnant

M Y DARKNESS WAS DEATH—SO I never feared it. Wielded it, delivered it, sought it, goddess damn begged for it....but never, ever, feared it.

And now...I stepped a foot inside of it—*alive.*

Bathed in twilight, Sheol was awash with vibrant fluorescent hues where the endless cosmos of the universe met the land. Swirling galaxies, faraway planets, numerous glowing moons, and millions upon millions of stars graced the very air around us---so close we could breathe it, touch it, taste it. And mirroring its surroundings above, a pure silver pathway snaked its way through vast and eerily shifting white sands. Like a haunting song, the sand's constant ebb and flow crested to form white phantoms, beckoning us with the promise of dark, sinful secrets—all we needed to do was dive in.

Where the white phantoms did not appear, lights flickered...like faraway beacons guiding us towards a destination that was not ours but seductively inviting just the same.

Sensing this, our group converged closer upon the reflective silver path, keeping distance between us and the soothing, yet deceptive, cascade of rustling sand.

My lips twitched at our fearsome bunch being cautious over shifting dunes, surprised to see that even Bane stepped inward. A stoic swordmaster and fire elemental with a grumpy attitude and loyal heart, he trailed reluctantly behind us.

Shifting my gaze, I watched Xi and Riley, earth and air elementals and my dearest friends, palm their blades, watching the sand warily. In unison they flanked our sides, just as they had always done—always true, always steadfast.

Whispered words drew my attention back to the front where Penina leaned towards Tyr, making them both laugh at whatever joke she had passed on. A shifter assassin for the The West Isle throne, Penina kept her deepest secrets close to her heart, hiding them behind her bubbly personality.

Opposite of her, Tyr laid out all his secrets bare just like the artwork of tattoos covering his entire body. A tiger shifter and Emon's best friend, as well as the general to the crown, his ego knew no bounds, just like his mouth and the pretty white tiger he hid inside.

And then there was Asher, one glance back at him and I knew his hand twitched to slap the inappropriate smirk right off Tyr's face. As my soulmate's father and former king of the shifters, Asher's silent strength prowled, ever watchful of the death god that guided us down this eerie path.

Turning back, I narrowed my eyes on my newfound *father* as well. I did not trust Shea, the god of death, and that distrust made my hand quiver—aching for the shadows and the comfort their protection would bring us while we ventured into the realm of the dead. No longer able to save us, the shadows were lost to the power of the Sanguine, and their absence was like losing an extension of myself, leaving behind tiny whispers of doubt.

What was I good for now, without them?

"We will get them back." Emon's soothing voice called to me, interrupting the immensity of my self doubt, his golden gaze also narrowed on the god in front of us, while our daughter, Riella, marched along, innocently ignorant of the dangers we faced.

Additional worry gnawed at my already grief stricken heart. How was I to protect her without the shadows on my side?

Being the first fae child to be born since the Blood Wars, she was a goddess blessed miracle, a priceless gift that I would protect with my last dying breath, and without my power, I feared this would be my resulting fate. Leaving her behind in a cruel broken world.

A world that she blindly explored without any recognition of the true monsters lying in wait. Her beautiful innocent acceptance and lack of knowledge of the fae was dangerous, even more so now, no longer being hidden in the deep waters of The Under.

Perhaps she would have been safer if I had left her there.

My teeth ground with frustration at this new thought, causing my jaw to ache along with my heart that was already drowning in emotional turmoil—no longer frozen to the world.

"The shadows are not our priority right now," I called out to Emon, glancing back down at our daughter. *"Riella's safety is."*

"Agreed." Emon's voice rumbled in my mind but I did not miss his worried glance and the sharp tug he gave the clothing the death god had dressed him in.

Lifting my chin, I summoned the indifferent mask I had perfected over my years of court life, locking away the anxious worries that plagued me.

Play or be played.

This was the game.

"Fear not, Sheol welcomes you, daughter," the death god called over his shoulder, misreading my blank expression and our converging group as worry.

The ache in my jaw renewed and I half wondered if I would make it out of Sheol with any teeth at all so fierce was my grinding. "I do not relish that death welcomes me, and I care nothing for this realm besides wanting to know why you insisted we come here."

"All in good time, my little chickadee."

Our group stilled and my mask fell as I stared hard at the death god's back, my lips peeling away from my teeth. "Call me that again and I will make sure it will be your last."

Shea's ring-adorned hand flashed in the cosmic light, as if my threat was merely a temper tantrum of no significance. "Someday you will understand exactly why I can, daughter. Now listen carefully, for this is your first lesson in learning your birthright you are so eager to deny."

I moved quickly, not needing the shadows to bring this asshole down, my anger and training would be enough, god or not. But a strong hand suddenly yanked me back and I spun, my hair whipping across my face only to meet a very different pair of golden eyes than what I was used to. Shea's continued monologue was lost in the background as I silently snarled straight into Asher's face.

The wolf shifter's grip tightened on my shoulder when I attempted to wrench away and he shook his head quietly, sandy blonde hair flying around him like wisps in the darkness. Darting his eyes back to the death god, he returned his golden gaze pointedly, tapping his hand to his ear.

Lips thinning, I easily registered what he was attempting to say—*listen and learn first.*

It still didn't mean I had to goddess damn like it.

When my arms folded across my chest, he smirked back, finally releasing his hold and patting my arm affectionately.

Turning back around, the twinkling sparkle in Emon's eyes was bright in my periphery. *"Now you know what it was like for me growing up with a truth seeker,"* he purred in my mind.

"Just...shut up shifter," I growled back.

Soft laughter of delight echoed in my head. *"I always fucking love that I can make you at a loss for rational words, my little umbra."*

I focused on the towering back of the death god. *"There is something wrong with you, shifter."*

"Are you listening, daughter?" Shea glared over his shoulder, shadows darkening over his face.

I could feel Asher's strong gaze at my back, warning me to not take his bait. "Sheol is not just the realm of the dead. It is the afterlife for all of Faerie's creations." I repeated his last sentence, my eyes narrowing on him, imagining what it would be like to send him into a true afterlife while ignoring the very obvious fact that in a moment's notice, he could swallow us up whole and I would have no way of stopping him.

Just then, I resented him more than I ever thought possible.

Glancing down at my own progeny, swinging her hand in Emon's hold, I wondered if she would one day feel the same about me?

I shook off the feeling, now was not the time for self doubt despite it currently running rampant inside.

"Yes. That is correct and what you see before you is Eithne," Shea continued, facing forward again with a proud smile that belonged on the face of a real father, not the god in front of me.

I glanced back over my shoulder at Asher with a hard glare, but he merely grinned, tapping his ear. Sensing the twitching smiles of the others and hearing another chuckle enter my mind from my soulmate, I rolled my eyes before schooling my face again, listening to the prattling of the death god and the hidden words he wasn't saying.

"This world is where souls come once their physical lives have been extinguished, but not all get to experience this side of it," he continued on like a goddess damn tour guide. "Like all things this world must have balance." The white sands arched up around him, siren-like in their evocative waves, and our group stepped closer towards Riella.

"What is the Eithne?" my daughter called out from between all the protective legs of her family, suddenly acutely aware of the conversation around her.

I frowned, glancing at the loyal fae who guarded her devotedly. Did I really consider them family now? It had been so long since I had any, that I almost didn't recognize it.

"Yes. We are your family," Emon's voice whispered inside my mind, reading me easily. *"You are mine, I am yours. Which means you will be getting all my baggage too. Will you still have me knowing this?"* he teased, but I could also detect the vulnerability in his question.

I shot him a glare but could not hold it fully. *"Does it mean I have to share you, because I do not like to share."*

"So I have experienced before, but that was with pastry...are you telling me that I am finally equivalent to your favored treat?" He purred softly in my mind.

That sound...goddess that sound, sent shivers down my spine and he knew it. His solid, powerful frame standing proudly and straighter within the light of low flying comets.

"The Eithne," the death god answered gently to my daughter while giving me a backwards look of annoyance, reading Emon and I's exchange easily, setting him off balance and placing the game more in my favor, "is a place of solace where a soul is able to rest peacefully and live out their purest pleasures without the burden and strife the world of the living causes."

"Wow," Riella gasped, leaning eagerly forward, reaching out to the white sands, stretching Emon's arm with her.

Captured by her stunning innocence and her swirling green gold eyes, I watched as she tracked the galaxies above, her long wild tendrils of blue black hair falling away from her cherubic face, her bronze skin shimmering in the twilight.

"Look." She pointed, her soft musical voice a command none of us could ignore.

Heads raised in unison, we all watched in stunning silence as hundreds of stars shot across the sky, raining colorful dust upon our upturned faces, falling silkily over our bodies in a sparkling shimmer.

Releasing her hold on Emon, Riella reached upwards, cupping her hands to gather the stardust with bright curiosity.

"Taste it, granddaughter," the death god coaxed her softly, sending more dust into her cupped hands.

Both Emon and I instantly latched onto her arms, shattering her enchantment and stopping her from leaning in to taste the stardust.

"No," we both growled, glancing at each other with reluctant amusement before turning towards the laughing death god, fury igniting in our eyes.

In one second, I pictured a hundred different ways I could eliminate that smile off his face.

"I promise you it is safe, daughter. See," he said ignoring our glares, gathering some of his own glittering dust and licking it. "Mine tastes like strawberries and cream."

Riella squealed with excitement planting her face head first into the pile of dust before we could stop her.

"Riella," I admonished but she could no longer hear me, squealing again and licking eagerly at her hands.

Catching Emon's worried look, he sighed. *Our cub trusts far too easily for this world.*

Glancing down at her, she laughed loudly, looking up at me with her face smeared in stardust. "It tastes like dragon fruit!"

I released her arm when her tongue came dangerously close to slobbering my own body. *I know.*

"It will put her in more danger but—" his lips twitched watching her lap up the dust like a kitten, *"I find I do not want her to be any other way, I want to protect this side of her—a side the fae lost a long time ago."*

Sighing softly, I whispered back in his mind. *"Me too but she must learn, Emon. She may not always have us."*

Emon frowned but before he could answer, Riella shoved by him, reaching with enthusiastic hunger for more stardust, her other hand now entirely in her mouth.

Snorts and chuckles soon followed while she skipped around us all with her newest addiction.

Even the death god laughed softly, watching her with softness in his jeweled eyes that I wish I did not see. "As I said, this is Eithne," his voice rumbled around us. "Everything here is meant to bring you joy and pleasure. Especially for my one and only granddaughter."

I pursed my lips with distaste and Emon growled low, reflecting my own thoughts. I couldn't even tolerate him calling me daughter...let alone claiming my child that I had only learned was mine just days prior.

Asher snorted with amusement behind us. "Reminds me of the first time Daemon experienced pastries."

Penina's eyes glittered, looking over her shoulder at me, winking. "That's all we need, another pastry pinching royal."

Emon snickered. "I am not entirely sure I can claim my cub's sweet tooth origins, Nina. I do believe her mother is far worse than I." A sudden smoldering gleam burned brightly in his eyes, ensnaring me just as easily as the stardust did with our daughter. But unlike her, I needed no stardust to be fully addicted to my soulmate. All he had to do was look at me like he was now and I'd succumb to my own selfish desires to possess him. *"You are covered in candied stardust my little umbra...and it tastes just like you."* He licked his lips for emphasis and I felt my legs weaken with his meaning. *"Don't you dare clean up before we get a chance to be alone. I plan to lap up the galaxies from your exquisite body and even then it won't compare to the real thing, so of course I will have to have that too."*

My legs gave way, unable to stay upright at the seductive purr Emon sent, enhanced by our new bond, I was unprepared for its magnitude. Multiple hands reached out to steady me and I hissed with embarrassed aggravation.

How could this shifter steal my very gravity with flowery words and a well timed purr when I was once the most feared being of Faerie?

"I'm fine." My lips pressed together and I shook their hands off.

Retaliating at the smug look he delivered, I sent him my own image of exactly how I would want him as he lapped the stardust from my body. Naked, on his knees, peering up at me while I threaded my hands tightly in his hair, a sharp command on my lips. *"Lick."*

Gasps sent everyone stumbling and reaching for one another this time, except for Riella who was still skipping happily collecting her dragon fruit flavored stars.

Tyr's laughter suddenly boomed in the twilight sky, doubling over in his mirth and Penina covered her mouth with a giggle, her deep brown eyes glittering back at me, while the others around us cleared their throats and looked away.

Suddenly nervous watching them, I licked my lips whispering. "Goddess please tell me I didn't say that out loud?" This day was getting far worse, evidently I was a kaleidoscope of emotions and lacked control.

The death god whirled on me then, his beautiful pale face constricted with darkness and disapproval. "Might I suggest you learn to use your soulmate bond appropriately, daughter," he hissed. "You did not say it out loud, rather you projected it to all of our minds. You'll thank me for sparing your daughter of such imagery before it reached her too!"

My eyes widened with dread before the world suddenly blurred and I blinked into Emon's burning gold eyes, blazing with heat and full of fierce devoted love.

I looked away with embarrassment coloring my cheeks.

"Don't," he purred, tilting my chin up to meet the swirling desire in his eyes. "Don't you dare be ashamed, Remnant Dark. You have no idea how sexy that just was. Claiming me for all to know, even if it was an accident. I wouldn't care if the whole universe knew that this is how you bring me happily to my knees, a king, kneeling to worship you." Kissing my lips softly, he groaned, swiping his tongue across them again. "Fuck, the glory of the stars taste good on you, little umbra."

I sighed. "You cannot mean that, shifter. My lack of control is a weakness we cannot afford." I was quickly becoming a liability.

He growled low and gripped my chin, forcing me to meet his stern resolve. "Then we will get stronger at it, but know this my love. Our bond is no weakness, it is our truest strength." Kissing me again, he stepped away with a mischievous shrug. "A strength that now your father knows the true meaning of."

"Indeed, is that what this little show is about?" boomed the death god. "You are mistaken if you think I'll allow this in my realm, shifter king."

Emon didn't bother to turn around to look at the death god, his eyes watching my reaction with feral intensity while I attempted to peer around him, seeing our family circling Shea with a precise formation.

The shifters had transformed, the elementals were poised with their power flowing around them, including Bane who had lightning flashing in his ice blue eyes. Riella sat confusedly perched on Asher's shaggy wolf, her stardust forgotten.

"I don't give a fuck if this is your realm, Shea. I've had enough of you and your fucking games. I have listened to you stake your claim as the father of my mate without permission, call her chickadee without her consent, ignore her demands on why you have brought us here, laughed at the protection she provided her daughter, and now you dare to chastise her as if she is a faeling to scold. As far as I am concerned, you are fucking lucky you're still standing." Claws unsheathed from his hands, Emon continued to watch me as his golden eyes burned brightly with power. "My mate and our queen may be patient with your disrespect, but I sure as goddess fuck am not, it is time to give us the answers we seek *death god.*"

Shea snorted but I did not hear his retort, one word ringing in my ears, loudly bouncing around in my head. "Queen…" I breathed.

"Queen of the shifter fae." Emon stepped closer, cupping my face, his burning warmth spreading all the way to my toes. "It's also part of my baggage, little umbra."

I leaned into his hand, not knowing what to say.

Sardonic laughter that sent chills down my spine erupted from the death god. "Queen? You insult my daughter, shifter king. She is more than your puny crown can hold, she's a goddess. Goddess of The Well of Souls."

Emon turned, fangs bared.

Dark shadows shifted across the death god's face. "I tire of this."

A swift flick of his hand had the white sands circling around us and within its granular swirl, and white hooded warriors rose from its depths. At the same time shadows from the cosmos above descended, their dark purpose obvious and I wasn't about to watch it happen—not again.

Stepping past my growling soulmate, I had but moments to study his manipulation of the shadows before I stretched my hands out, my heart thudding in my chest.

I could do this.

The darkness would respond, they had to respond, my new-found family depended on it...I depended on it.

I shot the death god a glare, "This is not just your world anymore," I whispered, wrenching the night sky from his hold and taking back control of my life.

CHAPTER 2

Remnant

I STOLE THE NIGHT from the death god—the darkened twilight sky, one massive shadow, and I bent it to *my* will.

Barely.

I could feel the strain, the threads slipping between my fingers, the shadows rebelling against my command, and the harder I held them the weaker the darkness became.

And Shea knew it.

His emerald eyes watched me, glittering with mocking amusement and a flicker of pride.

"Go on then, little chickadee, bend them, use them against me," his deep otherworldly voice taunted, rings flashing as he waved at me to continue.

Baring my teeth, I hissed through them, ignoring the bead of sweat on my temple. "I will not stoop to your level, death god. If you had ever been the father you claim to be, you would have known that I am no faeling, and I play by my own set of rules now.

So you can take back your darkness." Flinging the shadows back into the cosmos, I withheld the sigh and ignored the fact that I had truly lost all my power, "I never needed it anyway and I definitely don't now."

Stepping backwards, I allowed my friends to converge on him, taking Riella off of the back of Asher's wolf in my retreat—something I had never done before, but my daughter was the most important thing now, not my ego.

Emon slid in front of us and I caught his flickering worry for me before his fangs descended and claws bared in a protective stance. Growling, he commanded Penina's leopard and Tyr's tiger with that singular sound to prowl around the death god.

"Xi." I did not need to evoke a command, we had battled together long enough that I valued her quick decision making and keen strategy. She was a cunning earth elemental and that would hold true today when with just a flick of her hand, the white sand warriors threatening us shattered, their tiny granules of sand suspended high in the air.

Bane grinned, his teeth flashing brightly as he cracked his knuckles, sparks sputtering in his eager ice blue gaze. "I can work with this." Instantly, lightning crackled all over his body, and ignited brightly in a dazzling spider webbed explosion, targeting every single sandy grain and turning them into suspended glass.

Riley winked at me, latching onto the glassy shards with his air before they fell. "I do so love playing by your rules Rem."

My lips twitched with amusement, revealing the pride I felt for him and all of them as the glass shards spun in a whirling cyclone around the death god and the shifters followed.

Glaring at Shea through the dark strands of my wind blown hair, I snarled. "Your move, *death god.*"

Emon flashed me a feral grin. "*Savage,*" he cooed and I grinned back.

I had never sought the approval of others but for some reason hearing it from the deep growling tones of my soulmate made me want to seek it more.

Through a mask of indifference that I reluctantly had to admit must be a family trait, the death god stared back, past the threat, past Emon, and straight into my own gaze. The look itself was powerful enough to seize my chest, viciously hooking into me from across the white sands unmercifully.

"So be it," he finally said, crossing his arms in front of his chest, straining the black silk of his shirt while the intensity of his godly gaze still held me hostage.

Perhaps it was the dim light, or the reflection of the glass spinning around him but I could have sworn I saw sadness flicker in his emerald eyes and I snarled, he had no fucking right to play *victim* here.

"Eve, my love, please help our daughter see reason."

Inhaling sharply, I froze, this time not from the death god's fierce gaze but from the gorgeous splendor of my mother with her black hair flowing around her like the shadowy past she appeared from.

Fear, guilt, elation, joy. I felt it all in a span of seconds and it was enough to send me crumbling just like the last time I had seen her, in the City of Light, when I cut ties with my family to save them.

"Breathe, little umbra," Emon commanded softly in my mind, sensing the panic before it even began. *"Just keep breathing, I am here. We are here."*

I released the breath I had been holding, seeking Emon's spiced chocolate scent and allowed it wash over me, a warm blanket in the cold cruelty of this world.

Elegantly poised, even her tears looked regal as they flooded her eyes. "Hello my little chickadee."

A strong hand settled on her shoulder in silent support and I followed that swirling tattooed arm up to the green eyes of my brother smiling at me through ringlets of curly blue hair.

"Kadey Kins," I breathed.

"Hey Rem Rem." He sent me a tentative smile before turning a darkened gaze on Shea. "If you need additional help, I'd be more than happy to oblige."

The death god sighed exasperatedly. "Eve, my love, this is not helping. Our children. Reason. Now."

My mother sniffed, smiling softly at me. "Shea, *my love*, I do believe our daughter looks perfectly reasonable to me." Her head tilted towards my brother at her side. "What say you Kade?"

"I'd love a piece of him myself," he snickered darkly, and I frowned inwardly. What had happened here that made my brother hate our newfound father just as much as I did?

I shook my head, coming to Sheol was just as goddess damn backwards as the lands of Faerie, everyone wanted a piece of each other, masking the true lurking problems beneath the surface.

Lowering Riella slowly, I motioned for her to stay behind me as I stepped forward, my hands fisting at my sides, "I want answers, why have you brought us here?"

My mother looked back at Shea and shrugged a delicate pale shoulder. "Sounds perfectly reasonable."

The death god glanced over at her with amused shock, ignoring my question. "Are you not worried for my safety, my love? Our daughter and her friends are threatening to kill me."

Signaling to Asher to fall back to Riella, I strode forward, a brief flash was the only indication that Bane had thrown his sword to me. Without looking, I caught it with graceful ease, twirling it in my hand, getting a feel for its weight before adjusting my grip.

Nodding, I signaled to Riley to part the winds, while Emon slowly followed me at my back, Tyr and Penina snarling their support as they continued to circle around the three of us.

The entire action only took moments to execute, so when Shea looked back towards me and the three moons light glinting off my raised blade, he blinked slowly.

"I'll only ask one more time, *father.*" I spat the word like one would vomit from their mouth. "Why are we here?" The coldness in my voice seemed to chill the entire air around us.

My brother barked out a laugh that was just as cold as my words, snarling at the death god. "I fucking told you."

Shea's infinite gaze regarded me with sudden sorrow. "You have lost control of the shadows daughter, and without them, you will never defeat the evil that threatens your world."

I felt everyone still, as if we all stood on the precipice of fucking fate, and if we stepped forward we would find ourselves falling into its devious clutches.

Shaking his head, a lock of dark hair fell across his brow. "I am sorry for this next part though, daughter, just know it was the only way."

I hissed and Emon snarled behind me, a steady strong presence at my back as I laid my sword horizontally across my fathers throat, standing on my tip toes due to his towering height. "What do you mean you are sorry?" I narrowed my eyes on his, searching for the answers somewhere in the deep depths of this god.

Then the glass shards still hovering around us split back into grains of sand right before Xi's gasping voice called out to me. "General...Rem."

Alarmed, I turned away from Shea, knowing Emon stepped into my place, and caught the sight of my friend crumpling to the glimmering silver path.

"Xi!" I cried out stepping towards her, but sudden lightning and winds rushed by me, Bane and Riley immediately at her side.

Riley's panicked gaze looked up. "Her heart beats but I cannot *feel* her."

Tyr's tiger snarled behind me and Bane's face turned grim watching him. "Her light is gone."

At the swordmaster's words, Emon hissed, lunging for the death god, his claws tearing into the gentle silk of Shea's shirt. "What the fuck is this? What have you fucking done?" he roared.

Disgusted, the death god peered down at my soulmate and waved his hand sending him sprawling backwards. "I have done what I must," not even reacting when Penina's leopard and Tyr's tiger lunged for him, fangs and claws bared, he smoothed his shirt. As if knowing they would never reach him, he did not seem surprised when they fell mid attack, shifting back into their fae forms, deadly still in the white sands.

Blurring to Penina's side, Emon pulled her limp body into his arms. Leaning forward when her lips moved, he bent his ear down to catch the barely audible whisper before her head slumped back and her eyes closed. Stilling, Emon reared back, his bronze coloring turning an awful shade of gray as our eyes met.

Dread. Pure dread, seeped into my soul, we had fallen off the cliff playing right into fate's hands and for the first time in my life...I didn't know what to do.

"They are still alive, barely," Emon growled.

Then all at once our family crumbled.

First Asher's wolf fell, a soft whimper escaping his snout before he shifted back into his fae form with Riella clutching at his chest. "No! Papa Asher! Wake up. Wake up!"

Running to Riella, I pulled her into my arms when Bane's voice barked out.

"Dark."

I spun back around to see him catching the unconscious Riley in his arms with a grunt, sweat pouring down his face as he blinked at me, fighting whatever was taking them down.

"Make him pay for this girl," he half slurred, half growled before falling, still managing to hold Riley protectively in his embrace, his eyes falling on Penina before they closed.

Looking up at the death god and shielding Riella, I attempted to call the shadows to me, to find a way to stop this...I needed to stop this. But they did not respond, not even when I attempted to pull them from the sky, or the soft shifting sands.

Frustrated, I screamed at the death god. "Why! Why are you doing this? Stop this now..." Heaving with tears of betrayal, I looked past the death god to see the dark anger on my brother's face directed straight at our father and the sad eyes of my mother watching—just fucking watching. "How can you let him do this?" I whispered brokenly.

It was clear, I did not know them. The mother and brother I once knew would have never allowed this,

Riella sobbed into my chest, her tiny body trembling with fear and the death god shook his head sadly, but I didn't believe his sympathy for a second. "There is no way to stop what comes next, your mother and brother couldn't have prevented this."

"Little umbra," Emon gasped, crawling towards me, his chest heavy with panting breaths, his gold eyes shining with a fear I had never seen from him before.

Stumbling with Riella still tightly in my arms, I collapsed next to him, cradling his face with my free hand.

"Father!" Riella sobbed, falling from my hold into his chest.

Purring, his arms wrapped around her. "It's okay my cub. I'll find my way back to you." His blazing gaze burned up at me. "This isn't death. I'll find you my soulmate," he growled before his dark lashes fluttered closed.

I felt the world tilt the moment his eyes shut and I forced myself to look up at the bright emerald gaze of the god of death watching me. "Please," I whispered brokenly, the cosmos swirling in my vision, a harsh array of neon and moonlight as I fell to the white sands beside my soulmate.

Before I met the ground, strong arms enveloped me. The furious gaze of my brother staring back at the dark looming god.

"Fuck you and your fucking plans! This wasn't the way! She will never trust you or us ever again. Never! Just like I never will," he roared.

I whimpered and his furious face snapped down to me, softening slightly but still full of so much anger—just like the last time I saw him when he disappeared from my life in shadow.

"Don't worry Rem, Rem. I got you. Always."

Chapter 3

Remnant

"**C**ARE TO TELL ME *where you have gone, Remi darling?*"

I shivered at the soft caress of my former lover's voice and blinked, peering into the sunlight atop the parapets of the City of Light—intact and not riddled with destruction.

I shook my head, this wasn't right.

"Are you quite alright?"

I blinked again and turned to see Deirdre sitting in front of me wearing an elegant gown of silk turquoise, sipping on a cup of tea from a finely crafted, hand painted porcelain cup.

This wasn't right.

I stared at the cup, it was from one of her favorite sets. A set that she had thrown at me in a fit of rage for trading prisoners of war with the shifter king.

I frowned. This wasn't right...and then I knew.

We were in the spirit realm.

Narrowing my eyes, I leaned back in my chair crossing my arms. I was powerless here but so was she.

Watching my sudden mood shift, her red lips pursed with displeasure as she slowly lowered the fine porcelain, her long dark lashes fluttering with concern. "Remi? Darling are you alright?"

"I should have expected you would resort to this. Are you really that desperate?" I snorted back at her. "Really, De, out of all the possibilities you could have dreamed up in the spirit realm this is what you chose?" I waved my hand across the tea setting, watching it pass through my body.

The former queen's smile widened and her innocent astonishment shifted into one of cruel delight, the blood goddess was here to play now. "What gave it away?"

"Besides the fact that I never once dreamed of you?" I tapped my fingers on my crossed arms, stilling the sudden urge they had to rip her cowardly arrogant head from her shoulders—an attempt that would be fruitless in the spirit world. I waved my hand at the beautiful city before us, every ounce of it flawless but I knew better. I knew that the City of Light festered underneath its perceived glory. "You seek perfection in an imperfect world."

She laughed, the sound cold as it escaped her blood red lips. I wondered if it had always been that way? I had been so blinded by her beauty and power that I never saw the monster lingering beneath...too consumed by my own fear.

"It is unfortunate you will not bend to my will even here Remi darling, spirit is so beautiful when properly controlled. Just like your shadows." Snapping her fingers, deep burgundy shadows cloaked her in its smokey tendrils. "How do you like my newest accessory?" she purred, stroking them over her shoulder.

I forced my face to remain neutral even though my heart and soul called out to my faithful companions. "I think you look desperate and ever more the fake fool you have become. Stealing power, murdering your own, draining the life from Faerie, aligning yourself with the Sanguine—the very power that killed your own family." Leaning forward, I stared hard into her blood red eyes, gone was the turquoise that ran so deep. "I think you look pathetic."

Snarling, her face morphed into something so hideous it was all I could do but not rear back from the monster revealing itself. Red shadows sprung from her shoulders, wrapping around my neck and squeezing.

Arching a brow, I gave the monster a quizzical look of amusement. "What do you expect to achieve from this? You know as well as I that you cannot hurt me here...only influence me and your power to do so ended way before our relationship ever did."

Slowly Deirdre's face transformed back into her beautiful illusion and she flicked the shadows back into her hand. "You are such a bore." I ignored the way she caressed the shadows and the revulsion churning my stomach. "I have something you want and you have something I want. I propose a trade...the faeling for the shadows that have been lovingly devoted to you your entire life." Her hand snuffed them out as if she strangled them. "I know how much they mean to you, how much they are part of you...at one point I even believed I was jealous of them." She laughed, shaking her head, her silver hair falling around her. "How ridiculous of me. If only I knew my true calling back then."

Standing calmly and holding in my rage, I stared deep into her traitorous eyes. "No."

Red eyes burned brighter, pouring over the edges as if her eyes bled with her seething. "Is that your final answer?"

"After all these years," I said softly...deadly, "how little you know me." I turned my back on her, walking away from the illusion she had created, seeing it fade. Her control over spirits apparently not as strong as her control of the elements or the Sanguine for that matter.

"Oh I know you," she hissed at my back. "Do you honestly think you can be her mother? You who does nothing but destroy everyone and everything around you? You are death and you'll never be more than that, don't you remember?" She snapped her fingers as the rest of the illusion fell away and we stood upon the rubble of the City of Light.

I paused, staring out at the endless sea of crumbled marble and fake glory...no longer feeling the guilt like I once did not so long ago.

"This is your legacy," Deirdre whispered into my ear, having moved closer in my distraction. "It will always be your legacy. You will never be able to give either of them what they need. You are a relic, the past, and you belong in this rubble. They will have no future with you because you will destroy whatever is left of it...you already have."

I raised my chin, not bothering to spare her a glance as I walked away, latching onto my soulmate bond like it was a lifeline before

I allowed the sudden doubt in my heart to show upon my face. "You are wrong."

She laughed softly, a condescending sound that felt like ice running through my veins. "Then why do you run, Remi Darling?"

Chapter 4

Remnant

"WHEN IS MY MOTHER going to wake?"

I heard my daughter's worried whisper as I struggled against the remaining effects of Deirdre's spirit hold, panic accelerating my heartbeat, while I attempted to open my eyes. It felt as if the weight of the world would keep them shut forever and perhaps that would be for the better...but I fought it just the same.

I owed it to my daughter.

"Knowing your mother, it won't be much longer."

I scowled inwardly at the sound of my brother's low tone. He had *stood* by, he *watched*, he *knew* Shea's plan and he *let it happen.* And in doing so...he made my family *vulnerable,* he made me vulnerable. A condition Deirdre wasted no time in taking advantage of, pulling me into the spirit realm to spin her tales of deceit and half truths.

My voice wheezed through dry lips. "Away. Riella—get away from him."

I could feel rather than see my brother's frown and Riella's shift to my side, crying out and falling into my chest. "Mother!"

Mother, the sound whispered inside me—my new title, the sweetest, softest, most treasured kiss upon my soul. She had only used it a few times since waking and despite Emon and I discussing with her that we did not want her to feel the pressure of using such an honored title, she still bestowed it upon us anyway.

"You know, I would never harm a child, sister, let alone yours. She is safe."

Desperately, I attempted to move. "I don't know you anymore," I hissed back, ignoring the ache it caused to say those words. I thought the day I'd see my brother again would be a joyous one but now it was riddled with distrust and betrayal.

Finally able to peel my eyes open and feeling my body heal, I dragged myself upright, the pain jolting as I moved my numb limbs. Wrapping Riella as fiercely and protectively in my arms as much as my weakened body would allow, I gave her a gentle kiss on the top of her head.

"I am happy you are safe, my little chickadee."

She rubbed her face into my chest. "I was scared but Kade promised that you would wake up and so I decided to be brave like you."

I smoothed her hair back from her shoulder, the strands like the softest satin in my hand. "I am so sorry you were scared, little one."

Kade's sigh drew my attention to him, his hands rubbing down the front of his leathers, his expression still dark. "I promise you, Remnant, Riella has been safe the entire time."

"Depends on your definition of safe, doesn't it *brother*."

He pressed his lips firmly together, his emerald eyes flashing brightly at me in the dim twilight of the room. "You're angry at the wrong fae, *sister*."

If Riella wasn't in my arms, I would have him pinned to the dark glass wall that surrounded us right now. I knew exactly who to be angry at.

Baring my teeth, I hissed back. "Where is Emon?"

Narrowing his eyes at me, he nodded down to the bed next to me. "Your soulmate is safe, beside you."

Moving as quickly as my body would allow, I turned to my sleeping soulmate in all his bronze glory and studied him. His breath was steady, his power still radiating warmth like his body next to me, laying formidably upon black silk sheets despite his unconscious state.

Just like a fairytale, a sleeping beauty…oh how I would kiss him now and never stop, especially if that was where happily ever after was for us.

"Will he wake?" My hand trembled and I couldn't keep it from my voice either, reaching out to brush his light brown hair from his brow.

"I've been told he would," Kade bit out.

"Oh, I am, don't you worry, Kade Dark," Emon croaked, then his lashes fluttered open with gold eyes blazing up at me. "Hey little umbra."

"Shifter," I whispered at the same time as Riella flew from my arms onto his immobile body.

"Father!" she cried, landing heavily on him and I grimaced when he grunted, having just experienced the same numbing pain.

But he only chuckled, strength returning, his arms moved lethargically enveloping her. "My sweet cub," he purred, rising next to me, his hand reaching out to cup my face. *"Are you unharmed?"* He growled in my mind.

Inwardly I melted, wanting nothing more than to lean into his steady touch and soak in his powerful unfailing strength.

Except we were not alone, my brother watched us broodingly in the darkened shadows of the room.

"I am unharmed, Emon."

Leaning in he kissed me softly, sending fire burning into my blood, bestowing the very strength that I had just been aching for.

Riella giggled between us.

"Let us make sure it stays that way." Dropping his hand from me, he glared over at Kade, placing Riella between us protectively. "Give me one reason I shouldn't tear you into shreds and burn this place down."

I just caught the pain in my brother's eyes before he bared his teeth at Emon, folding his arms across his chest. "Because we both know I am not the one you want to truly tear apart," leaning forward his eyes gleamed, "and if it is Sheol you are looking to burn down, shifter, I'll gladly help you do so."

"Why?" I snapped, "you seemed more than content to let him weaken us before now."

Kade shifted, raising his booted foot upon his knee. "The sleep was going to happen whether Shea was involved or not. It was a mistake to not inform you though, one I warned him you would not take kindly to."

"What do you mean sleep?" Emon growled.

Kade's eyes shifted to my soulmate, his nostrils flaring, the same distrust in his own as there was in Emon's. "Sheol is meant for the dead, shifter. But I promise you, your court is well enough. They rest in another tower."

Emon's teeth bared, but I steadied him, my hand resting on his knee.

I understood how he felt, but I also could hear the truth in my brother's voice. Frowning, I looked around me, taking in the room we were in for the first time. "Tower? Where are we exactly?"

Heavy transparent black glass walls surrounded us, pitching upwards into a spiraling peak straight into space, stars surrounding us on all sides, shimmering against the glass. Behind me, Riella gasped, pulling on my sleeve and pointing wide eyed at a bright fiery comet shooting across the sky, casting shadows within the room in its bright light.

Reluctantly, I had to admit, this part of Sheol was breathtaking.

Kade grinned at my unveiled awe, "Welcome to the Voltum of Sheol, a city within the Eithne, where our mother and Shea live."

My brows rose, "Not you?"

Kade's eyes darkened. "I wouldn't call it living, but yes, I stay here as well. Someone has to."

Emon's claws slashed in the dark and he leaned forward. "I sense you are playing games, Kade Stellan Shea Dark. Are you sure this is where you want to take this?" he hissed.

Riella broke the tension between us, her question bursting from her loudly as if she could no longer hold it back in her tiny body. "You are so lucky you get to stay here!" She peeked around my body, "You get to eat all the stardust you want!" Hand placed on the bed, she leaned further towards Kade. "What does yours taste like?"

Kade's eyes widened and then a small smile formed on his lips. It was the first time I saw him without darkness in his expression—the Kade I used to know.

Clearing his throat, he winked at Riella, "I think I'll keep that one a secret little niece."

She looked up at me, "What is a nice?"

"Niece," I corrected her, "it means you are the daughter of his sister, which is me. You would call my brother Uncle, but he has yet to earn that title," I sent him a sharp look.

Kade's brow raised, "Indeed. Everything must be earned with you."

Both Emon and I growled our warning in unison.

"When it comes to my daughter, yes, brother," I snapped.

"Well then," he dropped his booted foot to the ground and winked at Riella, "I should start earning my keep so that your little bird may call me Uncle someday."

Taking a deep breath, I moved to drop my legs over the side of the bed and leaned into his space. "In that case, start talking Kade," I hissed.

He was far too relaxed for a fae that knew what I was capable of, brother or not.

Studying my face, he snorted and leaned back in his chair, slinging his arm over the top and stretching his dark gray shirt over his well defined physique—his build, I suddenly realized, was much like our death god father.

"Sheol is the land of the dead...and it is only for the dead...unless you're a god, then you may live amongst them," he frowned then, "if you call it living."

The ghosts were back in his eyes and it sent a chill down my spine. "What of the others? What about our court? Are you telling me that...that they are dead? Is this what will happen to our family?"

Emon inhaled sharply next to me and Riella whimpered.

"Mother, they can't die."

Emon slid forward next to me, pulling Riella into his lap, purring, "Of course not, my cub. We would never let that happen."

My brother sighed, his hand rubbing across his lips. "No. Not dead, they won't die. Not yet anyway, but not alive either. They are asleep...just."

My movement was quick, hauling Kade's body out of the chair by the collar of his gray shirt, I snarled into his face. "You are making this extremely difficult, Kade, and you are upsetting my daughter. I care not for your dark mood. Give us answers or leave. With or without you, we will have them."

Emon chuckled behind me, *"I love the vicious side of you, little umbra."*

Ignoring my soulmate, I shoved Kade away from me, watching him stumble with shock, before he regained his balance, his eyes cutting angrily in the abrupt space between us.

"What is your choice, brother, are you with us?"

He snorted and looked away. His eyes narrowed on the city of towers. "Even a straight explanation would not be enough, you would have to see it for yourself."

"See what Kade?" I ground my teeth, following his transfixed gaze, more goddess damn riddles, as if I didn't just throw him across the room demanding answers.

"He'd kill me if I showed them to you, but perhaps that would be better than this empty life," he muttered more to himself than to me.

Emon's warm hand cupped my shoulder and I glanced at him worriedly, seeing that he was studying my brother with intense scrutiny. Past him Riella sat quietly on the bed, a sad expression on her face.

"If I am following you correctly, your sister...our daughter, they both have God blood and because of that they are awake...so why am I, Kade?"

Kade turned and arched a dark blue brow at him. "How indeed? Anything you'd like to share, shifter king?"

Emon's supportive touch on my shoulder never changed even as a low warning growl vibrated from his chest. "Be very careful with what you are implying, *shadow brother*."

"Fuck you shifter, I'm not the one that needs to explain my misgivings. It is because of you we are all stuck here in the first place!" Kade sneered.

I snapped, lunging forward without thought, my fist connecting with my brother's face hard enough my hand broke. Shaking it out, watching Kade stumble with satisfaction, I felt my bones quickly heal. Although the act would have been much easier with the use of my shadows, I had to admit the actual physical punch was a bit exhilarating.

I frowned, except a well aimed punch wasn't going to take out Deirdre. I needed to find a way to get my powers back and I knew there was only one person that had the answers I needed.

Shea. My bastard of a father.

Emon's proudful voice broke my thoughts. *"I could watch that again one hundred times over and it still would be just as satisfying."*

Kade straightened slowly, sniffing through the bruising on his face, he snarled, "What the fuck Remnant."

Refusing to feel guilty, I hissed through gritted teeth, "There is only *one* person who is responsible for all of this and that is Deirdre. Should you lay such ridiculous blame on my soulmate again, I swear on the goddess it will be more than my fist laying into you Kade."

Kade's eyes roved over my face with his brows drawn. "You cannot honestly mean that, Rem. I kept a death god from breathing down on you for the past five hours...and even worse, I kept our own mother away. You know how hard that fucking is."

My fists curled again, the anew urge to punch him raging inside of me. "I am not the one acting differently, you are. Evidently a lot has changed and you are no longer the brother I thought you were."

His nostrils flared and his eyes burned. "And who's fucking fault do you think that is Rem? You chose her over us all those years ago and look what it fucking brought us." He waved his hand at the city rising into the stars, "You said you'd always be there Rem Rem, and then I was alone...you weren't there...you haven't been for years."

Feeling his words like a blow, I stepped backward, seeing my brother all those years ago on the balcony of the City of Light, the look of disgust on his face when I told him I vowed to serve the crown, leaving them behind.

He never knew I did it for him, for our mother, the shadow court. I thought I was playing the game correctly and I did...until I didn't, until I fell in love with Deirdre.

A roar ripped from Emon and he blurred across the room, sending Kade crashing into the glass by his throat. Snarling, Emon's fangs descended and snapped in Kade's face. "Too fucking far, *shadow brother.* Take your hateful anger out on me all you want but never—" Emon slammed him into the glass again, Kade's head whipping backwards with a loud crack, "fucking never at her. Understand me?"

Kade didn't even bother to acknowledge Emon's threat, instead he chuckled, blinking to orient his vision. "I didn't know I signed up to be everyone's punching bag today. No wonder Shea agreed to leave you to my care. The bastard must have known you'd be violent." His amused eyes settled on me and then widened at the tear that fell down my face.

Kade had never seen me cry. Until Emon, I had never felt safe enough to do so. Looking away, I swiped at my wet face angrily. While meant to be hurtful, Kade's words were true. I had left them, and I had been wrong, so fucking wrong.

"Don't let him get to you, little umbra. He is angry and confused. Your brother loves you, he just doesn't know how to express it anymore." Emon didn't look back as he spoke, but I felt his love wash over me just the same.

"Fuck, sister." Kade whispered.

I could not bring myself to look at him, more than ashamed I could not hold back my sorrow, realizing all my sacrifices had never truly saved my brother from the cruelty of this world. Instead, I focussed on the wisps fluttering just beyond the glass, bitterness burning at the back of my throat while another tear fell.

"I'm sorry. I didn't mean—" my brother's voice broke, "please don't cry Rem Rem."

A soft warm hand threaded through my own, Riella's musical voice whispering upwards. "Please don't cry, mother."

Exhaling, I smiled down at her through watery tears and dried my face again. "I am okay, little chickadee," I said, squeezing her hand reassuringly before turning back to Emon and my brother, with another sigh, the fight inside me dwindling, I signaled to my soulmate to release Kade. "Emon put my brother down, please."

Emon glanced back at me with his head tilted to the side and his lips thinning across his fangs. "Are you sure, little umbra? Personally, I would very much like to see if he can fly like you can...it would be so easy to throw him off that pretty balcony right over there."

I smiled sadly, looking out at the majestical balcony that inserted into the cosmic sky. "The thought does have merit, shifter, but I doubt that would be helpful to our cause."

"Oooo...can you really fly?" Riella spun to look at Kade, words tumbling from her mouth so quickly they were barely recognizable. "Can you teach me? Please! I've always wanted to fly!"

Kade stared at her in bafflement for a moment before he grinned, not even bothering to undo the grip my soulmate had on him. "Of course, I can show you how to fly, little bird, but I wouldn't want to show you from here. That drop is quite vertical and one can never trust the sands around here. Now if your father would be so kind as to release me on solid ground."

Riella squealed and jumped up and down, tugging at my hand while she looked up at me, "I am going to learn how to fly!"

Emon leaned into Kade, his hair falling over his eyes with his cold predatory gaze as he whispered harshly to him, "consider this your only warning, *shadow brother,*" then with a quick jerk of his hand, he released him, forcing him to stumble along the black glass wall.

Tilting my head to the side with curiosity, I regarded my brother who was now adjusting his clothing to its rightful place, grumbling to himself. "How high up are we exactly?"

Kade's head snapped up and he smiled like the sibling that I remembered from our past mischief. "Thinking of jumping yourself? Only the tallest towers are for the Dark family, sister. Go have a look for yourself."

Releasing Riella's hand I stepped across the room towards the crystal balcony covered by a thin barrier of glass, while the others watched on. As if it sensed me, the barrier shimmered and I raised my brow—it was an *illusion.*

Tentatively I pushed my hand through the transparent black wall, seeing it slide through with ease. Nodding to myself, the rest of my body followed and I was instantly bathed in an aurora of rainbow twilight that was Sheol's skies. Glittering stardust continued to fall, welcoming me in a gentle snow-like dust as it cascaded over the multiple towers of Sheol's city of Voltum. Their reflective surfaces spiraling upwards to sharp points that disappeared into the darkness.

I pursed my lips, knowing the others had followed me out into the night. "This glass—" I ran my hand along the smooth black surface, "it is the same as the onyx throne room, Lord Oberon's work." The ancient elemental fae's work was well known, his precise control over fire and earth made him a master craftsman of glass. There was no one better and he had passed on before I ever met him, in the Blood Wars.

I felt Emon approach, his warming power and delicious chocolate spice scent temporarily overwhelming my senses. His claw rang across the balcony's rail. "You are right, little umbra but how can that be?"

Riella rushed between us, leaning over the rail with her arms outstretched for more stardust without fear of the endless plunge below.

My soulmate grinned back at me, his gold eyes flashing. *"Our cub is fearless and has a sweet tooth."*

"Turns out Oberon is a friend of our father's and after his death, Shea granted him peace within the Eithne in exchange for building this city for our mother and our court. Voltum—the city of desires, wishes, hopes, and vows. Everything you would want in the afterlife right?" Kade said dryly.

Turning I regarded my baby brother as he stood leaning against the balcony entrance with his arms crossed, his stormy darkness back once more.

My brows pinched together. "Our people live within? These are their homes? I don't understand...they are not gods..."

Kade's face turned a shade darker and he shrugged, "Homes, shrines, stairs to the eternal..." pain flashed in his eyes, "tombs," he whispered.

Emon rumbled next to me, pulling Riella back from the railing the same time my command left my lips, "Take me to them, take me to my court—and my friends. Now."

CHAPTER 5

QUIETLY, WITH OUR DAUGHTER in hand, I followed Remnant and her brother out of our tower and back onto the mirrored silver path that connected the vast network of the city of Voltum. The predator in me carefully tracked the shifting sands while keeping a close eye on my soulmate's brother, Kade Stellan Shea Dark.

It came as no fucking surprise to me that Kade held his fathers name as was custom for the fae. Except, no one ever thought the Dark children could ever be half god's. It was always assumed that the shadow fae honored Shea, the god of death because he was more connected to their darkness rather than the bright light of Faerie and so Kade's name was simply in honor of that.

I waited for the voice of Ethereal to respond. Surely he would have a comment or two, but the fucking cat had been tediously silent since he almost burned our world down and that—goddess damn it, that concerned me.

"Father. Taste this." My cub stretched her slobbery hand up towards me, popping it from her dust smeared mouth.

I wrinkled my nose at the glittery saliva dripping from her fingers and gave her a wide smile, chuckling inwardly. "I wouldn't dare take away the source of your pleasure, my cub. You need not share, in fact..." I hoisted my daughter up on my shoulders and found myself falling in love with the way she laughed, just like I did when I first heard her mother's. "See if you can gather more from up there to support your little addiction and enjoy your stardust."

Remnant's shoulders shook with laughter in front of me but I could still see the tension in them. Her worry was practically palpable and it flooded our bond. She was shaken and I had no way of reassuring her that all would be well. Because that would be a *lie*.

I rubbed my bare chest, to ease the sudden ache I felt the same time her emerald eyes looked back at me. "*You finally got rid of your shirt. I'm surprised you had it on for as long as you did.*"

My brows rose, "*I can't tell if this pleases you or not.*"

Her laughter floated along our bond, and I held tightly onto Riella as she leaned to the side for what I could only assume was for more dust.

"*It did bring up some interesting possibilities...*" Her seductive tone purred inside of me and I swallowed hard.

Fuck.

Sighing, I shook my head. "*Maybe next time, little umbra. The fabric is much too confining for me to be able to kill your father if need be.*"

"*Who says you will be the one who gets to kill him?*" Flicking her hair back over her shoulder, I could not hold back the hungry stare at my soulmate's lush blue-black waves as they swayed just above her delicious ass.

Chuckling, I growled. "*Shall we make another bet then, little umbra? What shall we play this time? Winner gets the first attempt to kill your father.*"

Her soft laughter filled my mind and my heart soared at the sound. "*You certainly know how to court your mate shifter...the promise of death instead of a kiss this time?*"

I grinned both at her words and my new discovery while still watching the way her powerful ass flexed with every stride. Her worry had eased along our soulmate bond and just like that, I knew how I could distract her from the anxiety that plagued her every thought since coming here—seduction. *"Whatever it takes, soulmate."*

Remnant's steps faltered but neither of us had a chance to respond when our daughter shouted from atop my shoulders, practically falling off as she bounced excitedly. "Look father! What is that?"

Gritting my teeth, I gripped her body tighter to prevent her from falling again and followed to where she pointed. "What in the goddess is that?" I said, hissing at the creature in warning. Something just wasn't right about it.

The nondescript animal paused, morphing into several creatures before it at last settled into a petite black rabbit. Long twitching ears and blood red eyes glared back at me before zooming in on my cub.

I growled, my instincts telling me this *thing* was way too interested in my innocent daughter.

"It's a pookah," Remnant's brother said with disgust, shadows springing out from his hand to shoo off the creature. It hissed back at him, head turning while its eyes were still transfixed on Riella. "Their numbers have increased since we arrived with the shadow court. They are guardian spirits constantly seeking a soul to champion."

Riella giggled above me. "He is so cute! Can I pet it? Do you think we can keep him?"

The three of us exchanged baffled looks, knowing that the shifting creature was anything but cute. Reaching up, I patted my daughter's thigh. "It would be for naught, my cub. Their fates are entwined to the soul they are bound to, best leave it be so that it may find its destined partner."

Feeling, rather than seeing her deflate, I quickly added, "But if any fae has the ability to tame a pookah spirit, I would not be surprised if it was you, Riella. Be patient, perhaps what you wish for will come true."

And if she absolutely wanted the hideous thing, I would make damn sure I found a way to obtain it for her. All she needed to do was ask with those big swirling green gold eyes on her sweet little cherubic face and it would be done—as it would be for anything she ever wanted in this world.

Unicorns, done.

Pounds of stardust, done.

Burn this world down, done.

"And if she wanted you to find her a soulmate of her own one day and leave us behind?"

Startled, my head snapped up to meet Remnant's glittering emerald eyes, reading me so easily.

Gritting my teeth, I snarled irritatedly inside her mind. *"Done."*

Then as quickly as it appeared, the pookah was gone.

"Awe." Riella pouted, slumping further over my head with disappointment.

I patted her leg again, sympathizing but inwardly I was fucking relieved. I seriously did not like the way that thing looked at her.

Kade cleared his throat, glancing between us all quizzically. "We are here."

Holding Riella, I reached out to pull Remnant into me. Her startled reaction settled when I placed a soft kiss on the top of her head, her hair catching briefly on the scruff of my beard.

Fuck I needed to shave.

Sweeping the strands back and smoothing them into place once more, I fortified our soulmate bond with resolve. "Together." I reminded her.

Leaning briefly more into me, Remnant reached up and touched our daughter's booted foot. "Together."

Riella's soft hands reached down and cupped either side of my face. "Together."

Turning my mouth into her tiny hand I kissed it softly. "Always, little cub."

Remnant sighed and moved away, pulling us along with her as we stepped up to the swirling black building. There was no door but like the balcony the transparent wall was an illusion and it instantly transported us into darkness. A tiny light flickered in the distance, then another, and another. Soon, the tower was awash with lights, trailing and circling upwards, all the way to the seemingly never ending peak of the ominous tower.

Narrowing my eyes, I studied the spaces they illuminated—shelves, hundreds of them, spiraling up the sides of the room, each one holding a large glass case.

Growling, I stepped closer, seeing a glint of gold in the light from the petite silhouette of a fae enclosed in glass placed reverently on the shelf. "Fucking goddess." I whispered, my eyes widening with alarm.

"It's Penina." Riella whimpered.

"It's okay, little one," I choked. Instinctively, I plucked her from my shoulders, cradling her in my arms as she buried her face into my neck.

"This is a tomb." Remnant inhaled sharply walking past us and stepping up on the ledge to another glass coffin. "Tyr," she breathed, before carefully climbing up the next spiral step, "Riley." She touched the glass grimly with her fingertips.

I watched with a sinking heart as my soulmate continued to climb, naming off our friends while the glowing orbs of light floated delicately over each and every glass coffin like a ghostly guardian.

"Orly," she murmured, and I watched as sadness etched across her face, her hand stretching out on the glass. "We would play shadows and dragons together." Her eyes snapped up and then glared down at her brother, who had been silently watching in the shadows. "I don't understand. I see their chest rise and fall, I see their hearts beating."

"The end of your soul lies within Sheol," Kade quoted softly. "You know the rhyme mother always hummed to us. As I said before, Sheol is the land of the dead. It is not meant for the living."

"Yes. You have said that many times," I snarled back at him, holding Riella tightly as she whimpered with sadness. "But what the fuck does that mean?"

Kade sighed. "It means they are soulless, their light is gone. Their bodies are only vessels, preserved by the death god's powers in these glass tombs and the only way to return them back to their living state is to travel to The Well of Souls."

I frowned, where had I heard that name before?

Riella sniffed, rubbing her face into me more. "They will be okay though, right Uncle Kade? You're going to help us wake them all up. Help us get their souls back."

Kade stiffened at the title she bestowed upon him and so did my soulmate but I would not chastise my daughter now, all those years alone in The Under, she had yearned for a family. Unknowingly, she was jumping at any chance she could to build just that and there were worse beings than Kade Dark that lurked out there. Although he was different and clearly haunted, I could still see the fae beneath. Besides, was I not a collector of lost souls? My *own* family was a ragtag bunch of wounded fae, brought together by our wounds of the past and love for each other. A love that only strengthened us.

I shot Kade a warning look, stroking Riella's hair soothingly. "Of course he will, my cub. You need not worry about that, your *Uncle* Kade will make sure of it."

Remnant dropped from the fifty foot ledge she was on, landing in a soft crouch in front of her brother, standing with a fluid grace that was more shifter than shadow fae—goddess she never ceased to impress me.

Planting her hand on her hip, she stared hard at her brother, final judgment flickering in her eyes and we all stood on a precipice on if she would accept his wounded soul back into her life.

After a long pause, she spoke, "Of course Uncle Kadey Kins is going to help us wake them all Riella. Isn't that right, brother?"

I smiled. *"Well done, my love, he will never know what strength that really took, but I do. I see you, Remnant Dark and I am so proud of you."*

My smile widened when Remnant stood taller at my words.

Ignorant of our exchange, Kade's lips thinned in a flat line. "It isn't that simple. If it were, I would have already done so," looking over to me, his eyes settled on Riella and his voice choked, "but of course I will help if I can my sweet little niece."

Riella's head perked up from my neck and she wiggled herself from my arms to walk over to Kade, sniffing as she went. He watched her wearily approach him and then stiffened when she wrapped her arms around his leg. "Thank you."

Startled and a bit bewildered, he looked up at me.

I crossed my arms over my chest, immensely proud of my cub as well and nodded down to my daughter.

Kade released a shaky sigh, and looked down at her, patting the top of her head awkwardly. "You're welcome, little bird."

Startled, I tensed when my vision of them suddenly blurred. Shaking my head hard, I lost my balance and stumbled sideways with shock. What the goddess? I was a fucking shifter, I never lost my balance.

Catching myself on my knee, I panted, the room spinning at an accelerated rate. "Fuck." I groaned, right before my face decided to slam into the floor with no control of my own to stop it.

"Emon!" My soulmate's big green eyes, full of terror, were suddenly in front of me, and I blinked again. There were four of her now...goddess I couldn't handle four of her, I didn't have the stamina for that.

Desperately, I reached out to Ethereal, but he was still silent. I wished that damned cat would talk to me...he would have at least snorted at my predicament. Maybe even call me an idiot fairy boy.

Where the fuck was he?

"So goddess damn beautiful," I slurred, before I felt the room darken, this felt like before, but fucking worse, much worse.

"Emon? What is happening, what's wrong?" Remnant's strong arms wrapped around me, her voice frantic while I lay slumped in her arms. I was much too heavy for her but my soulmate was strong, fucking stronger than all of us combined.

Then our daughter called out my new favorite name.

Father.

I smiled at that. It took her very little time to adjust to us, a characteristic only a child would have. Such an easy acceptance, an innocent trust that no adult fae would ever have with a new-found family.

My soulmate's beautiful voice was sharp as she rapidly questioned her brother, but I could not focus on her words, only her hands that cradled my face, my eyes closing at the delicate touch.

"Stay awake Emon!" Her voice screamed in my head.

I smiled at her command and forced my eyes open again to peer through the darkness clouding my vision. "Little umbra," I breathed, instead of four of her there were two...maybe two and a half?

Perhaps I could handle two of her but what the fuck did you do with the half?

"That's it shifter. Stay with me now." She leaned over me, her eyes scanning every detail of my face. I could see her mind practically counting my breaths as she waited, cooing at me to stay and then...as quickly as it came the darkness started to dissipate.

Groaning with relief, I nuzzled into her touch. "I could never leave you. Not even in death, Remnant."

She hushed me, her eyes narrowing in anger. "Don't talk that way, Daemon Ash Strider. You just nearly became a glass coffin yourself." Her eyes widened then and her head snapped over to her brother.

I grunted, patting her hand, "let me move, my love, I am crushing you."

"You should rest, Emon," she scolded with a sigh before releasing me. Rolling over, I hauled my weakened body into sitting, feeling it heal like before and my vision clearing.

Then Riella was there, her face pale and full of fear, a half sob tearing from her little body.

I grunted as her tiny frame slammed into me and chuckled softly at the surprising strength she held. There was no doubt she was half shifter now. "It's okay, my little cub. I'm okay now." Smoothing back her hair, I kissed the top of her head, feeling guilty that I was the cause of her trembling fear. "Shhh. I am sorry for scaring you, my cub," I purred, rocking her and meeting Remnant's grim expression over her head.

"Are you alright, shifter?" she asked hesitatingly through our bond, her worry now evolving to full panic inside our bond.

"For now, little umbra, breathe for me please." I answered honestly back, my concern now for the way she was shattering in front of me.

Remnant's jaw clenched before she whirled on her brother, hissing. "Start explaining, Kade."

Her brother shook his head, scrubbing his hands over his face. "I cannot, because I don't know. His reaction was like all the others that fell into the soulless sleep but he has been able to stay awake. Only those with god blood should be able to do that."

"For now he will still be awake—but he is no god," boomed the dark voice of Shea, the god of death, as he manifested from the shadows with his mate, my soulmate's mother, on his arm, "he merely carries the essence of one."

CHAPTER 6

Remnant

M Y BROTHER SURPRISED ME, stepping quickly between my little family and our parents, cloaking us in his protective shadows.

The death god arched a dark brow. "A bit dramatic, don't you think my son."

Kade barked out a laugh. "Must be a family trait then...don't you recognize it, *father*?" he said scornfully.

Our mother sighed, releasing Shea and stepping towards us, touching the shadows that separated us. "Must you do this every day Kade?"

With a simple flourish of her hand, the shadows shattered into hundreds of black blossoms and with another wave, she directed the delicate blooms to each one of the glass tombs to lay peacefully on top of them. Sadness crossed her features as she watched her beautiful control of power displayed.

Turning back to Kade, she folded her hands in front of her, "Just because our people sleep, does not mean you must deny yourself a full happy life. Your scorn and guilt is eating you from the inside out, my little shadow."

Kade's expression softened slightly. "You may have found happiness here in Sheol when the curse broke and your love was returned to you—you deserve it after so many years of suffering and never knowing, but just because you love *him,* only the goddess knows why," he added sending Shea a glare, "does not mean I have to. What I do love is my court and my sister, and he knew...he knew what would happen to them when they came here and he does not *care*. He would do anything to fulfill his selfish desire for you."

Sadness descended upon all of us as his last words echoed in the hallowed tower and I reactively moved to comfort my brother, at last understanding his anger and the darkness that plagued him.

He blamed himself, just as I did.

Emon's strong hand held me back, the weakness that was there moments ago gone in his grip, but I could still feel the slight frailty in his power. Emon's attack had only lasted for a few minutes but it was enough for my heart to die a thousand deaths. The complete helplessness I felt was more than I could bear.

"This isn't something you can fix, Remnant. Trust me, I would know."

I frowned at him before my eyes fell on Riella, and then back on him. His look imploring me to stay. My hands fisted at my sides, he was right, I could not fix this but I could find a way to protect him and Riella, and the only way to do that was for my family to get over themselves and give us the answers we desperately needed.

The three of us looked back when the booming voice of the death god rang in our ears.

"Selfish," Shea spat, his face reflecting the dangerous god he truly was beneath, anger pouring off of him in waves of darkness, the room temperature plummeting to a biting cold, and the glass coffins frosting over beneath their shadow blooms. "And what do you call these tantrums? The pain you inflict upon your own mother with your anger and misunderstandings!"

Kade snarled back, watching the darkness lower down upon him. "Do your worst, perhaps then our mother will finally see the nature of who you truly are."

"Enough!" I stood with anger. This fucking shit was going to stop now. "I do not care for whatever this family drama is. What I care about is what is happening to my soulmate and how the fuck I stop it!" I turned with a snarl towards the death god, my teeth bared. "Stop this cold or I will make you. My daughter is freezing."

"I quite agree with our daughter, Shea," my mother said, placing her hand on his arm, looking up at him with a stern expression. "Comport yourself. You are a god among us mere fae."

Multi-faceted jeweled eyes studied my mother's granite expression, his nostrils flaring down at her before he growled and waved his hand, rings flashing in the multitude of orb light. Instantly, the cold air dissipated and warmth flooded through the tower once more.

My brows raised. He seemed to loathe being commanded but when it came from my mothers lips, he respected her enough to listen, although liking it was a whole other story.

Emon snickered. *"Not so god-like when Eve has him in her clutches is he? She makes him mortal, Remnant, and that's the angle we play."*

My nod was subtle. I agreed, especially since I had nothing else at my disposal to fight with. I had always been cunning and Emon was my match, although I never cared for his live bait tactics. "If you two are now finally fin—"

I choked on my words when my mother jumped the shadows, appearing before me with open tears in her eyes, her hair flowing with the lingering power she had used. I held my breath when her hand reached up to my face.

"My little chickadee," she whispered, her soft voice cracking—my mother never cracked. "You have suffered so much, I wish I could take this all from you."

I swallowed hard, fighting the sudden tears that mirrored hers. "I am okay, mother."

Her eyes seemed to bore into me, reading secrets that only Emon kept now. Knowingly, her penetrating gaze shifted over to my soulmate with a soft smile. "Yes I can see that well enough." Reaching upward with her other hand, she tilted my head down to plant a soft kiss on my forehead. "Know that I have missed you more than you'll ever know and I shall never forgive myself for not protecting you better."

Reaching up, I pulled her hands gently away, squeezing them reassuringly. "Someday, we will speak more and you will learn that you gave me everything I needed to protect myself and more. And when I fell, alone, I got back up, mother, just like you told me to. But right now, now is your chance to help me. How do I stop the sleep from taking Emon?"

A tear slid down her pale skin, staining her beauty in sorrow despite the gentle smile she gave me. "You will not like the answers I have to give. Let us leave this place, I have prepared dinner and I will tell you what I can."

Releasing my hands, she shifted back into the shadows at the death god's side, and I gritted my teeth. "Why not tell me now?"

Shea pulled my mother closer into him and I narrowed my eyes. He knew what we did, that my mother was the access we needed to all our answers and he would guard her until he was ready to share them.

"Because even the dead have ears, daughter. It isn't just them listening in."

Emon rose from the floor with Riella wrapped in his arms, his golden glow returned as he prowled to my side. Normally I would stand in awe of his presence but now all I could see was his death—where the light died inside him. It was only seconds before he came back to me but it felt like hours of agony, a slow torture without any end.

Bending down, he kissed my lips softly. *"I feel fine, my love. Slow your racing heart and ease your worry. I am still here with you as I always will be. Together, remember?"*

I shook my head softly, biting my lip, my words inside his head were like a vow. *"Where you go, then I go too, Emon. I am not me without you, do not ask me to be. It was you who said that I needed to live—and that cannot happen without you."*

His rough finger rose and released my lip from my biting teeth, soothing the swelling with his fiery touch. *"This world needs you in it, Remnant, Riella needs you too,"* he said softly back, dropping his hand.

"But, I. Need. You."

His golden eyes widened slightly with surprise, as if he hadn't realized that I could love him just as fierce and just as deep. *"And you have me, my love. There is no world, realm, or universe where you would not."*

"I must say, I am enjoying this immensely," Kade interrupted us.

Emon and I looked up at our family who watched with varying expressions. My mother was smiling softly, the death god was scowling, Kade was grinning, and Riella giggled in Emon's arms.

Kade chuckled darkly. "Do you know how many days I have had to sit awkwardly while they did their little mind speech shit? It's fun to see them get a dose of their own medicine."

Glancing at our parents and then back at him, I said dryly, "I think your boredom has led you to some dangerous pastimes, brother."

He grinned at me. "Oh you have no idea, stay awhile and you find out just how well I occupy my boredom, the havoc we wrought upon the City of Light has nothing to do with what I have brought to Sheol."

Our mother scoffed, her beautiful face wrinkled with mocking distaste but her eyes glittered at her son. "Here I used to worry that our daughter was always the bad influence on him, but now I do wonder...."

Our supposed father didn't look so easily amused. "Indeed. However, I expect you both to behave as you should, being the children of a respectable and powerful god." His eyes flashed a bright green in warning at us both.

I ground my teeth but it was Emon who stepped forward between us protectively, meeting the death god's warning stare with a lethal one of his own. "Try telling my soulmate how she should be one more time, death god. I fucking dare you."

Shea's lip curled, his teeth flashing brightly in the hovering lights. With a flick of his hand, my shifter soulmate was suddenly covered in a soft long sleeved shirt with dancing rainbow unicorns stitched gaudily upon the fabric. "It seems you need to learn your place as well, shifter king."

I snorted at the way Emon's thick muscle practically burst from the seams of the fabric, and how his snarling breath made the unicorns appear to be moving across his body.

Riella gasped, her hands tracing the dancing horned beasts on his pink shirt. "Look father, unicorns! I haven't seen one in real life before. Only the shadows showed me! Aren't they pretty? Is this their normal color?"

Emon's fury melted when he looked down at the pure joy gazing up at him. Shaking his head ruefully, his caramel brown hair falling across his brow, he answered her. "Yes, this is what they look like, although perhaps not always rainbowed." Then his eyes narrowed on Shea. "Who knew you were so insecure, death god."

And there it was...how we were going to survive our stay here was a goddess damn mystery to me. Between my violent seething, Emon's protective nature, Kade's glooming darkness, and the arrogance of a death god, I wasn't sure if it was possible.

My mother seemed to be the only neutral person here.

Shea's jaw ticked and flames rose in his eyes. "You wanted answers, shifter king. Here it is. The god essence you carry? It would have normally been more than enough to keep you awake here in Sheol, except you are no longer the host for my banished nephew, your panther has been ripped from you and my daughter is to blame."

I gasped at the way my heart plummeted into my stomach, stumbling into Emon's sudden still form, a sickening feeling churning my insides.

No, I couldn't have. I didn't. Ethereal was with him, wasn't he? I studied the stubborn set of my soulmate's jaw as he glared back at the smirking god of death, his eyes refusing to meet mine.

The blood drained from my face, I hadn't once seen him distracted or pause to listen like he normally would when his panther spoke the entire time he was here. "No..." I whispered.

"Shea—" My mother barked angrily, pushing herself away from him, her arms crossed over her chest and her darkness curling up around her like vipers. "This was not the place, this was not the way."

Except the death god's cruel smirk never left Emon's face while I attempted to pull my soulmate away. "Do not listen to him, shifter. It can't be true. He is a god, he can lie."

"Ethereal, is my sister's son. The great God of Beasts who destroyed his own world with his infinite power and then was banished inside of you as punishment for his dark deed." Shea continued, his voice cold, void of any emotion, and mocking. "You are nothing but the rotting cell for my wayward nephew to be held by, shifter king of The West Isles."

Spinning towards the heartless and cruel death god, I threw a silver dagger at his feet. The sound of it burying into the onyx glass from the sheer force of my throw grating. "Open your mouth one more goddess damn time and I will make sure you permanently can never speak again! It may not be now but one day I will see it happen, and take pleasure in doing so with that dagger." I nodded at the knife before tugging on Emon's arm and begging. "Emon, please, don't listen to him. We will find Ethereal, he will tell us his truth. You mean more to him than just a host, he loves you and he would never abandon you. He is likely trying to find his way back to you right now."

My shifter did not move, he did not blink. His golden eyes had grown brighter with every hateful word the death god spat.

I inhaled sharply when Riella's gentle hand reached up and touched his cheek. "Father," she said, her voice soft and musical, and goddess bless us, it was enough to pull Emon out of his trance. "It will be okay," she whispered.

Emon blinked at her but did not respond, he just stared, watching her without any emotion.

Riella's tiny lip quivered as she pet his cheek. "You'll be okay, father, don't be sad. You'll be okay."

"Emon..."

Slowly, so painfully slowly, my soulmate turned his eyes on me, finally revealing the devastation behind the blazing fury. My arms wrapped around him cradling his head into my body. Falling into me, he stooped his massive frame to get closer, the scruff of his beard dragging along my skin with a slow ragged breath.

"I knew he was gone, Remnant, I just didn't want to admit it. After all these years, just wishing he would disappear and now...fuck. I wasn't prepared for this."

"How could you!" My mother's voice was deathly cold behind us, her shadows swarming around her just like the fury in her eyes.

"Get out," I whispered, over Emon's head at all of them.

The blaze in Shea's eyes snuffed out and it was only then that he registered his own mate's fury and the looks his children gave him. He stepped towards my mother, "Eve..." he growled but she only stepped further away.

"This is unforgivable, Shea." Her shadows cut through the air with her icy words. "Our children are not the Gods, we don't destroy each other for bragging rights and glory. This was an asshole move, even for you."

Emon's breathing became more ragged, similar to the night on the Balsam Plains when he relived the nightmares of our past.

"Breathe Emon." I held him tighter to me before I said with cold calculated violence. "I said. Get. Out." My words deadly whispering off the onyx glass making the death god wince and Riella to hold tighter onto me.

My mother's fury crumpled into empathetic sadness. "I am so sorry, my little chickadee, of course we shall leave. Take all the time you need and I will be here when you are ready to speak again." Then in a whirl of shadows she disappeared, leaving just Kade and her frustrated mate behind.

"Sister..." Kade took a step towards me and I shook my head.

"Leave," I seethed.

His face darkened but he nodded, leaving the same way my mother had.

In smoke and shadow.

Now just the death god remained and I bared my teeth at him, releasing a growl even a shifter would be proud of.

Shea flinched. "Fuck," he grunted, regarding my feral defense, his lips pressing into a thin line. "When you are ready, daughter, I will explain everything. Be at ease, your mate is safe for now, he has time before—"

I cut him off with a snarl. "Do not call me your daughter ever again, you are no father to me. Now get the fuck out of my sight."

Shea frowned and ran his hand down his face, spewing curses I had never heard before. I did not care. If I had my shadows there would be no possibility in all of this goddess damn universe that he would be standing right now, it would be a miracle if he was even left breathing, but I did not have them.

All I had was my rage, and it was enough.

Sending me one last remorseful look, he cursed again. "Now I know why children were forbidden for the gods," he muttered under his breath before he disappeared from our presence.

I stared blankly into the space where Shea had just stood and the knife that marked it, counting the seconds before feeling that we were safe from his manipulations, I raised Emon's head to look deep into my eyes, Riella still petting his cheek.

"Breath shifter, inhale...exhale."

His gold eyes blinked at me and before he calmed his breath, he inhaled and then we all exhaled together.

Chapter 7

I HADN'T LOST CONTROL of my emotions since Remnant stalked into my life with her cloak of darkness and kiss of shadows, but today it was as if my reprieve of my nightmare hadn't been days, but hours. The news of losing Ethereal left me bereft and lonely...something I hadn't felt since my mother was murdered and I exiled my father, and now here I was, relying on my already shattered soulmate to patch me back together.

That wasn't her job, it was mine...I fisted the pink unicorn shirt in a ball, growling.

Remnant's voice was soft within the room of our tower, soothing like the twilight that surrounded us. "Riella will be sad if you shred that shirt, Emon."

I grunted and looked up to see our little cub dancing on the balcony collecting stardust, still feeling her fear and gentle touch on my face when I lost control.

This could not happen again.

Forcing my hands to uncurl, I smoothed out the pink fabric and began meticulously folding it, so that the unicorns would show for her to see and admire.

"Are you sure you want to go to this dinner?" Remnant sighed, moving towards me from where she had been leaning against the glass wall, watching our daughter play.

"We need more answers," I said, setting the shirt on the counter of the large kitchen that occupied half the room of this tower, realizing it was the perfect surface for kneading dough. Drey would have loved it. "What we learned earlier today has just left us with more questions than answers."

Her hand reached up and turned my face towards hers and I fucking wished I could erase the worry that now was a permanent part of those emerald depths. "You need your rest, Emon. What you have experienced today...most wouldn't even be standing."

I turned my lips into her hand, "you would be, my little umbra." Stepping into her, I pulled her flush to my body, kissing her sweet sinful lips like they were my salvation. When she melted into me, I purred with satisfaction realizing quickly that she was all I ever needed to feel whole, her and Riella.

Delving deeper into our kiss, I gorged myself on the strength of our new love. The shock of today's events disappeared and instead was replaced with the taste of her, the touch of her, the smell of her—she was my cure, every part of her.

Pulling away, I grinned at her unsteady breathing and the sound of the thundering race of her heart. "Do not worry over me, Remnant. Worry more about what will happen after this fucking dinner, when I am eager for dessert." Pecking her lips one last time, I left her standing imprisoned in her own desire and my seduction.

Her worry eradicated.

For now.

I grinned, burying my own deep inside me, just like I used to with the cat, locking it all in a fucking box before calling Riella to come back inside.

It was time for another show down with my in-laws, and this time I would be fucking ready and I would get the answers my family needed.

***

Dinner was a fucking affair that I would have expected for an entire court, not for our party of six.

I glanced at it with mild disgust, never a fan of such finery. To say that Eve had outdone herself was an understatement. The table upon which I wanted to feast on my soulmate was surrounded by cloud chairs that floated above a balcony extending into the cosmos, providing the sweetest, softest mood lighting within this twilight world. Even the stardust was somehow directed to arch around us by an invisible barrier, and encased us in a sparkling curtain that was simply impressive.

None of it compared, however, to my soulmate sitting next to me. Remnant's not so discreet gaze roamed over my bare skin, and I shifted in my seat beside her. Her wandering emerald eyes were like an exquisite fire—a hot sear that did not burn but whispered promises of sweet seductive pleasure that you could barely hold back from.

Ever since I had kissed her in the tower and left her needing, her looks of longing had only intensified. The urge to snatch her from the delicate cloud she sat upon and devour her the way her eyes were begging me to was so fucking strong my arms strained at holding back.

I leaned into my soulmate, my nostrils flaring as I fell into a cloud of her unique scent of lilies and night, purring huskily, "Eye fucking me isn't going to get us the answers we seek, little umbra, but just say the word and I will whisk you back to our tower where you can do more than just look."

Licking her bottom lip, I watched the blush form across her fine porcelain skin. The fact that she even paused had me to the point of breaking, fuck this dinner shit.

"If you remember correctly, shifter, I didn't even want to come here tonight but you thought it to be a *good idea.*" Her eyes sparkled, "Alas, I'll just have to make do with looking," she murmured softly.

A slow smile spread across my face, before I leaned back, lengthening my large frame and stretching my legs in front of me, her roaming gaze setting my body on fire again—pure male satisfaction had me purring in my seat. "Whatever my little soulmate needs, my little soulmate will get."

"Gross. My ears may not be like a shifters but some things I do still hear," Remnant's brother gagged from across the table.

Smirking back, I watched as Kade fell into the dutiful role of uncle. The moment we arrived here had been...tension-filled to put it lightly but Riella's bright enthusiasm for the vast array of new foods laid out before us was more than enough to set our differences aside—for now. Besides, it seemed Kade was enjoying his new role.

"What is that called?" Riella pointed at the large centerpiece of chocolate cake decorated with mouth watering raspberries that I had been covertly eyeing since we sat down myself. It was the only thing here that I even remotely came close to wanting to eat if it wasn't going to be my soulmate.

"That is called chocolate cake, it is sweet and slightly bitter, with hints of spice, and the fruit on top is also sweet but tart," Kade explained to her while slicing a small piece to put on her plate.

She looked up at him eagerly. "Do you think I will like it?"

Kade laughed and tapped Riella's nose, smiling wide. "Judging by the way you eat stardust my niece, I think you will like it well enough."

I chuckled silently. Watching my daughter had become my second favorite pastime. The first was so easily denied recently by my soulmate that I had to make do with seconds. I gave the fitted black shorts Remnant wore a longing side glance—knowing she picked them in retaliation for leaving her full of desire in the tower.

Swallowing down a torturous groan, I refocused on Riella, leaning forward, eager to watch her take her first bite of chocolate cake. She had already proven to have a sweet tooth with her most recent stardust addiction, and she was our daughter after all.

Rotating the plate one way then back, she assessed the best attack for this newfound food. Then throwing all hesitancies straight off the very balcony we sat upon, she scooped up the chocolate cake and shoved the entire piece into her mouth.

I grinned. Definitely our daughter.

Her eyes grew wide and her mouth opened with awe, displaying the half eaten piece of cake for everyone. "Can I have another?!"

Kade roared with laughter.

My soulmate laughed alongside him and I relished the sound, fully loving the way my daughter's cheeks puffed widely out to the side when she closed her mouth to voraciously chew and swallow.

Leaning sideways, I mouthed from the corner of my smiling lips to Remnant, "This looks familiar."

"Indeed." Eve replied, materializing from the darkness beside us with a bottle of ambrosia in hand. Stepping between my soulmate and I, she glanced down at me before she poured the pink drink into the fine crystal glasses. "That was exactly how Remnant was at Riella's age, always stuffing her face full of treats." Pouring her daughter's glass, her eyes softened, "I am thankful you decided to come, my little chickadee. I know it was not easy and that you have many questions," she glanced at me, "I will do my best to answer them."

"Thank you, Eve." I nodded to her and she gave me a small smile back before moving away from us to sit at the head of the table, where a second cloud-chair sat unoccupied.

I could no longer hold back the burning question escaping my lips, staring at my soulmate's profile. "Is this where your obsession with chocolate comes from then, little umbra. Because, I haven't forgotten, you never did answer me that day in the garden." That moment would stay with me forever, it was the first time she had voluntarily been vulnerable with me, sharing her demons as I shared mine, something we did again today.

Her emerald gaze turned on me, her long dark hair falling over her shoulder as she rested her chin in her hands with her elbows propped on the table, her scrolling tattoos beckoning me.

Fuck.

"Tell me your majesty, are shifters aware of their own scent?" she teased.

I frowned, I never even thought about my own scent aside from when I needed to bathe blood from my body. Turning my nose down I inhaled deeply, confusion whirling inside my mind. I could practically hear Ethereal's laughter but I shoved that thought aside, I would not dwell on it until I had all the information at my disposal.

"Is this your way of telling me I stink, little umbra?" I said, my face wrinkled with amusement and confusion.

She smirked and her voice was a whispered caress inside of me. *"Of course you stink, shifter. You reek actually...reek of delicious spiced chocolate...you are my new sweet obsession, just as I am yours. Nothing else will ever taste as good as you again."*

Without any thought, I moved with my shifter speed, pulling her into my arms and devouring her lips with mine, that kiss earlier wasn't fucking enough and I cared not who saw. I craved her, I wanted to strip her down till there was nothing but her soul to intertwine with mine, where there was no fate of the world on our shoulders, there was just us and our love.

Pulling away and breathing heavily, I rested my forehead against hers, growling. *"That's shit I'm supposed to say, little umbra."* Brushing my lips along her now swollen ones, I added with a smirk, *"I can't wait to see what else of me rubs off on you."*

I brushed her hair back over her shoulder. She had changed it, instead of waves it was straight silky strands of black and blue and I loved how it fell like a curtain from my fingertips. Glancing back at her, I saw the shadows of fear flickering in her eyes, and I knew just where her mind had gone.

"Don't think of it now," I whispered gently through our connection. *"Lets try to enjoy this night with Riella and the new world she is exploring. We are sitting in the fucking stars. You're a fucking goddess and you are even more beautiful in this world than the first time I saw you."*

Her hand rested on my chest, spreading wide over where my heart beat fiercely for her. *"My world isn't a place, shifter. It's you and Riella. It is all I will ever need. Not a title, not power...just you both. I cannot lose you."*

I picked up her hand and kissed it tenderly. *"There you go again, little umbra. Saying shit that I would. Fuck, you're stealing my game, soulmate."*

Worry formed a tiny crease between her eyes. "Emon."

Smoothing the frown with my fingertips, I trailed them down the softness of her cheek, the flawless skin of her neck where her pulse beat wildly, and then brushed it softly against her collar bone careful with the words I chose. "Remnant, I am fine, I feel fine..." glancing over her shoulder, I smirked at her father, the death god who had made his silent entrance at the same time I had devoured his daughter's mouth with mine, payback was a fucking bitch. He would pay for the shit he pulled today. I would make sure of it. "For now that is, the death god looks like he might murder me again."

Remnant shot me a stern look before her face took on the neutral mask she wore so well...and just like in The Under, I marveled at her performance. Turning to her father and sliding from my lap she addressed her father, "Shea," she said formally.

Still smirking, I shot an assessing quick look at my daughter, finding Kade had been occupying her strategically with another slice of cake, this time teaching her how to use a fork properly to eat it. The water fae had no use for such things, using their clawed webbed hands and needled teeth to eat.

Edging my cloud closer to my soulmate, I threw a possessive arm over her shoulders and leaned back in my seat. "Nice of you to finally join us. Now start talking, death god."

If he thought I'd allow myself to be ashamed for breaking in front of him then he was sorely mistaken. When I broke, I only rose up stronger than before, it was the only way for me to live.

The death god snorted, sitting beside Eve. "Would it kill you to keep a shirt on, shifter?"

I scrubbed my hair back, puffing out my chest just to piss him off more, and smiled down the table at him. "You tell me Shea, you are the God of *death* after all."

The death god growled and flourished his hand. Immediately, I was confined in a heavily furred rainbow sweater.

I bared my teeth at him in a silent snarl. I much preferred the hideous unicorns over this shit.

The death god tilted his head in response, watching me tug on the damn thing to loosen it from my body with both satisfaction and disappointment. "A pity," he sighed. "It would seem clothing does not kill you."

Eve shot him a look of disapproval.

"Just a bit of fun love." I heard him mutter the excuse towards his mate, her eyes burning with fury.

I was fucking glad I wasn't around for that showdown, the tension between them more palpable than the one between him and I.

"Fun?" Eve hissed. "You promised Shea, you promised you would apologize and I am still waiting for those words to leave your mouth."

CHAPTER 8

G RINNING, I RAISED MY brow at the death god, watching him fumble to say any words, his eyes saying the opposite of what was caught in his throat.

"I—" he snarled, snaking his tongue across his teeth with glaring eyes in my direction.

Eve's arms crossed her chest, darkness pluming around her, moving in tandem with her dark hair. "Anytime now, *my love*," she mocked, the hard edge to her voice unmistakable.

Sparing her a glance and seeing no mercy in her stare, he turned back to me, pinching the bridge of his nose and huffing out a breath. The rings on his hand flashing in the moonlight. "I apologize for my godlike behavior earlier, even though that is what the fuck I am." Pulling his hand away, he sent his soulmate an irritated look before glaring at me. "I didn't think you'd be so delicately emotional about it."

I chuckled darkly, "Thank you Shea," I said while ripping the sleeves off the newest piece of clothing he bestowed me. Thank fuck Riella was too occupied with her cake to notice because I was going to end up with a stack of rainbow colored shirts that she *loved*. "For such a heartfelt apology," I added, drawing my sharp claw down the front of the monstrosity of dyed fur, freeing my torso once more.

Remnant snickered next to me and even Kade let loose a dark chuckle. "A vest. Clever shifter, Penina would be so proud—" The moment Penina's name left my soulmate's lips, her sweet laughter died off like the stars falling from the evening sky—it was just as painful to see as the sight of my sister laying lifeless in a glass tomb.

And now I battled with time, an unknown clock ticking down the moments I had left before I suffered the same fate as her and the rest of my family.

I tightened my arm around Remnant's shoulder, drawing soothing circles with my fingertips on her exposed skin.

"I think we both have had our fun for now." Turning my fierce gaze on Eve, I addressed her simply. "You said you would provide us with answers and we are here now seeking them."

Sending one last scathing glare in Shea's direction, her calm voice carried across the table like a soft breeze. "I will do my best, Daemon but know some things..." her eyes turned inward, "some things I am bound by the universe to not speak of, if I do it could mean catastrophe for the rest of us."

I grunted my agreement but Remnant did not.

Her fist connected with the table, causing even Riella to look up with wide eyes, chocolate smeared all over her face. Kade leaned in and whispered something in her ear that made her giggle. I had been right about him and even though he didn't know it yet, Kade Dark would soon become part of our ragtag family.

Remnant seethed, "that's not good enough, not even close. Not when it comes to my family."

Shea's deep voice rumbled and he looked down at Eve. "Now where have I heard those words before?"

Eve's eyes widened. "That was a long time ago Shea and—"

"And I broke the universal rules for you my love," he interrupted with a smug smirk.

"Our very world was at stake," she snapped back.

Shea reached for his own glass of ambrosia, "As it is now once again."

Eve narrowed her eyes. "Your sister was dying and called for your aid, you refused."

"And she sent you to convince me...except you had an even bigger secret, one you thought I knew nothing about—our daughter," he sipped from his glass, totally forgetting that the rest of us were still watching.

Remnant's body stiffened and my hand resumed its soothing strokes over her skin.

Eve sighed, relenting. "I shall never live this down."

"With all due respect to you both," Remnant said through gritted teeth. "I don't care to hear about your tragic love story. I care about what is happening to my soulmate and how I can stop it."

Eve's green ringed eyes turned on us both, her gaze patient. "A pity daughter, since our love story holds the answers to the questions you desperately seek."

The truth snapped into place and I gave her an assessing look. "You're alive. The sleep has not taken you." A singular claw rapped on the table. "Unless I am mistaken you hold no God blood in your veins, and yet you have not become soulless. How do I stay the same?"

Shea sipped on his drink once more, sniffing. "Not the dumb witted animal I assumed you to be."

My fangs lengthened in a silent snarl and Remnant's face darkened.

Snickering, Kade rose from the table with a sigh. "Well before the morning repeats itself, I think that is my cue. Rem, if you can trust me enough, there is a herd of camphor below, not quite the unicorns my little niece has been wishing to see but I thought they'd be close enough to entertain her while you four work out...whatever the goddess this is."

Riella bounced in her seat, chocolate frosting covering her face, hair, and hands while her swirling gold and green eyes implored us, "Oh can I please?"

Remnant's eyes flashed with both interest and discord, and I hummed, drawing that conflicting gaze into mine. I knew Remnant would never deny our daughter the sight of any beast, having a similar passion for them herself.

Except now she was terrified, the anxiety of losing us at any notice so plain to see that indecision plagued her—her answer lost on her tongue.

"She is fae my love, and no fae ever survived being sheltered in this world. She will be safe with Kade despite your falling out and our daughter deserves to live freely just like you and I had at one time...or else what is it that we are actually fighting for?"

Remnant took a deep breath. *"I know you are right..."*

Leaning in, I kissed her shoulder softly and then turned to the pair both waiting anxiously on our answer, Kade looking like the young chocolate covered faeling next to him.

"Of course." Shooting Kade a warning look, I added, "Do I need to remind you of what would happen should anything happen to our daughter?"

Kade rolled his eyes. "Relax shifter, camphor are not dangerous here, they are but horned amphibian spirits searching for their lost water in this world. It's the nuckelavee you really have to worry about, those demon horses like feeding on their souls."

Remnant leaned in eagerly this time, all worry gone from her bright eyes. "There are nuckelavee here?" she whispered excitedly.

Riella's eyes widened even further as she glanced between her mother and her newfound uncle. I scrubbed my hand through my hair with a quiet groan.

Goddess help us.

Kade's eyes gleamed, evidently sharing the same interest as his sister. "Yes and they are much easier to catch than the nightmares of the Nocturnes."

Remnant smirked, "Do tell, brother. You have caught some yourself? Did they grant you the eternal flame?"

"Remnant..." I said with half irritation and half amusement. The eternal flame was a myth...*wasn't it?*

Glancing back at me and seeing the amused worry now on my face, she reigned in her excitement and leaned back into my arm slung across her seat. "Don't worry yourself Emon, of course we will kill him if anything happens to our daughter on his watch."

Kade winked, "That's the spirit." Reaching for Riella who happily jumped into his arms, "But you're old now sister, I don't think you can actually catch up to even attempt to kill me, Rem Rem." Shifting our daughter in his arms and attempting to avoid the chocolate massacre all over her tiny body, he looked down at her with a grin, "Ready, little chocolate bird?"

She nodded happily and then shadows swirled around them, shifting through the darkness leaving behind a singular tendril of black smoke floating on the air.

My soulmate stiffened and reflexively, I reached for Riella and I's shared bond, the one she had solidified while in her healing sleep before I even knew her. Feeling her sudden euphoria like a bolt of energy racing through my body, I smiled.

Chuckling, I winked at Remnant. "She is ecstatic with her new beasts." Tucking a stray strand of hair from my soulmate's face, I trailed a single claw down her porcelain skin following the relief spreading over her fine features. "Just like her mother would be."

Eve cleared her throat and a soft blush filtered through my soulmate's face and I smirked, loving that color on her pale skin.

"You are different with your shifter, my little chickadee, and I am happy for you. You are good together." We both looked up to see Remnant's mother studying us intimately. She gave me an approving nod. "Which makes what I have to say that much harder. To answer your question Daemon, I am awake because of the *extremum vitae spiritum edere,* to death I give my last breath."

Remnant inhaled sharply, the blush immediately gone and her face paling. "You forfeited your soul to him?" Remnant turned a hateful glare on the death god. "That is worse than even a soulless sleep, mother. There is no afterlife for you now, should death take you, you will cease to exist and we shall never be together again. It erases you from the wheels of fate instantly."

Her blue green eyes glittered with emotion but her features remained reserved, Shea more than deathly quiet next to her. "Shea is my soulmate, daughter. We are already entwined, the only difference now is that I exist only because he does. It was the only way for me to be here for you when the time came, otherwise I too would be in The Well and as your father so nicely pointed out, I am needed to break the rules..." I didn't fail to miss the subtle way her eyes flickered to me pointedly before falling back on Remnant.

Remnant's hand slammed down on the table again, the damned thing taking a beating with her frustration tonight.

"He is a death god for Faerie sake!" she turned her fury on the solemn Shea, his lips thinning and his face darkening the more Remnant raged. "You! You are a death god with unlimited power! Surely you could have found another way!"

He narrowed his eyes at his daughter and all my claws extended slowly, preparing to fight the god of death, I knew the vest was the right choice. "I am bound by rules just as all gods are. My power, while mostly unlimited, cannot be abused without serious repercussions. If it were not so, I would have saved us all from this misery thousands of years ago." Shadows spread across the table. "I knew of you the exact moment you were born and I paid the price by watching you grow up without a father. Then I watched my son have to do the same as the price for my involvement in the wars, but it was even more than that, all memory of me was wiped from the mind of my soulmate, while I remembered our love, she did not." The night sky lowered down upon us as his anger built. "Then I was forced to watch as she raised two children on her own, forced to watch and wait while you suffered because I was terrified of what the cost would be should I interfere again. You think my power great but it is a prison, a prison of the worst kind of torture. A prison of no power over what really matters."

Remnant jumped to her feet, shadows flickering around her and dying out. It was the first time I saw them respond to her since we came here. "Am I supposed to feel sorry for you then, death god...*father*?" she snarled. "You brought us here in deceit, forcing us to make the same sacrifices as you. Does that make you feel better somehow knowing that we shall all suffer the same as you?"

The night sky lurched and the death god glanced up with his eyes shifting to gleaming pride and it was then that I realized he no longer controlled the night, Remnant did.

Ignoring her accusations, but fascinated by Remnant's power he encouraged her. "That's it daughter...show me," he said, still watching the night, "show me how you can pull down the night, just like you did when you first came here."

Glancing back at my soulmate, my brows drew together. Remnant usually commanded her shadows with ease, vast amounts of shadows, without strain, but watching her now—her body shaking, her chest rattling with quick breaths, sweat pouring down her brow and the shadows flickering in and out, I knew...knew something was horribly wrong.

Shea's dark look while he watched her also narrowed with concern and confirming that I wasn't delusional.

Remnant truly no longer had control over her powers.

"You were already coming here daughter," Shea continued, his voice gentling, to ease the strain and her anger, the night swirling dangerously over us without control, "your shadow sphere made it possible for me to finally come to you, a way to hide from the universal laws that would punish us more had I stepped a single foot in Faerie. Your mother and I have been waiting for an opening to retrieve you for years. But after the loss of your lilin—"

"Lilin?" Remnant staggered, the darkness wobbling towards us. "Is that what they are called? What does that mean?"

The death god growled, glancing upwards. "Sit down Remnant and release the night slowly, you are not ready for this power and it is putting us all in danger—your daughter in danger."

Startled Remnant glanced up at the sky. "I—I don't know how," she whispered shakily.

But I did.

Purring softly, I pulled my soulmate into my embrace, her legs straddling my lap as she fell into me, her face imploring me desperately for help. Gripping her hands and turning them over, I rubbed my thumbs into her palms. "Breathe with me, my love," I whispered. "Inhale." She inhaled and I smiled encouragingly at her. Kissing her lips softly, "Exhale," I breathed against them.

Her eyes fluttered closed, her dark lashes brushing against her pale cheeks while she exhaled.

"It's just you and me, in a bed of clouds, rainbow crystals dance across our skin, you're listening to my heart beat, the way my chest rises and falls where your head rests, fitting perfectly into me." I kissed her again and her eyes snapped open, blazing with resolve, her fear gone. "Now, little umbra. Release it, release the night."

She blew out a shaky breath before the sky slowly receded back into the cosmos.

I grinned at her, nuzzling her nose with mine. "Well done, my fierce shadow savage. Pulling the night sky on your father...I am in awe of you."

She relaxed in my hold, her hands splaying across my chest beneath my rainbow furred vest, brushing her lips conspiratorially against mine. "Barely Emon, he was right. I didn't have control."

"But you did in the end."

She sniffed, "I really don't like him."

I chuckled darkly seeing Shea's gaze flicker with hurt before smiling against her lips, "Sometimes we have to play nice to get what we want." Leaning away, I swept her hair aside, before brushing my lips against the shell of her ear. "But you can play dirty with me later if that is what you still need, my little umbra."

Remnant blushed but it was the intensity of the look she leveled on me that had me holding my breath. "You're not giving him your soul, shifter. There will be no Sheol for you in the afterlife if you do this, Emon. That is what my mother gave up. An eternal life if she dies. Your life will just come to an end and you will leave me here. Alone. Always searching for my other half but never finding it. Selfishly, I will not let you do this, we will have to find another way."

"I know," I sighed.

Tilting forward, I gave her one last lingering kiss, one that promised of whispered worship, and watched as her eyes fluttered closed in sweetness. Exhaling softly, I forced my limbs to move, pulling away and determinedly placing her back on her cloud perch.

Her eyes opened, studying me, a small smile playing on her lips when I pulled her seat closer, grunting irritably, unable to tolerate not even an inch of air between us. Our thighs brushed, my hand searched for hers, holding it in tenderness, resuming my tracing on her soft pure skin.

Giving me one last assessing look, that pulled a smirk from my lips, Remnant turned back to her parents, squeezing my hand gently. "I will be okay now," she said softly.

I squeezed her hand back, my other reaching for my own tall glass of ambrosia, delicately pinching the thin stemware between my fingers, annoyed with the worry that I may break the damn thing before it even reached my lips.

"Let's start over, can someone please explain to me what the lilin are?"

I arched a brow over the rim of the glass, my lips smirking against the cool surface. *Did you just say please?*

I am attempting diplomacy, she snapped back.

I snickered, my laughter rumbling along our bond before slugging back the sweet ambrosia liquid, confident that I was not going to turn into a rutting animal this time like I had back in The Under.

"The lilin are not shadows like you believe, daughter. They are souls. Vengeful female souls that serve only one being. The God or Goddess of The Well."

I frowned, setting the glass down, tapping it lighty with a singular claw. "What is The Well?"

The death god's eyes gleamed hard as they fell on me. "The Well of Souls is where all of us go upon death. There we are judged and if deemed worthy, given permission to live our afterlife however we like. Some remain in The Well along with the soulless, having never truly died. Others choose the Eithne, and some...some choose vengeance, they pledge themselves to the God or Goddess of the Wells, waiting for him or her to collect them. Those are the lilin." He paused and looked at us thoughtfully. "I was once that God, conquering the lilin nearly a millennium ago...but then you were born daughter," his gaze shifted to her with a soft smile, "I passed the lilin down the moment your eyes opened, ready to champion your world. Thus crowning you Goddess of The Well of Souls."

"The Goddess of The Well of Souls. That is what you called me when I came here," Remnant murmured.

I squeezed her hand and purred proudly, "Your fan club just became so much more interesting, little umbra. At this rate I am going to have to fight off your admirers when they come sniffing around."

She snorted and I chuckled again, refraining from adding that it didn't matter who the fuck came around. I was the one and only in this fan club, and anyone who challenged me on it would meet a swift defeat.

"So the lilin are vengeful souls but for what purpose?" Remnant continued.

The death god nodded. "To rectify the wrongs of the past by preventing it in the future. Their power is vast, in all my years of godhood, I have yet to see anything else like it. Because of this, they can only be conquered by overpowering The Well itself, and only then, can their master abdicate them to others—like I did for you." He leaned in gravely, "I must warn you The Well is treacherous, it does not give up its own easily."

"Neither do we," I snarled.

The death god glanced at me, before his eyes fell back on Remnant. "Only a few things can destroy the lilin. One of them is to obtain more lilin inside The Well to defeat the original."

"And the other?" Remnant asked, her head tilted to the side, her hair falling silkily over my arm, studying her father with calculated calmness.

My fingers twitched on my glass, wanting nothing at that moment then to run my hands deeply through it.

Shea leaned back in his chair, "It's a myth only."

"The choice to travel to The Well is yours," Eve added quickly, her eyes flickering briefly at me, before gravely settling on Remnant, "but I have seen both paths, with and without the lilin. And when the time comes to face Deirdre, as I know you plan to do, without the lilin—you will not defeat her, daughter."

I swirled my glass, noticing that it had refilled itself. "Yet, your visions could be interpreted in many ways, Eve."

Eve turned her gaze on me. "Yes, King Strider," Eve said solemnly.

I drank deep into my glass before setting it down. "But you believe this is not one of those cases."

"I do," she pragmatically replied.

I licked at my fang glancing at Remnant, her eyes flashing at me like fierce emeralds before turning back to the death god, her body tensing as she spoke, "Is this why you orchestrated my arrival here? Why not leave the others out of it? Why bring them here if you knew the cost?"

Shea picked up his glass, his expression unreadable, "I did not intend for your friends to get involved but they refused to give your daughter to me and it was imperative for her to come to Sheol—as it was for your soulmate as well. You will need them both should you choose this path. Although, I hadn't anticipated that your mate would no longer have my nephew inside him, leaving him vulnerable." Tilting his drink at me he took a long swallow, before shaking his head, "I simply did not see that one fucking coming."

CHAPTER 9

Remnant

"You didn't see that one coming?" The deadly whisper hissed through my lips. "That's your excuse?"

Shea regarded me with a simple tilt of his head and a tapping of his rings on his glass. "Yes."

Emon's hand tightened on my thigh, whether he felt my muscles coil or the initial movement I did not know but his hold wasn't enough to stop me. Plucking the silver knife hidden within my boot, I threw it with a snarl. A flashing silver blur that split the fine china elegantly placed before Shea. The blade vibrated from the force of my throw, its lethal edges already buried halfway within the table before my mother released her gasp.

"Remnant Dark," she hissed, staring at me in shock. I did not look at her, I only saw Shea in my rage.

The slapping of my palms on the table was harsh as I leaned in, baring my teeth. "Did you see that coming, death god?" I purred dangerously. I could practically hear Xi, muttering trouble was coming with this tone, when all my words came out as feral questions.

Shea's eyes drifted up from the blade, his smile widening the further they rose. "Of course. You are half your mother after all."

My nails dug into the table, stopping myself from throwing another blade, "And what are you then? Care to take a look at your own reflection or are you afraid of what you will see?" I nodded to the silver dagger, seeing my own snarl on its deadly edge even from here. "Because I can tell you what I see. I see an arrogant, self centered, and callous god who has lost touch with his own emotions after living a lonely life with only power to keep him company."

The air stilled around us, the star dust paused its descent, and even my mother and Emon seemed to not breathe.

Shea's eyes flared bright green, penetrating with their intensity, "All I *need* to see, daughter, is a way to make sure you survive," he seethed. "And if this is the role I must play, where I am the villain to you, then I will."

I snarled, pushing away from the table, hating the fact that what he said made me feel something different than pure rage. "And your solution for me to survive was what exactly? Send me to The Well of Souls to obtain the lilin, the souls of my friends, and those of my people to rectify your wrongs?"

Plucking the blade from the table as if it hadn't been deeply embedded, he twirled it over his fingers, the blade pinging against his numerous rings. "Yes."

Folding my arms, I bit back another angry retort knowing it would not get me anywhere and settled a leveled look on my mother, cold anger still evident in my voice, "And you have seen that I need to bring Emon with me? Can I not leave him and Riella here, where they can be safe?"

Emon growled, rapping his own claws on the table, sending dishes rattling, "That's not fucking happening, little umbra."

My mother looked between us, her lips pressed together before she spoke, "If you leave them both here you will not win over the lilin at The Well."

A whirl of bright shooting stars flew over our heads, illuminating my growing darkened expression. "How long does Emon have?

Shea's eyes held mine, never wavering, "Days."

My heart pounded in my chest, the tightness creeping. "How long does it take to reach The Well of Souls?"

"Days," he shrugged. "You will need to leave by tomorrow if you plan on making it to The Well before the sleep overcomes him."

I bit the inside of my cheek to keep myself from exploding, the blood welling inside my mouth. "And what of Ethereal, you said Emon was his host. What has happened to him?"

Shea's brow rose. "What happened to him was *you*, daughter."

I stilled, a sinking panic pitting deep in my stomach, the race of my heart now a fierce sprint. Deirdre's taunting words rung all too loudly in my mind.

"They will have no future with you because you will destroy whatever is left of it...you already have."

"What do you mean?" my voice shook, fear quickly replacing my rage.

The death god observed me thoughtfully before he grunted with self affirmation, waving his hand to create a swirling cloud of shadow that circled above the table forming a black orb. "What I mean...is this." He nodded towards the mass with both pride and sympathy.

Emon reached out, trailing his hand through the shadows with a deep frown. "These are the shadows from when you saved me," he growled softly, his hair falling over his brow as he glanced back at me questioningly.

Tearing my gaze from him, I studied the weaves with a deep sense of foreboding, the tightness in my chest growing. "Yes, it's a replica of the shadows I created to stop Ethereal from crossing into the gateway to the Sanguine," I said slowly.

Shea hummed, stroking his fingers across his lips in thought. "Indeed it is daughter...a new shadow weave that I have never seen before. Shadows that don't just stop or deflect an enemy but strips them of their very soul and locks it away. What you created was a prison or a weapon that separates a soul from its physical body." He tilted his head and I shivered at the intensity of the cold calculated look glittering in his eyes. It was a look that told of future dark plans. "Fortunately for your shifter," Shea continued, "he had two souls to give and Ethereal was the one stripped from him. My nephew is now free and irrevocably trapped in those shadows—until he learns how to escape them, that is," he smirked and a brief flash of shadow delivered my silver blade back in front of me, resting next to the butter knife like it belonged there, "I'll be ashamed to call him my nephew if he does not soon enough."

"We are no longer bound?" Emon's hand shook slightly as he trailed it through the shadows again, his hushed tone full of disbelief and uncertainty.

"Yes," Shea said with a shrug. "I do believe that was what you always wanted, correct shifter king?"

"Shea," my mother murmured, drawing the death god's attention with a frown.

"What have I done now?" he sighed, looking back towards us, trying to understand.

Emon ignored them, his gaze never leaving the shadows, his profile strong and unwavering, his golden eyes losing their playful twinkle.

"Emon," I said softly, my trembling hand falling on his shoulder, my heart breaking while my parents whispered heatedly in the background. Their attention drawn away from us.

"He really is gone," Emon whispered, more to himself than in answer to me. His hands curled into fists, the claws breaking his skin and causing tiny beads of blood to drip down onto the fine tablecloth.

I could not breathe. I had done this...it was just like before. In my attempt to play the hero I also destroyed what mattered most. "Emon, I am so sorry. I didn't know...goddess, I am sorry," I choked.

"He's right, you know. I always did want to be free of him." Emon's deep rich voice said flatly in my mind not even hearing my words. A sudden bark of dark laughter burst from him, and my hand tightened on his muscular shoulder. "Of course he would be gone when I need him the most," he sneered.

I could not stop the tear that fell down my face. The cycles of his loss rapidly dictated his mood while he struggled to come to terms with the panther being gone.

Sobering, he ran a ragged hand through his hair, "I hate the silence," he whispered.

I could not stop the trembling, my breathing short, and my hand fell from his shoulder, my body collapsing into the seat with defeat. I really was a monster. "I'm sorry, Emon."

A frown pinched his features before he moved so quickly that I found my watering eyes drowning in his fierce stare, I could see nothing else but those pools of golden light. *"Stop,"* Emon said soothingly, reaching for my trembling hands, swirling his thumbs rapidly over them, breathing slowly in and out, reminding me to do the same. *"Stop, my little umbra, I see these thoughts, I know these thoughts. You are not a monster Remnant Dark, you are my soulmate, Riella's mother, a daughter, a sister, a friend, a goddess. You are everything you need to be and more—but never, ever, ever, a monster."* His hair fell between his eyes and he dropped his forehead to mine, drawing another ragged breath, "If anything this is my fault for being so afraid of my damn power. If I had learned how to control it then maybe none of this would have happened."

Shea sniffed behind us. "That's an understatement."

Ignoring him, I shook my head, devastation still cutting up my heart for what I had done. "Shifter...I saw that power, it opened up the sky, it tore through the universe. You wouldn't have prevented anything but you most certainly would have destroyed everything."

He smiled sadly at me, sweeping my hair back, a bit of brightness returning. "Then thank the goddess, you were there to save me. How many times is that now?"

I smiled sadly through watery eyes, "I've lost count, shifter."

"Four," Shea growled across the table like a child that was being denied attention.

It helped though, to shove my grief aside and refocus on the loathing I felt for the being that was my father. I gave my mother a questioning look, seeing that she was rubbing her temples muttering to herself.

"How do you even live with him?" I asked her and Emon snickered next to me.

She lifted her hands from her face, folding them neatly back in front of her and gave me a playful smile, "Why do you think I left him the first time?" she said laughingly.

Despite myself, I laughed with her, the sound of it lifting the darkened mood and the stifling grief.

Shea looked between us, his brows pulled together creating a small v on his flawless beauty as if he had never seen the sight of his soulmate and daughter laughing together.

And once upon a time, we always did---those memories so far buried in pain and loss that they were difficult to recall.

Emon's thumb swirled over my hand, *"Fucking beautiful,"* he purred, *"goddess help me there is no symphony that could ever be composed that is more beautiful than the sound of your laugh Remnant Dark, and it cures the silence."*

CHAPTER 10

Remnant

"WILL YOU TELL ME a story?" Riella sighed softly as we tucked her into our bed. She had spent most of the evening chasing the camphor with my brother, and now she had declared the beasts were her new favorite but was quite disappointed she did not get to see any nuckelavee.

I couldn't help but share her disappointment..

She fidgeted nervously, her hands twisting in her lap while her swirling green and gold eyes watched us both carefully, biting her lip waiting for our answer.

Glancing over at my shifter soulmate, I saw his eyes soften watching her, realizing, just as I did, that it was likely she had never had a tale told to her in the seven years she has graced this life.

"Of course," I said, tucking her in more, to hide my sadness, "I hear that your father is an excellent archiver of stories, perhaps he has a few stories he'd share."

Emon pounced on the bed then, sending us both bouncing with squeals of laughter that echoed in the great open room. It was a beautiful sound, a sound to be cherished in these darker times.

"What kind of story does my little cub want to hear I wonder?" Emon purred, flourishing his hands dramatically, his brows raised, "Tales of her mother's great battles or of her father's unparalleled strength?"

I snickered, "unparalleled?"

"Apologies soulmate, of course Riella is the most powerful one here." Emon flopped onto his back, placing his hands behind his head, and grinning when Riella covered her mouth snorting with laughter.

Laying down on her other side laughing, I tickled the beautiful creature that was the truest and purest form of the two of us. "Of course she is."

Giggling, she thrashed to escape the tickles, her small body flailing wildly only to smack Emon straight across the face.

My soul mated shifter, with his *unparalleled strength*, howled, clutching his nose, groaning with watering eyes, "goddess."

Riella stilled, her lip trembling. "I'm sorry," she whimpered, shrinking into me.

Emon quickly stopped rubbing the bridge of his nose and blinked hard at our cowering daughter. "Do not cry my cub, I know it was an accident," he winked at her, "I think all I need is a kiss right here. Then my nose will finally be cured and straight again."

Riella's lip trembled more, her eyes full of alarm. "I broke it, I made it crooked," she gasped.

I snorted and hugged Riella into me, kissing the top of her head. "Your father's nose was already crooked, little chickadee, he is just acting like a baby nymph right now."

Emon shot me an innocent look, "heartless soulmate, I am practically wounded by our daughter's unparalleled strength and this is how you care? Comparing me to those terrorizing beasts," he gave her a grin, "our daughter has the power to fix me, what say you my cub? Will you heal me with a sweet kiss? Just here," he pointed at the slight wayward slant of his nose.

I rolled my eyes but our daughter nodded, a stern concentrated look on her face as she leaned in to place a sweet delicate kiss on the bridge of her fathers nose. I prayed I would never forget this moment.

Looking up at me, his chocolate brown hair fell in his mischievous golden eyes. "What do you think soulmate," he angled his head for me, "am I handsome, has our daughter cured my un-fae like imperfection?"

Riella's face fell in dismay. "But father I did not fix you, it is still crooked."

Emon ruffled her head and leaned back with a sigh. "Worry not my cub, I am truly cursed to spend an eternity with this crooked nose!" He raised his hands up to the glass ceiling where stars showered above us. "Why has the goddess forsaken me so?"

I laughed and reached over to swat the dramatic shifter on his bare chest, the slap loud in the quiet twilight of the room. "Hush shifter. You are upsetting our daughter, she does not understand."

Emon chuckled and caught my swatting hand, kissing it softly, then glanced at our daughter questioningly, "Shall that be your story tonight? The tale of how, your father, the strongest shifter, with unparallelled strength, ended up with a permanent crooked nose?"

My brows rose and I looked down at Riella. "What do you think, is this the tale you would like to hear tonight?"

Our daughter bit at her lip worriedly. "It is not my fault then?"

Emon chuckled, "Nay, it is not your fault."

Releasing her lip she grinned widely, relief shining in her eyes, "Yes please, I want that story!"

I grinned, finding I too desperately wanted to know this story. Penina had teased that I should ask him sometime...and now that time was finally here. I only wish I could share my reaction with her in hearing it, she would likely laugh at every expression crossing my face.

Emon lifted up the covers that had fallen off of Riella. "Snuggle in my cub."

Instantly diving in with her overly large nightshirt, Riella curled her small body into his large frame. Laying down alongside her once again, Emon and I faced each other with our heads propped on our hands while our daughter's rapt attention never left Emon's face.

Brushing her hair back from her sweet innocent face, Emon's voice rumbled as he quietly began his tale. "This story starts, how all stories start. With a curious little faeling..."

Riella purred, "Like me?"

Emon smirked, "Just like you because that faeling was me." He tapped her nose and then continued to stroke her hair away from her face, his eyes taking on a distant look, lost in the memories of his tale. "When I was young, I would run wild in the wilderness of The West Isles, dreaming of the days I would become a true shifter and roam my country just like my father did before me. I wanted to know everything about it, just like the back of my own hand." Emon held up his hand in front of him and frowned. "Huh, what are these things, I wonder?"

Riella giggled, "Silly father! That is your hand!"

I shook my head, my shifter soulmate was in his element...he was meant for this. Not only for the way he strung his words, commanding a room with just a tone of his voice both in jest and in importance but also he was meant to be a father. Just like his role as my mate, he slid into fatherhood with ease while I? I struggled to see past my fear.

Deirdre's haunting voice echoed in my mind. *"Do you honestly think you can be her mother? You who does nothing but destroy everyone and everything around you? You are death and you'll never be more than that."*

"Where have you gone, my little umbra. Stay here, stay present." Emon's voice called out to me, shattering the hold Deridre's hauntings had ensnared me in all while continuing his story. "Oh, yes of course." Emon continued, narrowing his eyes at this hand, "I almost forgot what my own hand looked like." Winking at her, he laid it softly on her shoulder. "One day during my travels I lost track of time and was not home in time for our mandatory family dinner. My father was furious—"

"Papa Asher," Riella interrupted.

Emon smiled patiently. "Yes, Papa Asher was not happy with me. I think that I had scared him. This was not the first time I had disappeared for days and so they thought of the most heinous unthinkable punishment. Can you guess what that was?"

Riella bit at her lip, whispering, "What did Papa Asher do?"

Emon gave her a serious look, "I was sent to bed without any dinner."

"No!" Riella gasped and I snorted, the drama demonstrated by both of them was too much, but also if there was one thing that our child inherited from both of us it was an appreciation of food.

After she had returned from sightseeing and joined us again at the table, Riella had begged Kade to tell her about every piece of food and made a point to sample it all. There was not a single thing she did not like, and the rest of our entertainment for the evening was watching our daughter explore. Everything was new to her above the surface and to watch her live our world in a way we had long forgotten was beautiful and humbling.

"My thoughts exactly, my cub. Fortunately for me, I was a skilled climber and escaped my prison in search of food...and there was only one place that I knew would be close enough to home for me to sneak in and out unnoticed before my parents missed me, and it had the best baked desserts for its morning customers when the sun would rise."

"Were there chocolate cakes?" Riella's eyes glazed over.

Emon hummed, "Oh yes. The best cakes, but also cookies, ice cream, and your mother's favorite...pastries."

Riella pouted, "I haven't had pastries yet."

Reaching out I entwined her fingers with my own. "When we return to Finlandia, I will take you to Griffins Gateau. Drake the baker there will likely make a very special pastry in honor of you."

Riella rolled over to smile up at me. "Really?"

I kissed her sweet little hand, knowing it had the makings of a future pastry pincher. "I don't see why not."

Emon watched us, his gold eyes brightening in the dim light and I was suddenly ensnared by the pure beauty of him.

"What happened next, father?"

Realizing he had become just as ensnared, he shook his head. "Where was I? Oh yes. Pastries." He shot me a heated look before continuing. "I was resolved that if I could not have my dinner then I would take matters into my own hands and have dessert instead. So I snuck out and broke into the bakery where I knew the desserts were there waiting for me."

"That is bad right?" Riella looked between us both, "It's not good to break into things and steal."

My soulmate snorted and tapped her nose again. "It is very naughty but it also depends on why you are breaking in. That is the hard part about learning right from wrong, my cub, sometimes they look exactly the same and are, at times, just as sweet." Chuckling at the way she pondered his words, he continued, "unfortunately, I did not know that earlier that day the baker had asked a powerful warder to protect his shop against rodents that were stealing his baked goods nightly."

I raised a brow, "Rodents?"

Emon smirked, "Yes rodents, what could possibly make you think otherwise, little umbra?"

I shook my head and Riella laughed.

"To catch these rodents," Emon shot us both a sharp look, "the baker had it warded so anything or anyone trespassing would be frozen still under its spell. Even that would have been fine, except the baker also placed a slippery trap, one that caused me to fall face first into the floor the moment the wards were activated. I was found that morning, my face smashed still on the floor in my own blood, with a crushed nose, and a half eaten pastry in my hand."

I sputtered before bursting out in laughter at the same time as Riella gasped with alarm. "Did it hurt, father? Were you okay?"

Emon leaned forward and kissed her head softly. "Yes, of course I was okay. Remember I am the strongest shifter in the universe. It was my ego that hurt more than my nose ever did that morning." He stroked her hair again with a fond smile on his face. "The baker was horrified that he had caused harm to the golden prince though and he did not hesitate to find help, which included my parents. When the wards were finally lifted, some of the spell lingered because it had mixed with my own blood, leaving my nose to heal out of alignment." Emon wrinkled his perfectly imperfect nose, but to me, the defect, had only made his roguish charm even more alluring.

I laughed softly. "Daemon Ash Strider, King of Shifters, Thief of Pastries."

Riella rose up suddenly and kissed Emon's nose one more time and he blinked down at her with surprise, "What was that for, my cub?"

She smiled shyly at her father, lowering herself back down into the covers and snuggling against his chest. "Making sure my kiss will be frozen on your nose forever."

I swallowed hard against the burning emotion rising in my throat and for the sweet innocence that was our daughter. Such a goddess blessed miracle that I was just honored to be in the presence of, let alone be allowed to grow a bond with her and to be a part of her family...to be her mother.

Emon gruffly cleared his throat, "Thank you, my cub. It will always be with me now."

Riella yawned, her eyes closing, lashes fluttering over her bronze cheeks, "I never had a bedtime story before," she admitted. Blindly reaching back, she pulled me closer to her, sandwiching her body between the two of us. "They are just how I imagined them to be. I think I will want one every night."

My eyes blurred as they met Emon's. Tears of both sorrow and joy threatened to spill over my cheeks. "Then you shall have them every night for as long as you wish, my chickadee," I choked out.

She yawned again, her voice barely a whisper as she fell asleep. "Then I wish to have them every night for forever."

Emon kissed her softly, "Wish granted, my cub."

CHAPTER 11

I STARED OUT OVER *the horizon at churning seas where flying fish jumped in and out of the aquamarine waters, while a pod of nymph's shot out of the depths to catch them with their needled teeth.*

Frowning, I tracked the sun falling to the west, its rays glittering across the waves...but that couldn't be right. In my homeland the sun set upon The Red Caps, not an ocean...and it rose across these very waters in the east, which meant, this wasn't the West Isles, it was Faerie.

Spinning, I cataloged the white marbled city I only had the misery of seeing one other time in my life before I stood upon its ruins with a mixture of satisfaction and heartbreak almost one hundred years ago.

"The City of Light had such beautiful views." A voice sighed with nostalgia behind me—a voice that sent a dark sense of dread down my spine and made the hairs on the back of my neck rise.

Snarling, I turned on the voice, wanting to rip it from its owner more than anything else in this world. "Deirdre. I was wondering when you would show your cunt face."

She grinned in her silver splendor, her turquoise eyes, much like the waters I had just admired, glittering with pleasure. "Perhaps it was your wondering that allowed me entry. Even now you have not stopped thinking about me, shifter king."

"You are right about that Deirdre." My fangs lengthened. "I have not stopped thinking about all the ways I will kill you one day, if I could I would do it now."

Her cold laugh affected me more than I cared to admit, nausea rolling in my stomach. The sound so similar to the days I spent under her evil torture.

"You will have to keep dreaming about me then shifter king, since neither of us can hurt one another in the spirit realm...physically that is."

My brows rose. "You intend to impart some sort of fucked up psychological warfare on me now, is that it...haven't you tired of your monotonous games?"

She pursed her blood red lips, the same color bleeding into her eyes as burgundy shadows whirled around her. I narrowed my gaze on the umbras that had once been my friends, feeling their desperate cries for help beneath the corruption of power that dominated their greatness.

"I hear you have lost your beast. You should be really careful around those who have lost their souls...you never know who might be listening. Quite the family drama you have had recently." She circled around me, her tiered silver gown flowing with her sensuous stride that made my dick shrink inside myself. "I can help you get him back, you know." Her eyes gleamed. "Give me the child and you can be whole again."

My claws extended as I tracked her movement with a vicious grin. "You had your chance at being a mother. Your son died in the wars, perhaps you should have taken better care of him instead of scheming for a crown."

Her eyes bled red, "so the healer shared the secret story after all did he? What was it like to watch his head roll from his body I wonder?"

I sent her a silent snarl. "That was part of your plan, wasn't it?"

She grinned. "Clever shifter, smart and handsome...you must get it from your mother's side." Gliding past me she stared out over the seas, the sun dipping into the water. "It really was a beautiful view."

I stared at her back, imagining my claws wrenching her cowardly spine straight out from her body.

Her red eyes gleamed sinisterly over her shoulder, as she looked back at me. "It was the last view your mother had, you know. She was standing right where you are now...before I killed her."

I lunged, unable to hold back. Deirdre's laughter echoed around me and the picturesque ocean scene spun as I fell to my knees upon a shallow grave of diseased ridden earth with my mothers dead unseeing eyes looking up past me. She was barely recognizable between the burns and the rotten decay where she had been cruelly tossed away without any remorse or respect even in death.

And yet, I could not pull myself away from the horror of it all. Frozen, I stared down at her lifeless body, bile rising upwards and burning the back of my throat.

"I thought you might like to visit your mother's grave, since you never did get to say goodbye. She did make quite a charming decoration hanging on my city gates, finally giving purpose to her pathetic life, a warning of what would happen to any and all who opposed me."

I couldn't look away, Deirdre's words like a distant echo in my hallowed mind.

Then the image of her blurred, her body disappearing only to be replaced by the shredded remains of my soulmate.

"No," I choked.

Remnant's flawless pale skin was marred by hideous slashes and puncture wounds, dark red blood splattered across her skin, and her throat had been completely slit open, blood still pouring out of the mortal wound.

"My my, someone lost their temper," Deirdre tutted behind me. "I dare say she had it coming. All that time you spent caring for her, protecting her, loving her even...and still she betrays you? I do not blame you for snapping but I do know what it is like to have a soulmate who betrays you, sometimes love simply cannot change nature."

Roaring, I stood to face her. "You are insinuating I would do this to my mate!" My body trembled while I prayed feverishly for the universe to change its laws and to allow me just this one time to rid it of this evil filth.

"There is no insinuation...you will do this." Her eyes gleamed. "You will not be able to stop yourself...especially since Remnant Dark is the reason your mother is dead."

I threw my head back and laughed. If this fucking cunt expected her words to do more damage and break me so easily than she was sorely underestimating me...which meant when the time came she would be an easier prey than I ever expected and I—-I was a patient predator.

Waving at her while still laughing, I turned my back on the pathetic creature. Not understanding at all why the fuck the ancients put a crown on her head in the first place. "You can play your fucking games by yourself, pathetic goddess of nothing." Walking away from the image of my slain soulmate and the furious glare of the manipulating fae behind me, I stated, "now how the fuck do I get out of this place? You bore me."

CHAPTER 12

M Y EYES SHOT OPEN the moment I left Deirdre behind in the spirit realm. Blinking up at the twilight sky, I allowed the soothing moonlight to steady my pounding heart, unsure of what was worse. The nightmare memories of my soulmate's screams or the decaying of my mother in an unmarked grave.

Next to me, my cub snored adoringly, her heartbeat soft and steady in her peaceful sleep. There was no indication that she suffered the same dreadful sleep as I but there was for her mother...who was absent from the bed, her own soft breaths no longer adding to the melodious sound that seemed to become my new heartbeat.

Immediately my gaze searched within the room, finding it empty as shadows crept across the wall. Sniffing, I scented the air, knowing my soulmate was not far as her scent was still strong. My eyes fell on the balcony that was across the room, semi transparent black glass blocking the tantalizing silhouette of my mate.

Easing myself carefully from Riella's side, I stiffened with gritted teeth when she stirred then rolled away from me, trailing all the covers with her. Smiling softly, I was transfixed by her sweetness cocooned in soft bed sheets, her dark hair spilling across a bed made of clouds, her cherub face from which tiny snores escaped was what blessings were made of.

Gently, I pulled the bed sheet down under her chin to allow her to breathe easier and left her to her peaceful sleep. Padding across the moonlit room, darkness danced with each prowling step I took before I stepped through the enchanted glass barrier out into the night. A comet burned brightly overhead, highlighting the gorgeous figure of Remnant as if she was just beamed down from the skies for me to soak in her splendor. She was in her element here—her long blue black hair flowing around her in silky straight strands, calling for me to run my hands through them just like I had at dinner while her exposed legs peeked out from the billowing night shirt she wore. Everything about her standing here was a fucking tease, beckoning me to reach out and touch that soft moonlit skin.

I shivered with sudden passionate need that had nothing to do with the night breeze that was neither cold nor warm. If it wasn't for the sinful desire that just the sight of my soulmate caused, I would have said that the temperature was peaceful...relaxing even—the kind of lazy happiness that sated lovers could sit together in for hours never wanting anything more from its dark caress.

"I couldn't sleep," Remnant whispered, sensing my presence, her arms hugging her body, forcing the black silk shirt to ride higher up her legs, just before the delicious curves of her ass met her thighs.

I inhaled her lily scent deeply and burned it deep into my mind before I shoved my raging desire down and prowled, closing the space between us. Circling my arms around her small frame, my body engulfed hers, and I relished in the way she submitted into me. It was powerful and sweet at the same time, especially when a shaky sigh escaped her lips.

Dropping my mouth to her soft hair, I breathed against the strands. "Nightmares?"

Her fingertips traced along my forearm that rested over her chest, drawing swirls along my skin making me shiver. "Not since we solidified our bond...I keep waiting for the panic to start anew but it has not. What plagues me is something entirely different." Her confession ended in a soft whisper and I knew then this was difficult for her. To open up and speak about her fears.

I squeezed her tightly to me, trying to permeate my own strength into her. "This is likely the only sleep any of us will get for some time, little umbra. What remedy can I conjure so that you can be sleeping restfully in our bed?"

Her head fell back into my chest and a worried frown creased her forehead while we both stared out into the exposed cosmos. "I could say the same to you, shifter. I know that your sleep just now was anything but restful. I can feel your fear and unease in our bond too, Emon. It's Deirdre, she has come to you in the spirit realm hasn't she?"

I hummed, turning my nose into her hair and inhaling her scent to burn away the image of her dead body, her throat torn open by animalistic claws. "Yes," I breathed.

Her body tensed and I could feel the anger vibrating throughout. Remnant Dark may be small but like our daughter, she was powerful and when it was unleashed...goddess help us all. "She visited me as well, when we passed out from entering this realm. What does she possibly think she can gain from this?"

"To create discourse, sow doubt, to weaken us. She fears us and what we are capable of together."

"Do you...do you need to talk about it?" she asked softly.

"I fear it will only upset you more," I kissed her hair and purred down at her when she started to protest, "why don't you tell me what is really keeping you up, since it is not your psychopath ex lover that haunts your thoughts. Thank fuck for that."

She snorted and her lips pursed in thought. Tactfully, I allowed the silence to grow, knowing it would eventually spill her secret musings only if I gave it the space to come forth.

My father would be fucking proud. I could almost feel his truthful gold eyes shining with it, watching us.

It didn't take long.

"I don't have full control of the shadows," she finally confessed, her voice so soft I barely heard it with my shifter ears as she reached out with her hand to the night. The moonlight cast hundreds of shadows on the glass tomb towers that made up the Sheol's city, Voltum.

A grouping of shadows jumped off the building, floating in the air towards us. I narrowed my eyes, watching the way they quivered, resisting the call of my soulmate before completely shooting back to the resting place.

"I have been trying for hours, I can't even pull the smallest shadow to me now."

I had known, of course but was waiting for her to discuss it when she was ready. "Has this ever happened before? Could it be tied to the lilin?" I questioned, tucking my chin on top of her head again.

Her head rocked back and forth, her hair catching on my beard. "Never," she said vehemently, her teeth flashing in the night, her sudden violence stirring my blood and unleashing the desire I had pushed away just moments before. "The Lilin were never shadows," she added, gritting her teeth, "losing them should not have affected who I am—who I should be." Turning in my arms, her hand rested on my chest, her eyes lost in thought, staring through me unseeing. "My shadows are gone and I cannot even rely on my power to help us, shifter."

I growled low, sensing more. "Say it."

Slowly, she dragged her eyes up to my own and the uncertainty within those emerald depths was like seeing the sun falling from the sky, dooming us all. "Emon...can you shift?"

Raising my hand up, I unsheathed my claws and trailed them dangerously over the soft pale skin of her face, over the vulnerable exposure of her throat, and then across the swell of her breasts that started to rise and fall with her quickened breath, her shirt unbuttoned tantalizingly low. "I still have my claws." I smirked and allowed my fangs to descend over my lips, watching her eyes dilate as I slowly ran my tongue over one of them. Bending, I grazed them over the pale column of her neck, her breath catching as I bit down, stopping just before I broke the skin and then stared possessively at the red markings. "I still have my fangs," I breathed across her porcelain skin.

Shivering in my hold, she looked away, her voice quivering. "I can't lose either of you..."

Snarling, I straightened, gripping her chin and forcing her eyes to see my hardened resolve. "I know those words, I know that tone. You're not fucking running again, Remnant Dark and you sure as goddess fuck are not doing this alone to spare us. Our daughter is too much like the both of us to be left behind and you know I will hunt you down anyway. How do you think that will end, hmm little umbra?"

She gave me a sad smile, "With you cheating of course."

I grinned, goddess what I wouldn't give to run on the parapets of my city with her, that moment when I saw her come back to life burned so brightly in my memory that I almost was there again.

Her eyes searched my face and then fell on my nose. Reaching up, she traced its profile, smiling softly when I wrinkled it at her. "This really is from pinching pastries?"

I grinned, "I have a feeling our daughter will be much better at it than I ever was, inheriting her mothers stealth and strategy, she will bleed Drey's bakery dry."

My soulmate laughed, shaking her face from my hold, peering through the glass where our daughter lay sleeping safely. "I still can't believe she is ours...I never aspired to be a mother. It seemed foolish to even think about, but now that I am...she is so magnificent, how can I ever be good enough for something so innocently sweet, Emon?"

Pulling her in closer to me, I brushed the tip of my claw against her plump lips wanting nothing more than to claim them. "You are good enough, my love, because you are just as magnificent. Do you want to know how I know that?" I purred, dropping my tone low.

Her breath quickened, "How?" The sexy gasp she released setting my body aflame.

"Because I think the same every time I look at you." With great restraint, I kissed her lips softly, retracting my fangs, and rubbing my mouth against hers. "I know you have more fears," I whispered to her. "Confess them from this gorgeous delicious mouth so that I may either purge them from your soul forever or keep them until you have the strength to face them yourself. "

Her eyes fluttered closed and she leaned further into me. "Riella has no power to defend herself, I have no shadows to protect her, you are no longer connected to Ethereal, and I can't...I can't even think of you half dead laying in those tombs, Emon." Her lip quivered, "I don't know another way to prevent the soulless sleep from taking you without taking your own soul."

I kissed her eyelids. "Do you not think me formidable enough, now that the cat is gone?"

Her eyes shot open, her hair blowing across her beautiful face in the soft night wind, "Of course not. Never would I think such a thing. You are a powerful shifter...even in irons, I've seen what you are capable of." She shivered and shook her head. "Ethereal is...was a destroyer but you, Emon, you feel like life. Life that is too precious to lose to death."

Exhaling the relief I felt that she did not doubt me, I brushed back her hair, "Then you shall never lose me. Nothing is more powerful than us together, Remnant. Nothing."

Her arms clutched at me as I licked at the fluttering of her pulse, breathlessly her words spilled out of her in a hushed whisper—perhaps it wasn't silence that spilled fears from my soulmate after all. All that was needed was carefully crafted seduction we both could enjoy. "We don't know what is in The Well, Emon, what trials we will face. What if it is a mistake bringing Riella with us, we can hardly protect ourselves."

"Can you not wield a sword? Were you not a war general of an entire fucking continent? Am I not the king of shifters, still strong and a worthy bait?"

I snickered at the last part, licking her skin again and groaning at the taste of the lingering stardust—it was the exact flavor I thought it would be, my new favorite sweet treat that only my soulmate could fulfill.

"There is no safer place for our daughter than at our side," I continued, "besides we are more than our power and even so, that is *not* what makes us formidable—our love is, and no one can take that from us. Fucking no one." Hooking my claw on the low button of her silk shift, I popped it open, brushing the soft material aside to reveal her pale defined shoulder, the swirls of ink beckoning my lips to trail along its secret path.

"Vengeful souls are unpredictable with no honor, they have no need of such restraints," she continued her confessions rapidly while I continued to rip open the buttons on her shirt one at a time, my mouth trailing over every inch of gorgeous skin that was revealed before descending on her breast.

Groaning, I waited for her hands to bury in my hair, her nails raking against my scalp as I suckled her. "We are fae," I whispered against her hard swollen nipple, licking it and loving the fucking sweet whisper of my name on her lips that was half begging and half praying.

Growling, I ripped the rest of her shirt from her body, smoothly dropping to my knees, her hips held firmly in my hands while I peered up at her through the hair that had fallen across my eyes.

Raking it back, the multiple moons of Sheol highlighting the beautiful fire in her eyes, she smirked at me, "What exactly are you about, shifter?"

"Making my soulmate's daydreams come true," I winked up at her, then licked the smooth skin of her belly, watching it clench with the slow draw of my tongue before drawing my nose from her naval lower.

"Emon?"

"Hmm," I growled, inhaling the sweet desire between her legs that I knew would taste the same as the candied stardust on her skin.

Wrenching my head back, she grinned down at my petulant snarl—like a faeling having his candy taken away. "I believe in my daydream you were naked on your knees, shifter."

I chuckled, shaking her grip from my hair and nipping at her hand. "Indeed."

I was a blur of movement. Quickly shedding my clothes, I knelt before her again, this time taking in every exquisite detail of her bared moonlit body.

Breathing heavily, I rubbed the faint stubble of my beard against her soft skin, "Your father was right about one thing," I whispered. "You are a goddess—my fucking goddess." I kissed her upper thigh before peering up to meet her passion blown eyes, my own body shaking from holding back from her. "I will worship you forever." The words were like a fucking vow echoing from my soul and our bond flared brightly within my chest.

"Emon," she whispered and I shivered at the way my name left her lips. Her hand reached down to cup my face and I tilted my head into it. Slowly, she ran it over the scruff of my beard and then reached back to cup the back of my neck. A seductive gleam, brighter than the shooting stars across the twilight sky, flickered in her heated gaze, her voice husky when she finally spoke. "Lick."

I had no words left to give, only a deep low growl before I buried my face between my soulmate's quivering thighs, groaning in ecstasy when the taste of her exploded on my tongue. My last thought before I completely lost myself was that she tasted better than any cosmic stardust this realm could ever rain down upon me.

CHAPTER 13

I WATCHED THEM BOTH sleep.

My daughter had somehow unwrapped herself from the covers and was sprawled out on the bed like a starfish in a sea of clouds, leaving very little room for her mother who slept soundly on the bed's edge. Remnant's breaths were slow and soft, a fae deep in satiated sleep, and I was the one who put her there.

I licked at the delicious taste of my soulmate still on my lips with the memory of her screaming in pleasure, a symphony that was the best kind of music. She had collapsed in my arms, exhausted and sated with her monosyllabic speech before falling into a deep rest.

A rest that she needed badly.

As fae, our health regenerated rapidly on its own, but the mind...that was a different thing entirely. I prayed that the deep sleep overtaking her now would lift the cloud of doubt she was drowning in. Perhaps then the fears she confessed would ease their grip, the worry in her beautiful emerald eyes tonight—fuck it was almost more than I could bear.

And it had been too goddess damn close to how I had been feeling as well.

Snarling softly, I started to pace the room. With Ethereal gone I had no fucking idea who I truly was, no idea *what* beast lurked inside me and—*if I even had one*.

That little fact was something I avoided revealing and I knew it would come back to bite me in the ass with swift retribution, but still I would do it again. Remnant had enough to goddess damn worry about and I was already a big part of that with my lack of god blood.

Fuck Shea.

The death god took her choices and shoved her in a corner to fight her way out without anything to protect herself with. His actions went against every fucked up morally gray fiber of my being, the one thing I never take from anyone—choice.

Dark anger and wild fear seized my chest, squeezing me like a vice that left my breaths shallow.

Still I paced.

I wished that I had my family awake and well with that damn cat buzzing in my ear. To have some fucking advice or outlet to work my way through this mess we found ourselves in, to find a way to stay at Remnant's side. For if she had no choice then I would goddess damn make sure she at least had the tools at her disposal to fight for another day.

My steps faltered.

Slowly I turned to stare at my mate. I always knew she had strength that was superior to any other and her strength ran deep. It never wavered, and I thought—I thought I understood it but what was clearer now more than ever was that I had just scratched the surface in understanding its depths.

The empty ache I felt now, with its hopelessness and fury—Remnant had felt this for fucking years. Her friends, her family, her love, her life, everything that she had known was stripped from her within seconds. She had been left shattered, she still was when I finally found her and still—she followed me out of that cabin to live again.

And here I was, fretting like a goddess damn faeling when I had everything I would ever need.

My daughter and soulmate.
I lived them.
I breathed them.
My heart beat, my power flowed, my soul ascended, *for them.*
The quiet flutter of soft wings had my head jerking up, the sound easy to detect for my shifter ears and the culprit knew it. Prowling towards it, I stepped outside our lavish rooms and into the corridor. A long spiral staircase descended down to the ground floor of the tower we slept in and I searched its shadowy alcove. When the wings ruffled again, I narrowed my eyes on the fluttering sound seeing a small chickadee hop up on a step below.
Chirping once, it took flight, flapping its wings to disappear downward into the darkness.
It wanted me to follow.
Running my hand through my hair, I glanced back. My daughter and soulmate still rested peacefully in their slumber. It was likely my absence would still keep it that way since there was no chance I'd be sleeping tonight, my frustrated prowling only risked waking them up.
Sighing heavily, I stepped down on the onyx glass steps and despite my light footfalls, I felt heavy. An ominous feeling weighing me down with each passing step I took. Every instinct told me to go no further but still the soft chirps and light wings taunted me to follow.
When my feet finally hit the landing, shadows swirled in the dim light to reveal Remnant's mother. Dressed in fitted leathers, hair unbound...she looked too goddess damn much like my soulmate.
Raising my brows, I addressed her with a short nod, "Lady Eve."
A soft smile fell on her face, "King Daemon."
I crossed my arms in front of my chest with disappointment. I had expected someone else entirely, someone who would appreciate my half nakedness as much as he would appreciate scat on his boots.
Where had that damn chickadee gone?
"Where is your lesser half, the death god?"
Eve's smile widened and she tilted her head towards the doorway, "Walk with me, Emon."

I glanced back up the long glass staircase, still able to hear Riella's soft snores and Remnant's slow breathing. Looking back at her I shook my head. "No. Say what you need to here."

"What needs to be said, what needs to be done, cannot be done here, shifter king." Her blue green eyes bore into me, her hand raised at my attempt to protest, "I know that you do not trust him, Emon, but Shea watches over your heart without any selfish intent or intrigue tonight. Although you have made that task difficult with your most recent choice of activities."

I smirked. "A little exercise never hurt anyone."

Her eyes narrowed but still glittered with amusement, "Indeed, an interesting choice of exercise...on the balcony, a display for the entire realm to see."

My smile widened. "Balconies have always held a wonderful array of possibilities...I was inspired by the stunning view. Be sure to convey my thanks to the death god for creating not one but two exquisite views for me to indulge upon."

Eve threw her head back with laughter. "Have care, shifter king, one of them is *my* daughter too. Do I not get credit for at least half of the view?" shaking her head, she waved me forward, her hand extended in invitation.

Sighing, I relented. The heavy feeling returning the moment I took her hand, tucking her arm into me as she led us out of the tower.

"I will not deceive you Emon, son of Asher. Tonight, I am bending the universal laws." Eve's voice carried through the silence of Sheol's night. "I shall accept the repercussions of this decision for I no longer wish to see my daughter suffer."

I frowned. "I am not entirely sure Remnant would want you to do this then."

She shook her head sadly while we continued to walk. "Yes, you are correct with your assumption but my daughter has sacrificed enough for me, it is high time I do the same. Now listen closely, Daemon." She waved her hand out before her, "I have had a vision of you and my daughter, one that I cannot ignore. As you stated tonight, visions can often be interpreted in many ways, and mine even more so. Rarely are my glimpses of the future concrete. They are more like timelines, feelings—so fleeting that I had learned to not invest too much time worrying over them, usually allowing the fates to play out the future as it should be. But with Remnant..." she looked away, her voice wavering, "I have made so many mistakes—mistakes that caused her to suffer greatly in my arrogant understanding of my secondary powers and my stubborness in adhering to the rules of the sight."

I studied the wretched pain etched on Eve's face, full of regret and guilt. "You could not have known, Eve."

She glanced over at me and then back to the silvery path we walked upon. "Some of it I did. I knew Deirdre would someday harm her...but to what extent I did not know. I should have never allowed her to stay there. I should have forced her to break her oath and brought her home. It was within my power to do so but I thought, in my arrogance, I still had time to guide Remnant away from Deirdre's manipulative clutches. Except it only served to push her further away from me. Newly out of her centum, Remnant was so eager to prove herself and to help her court. Deirdre was also eager but not for the right reasons. She wanted power and my daughter was that power."

"Until Deirdre realized that she would never be able to truly control Remnant, not in the way she really wanted to and decided to destroy it instead." I snarled into the night and watched a lone ice phoenix blazing across the sky, releasing fiery snow that fell down in front of us.

"Yes." Eve said simply, watching the ice phoenix snow as well.

"She is not meant to be controlled," I added, reaching out to the icy flakes and closing a tight fist around it with a snarl, feeling it burn my hand with its fierce cold. When I opened it, the ice remained, but my flesh had been burned. Blowing softly on my palm, the phoenix snowflake drifted back out to the white sands of Sheol. "She is meant to be unleashed."

Eve studied the snow for a moment before she whispered softly, "You will not make it to The Well Emon...and without you, Remnant will not either."

My lips thinned and I raked my hand through my hair, "I sense an unless..."

She sighed, weaving shadows around the chilling fire and cradling it in her hand softly so it would not burn her, she stared down at it thoughtfully.

As if the past slapped me in the face, I was suddenly struck with the image of my own mother holding a wisp all those years ago as she confessed her worries of the future. My brows furrowed, Eve and her were not that much different. Both of them mothers in a dangerous world, searching for ways to protect the ones they loved.

"I should clarify. Your body will not make it...you will succumb to a soulless sleep no matter what path you take. But there is a way for your soul to stay tethered to my daughter instead of going straight to The Well, and in this future the odds are more in your favor."

I shook my head, growling, "I will not forfeit my soul to the death god, your daughter would never forgive me for that."

Eve nodded, releasing the shadows to allow the blue phoenix fire to fall and sizzle onto the silver path. "What I speak of is not the gift of the last breath. It is a binding oath of the shadow fae." She arc'd her hand over her head at the stars, the shadows forming a sign of infinity. "Darkness has no beginning or end, it is infinitely connected and each shadow fae binds themselves to a part of this darkness, in your case you would bind your soul to my daughter's. Your soulmate bond can be destroyed but darkness cannot, through it your soul can continue on at my daughter's side until your body finally leaves these lands."

I stopped her from walking forward, my voice cracking with emotion, "You're asking me to take the eternal oath to the shadow fae court? And by doing this, I will ensure my soulmate succeeds?"

Shaking her head, she pursed her lips. "I have never had a clearer vision than that of the consequences of the choices you make tonight, but that does not mean my visions are foolproof." She looked up and studied me through worried eyes, "Daemon, you must know what it will mean if you do this—"

I cut her off, my hand slicing downwards with finality. "I accept."

She pursed her lips again and again the reflection of her daughter was far too akin for my own comfort. "King Daemon, I feel that I must speak plainly about what it is you will be giving up, what you might become—"

I growled low. "I am well aware of what I will give up to make this oath. I still accept." Then I tilted my head, "But I will ask for one favor."

Eve nodded. "I think I know what this request is but whatever it is you ask of me, I will try to grant it."

"I need paper and ink." Sighing deeply, I shook my head, running my hand through my hair again with a growl. "A lot of paper and ink."

Her sapphire eyes ringed with green sparkled and I swore I could see the future unfolding within them. "This will not be an easy path for either of you to take, but I can see now that the fates have chosen well."

"No," I turned and looked upwards at the swirling black tower of glass where my soulmate slept, making out the outline of the balcony extending into the stars, and spotting the chickadee perched upon its railing, "your daughter chose well, the fates had nothing to fucking do with it."

Chapter 14

Remnant

My eyes cracked open from my slumber at the sound of deep laughter and innocent giggles. Staring at the steam hovering above a warm beverage lovingly placed on the bedside table, I listened to the continued giggling of my daughter, allowing it to pull me back to the waking world.

My sleep had been deep and I felt groggy as my bare feet dropped to the cool glass floor. The feel of it was soothing and I took a few moments to relish in the sensation, allowing the lingering sleep to dissipate and my senses to awaken. Drawn by the delicious aroma of hot liquid steaming at my bedside, I blinked through the slightly brighter twilight of Sheol's morning and picked up the cup to gaze across the room. Smiling, over the rim of the glass, I basked in the vision my soulmate and daughter made as they conversed in the kitchen across the wide open room.

If only every morning could be exactly like this one.

Absentmindedly, I sipped at my drink, before my brows rose with shock as decadent chocolate liquid hit my tastebuds. A symphony of subtle hints of cinnamon and chili lingered with the rich bitter sweetness of cocoa, and I savored the taste long after I had swallowed. Smiling into my cup, I took a deeper and more appreciative drink this time, not caring if the liquid burned my mouth.

It reminded me of Emon—everything that was good and sinful about my mate all in one cup of warming liquid that heated me thoroughly on the inside just like he did.

I hummed my pleasure.

"Oh to be that hot chocolate right now, little umbra," Emon's voice whispered in my mind.

My heart skipped at his growling sultry tones and I looked up to see his golden eyes cutting across the room, watching me intensely. Unaware, our daughter chatted away, her legs swinging on the countertop from which she sat upon.

"You are a clever shifter, except...I woke up alone. So perhaps not too clever," I purred back, licking my lips at the lingering remains of the cocoa, and watching his eyes glow brighter in the dim light.

"Apologies soulmate, but our daughter was hungry and I did not wish to wake you. You needed your rest. Come join us when you are ready. Clothing has been set out for you by the enchantment of the tower."

When I was ready? I was more than ready to ditch the spiced hot chocolate and drink in the real thing that was watching me with bright eyes from across the room—but he didn't need to know that.

Emon smiled when I took another long sip, teasingly holding his gaze and licking my lips afterwards. If it wasn't for the distressed cry from our daughter and Emon's natural instinct to catch whatever Riella had accidentally knocked over, I knew my soulmate would not have been able to stop himself from pouncing on me from across the room.

"Cruel," Emon growled low to me, distracted by our daughter's apologetic stumbling as he frantically attempted to clean her up.

Grinning, I rose from the bed and stretched out my rested body before dressing quickly, sparing my soulmate any more sensuous torture.

Tying off the last laces of my thigh high boots, I eyed my reflection in the onyx glass. There was something different about the fae that stood before me in a tight fitted bodice of leather and black shorts—something darker and more unhinged. A wild creature with no direction. Emon had recently freed me from the cage that had smothered my soul for all these years, and now I was back in another one, this time supplied by my would-be father.

And me being cornered and trapped was a recipe for destruction.

My eyes flickered with doubt in the dim light as I attempted to draw the shadows to me—failing again, not even a twitch this time and this was what terrified me more than the cage ever could.

Turning away from my dark reflection and my self inflicted uncertainty, I stealthily moved across the room where the light was not nearly as dim, revealing the disorderly state of my daughter and soulmate who grinned when I approached.

Was that flour covering them and—sweet goddess, was Emon wearing a shirt?

Frowning up at my grinning soulmate, I trailed my finger down the familiar fitted pink unicorn shirt he had been forced to wear just yesterday. The definition of his muscular body could still be seen molding the fabric, but it was not the same as seeing and feeling his delicious bronze skin.

"A shirt?" I arched my brow suspiciously.

He winked, a sheepish expression on his face that reminded me of when he destroyed my mirror within my cabin. Emon was up to no good. "Anything for my cub."

"It's my favorite," Riella added happily.

I hummed, rubbing the abnormal amounts of the white dust that had transferred to my fingertips when swiping his shirt, confirming it was indeed flour.

Looking between the two of them both dusted thoroughly, I held back my questions for Emon later.

"What are you two about?" I said curiously, taking in the sight of Riella's dark hair now a unique shade of gray. Not to mention, there was a delicious aroma that was not just my hot chocolate but something even more tantalizing.

Riella's legs swung excitedly, her flour covered hand streaking more of its dust into her hair as she swiped it back from her animated face, the words gushing out of her all at once. "Father was teaching me how to make pastries." She looked back at Emon with wide questioning eyes, "Mother is awake, may I have more now?"

My soulmate chuckled and attempted to wipe her hair with a damp cloth, failing miserably at his mission. Her excited bouncing only a fraction of the reason for his unsuccessful attempt. "I don't know how you are still hungry, my little cub. You ate half my filling and had two full pastries already."

I stifled my laughter into my cup, watching over the rim at the way she enchanted Emon with wide innocent eyes and fluttering dark lashes. "But I really want to try the custard one...you said it was your specialty and that we had to wait for mother to eat it." Then she extended her bottom lip in the most adorable pout.

Emon snorted, struggling against his need to give her everything she wanted and being a stern parent. "Let's make a deal then my little cub. How about you go get cleaned up and dressed for the day, then we will all eat that one together?"

Her excitement deflated for only a brief moment before she straightened, clapping her hands. "Okay! Can I use that thing that sprays water out at me?"

I lowered my mug. "The sink?"

She shook her head with exasperation, rolling her eyes. "No, not that one, the one that is like a waterfall."

My brows rose at her snarky response and Emon chuckled, sparing me having to answer back to our daughter's sudden attitude. "You mean the shower?"

She nodded eagerly. "Yes that."

He grinned, lunging quickly to scoop her up off the counter top and launched her into the air. Her loud squeals of laughter reverberated off the black onyx walls as she descended down into his waiting arms, nuzzling her flour covered nose lovingly. "It is likely best that you do, my cub, but remember to take your clothes off this time. The bathroom will provide you with everything else that you need, soap, a towel to dry off, and new clothes to wear." Setting her down, he crouched low to whisper in her ear and then both turned to look at me.

She nodded once before skipping towards me, closing the distance between us. Smacking into me, she hugged my leg, looking up with her swirling gold and green eyes. "Good morning, mother!"

I chuckled and bent to embrace her, not caring at all about the white flour that now covered me too. Bowing my head to hers, I placed a kiss into her gray hair. "Good morning to you too, chickadee."

Pulling away, she grinned up at me. "Don't eat without me, please!" Then spun off, racing towards the bathroom, shutting the door behind her with a soft click. Moments later her squeals of delight could be heard with the rush of water.

Snickering, I glanced back at my soulmate, my laughter trailing off at the predatory stare he instantly captured me in. I licked my lips, feeling the need to run, marveling at the way he heightened all my senses.

Nodding at the platter of buttery golden brown pastries that appeared to be filled with various types of custards and jams, I teased him, "So the thief became the chef?"

He grinned, wiping his shirt and flour covered hands off on a wet towel before throwing it back down on the counter. He stalked towards me while he answered. "Of course I did. I had to work every summer until I reached maturity in Drey's kitchens as my punishment for my thievery."

I backed away slyly, clutching my mug to my chest to hide the way his prowling made my body tremble. "Alas it still did not cure your habit of thieving pastry?"

His hair fell across his brow, pausing to assess me. "It did not."

"You must have been up all night baking...did you not sleep at all?" I said breathily, damn my body for betraying me to this shifter.

Emon's eyes glowed brighter at the sound, his nostrils flaring at the scent of my increasing need for him. A need that I both feared and prayed would never leave me.

His grin widened and his fangs lengthened past his lips. I shivered at the memory of what he did with them last night, my body clenching hard now with raging need. Sensing the danger, I shifted to move quickly, but I was no match for his speed, not this time anyway.

Squealing much like our daughter had moments before, the world spun before I was pressed up against the frigid steel of the ice box while the hot body of my shifter growled sexily down at me.

Through disheveled hair, Emon slowly raised my cup up to his own lips. Somehow, he had managed to take it from me and not spill a single drop. Now it was his turn to watch me over the rim as his hard thigh wedged deliciously between my legs, lifting me to his own eye level.

"You keep forgetting that your soulmate is a shifter, little umbra. I am faster and more efficient than any other fae you have ever known." Tipping the cup back, he drank deeply and then set it down on the counter beside us before gripping my hair with his clawed hand, tilting my head back to slam his lips against mine.

Shocked, I moaned loudly when the spiced hot chocolate filled my mouth forcing me to swallow hard before his tongue swooped in to claim it for his own. He was devouring me so thoroughly that I could feel the scrape of his beard against my flushed skin, the hard length of him pressing into me, sending my core into euphoric spasms while I clutched desperately at the soft pink fabric of his shirt.

Pulling back, he released my hair, planting both his hands on either side of my face, while we shared the same gasping breaths.

Panting against my mouth, he purred. "Good morning my little soulmate goddess."

I shivered at the sound of his dark husky voice. "Good morning, my soulmate king."

He chuckled and then ran his tongue sensually across my lips. "Drey also taught me how to make his award winning hot chocolate," he purred. "Tell me, little umbra, what tastes better..."

Kissing me slowly this time, his tongue swept inside my mouth like a dark caress and I arched further into him, needing to be closer, to bury myself beneath his skin, or at the very least beneath the damnable clothes he now wore.

Why choose this time to wear a goddess fucking shirt?

Groaning and releasing my mouth, Emon kissed sweetly along my jaw up to the shell of my ear whispering, "The hot chocolate or me?"

Blinking, it took a moment for my head to clear in order to completely understand what he was asking me. He chuckled, his lips descending on my skin again.

Swallowing, I breathily answered him. "You," I gasped quietly, as his silky lips grazed my collar bone. "Perhaps if you add in more spice next time it would have been closer."

Emon's chest rumbled, rubbing his beard against my sensitive skin, knowing how it would send shivers down my spine. "I think...that perhaps the spice should stay with me...what do you think, my little umbra."

"I—-I think I'm okay with that," I whispered, reaching up and running my hands through his flour dusted hair.

His head pulled back to look at me then, his gold eyes shining with depths of happiness I could barely comprehend. "Today is a new day, which means, I get to tell you how much I love you all over again."

Captured by his purity, I stared at him before leaning forward to kiss his lips softly. "I love you too Emon."

He inhaled, wrapping his arms tightly around me, and I gasped when the world blurred, finding myself now perched on the cool marble countertop.

Watching my lips press into a thin line of disappointment, Emon laughed. Placing my mug back into my hands he leaned forward to kiss my forehead softly. "Our daughter has finished her shower."

Sighing shakily, I growled with irritation. "Then you shouldn't have started this."

Emon's eyes trailed over my aroused state—the way my chest rose and fell quicker than normal, my disheveled hair, the red flush of my skin that I knew still colored my cheeks.

Slowly, he slid over the plate of delicious smelling fresh baked pastries. "I have a feeling you'll forgive me." When I reached for one, he stopped me purring low, "Be patient my love, our daughter has not returned."

Sighing harshly, I drank my hot chocolate instead, glaring at him over the rim.

Smirking, his golden eyes twinkled in the cosmic light. "Waiting makes everything that much sweeter, little umbra. Remember that, when I worship you again under the stars and you lose your voice screaming my name."

CHAPTER 15

Remnant

M Y SWORD FLASHED IN Sheol's cosmic light and swept outwards the moment I stepped outside our tower. The sound of steel ringing against shadow traveled down the hallowed paths of Voltum as I turned to see my brother's power crossing my blade.

Kade grinned, leaning casually against the tower wall, his eyes trailing behind me with expectation. "Trying to start the day off with a kill I see. Where are your little sidekicks today?"

I snorted and sheathed my blade while my brother dropped the shadows. "Emon and Riella are eating pastries on the balcony watching the herd of camphor you showed her yesterday. What are you doing here Kade?"

He looked slightly deflated, like he was looking forward to seeing his niece, his new little shadow. Curly blue hair fell across his face when his eyes darkened. "You are leaving. I thought it would be a good idea to visit my sister before I don't see her for another century or two."

"Kade—"

He shook his head, pushing off the building with his foot. "I didn't come here to rehash this. I actually came here to see if you wanted to play shadow league before you go. For old time's sake."

I frowned, "Shadow league...I haven't played that since—"

His brow arched mischievously and his emerald eyes so much like mine twinkled. "Since we destroyed the throne room of the City of Light after too much ambrosia wine?"

I bit my lip smiling back at him. "I seem to remember you just could not accept the fact that my shadow warrior was far superior than yours. I was going to win and you purposefully set fire to the frozen stone trolls on display there."

Kade snickered, "It was worth it seeing the queen of Faerie's look of disgust when they woke from their slumber farting."

I laughed and pointed at him, "Half the court was left unconscious for days by that stench. It took me weeks to get the smell from my nose!"

He grinned, "Those pompous court fae needed a little bit of stench for their upturned noses, Rem Rem."

Shaking my head I answered him truthfully, "Perhaps." Then my smirk grew wider seeing that knowing sparkle in his eyes. "You're hoping that we do the same to *dear old dad's* realm aren't you?"

My little, not so little brother crossed his lithe muscular arms over his chest. "Such an accusation, sister!" Tapping his fingers, his teeth flashed in the twilight. "But now that you mention it..."

"As much as I'd love to play shadow league with you Kadey Kins, my power has not been reacting obediently to me lately. I have no control over the shadows." It goddess damn hurt to admit that. The ache of that knowledge vast inside my chest.

Kade chuckled darkly, "Oh I know it and it's perfect, who knows what kind of wondrous things would happen with rogue shadows. Besides, I spotted some nuckelavee not too far from here. They are hunting the camphor this morning. So what do you say Rem Rem? Afraid you'll finally lose to your baby brother?"

I tilted my head, studying him. For a better part of a century Kade had been trapped here, the people he once loved and cared about were in a soulless sleep, leaving him alone in a world of death while our parents rekindled their former love.

And here I was—less than a day since I had arrived and was already planning on leaving...

I smiled wide at him and cracked my neck side to side. "Alright. You're on but tagging instead." I wasn't even sure I could handle that. "Hand to hand combat or weapons..."

Kade grinned, his eyes gleaming with renewed light. "I was thinking given the unknown way your powers are manifesting...explosives."

"Explosive tag sounds...*dangerous*." I reached out for the smallest of shadows. I could feel its initial resistance, but then it finally conformed to my will morphing into a sparking ball of shadow. It would have to do. I looked up at him and nodded, "You're on." Tossing the shadow bomb at his feet, I ran before it exploded in the white sand. "Best me if you can, little brother!"

Stepping off the silvered path, I ran lightly upon the white sand out away from the city. Kade was right, there was no telling what I would do with rogue shadows that I could not control. I scowled when I attempted to pull ones that were trailing across my path following a soaring fiery comet, but its shadow barely budged.

"Shit," I hissed, feeling rather than seeing Kade's darkness descending.

Skidding to a halt, I raised my brows at a dozen shadow gnomes waddling towards me, complete with their long beards dragging across the sand and biting needled teeth.

"Tick, tick, tick," Kade called behind me, his voice slightly unhinged.

"Oh come on, that is so fucked up!" I cried out, diving down into the white sands just before they exploded one by one.

Waiting for the attack to end, counting down each explosion, I rose after the last one buried my entire body in an inch of sand. Normally, I would have just disintegrated the shadows, just last night I could pull them down from the goddess damn sky. Now I couldn't even use them to shield myself for protection.

"Awe, is little Rem Rem feeling sorry for herself. "

Wriggling from the sand and spitting it out from my mouth, I glared at my baby brother standing over me, then kicked out my feet. Kade's ass hit the ground in a puff of dust and I sent another small spark of shadow towards him that wriggled and then puffed in the cloud of smoke.

He stared at it before looking at me, laughter bursting from us both at the sorry state of my powers.

Swiping sand at him playfully, I eased my laughter, reclining back on my elbows.

Kade's laughter trailed off as well and the silence stretched between us.

I gazed up at the colorful twilight feeling the star dust fall upon us. "It really is beautiful here."

Kade snorted. "Until you realize you're literally living in a tomb."

My lips pressed together grimly and I shot my brother a side glance, seeing the pain and darkness creep into his features. "Our people didn't have a choice when they became soulless, but you do Kade. You still have a choice."

He snarled, leaning back on his hands. "What kind of fae would that make me then, Rem? How could I possibly ever feel any ounce of joy when I know they are there, half dead, their lives being stolen from them with each passing of the moons."

I tilted my head to the side, letting the stardust kiss my face. "I felt the same once. For almost a hundred years, I exiled myself in the Wildwoods, staring into a soul mirror every hour of every day, reliving what I had done. I destroyed half our world Kade and I loathed myself, a monster of all monsters, not fit for redemption, not deserving of death."

"I hate that our mother led our people here," Kade said after a long pause. "But what I hate more is that she forced me to leave you behind Rem. After that day on the balcony, when you told us your decision to take your vows with the queen. I left you there, left you in that bitch's shadow and if I hadn't been acting like such a damn faeling I would have seen clearly what you were trying to do, who you were trying to protect. I vowed I would never make that mistake again...and then I did."

Tears blurred my vision, "I know Kade, Emon showed me the memory of that night. But they were both right to force you to go. Deirdre would have destroyed you just as easily as she destroyed me and I promise you there is more than one way to kill someone without stopping their heart and Deirdre...goddess she is a master at it. Even our people are better off as soulless than in her hands."

Kade stared back, his green eyes a turbulence of emotion. "I always had a purpose. Protect you, protect our court, protect our mother...who for years walked alone in her darkness. But here, I protect nothing, I do nothing, I am nothing."

I reached for his shaking hand and pulled it into mine. "That is not true, you are my brother, you are our mother's son, you are half a god, and most importantly you are the ever vigilant watcher of our people, keeping them safe and their memories alive while their bodies sleep. Sometimes the mark of a leader isn't about what you do but about what you don't do that matters the most." I squeezed his hand, "I am proud of you for taking care of our people all this time Kadey Kins, and I swear to you, I will return from The Well with every single one of them. Your story doesn't end here, it's just beginning. I can feel it."

Kade pulled his hand back to sweep the curls off his brow, his face scrunched up tightly, "Fuck Rem Rem, when did you start becoming so philosophical," he chuckled softly through the glistening of tears he would never admit were there.

Shrugging, I looked back at the cosmos of Sheol, "Well when you spend that many years alone in a cramped cabin with nothing but shadows you tend to think harder than normal. Plus I'm goddess damn older than you, which means I am wiser."

Kade snickered. "Not wise enough for this sister." Quickly rising, I stared idiotically at him sprinting away from me before I noticed the shadow bomb. Diving away, it exploded. Dark spots and sand blurred my vision while I cursed at his retreating form. "Goddess damn it Kade! You cheat like a fucking leprechaun!"

He laughed maniacally, "Takes ones to know one!" he hollered back, his heels kicking up the sand as he ran.

"Takes one to know one..." I repeated back with a frown, staring at my little brother, actually worried now that he had lost his goddess damn mind because he was starting to sound like Emon.

Shaking my head, I jumped to my feet, spitting out more sand, and narrowed my eyes on the shadows in front of Kade. The ones he was running directly towards. Forcing them to answer my call, they fought against my hold but I still managed to draw up a thin small line—one Kade was speeding straight towards. Sweat dripped down my brow as I struggled to hold the rebellious thread of darkness. No more than six inches long and as thin as a piece of my hair, it was all I could manage—but it would be more than enough.

Like a tripwire, the moment Kade's lithe frame crossed the line, a wall of sand blew up into his unsuspecting face. His loud curse was the last thing I saw before a massive pile of exploded dunes fell hard upon him like a heavy snow from the bough of a tree.

Unlike my brother, I didn't waste time laughing as I took off running, although my grin was now just as wide as his was a moment ago...before I buried him alive.

CHAPTER 16

Remnant

"WHAT WERE YOU TWO thinking!?" The death god's voice rattled my already ringing ears and I wrinkled my nose at the unwelcomed noise.

Was he seriously scolding us like faelings right now?

Kade stood silently shaking next to me with laughter, his blue curls hanging off his sweaty sand-covered brow as he stared straight down at the dunes.

I could not look at him, if I did, I'd be risking bursting out into fits of laughter as well. Nor could I look at my soulmate standing behind me with our daughter in hand. His dark chuckling and amused pride radiating through our bond was hard enough to ignore.

I raised my head and sighed. "It was just some harmless shadow league tag."

Green fire shot from the death god's eyes and I tilted my head—that was new.

"I don't give a Sheol fuck what it's called. You released dangerous nuckelavee into my home—your mother's home, and then blew them up to the fucking well and back! Just look at this mess!" he roared, his rings glinting in the twilight as he waved his hands erratically, the sky darkening as the shadows rose from the entire realm to greet it.

Both Kade and I smirked at the shattered black glass speckling the white sands of our parents home. Some pieces stuck out like lethal shards, others disintegrated into fine black dust, and what was left of the foundation spiked upwards in a surprisingly prism formation, still stretching more than hundreds of feet into the air.

Briefly, our eyes connected with each other—it was a mistake. Together, fits of guffawing laughter exploded from us and only served to fuel the death god's anger more.

Sheol suddenly pitched into a deep night, the entire realm falling into a darkness that was so thick it was difficult to see. An effect that sobered our laughs quickly.

Wiping my eyes and exhaling steadily, I attempted to compose myself before we would be completely smothered by his power over the night.

"What if it had been a glass tower of the soulless, daughter?" Shea continued to rage, "...what kind of game would you call it then?"

I waved him off and rolled my eyes, still trying to control my laughter while my brother hadn't bothered. "Please we are not amateurs. We knew your tower was empty before the nuckelavee were trapped there."

Emon snorted in my mind. *"Pity he wasn't within."*

"Dear old dad has a point sister," Kade chimed in, "We might need to officially change the name of this game. Maybe Demolition Dick since you did after all, create a giant shadow penis that blew up the nuckelavee and our parent's home."

I grinned at him. "I blame you Kade, you were the one that told me to *fuck them up.*"

I felt my brother's amused look assessing me. I could *not* look at him. I would completely lose it again. "I suddenly find that I am fearful for your soulmate's health, Rem Rem."

"There is no need to worry for me, shadow brother. Your sister is exactly what my health needs." Emon responded smoothly, snickering at my brother's sudden look of disgust, before his voice purred sinfully in my head. *"I'm all in for shadow dicks just as long as they don't explode, little umbra."*

My heart started to race then for a whole different reason and Emon chuckled behind me, detecting its accelerated rate.

"What is a dick, father?" Riella's tiny voice decidedly cut off his amusement. Their laughter stopped short.

I grinned, turning to wink back at Emon. *"Have fun with that, I'll opt out on this one."*

The death god eyes looked as if he was truly considering putting us down like the crazed beasts we were.

Before he could make good on the murder in his eyes, the shadows swirled and my mother stepped from them, perfect timing per usual. She quirked a brow at the dark skies. "Shea, honestly, release the night, it's already dark enough here and what are you planning to do exactly? Kill our only children and grandchild?"

He growled through his teeth. "Not kill, maim maybe...and never our granddaughter, she would be spared from this circus." Then glancing over at Eve, he rolled his eyes at her stern look and I realized then just how much we were alike. Sighing, he released the night. "They would have healed...they are half god after all."

Dressed in a fitted black dress, my mother placed a delicate hand on her hip. "And they are also sister and brother, Shea. Our children have not seen each other for more than a few centuries when at one point they were all they had, growing up without a father."

Shea flinched.

Sighing, she placed a hand on his arm. "I don't blame you my love, but I will blame you if you don't start using your godly powers to fix our home. The damage is reversible and you know that." Turning towards us, she folded her hands in front of her. "Am I right to assume this has summed up your mischief for the day?" Shaking her head, she added, "No need to respond." Her eyes fell on me. "I'd be remiss to not encourage you, daughter, to review basic shadow forms again, until your powers balance." Her lips pursed at Kade. "You as well, I find it alarming you did not know how to stop an exploding penis, and lost in your game because of it. One may think you lost on *purpose* but that could not be since we all know you loathe losing to your sister. Alas, losers must fetch the provisions. Run along now Kade, and make haste."

Kade snickered and then bent to give me a quick kiss on the cheek. "Most fun I have had in a century. Thank you Rem Rem."

Then he grinned, throwing another bomb at my feet that left me coughing in a billow of smoke, Kade's laughter disappearing into the shadows.

"Goddess damn it," I cursed.

My mother shook her head, watching my face morph from disbelief to pure vengeance. I was going to get that little shit back somehow...someday. Turning towards my soulmate she arched her brow, "King Daemon, give me my granddaughter before you answer her question the way I know you will. I'd like to spend some time with her before she leaves me."

Emon scowled back before crouching down to our daughter, nuzzling her nose and shooing her over to my mother with an encouraging nod. Relief that he was avoiding having to answer Riella's question poured throughout the bond making me grin harder.

Shea stared after them as they passed, a painful longing in his eyes that had me feeling unwanted sympathy towards him. Shifting in my discomfort and feeling sand in places I wished I hadn't, I cursed my brother again for his ridiculous games.

The death god's melancholy was short lived however, my mother sensing his sudden change in mood, glanced over her shoulder and blew him a kiss, her blue green eyes gleaming before turning away with my daughter in tow.

Shaking my head, I swore softly, amazed to see how easily my mother could strip the death god down to his core and in that moment he looked almost fae...just a fae that loved his mate.

"Our females have a way of keeping us true and humble to our basic selves, little umbra. You do the same to me."

Meeting his eyes, I did not need to speak to tell him that he also did the same. He could see it there, in my gaze, in the way that even though we stood separate, I still leaned towards him with a vulnerable reliance that would be dangerous if it ever left.

Sighing the death god turned towards me, the softness he held for my mother now gone and replaced with his godly self righteousness once again. "You will listen as I attempt to fix what you destroyed. What I have to say next is vital for the survival of your journey."

I folded my arms across my chest and frowned. "As you wish."

He grunted and faced the prism of glass that was his demolished home. Stretching his arms out the glass shifted, breaking down into thousands of pieces of fine black sand.

"When you first arrived," he said casually, as if what he had just done was mere child's play, "I explained to you that this part of Sheol is called Eithne, our home."

"Yes" I said with my eyes narrowing, watching the way the bared markings on his forearm that were so much like my own, started to glow with a soft ethereal light similar to the three moons that were now lit in the far distance. "Is this the part where you tell me that Eithne has a counterpart?"

The death god's eyes shimmered with pride when he turned to look over his shoulder at me. "Yes. Well done. It is called the Vagari."

"Wandering," Emon stated simply, stepping closer and pulling me into his side, the backs of his knuckles brushing sand gently from my face. I relished the pleasant warmth of his body touching mine, our souls singing at the physical connection, although he could have forgone the damn pink sweater he was wearing.

Shea snapped his fingers and the black sand rose, swirling, morphing and twisting until emerald flames engulfed it in a single blast that reformed their glass tower of a home. "There. I suppose there is an upside to this...I've been meaning to make a few adjustments, ones I am sure your mother will thank me for tonight." He winked at me.

I wrinkled my nose. "Eww."

Shea's brows rose, his multi-faceted eyes shifting from Emon to me. "Hypocrisy doesn't look so great on you, daughter."

I gave Emon a side glance, shocked that no growl came from his lips. Instead, he shrugged, pulling me in closer, his hand on my hip searing sinfully through the fabric of my clothing, a lovely burning that made it difficult to focus.

Emon however, had no difficulty at all. "What should we expect in the Vagari?"

"The Vagari..." Shea growled, shooting him a murderous look. "Is more than just the souls of the fae banished there...it is the realm of *all* banished souls. Shared by myself and one other." Looking at me, he said pointedly, "You may call him a *cousin*, I suppose, since it was my actual god cousin that favored him and sent him there to rule. He is...*unique* and runs his half of the realm well enough."

"Family relations that your father does not approve of? Let's go now," Emon cooed in my head, his fingers sliding under the hem of my shorts teasing my upper thigh with his soft stroking touches.

I inhaled his intoxicating scent, Emon was like a drug to my system and I needed more...always more. I gripped his hand, shooting him a stern glance. *What did you say earlier, shifter? Patience. Time to exercise it. We must be prepared for what to expect, my power is no longer reliable and we do not know these lands at all.*

"Daughter, are you listening?"

I sighed irritably, looking back at my father, his jaw ticking on his otherwise flawless features, "Of course I am listening. What dangers will we face in the Vagari, and can we rely on this *cousin* of ours?"

Shea's eyes narrowed, studying me briefly before answering. "I cannot say, the realm shifts constantly and you would only waste time seeking our cousin's aid. But if he comes to you, I am fairly certain he will be accommodating."

"Fairly certain?" I growled, my teeth bared at him.

Emon hand tightened on my hip. *I love it when you go savage. Sometimes I forget you are shadow fae.*

The death god gave an exasperated sigh, "As I said before, I do not venture that realm, unless it's to seek The Well. Those souls torture themselves." Then his head tilted to the side and I could not tell if he was listening for something or thinking hard but when his eyes did snap back up to meet mine they glowed again. "Excuse me a moment, daughter." A cyclone of shadow swirled around him before he vanished.

I stared blankly at the shimmering black tower he had just created with a snap of fingers where he was once standing.

Emon dropped a kiss to my bare shoulder, *I can feel your worry, soulmate, but all will be well, I promise.*

I looked up at Emon suspiciously, clawing my way out of the carefully set seduction he was implementing upon me. *"You're hiding something."*

His eyes flashed briefly and in that moment, I saw the same reflection of worry I held before he masked it with a roguish grin, his hair falling between his eyes. *"You mean aside from my urge to throw you against your father's newly built home and have my way with you?"*

I licked my lips, his growling tone in my mind pooling more heat between my legs, a desire that had been there since the morning when he left me a complete mess in the kitchen, snickering with satisfaction. It was no wonder I created a giant shadow dick to demolish the city of Sheol...I needed his dick to demolish me...thoroughly.

A thought I sent to him through our bond.

Grinning, Emon's hand brushed against the look of yearning on my face, trailing through the strands of my hair, then behind my neck where he gripped me tightly. A show of sensual dominance done so discreetly in our stolen quiet moment together.

Whispering against my lips, he purred, "Trust me, when we get another chance to be alone again, there will never be any doubt of just how thorough I can be, little umbra."

CHAPTER 17

"**A**POLOGIES, THERE WAS SOMETHING I had to arrange in preparation for your departure," the death god sighed behind us, appearing just as he left, in a violent swarm of shadow.

I released my soulmate, before Shea started to glare murderously at me again, and relished in the way Remnant's eyes were blown with desire—desire that honestly was driving me fucking crazy. I hadn't planned on seducing her. Most of the time I never did, but it was fucking impossible not to respond to her without impulsive need. My shifter nature was a fucking beast with the early stages of our mating bond and I barely controlled the craving to possess her thoroughly, fully, extensively. Even now, with but seconds since I released her, I ached to feel the softness of her skin again, to make it burn with the same passion that was a furious inferno inside.

"And what exactly would that be?" Remnant crossed her arms in front of her chest, pushing up her breasts high and tight in her leather corset and I fisted my hands at my sides.

"You shall see soon enough, daughter."

His response made Remnant snarl. "Tell me more about the Vagari. What of the climate, the terrain, beasts we may encounter?"

I held back a groan at her vicious side. I fucking meant it when I said sometimes she acted more shifter than shadow fae. Her most recent reaction was the perfect example and the reason why I struggled to keep my hands off her.

Sighing, I ran my hand through my hair. I would overcome this.

I was a full grown shifter fae, I should be able to control these urges...except my soulmate was no mere fae female. To resist her was like holding my breath since she was the air I fucking breathed and without it I could not function either.

So I chose to breathe—only her, always her, till she could no longer supply me more air. But even then, I would find a way to make sure that fate never happened.

Unfortunately, true to her character, my soulmate did not make my lusting need for her any easier. The shorts she wore were the same she had on when we ran my city's parapets. They wreaked havoc on me then and they were wreaking havoc on me now. She knew it too—with every passing look she gave me. Each time, her gaze trailed over my body, she set it ablaze, making me want to rip this damn shirt right off of me and fall straight into her trap.

I sniffed, my soulmate was clever, already sensing that I was hiding something but I was still a predator, never prey. She would not get what she wanted from me so easily. At least not until I decided to become trapped. Which was going to be a problem of fucking epic proportions.

"You must keep it hidden for as long as you are able to, Emon, or you both will fail." Eve's words from last night perseverate in my mind, altering the entire course of what I had hoped Remnant and I's future would be.

I ground my teeth at the word fail. As a shifter fae, I had never been afraid to fail. Our experiences were what made us formidable and failure was part of that. If I had succeeded at everything in my goddess damn life the first time, it would have never made me the fae I was today.

Except now there was too much at stake to even fathom the possibility and I would do everything in my power to make sure we got it right the first time.

We were not going to...*fail*.

Normally, this would be the time I'd rely on at least a snide comment from Ethereal but there was only silence and I hated that more than I ever thought possible.

Shea studied Remnant briefly as if he was considering his answer before he spoke. "The environment and terrain changes based on the location you enter. A location that changes constantly, just as much as the beasts there. As I said before, souls in the Vagari torture themselves, and morph into many grotesque creatures. There is no telling where or what daughter, but what I can tell you is that there is not a single area within that side of Sheol that is not highly dangerous."

"Typical, always the vague answer, you'd be better off going in blind Rem Rem for all the help he is giving you." Kade's voice sounded from behind us, having shadow shifted back with a heavy leather sack strapped to his chest. "Here," he said, lifting it from his back and hurling it at me without warning.

If Kade Dark was trying to get a jump on me he would have to try much harder. Easily catching the pack with my own speed and strength, I swung it over my shoulder, marveling at its lightness for a party of three traveling, and gave him a smirk.

He sniffed and rolled his eyes.

"So I noticed," Remnant replied dryly.

The death god growled at his son, completely ignoring my soulmate, but the dark look he had now had me moving subtly closer to her. "Every day, Kade. Every fucking day, I have to listen to you bitch—"

"Shea," Eve warned off in the distance. Remnant's mother never looked his way, she didn't have to but we all did. Her tone, commanding and stern, said more than enough and I couldn't stop my lips from twitching at the hideous contorsion the death god's face took on. If Eve noticed, she did not react. She just simply continued to entertain our unaware daughter with the shadows. Her hands moving like a puppeteer, morphing the darkness to dance enchantingly and completely enthralling my cub with her silent picture stories.

Breathing deeply, Shea plucked at the silk sleeves of his shirt, rolling the cuffs higher up on his arms, revealing the same tattoos as my soulmate. "Despite your brother's belief, I do not purposefully mean to be vague," his eyes bore into us both, "if the Vagari was meant to be understood then it would not be much of a realm for the damned, now would it?"

I crossed my arms in front of my chest, "yet still you are willing to send us there."

His brows arched high on his head, "I have no qualms with you falling into the soulless sleep if you are too afraid to venture into the wandering."

I could practically hear Remnant's teeth grind.

I chuckled darkly, pulling my soulmate into my side should she attack her father with her bare hands. "Is it really me that is afraid, death god? Because I haven't once heard you sacrifice your time to assist us in getting to The Well."

"You dare?" his hissed voice was sharp.

My claws unsheathed and rapped on my folded arms. "Oh I fucking do."

After listening to the tragic love story of Remnant's parents last night I realized that there was one major difference between me and the god of death. I glanced down at the stern warrior face of my soulmate, taking in the way the cosmos shimmered off every part of her exposed pale skin and the way the white sands rose around her in silent beckoning—every part of this realm silently whispered its devotion to her.

Just like my fucking heart and for that alone, I would have burned down every world to get to her—I still would.

Rules be damned.

But not Shea, his dedicated love for his soulmate was obvious but his ultimate immortal self had no concept of time. For him, thousands of years was a blink, barely worth sacrificing a world for—obviously I fucking disagreed.

Eve was goddess damn virtuous for accepting it.

The death god's nostrils flared and I could hear Kade laugh darkly behind us. "I should not have to explain myself to you, shifter king." He looked at Remnant imploringly, "but I will for you daughter. I cannot enter the Vagari because it will put your mother's soul at risk if I were to linger too long. It will change her and I will not allow that to happen."

Glancing over at his mate, his eyes softened when she looked up at him with a sad smile while the shadows swirled around her and Riella in a dazzling display of fireworks, butterflies, and pixies.

The control of Eve's power was simply beautiful and gentle. It was hard to believe that she was once the hardened warrior leader of the shadow fae...one of the heroines of the Blood Wars that delivered the god of death on the doors of the Sanguine.

"But I can assist you..." his eyes narrowed on me, "all of you." Then turning sharply, he whistled into the swirling galactic sky.

"Oh this is going to be good," Kade snickered and Remnant glanced at me sharply before setting her eyes on the horizon.

Like fucking bait we waited and my fangs slowly descended, to prepare for whatever fucked up way Shea was using to earn his daughter's graces in own his favor.

I snorted inwardly, as if that would ever happen.

The haunting white sands rose slowly, arching over the widening silver path without a granule dropping on its reflective surface. From it descended two flickering lights, floating down from the sands like hot ash sparking from a fire, burning bright before darkening and sizzling upon the silver surface. Smoke rose from the burned embers, swirling and morphing into the outline of two very large beasts.

My nostrils flared at the scent and instinctively I edged even closer to my soulmate,

"Oooo what is that!" Riella's excited voice reached me before her running legs did, and I swooped down, catching her before she ran straight into danger.

"You must be more cautious my cub, not everything here is safe or kind. You must be more aware, Riella," I growled down at her.

When her lip trembled up at me from behind my leg where I placed her I immediately regretted my scolding. "I just wanted to see." Those big swirling green and gold eyes undid me.

Fuck.

"I know," I said gently, "and you can, from here, where I can protect you. Understand?"

She sniffed and nodded, "Okay. But what are they?"

I didn't need to look back up to see the beasts walking towards us, their scent was strong enough. "They are called cù sìth."

"It cannot be," Remnant whispered.

Reaching out I placed a supportive hand on my soulmate's shoulder, feeling her heart race rapidly, smelling the radiating sadness and shock like a sharp bite on my tongue.

"There is a special place in Sheol for honorable beasts," Shea explained, "especially ones honored by my goddess daughter. Your prayer was heard, chickadee."

"These are your cù-sìth little umbra," I hummed, watching the two great black hounds of death stand towering over us and I squeezed her shoulder in support, attempting to ease her racing heart. Remnant's hand shook when she placed it over mine, her grip just as tight.

Releasing the now wary Riella from behind me, I gently placed my hand on her back to push her forward. Remnant looked down at our daughter with tears in her eyes. "The cù sìth are the great death hounds of Faerie daughter, and these two were once my friends."

"What happened to them?" Riella whispered, her brow furrowing intently as if she was seeing or hearing something from the great beasts.

Remnant glanced at me worriedly before answering her. "They died, little one. They were killed by the Sanguine."

Riella leaned in and rested her head on my soulmate's hip soberly but her eyes wide with wonderment. "That is sad. But she is beautiful and I think happy now. Isn't she, mother? And her baby—so cute."

"Yes," Remnant whispered, squeezing Riella's hand and stepping away from us towards the deadly beasts.

Two sets of red eyes, through a black silky coat, watched her steadily, never leaving my soulmate as she approached. Her painted red ear twitched, but I sensed no threat from the death hound, only patience and acceptance. Standing before the beast, Remnant's head extended far back, to stare up into the great menacing face. The moons above highlighted the beautiful planes of Remnant's profile, absent of fear with just as much awe as our daughter.

A swell of pride swirled inside my chest. Remnant had done this, she had instilled eternal peace for a creature that one would not have given a moment's thought for, too selfish to see them as anything more than a dark omen of death.

The pup shifted excitedly, no longer able to hold back her own excitement, much like our own faeling. Identical to her mother but half the size, the pup barked happily before pouncing with its head low, its long black shaggy tail sweeping back and forth into the night sky.

Shea moved to stand next to Remnant's side to speak. "Greetings Sadhbh," brushing his hand against the bowed pup head, he smiled, "and Blaithin. Thank you for coming. I have asked you here to assist my daughter across the plains of Eithne. I do believe you know each other well."

Shea stepped aside then, next to Eve and Kade who had moved silently closer to see the great beasts themselves.

Remnant inhaled, "Sadhbh." Her head bowed, the name a mere whisper from her lips.

Suddenly, I was taken back to the day I had delivered Xi and Riley to her, how her heart broke with grief because she had blamed herself for their deaths...just as I knew she did now with the cù sith.

I swallowed down my need to tilt her chin up, to reassure her that their deaths were not her fault, and to rekindle the fire in her eyes rather than the immense sadness. The memory of Tyr's restraining hand like a ghostly shadow on my shoulder, his voice calm and so fucking distant. *"She needs this, brother."*

"I am sorry I was not there to save you and your little one," Remnant choked, reaching out to the panting pup that was more than eager to greet her. The not so little beast circled her energetically before licking my soulmate from head to toe. Riella giggled beside me, I could practically feel her body vibrating with equal amounts of enthusiasm...she was after all her mother's daughter.

I growled through our soulmate bond. *"Take note, little umbra, this is the only other soul I'll ever allow to lick you from head to toe in such a way. That right is mine and mine alone."*

"And now Blaithin's," she cooed back to me before shoving the large pup from her, smiling and swallowing down her guilt. "You have grown much since last we met Blaithin...I do hope you have been staying away from large bodies of water this time."

The pup barked energetically, a sound that was fierce and loud, sending us stepping backwards while her mother looked on, ever watchful.

Riella giggled, tugging on my pant leg. "Oh father, please! Can I meet her?"

I chuckled, tapping her nose. "Just like your mother." Engulfing her tiny hand with my own I led her to stand directly in front of the two great beasts, nodding my head in greeting. "Sadhbh, would you do us the honor of allowing our cub to meet yours?"

The cù-sìth mother bowed her great dark head, then lowered to the ground, her red eyes fixated on Riella.

"She is ours," Remnant said calmly, reaching for me to stand on her other side. I did so, wrapping my arm around her and swirling my thumb in soothing circles along her hip. "We are here to try to stop the darkness from spreading in Faerie. So that she may have a world to live in."

Red eyes flickered with understanding and then she growled low, her breath cool against our skin like fresh rain.

I grunted, understanding her growling acceptance of our little family and then inclined my head towards our daughter. "Give them your name if you wish to, my cub."

Wide eyes glanced up at us before she turned back to the great beasts. Biting at her bottom lip, she took a hesitating step forward.

The pup however had no hesitations in her greeting, immediately dropping to the ground and rolling onto her back, her great tongue flopping out and drooling on the silver path.

Riella laughed then and dropped to her knees, having to stretch her whole body across the great beast to sink her hands into its black fur. "I am called Riella," she said grinning as the pup barked happily.

Remnant's eyes met mine and I simply adored the soft tenderness in her emerald depths as we witnessed our daughter take on this strange world with a purity unmatched by any other. Her laughter, like tinkling bells floating in the twilight skies, was a sweet melody of promises, a hopeful future we could have never predicted.

I swept Remnant's hair back from her face, letting the back of my hand gently graze over her soft pale skin. Inhaling her scent, I allowed it to penetrate my soul, to strengthen my resolve in cherishing her forever. Unable to deny myself any longer, I leaned in to chastely kiss her sweet lips, pulling away slowly, our breaths mingling. It was a kiss full of meaning—a thankfulness for the best two gifts that only she could have ever given me.

Eternal undying love and a cub to share it with.

CHAPTER 18

Remnant

PULLING AWAY FROM EMON when I could see everything promised in his eyes was as if someone was stealing my air...only being close to him could I ever breathe.

How did I ever live without him before?

Shaking my head to clear my thoughts, I knelt on the other side of the not so small cù-sìth and smiled at the sheer excitement in Riella's eyes. "Give her a good scratch, pups love belly scratches." Dragging my nails over Blaithin's underbelly she stilled, her tongue hanging out even more and her red eyes rolled with pleasure.

Riella's tiny hands disappeared in dense thick black fur as she stretched her whole body across the giant pup to give her a good scratch. She giggled as Blaithin squirmed, rolling Riella further onto her body where they were now pressed belly to belly. Both of them sighed, and Riella's tiny arms did their best to wrap around the gigantic beast.

Sadhbh snorted, rolling her eyes at her own daughter's antics. When she turned her dominating gaze on me, I sighed, seeing only love and acceptance there. Patting her great muzzle, I kissed her large wet nose that was half the size of my head then searched for the death god.

I found him watching us with a face of granite, hard and impassive, with his arm poised gently around my mother. I recognized that look and knew it well. It was one I had worn many times myself. It was a guarded expression, one that kept violent emotions at bay—as a god and my father he was used to only watching happiness from afar, never able to participate in it.

My eyes trailed over to my mother, the blue circling her green gaze sparkled knowingly, and she nodded encouragingly to me.

"Thank you," I said.

Startled, Shea's penetrating stare landed on me, confused and calculated at first, and then he grunted. "All those adventures you had when you were young, when you dreamed of faraway realms and new worlds with naught but a chickadee to guide you...they were not dreams daughter, they were real. Together you and I traveled the universe..."

I blinked, unable to take my eyes away from the raw confession I saw on Shea's face.

A deep purr cut through my mess of emotions bombarding my skull, and soothed its storm. *In the cave, you shared with me that you used to dream about going to distant lands following a chickadee. Remnant...it was your father. He found a way to be with you the only way he knew how. Fuck, I despise this bastard but goddess help me, I would have done the same.*

Still processing what this meant, I shook my head, "It was you. All that time."

Shea nodded slowly, "Yes. As you got older it was harder to reach you. You see...a faeling's soul is wide and vast, innocent and open but as we age we harden, and those once beautiful realistic dreams," he shrugged, "they rust, they shatter, and they disappear."

I swallowed down the emotional burn rising in my throat. I wasn't sure how to respond or even what I was feeling now so I simply nodded, my own face turning to granite. Absorbing one simple truth from all of this—a parent would go through any lengths and find any loophole they could to ensure the happiness of their children.

A small smile graced his lips watching my expression change and he nodded back. For the briefest of moments, we understood one another, a connection that was once severed had reclaimed its place—I had a father.

Clearing his throat, Shea turned his gaze on Sadhbh who was also receiving a good scratch from my soulmate. "I believe we cannot stall any longer, the sands are shifting." At this, the white dunes rose in an eerie ghost-like wave to part a brand new silver path. "It is time for your journey to begin."

Barking happily, Blaithin rolled to stand and I snatched Riella quickly from her large body before she was entirely crushed. Her mother huffed hard in reprimand at her offspring before rising fully to her own great height.

I smiled in awe at her beauty. Her fierce red eyes boring down on all of us were menacing in the Sheol twilight and the whispers of bad omens clung to every soft panting breath she took. But to me she was sheer perfection—an example of beauty found even in death.

Shea approached, patting the beast's front leg. "Sadhbh and her pup will carry you through the Eithne upon the silver path only, they cannot enter the Vagari which is where you will need to go in search of The Well of Souls." His jeweled eyes turned on me, harsh and firm. "Have care, as I said before, once you enter the Vagari, I have no control of the chaos there, it is wild, untamed, and violent for a reason." His chin rose proudly. "If you stay true to your course, you should be there in a few days."

I crossed my arms and clenched my teeth. "How will we know which direction to take?"

My fathers eyes gleamed. "There are a great many paths towards a destination, follow your instincts. You are its goddess after all."

My brows rose, *he could not be serious.* "If I followed my instincts, I would have never come here."

The god of death smiled knowingly. "It is instinct to not always follow your instincts."

My mother snorted, shaking her head while Kade barked with laughter. My brother had stayed petulantly silent this whole time and I knew why. He was preparing for the sharp cut of abandonment again.

"Riddle that one, sister. Again he somehow answers you with no answer at all. Good luck with those instincts—I'm sure there will be a few more shadow dicks if that's the advice you take."

Eve rolled her eyes, patting Shea's chest, keeping him firmly in place while he looked on at his son with death itself clinging on his rising shadows.

I laughed softly, shaking my head at my instigator of a brother while at the same time, Riella tugged on Emon's shirt

"Grandmother told me that a dick is the word for penis. Also that you have a penis and I do not. She told me it is a good place to aim if someone ever tries to take me from you and mother."

Brows raised, I sent my own mother a sharp glance, which she returned with a leveled one of her own.

Running a hand through his hair, Emon crouched down. "Eve is right, my cub, and if someone ever does try to take you away from us, make sure your hit is swift and hard. Then you run. Understand?"

Riella's eyes widened and she nodded quickly.

Emon sighed. The relief tangible before he nuzzled her nose. "Would you like to ride Blaithin on our journey?"

She nodded with a wide smile splitting across her face, almost too big for her petite features. "Yes, please!"

I marveled at my soulmate, how easily he fell into the fatherly role, and the grace he held with every new challenge. It was no wonder his aura was so fiercely bright and golden because that was what his love felt like and it touched everyone around him, thoroughly.

Rising, Emon shifted the pack on his shoulders, sending me a heated knowing look before turning on Kade. "I expect we have everything we need?"

Kade snorted. "Everything *you* need you mean?" His eyes narrowed and Emon bared his teeth, "yes shifter king, I've packed enough provisions for the three of you—although your shifter ass made the task a bit more challenging than normal." He eyed Emon speculatively again, "make sure he doesn't eat all of your portions Rem Rem." Kade called out to me, snickering at another growl he received. "Your canteens will refill themselves automatically. You'll need them once you pass into the Vagari. It's hotter than a demon's taint there." Then my brother swiped back his curls, the darkness taking over his features of a tortured lonely soul, "I would go with you Rem Rem, but I have made a vow to watch over our court—"

His words trickled off as I moved quickly, pulling him into my arms, and hugging him fiercely. He stiffened for a moment, before letting out a long sigh, a sigh full of agony and frustration while his arms wrapped around me.

Our embrace was brief but it was enough, enough to tie us tenuously back together after being apart for so long. "You don't need to explain to me Kadey Kins." I said softly.

Stepping back alongside my soulmate, I could feel his pride in me as he placed a gentle kiss on my head.

"I wish we had more time," my mother said softly, before kneeling in front of our daughter in a wave of black finery just like the shadows dancing upon an ocean surface. Leaning forward, she kissed either side of Riella's cheeks. "I will think of more stories for us to share with the shadows the next time we see each other, alright?"

Riella beamed at her and nodded quickly before launching herself into my mother's arms. Returning her embrace, my mother's eyes fluttered closed, a painful expression crossing her face briefly and then pulled away, smoothing back Riella's hair from her face, and smiling. "Be brave." Rising she turned to me, repeating the same actions—a gentle kiss, a sweep of the hair. "A mother will always wish for more time but in the end it still flies away with her heart just the same."

I took her hand in mine, and for a brief moment I soaked in her dark commanding presence that was soft, embracing, protective. Nothing like what most thought darkness represented. "But we do leave behind our love, always."

My mother smiled softly, a lone tear falling down her face, making my heart ache for the loss she was now feeling. "Indeed, and it is cherished, my little chickadee. Always." Squeezing my hand she let it go. "Fly steady, pure, and strong," she said, her chin tilting high at the same time as Shea stepped to her side, throwing a comforting arm around her shoulders.

"Remember the verses, daughter," Shea said, "To the city of death..."

"Where love is regret." Kade nodded, reciting the next lines. "The end of your soul lives within the Sheol," he whispered.

"Beware and *behave*." I gave my brother a wary look.

Kade grinned, stooping down to kiss Riella's forehead. "The darkness you will obey," he said, tapping her nose before he gracefully slid away on the silver path. "Stay alive Rem Rem and keep my favorite niece safe." He winked down at Riella, "I have yet to show her the midnight pegasuses."

Riella leaned in excitedly. "Oooo what are those Uncle Kade?"

He snorted and his smile widened with pure adoration. "Think flying unicorns, my beautiful niece."

Riella squealed with excitement, jumping excitedly, inciting the cù-sìth pup to do just the same. Barking her joy in the chaos, Blaithin pounced around us, stirring up the white sands that hovered in the cosmic air before swirling back down on itself.

Emon chuckled, scooping up our daughter in his arms. "I think we already have a flying unicorn right here!" He tossed her tiny body high into the sky, leaving behind her charming laughter before she came rushing back down.

"Do I look like a pegasus, Uncle Kade?" Riella called when Emon tossed her one more time causing her to flap her arms like wings.

My heart soared along her flapping arms and I knew this image would always burn bright in my memory.

"One better! You are a fairy princess flying in those stars," Kade shouted up at her.

Emon grunted when he caught her, nuzzling her nose affectionately, a feverish light glowing off her bronze skin. "The most beautiful fairy princess in all the lands...worlds...universes," he said softly, then set her down.

"How could I have forgotten?" Shea spoke, stepping forward with his arm resting on his knee, gazing at Riella with a soft smile. "Every princess needs a crown does she not?" Waving his hand still heavily adorned with the same rings I saw him wear yesterday, he produced a pure glass crown with a bright spark burning like it was alive in the center.

I watched as our daughter took the delicate headpiece, swirling green and gold eyes glittering in the twilight. "Is that for me, grandfather?"

He laughed softly. "It was made for you and only for you, crafted from the stars that danced the night your soul was born, this one right here," he pointed to the shimmering middle, "glowed and danced the hardest. I knew I had to capture its light for you."

I swallowed hard with burning emotion and Riella's bottom lip trembled before she flew herself into the death god's arms. He grunted and stilled, his eyes full of shock and wonder before they closed softly while engulfing her into his formidable hold. The crown dangled in his hand, forgotten while the painful sad expression returned on his face.

I felt a wet nudge on my shoulder and looked up into the knowing red eyes of the death hound Sadhbh. I could tell that she sensed this was the right time to leave and I was inclined to take heed of the hound that delivered death omens.

"We must go," I said softly, watching my mother wipe away her own tears.

The death god cleared his throat. "Yes, yes, daughter, it is time." Pulling Riella away from him, he plucked the crown from her hands and placed it upon her flowing raven hair. "It is enchanted to stay on you. Don't take this off my sweet little bird. It will protect you even in lands where I cannot reach."

Riella nodded determinedly, absently clutching another memento that hung in a chain around her neck through her shirt . "I will wear it forever, grandfather."

"See that you do," Shea responded gruffly, then whistled softly. It only took moments for the death hound cub to plow through our little group, knocking every single one of us over with her clumsy excitement. Her mother barked roughly before the young pup stilled, then sat, her tongue rolling out again. "Blaithin," Shea scolded, "you must listen to your mother and take care of my granddaughter for me. She will ride with you on the path." He wagged his finger at her. "Do not veer off the path."

Blaithin barked happily and then turned to Riella, her ears pulled back as she bowed with sheepish eyes at our daughter.

Riella grinned. "Don't be sorry Blaithin. I am excited too!"

The cù-sìth pup grinned her lethal canines before standing and barking again, looking at her back and then at Riella expectantly.

Shea waved his hand and suddenly a soft blanket of silver was laid across the pup's back. Picking up Riella, he gently placed her up on her perch. "You wont hurt her holding onto her fur, but if you don't the blanket is enchanted to keep you astride."

The sky shifted and suddenly the stars swarmed, dancing happily in merriment around Riella and covering her in glittering dust. In that moment she captivated all of us—her innocent cherub face tilted up to watch the stars swirling, her eyes wide with pure wonderment, her mouth parted with an inhaled awe, and her hair flowing around her, illuminated by the shimmering glass crown upon her head.

"She is her mother's daughter," Emon's deep sultry voice whispered in my mind as he shifted closer to me.

I blinked and turned towards him, realizing his eyes had been watching me this whole time. *"I don't want her to ever lose that—the feeling of this moment."*

Emon nodded solemnly, kissing my forehead. *"We will protect it, protect her..."* Then he snorted. *"As if anything can stop us."*

The cù-sìth hound nudged me one more time before my father raised his hand and both Emon and I were being lifted by the shadows to sit atop her massive form. She was not as large as Emon's fierce panther but she was close.

The pain that ached deep in my chest intensified, thinking of Ethereal and the destruction we left behind in Finlandia, what I had done to Quinn...Jar. I was even worried about Eshe, her bitchiness must have grown on me.

"Say goodbye to your family for now, my beautiful soulmate," Emon's voice rumbled behind me, dropping a kiss to my shoulder. "Our worries can wait at the very least for that."

Sniffing, I looked downward, meeting the eyes of my brother, mother, and my...father. Yes, I could accept that now...just. I placed my hand to my heart. "Till we meet again."

"We love you, our little chickadee," my mother called out while all three of them placed their hands on their hearts as well. "Stay safe on the path."

"Abeamus Sadhbh." Let's go, Sadhbh. Leaning forward, I patted the space between her ears.

The stars that danced around my daughter shot back into the sky, exploding around her into bright bursts of color, saying their goodbyes.

The cù-sìth howled.

A haunting and foreboding sound. Its eerie call sent an unwelcome shiver down my spine—and I prayed it was not an omen for what was to come.

CHAPTER 19

I NARROWED MY EYES when I saw our cub slowly slump in her perch. She had been riding with such ease for the past two hours that I hadn't given a moment's thought that she had been tiring until now.

Tucking my chin over my soulmate's shoulder, I growled low. "We should stop for a bit. Riella is not used to this type of travel."

Remnant nodded. "I agree, a break is well needed." Leaning forward, Remnant softly patted the death hound between her ears. "Sadhbh, let us rest for a few, beautiful one."

The cù-sìth hound barked once before slowing to a trot. Following her mother, Blaithin fell into step beside her, taking her new role seriously although she could not contain all her excitement by the way her large black tail wagged, stirring up the sands that rose up to inspect us.

Dutifully staying on the silver path, I vaulted off the beast that had finally come to a halt and landed lightly in a crouch, my feet only a whisper on the smooth reflective surface. I rose to my full height and looked up expectantly. Never to be one upstaged by my antics, Remnant did not disappoint.

Dismounting on the silver path with a graceful flip in the air, she landed in front of me with a sultry smile on her lips.

"Well done, little umbra," I purred.

She grinned and winked, her hips sashaying as she walked over to the cù-sìth pup to assist our daughter down. I licked my lips, suddenly back in the Wildwoods, that first day when she truly smiled at me, life igniting in her eyes—sweet goddess I would never tire of seeing her this way—

Distracted by my mate there was no way for me to avoid the large black tail crashing into my face. Cursing, I was sent stumbling sideways, spitting out a mouthful of coarse hair.

Did I just get fucking slapped to Faerie and back by a damned cù-sìth tail?

Righting myself, I met the innocent eyes of Sadhbh, I snorted at her facetious demeanor as if she hadn't just purposefully annihilated my face with her powerful tail for drooling after my soulmate.

"Mother, my body hurts," Riella whined, as Remnant steadied her wobbling legs.

"That makes two of us," I muttered, rubbing feeling back into my bruised face.

A huffing sound came from the death hound mother and I quirked a brow at her, shocked to realize that she was laughing, amusement sparkling in her bright red eyes.

"You played your card now, Sadhbh. I am on to you." I winked at her and winced inwardly at the soreness it caused.

Shaking it off, I peeled our bag of supplies from my shoulder, and reached in feeling exactly what I was looking for. My shadow brother was more clever than I thought, an enchantment on the bag delivering whatever my thought desired. Opening a canteen of water, I knelt before Riella and handed it to her. "Drink, my cub. Your body will heal soon. When you are done with that then walk around to ease the soreness."

Riella nodded, her crown creating reflective rainbows on the silver surface and white sands. I frowned, weary of the beacon its shimmer created but admittedly was inclined to heed the death god's words. If the crown served to protect her then it stayed on her head no matter what. There was no telling what kind of creatures lurked here.

Standing I handed Remnant a canteen, noticing she was scoping the area just as much as I had been since we stopped. She took a long sip watching the shifting sands and glittering twilight before handing it to me.

"It's calmer out here than in the city," Remnant said slowly, watching as the waves of sand crested up to the silver path and then crashed back down away from us. Then her eyes fell on Riella. Our daughter was walking around the happy cù-sìth pup scratching and petting her into a panting slobbering mess.

Taking a long swallow of the sweet clear water, I capped the canteen, grunting. "I've noticed some flickering lights out upon the sands but just as my eyes settle on them they disappear, could be wisps but you are correct. Even the cosmos above us seems quieter, the star dust less."

"I've noticed them too and I don't think they are wisps," she frowned and tilted her head. "They have an enticing pull, as if they want us to come towards the light."

I snorted, offering the water to Sadhbh who shook her dark head at me and laid down with a soft huff, her red eyes closing to rest. "Well that just sounds like trouble we don't have time for." I tossed the canteen back into the bag and reached for a pen and paper and began scribbling my thoughts upon the parchment.

She eyed me curiously. "Taking notes, shifter?"

I shrugged, holding my face impassive, "Someone needs to keep adding to The Unaccounted Life of the Last Shadow Fae." I blew on the paper, this was only partially true. What I was writing was much more important.

She snickered and looked away, her gaze getting lost in the distance. Folding the parchment and I placed it back into our pack and slung it over my shoulder, watching as her dark brows furrowed deeper on her beautiful face.

Chuckling, I shook my head. "You're thinking about investigating them aren't you?"

When she didn't answer, I stepped closer, cupping her face to look up at me and eased the frowning wrinkles away with my fingertips.

"I would be the first fae to volunteer to go with you on this, little umbra. But we have a job to do and very little time to get it done. Besides, your father said to stay on the path."

Her emerald eyes glittered mischievously. "And you were planning on following his orders were you?"

I grinned ferally down at her. "Of course not, but the first part of what I said is still valid."

"I can't help but feel like they are important somehow." She sighed, ensnared by the distant horizon again.

"Riella, don't step off the path," I scolded seeing our daughter step a small foot onto the shifting sands.

Startled, her head snapped up with wide eyes but her voice was strong, "I know father, but look, I see something."

Instantly, Remnant and I were by her side, following where her small hand pointed straight ahead to a high sandy dune in the distance.

"There atop that far hill," she whispered, "Do you see?"

Sniffing at the air, I smelled the forest and sun first, then I spotted what she had. My fangs bared and my claws unsheathed, I reached over my head to the pack where two swords launched into my hand. "I do," I said softly, handing the second sword to Remnant, all the while not taking my gaze off my target in the distance.

Two crystal blue eyes stared hard in our direction and just like the pull Remnant described moments before, it was almost like it wanted us to come to it.

A gentle pat on my leg from my daughter's delicate hand gained my attention.

"I think it wants us to go to it," Riella said softly to me, her swirling green and gold eyes wide and innocent.

Remnant raised her sword, her dark hair falling over her shoulder, her body shifting defensively. "Emon..."

Looking back at the penetrating blue eyes, I snarled. My entire being wanted to take care of this threat head on and I knew Remnant felt the same, but we had Riella now.

"It seems content with just watching us for now," I growled. "Let us rouse the hounds and move on." I frowned at them, surely they would have been alerted to it if it truly was going to harm us.

Remnant nodded, lowering her blade but not her stare. "I agree."

Riella pouted at me as I scooped her up and walked towards Blaithin who barked happily at our sudden attention. "But father, I do think it wants us to go to it."

I looked down at her innocent face, the sweetness there with her little crown and dark hair flowing around her face. "I know my cub, but we cannot risk it right now. Let's see if we can learn more from afar first."

Sighing, Riella nodded, gripping onto the black fur as I placed her on Blaithin's back. Settling into her perch with her back straightened and her face set with disappointment, she looked down upon me so regally that I had to blink hard in order to verify what I was seeing.

But by the time I opened my eyes again, she had looked away, leaning low to pet the pup, giggles escaping her as Blaithin attempted to slobber her hand.

"Shifter?" my soulmate said from above the giant cù-sìth beast.

Hissing, I crouched low before launching myself high up into the air, my soulmate's hand captured my own and swung me steadily up behind her. Immediately, I inhaled her scent, calming my animal instinct to rip whatever it was watching my family to utter threads.

"Abeamus Sadhbh," I snarled.

***

We rode as far as Riella could manage, then pulled her atop Sadhbh with us, and rode longer still. Silently we all watched as the twilight of Eithne dimmed and lightened, the white sands rose and fell, and the lights flickered on and off in faraway distances. When we finally did stop to rest again, it was only because the young cù-sìth pup was falling behind.

But it was all for naught, I could still scent the same smell as before...it was of the forest and sunlight and when the bright crystal blue eyes appeared again atop another dune, my fangs lengthened.

"Rest now Blaithin," I purred, patting her head affectionately while she curled up beside her mother, never taking my eyes off the watchful entity.

"It's still there, father," Riella whispered to me, leaning into my side.

I nodded, running my hand through her hair soothingly. "Yes, my cub, I see it." I narrowed my eyes, finally making out a shape of the creature in the distance.

"Here, my love, have some dragon fruit. I do believe your uncle packed it just for you," Remnant said, kneeling down to place the pink skinned fruit into her hand.

"My favorite!" she squealed, breaking it open its pod with ease and munching on the soft flesh with enthusiasm.

Remnant rose beside me, her arms crossed over her chest, the toned muscle in her arms making her scrolling tattoos ripple. "It hasn't dared to come closer, can you make out any further what it may be?"

I ran my hand through my hair, grinding my teeth at the way the pink fabric of my shirt restricted my movement. But it was necessary for as long as I could make it that way. "It's a predator feline of some sort." I tracked the long twitching tail, "it's not stalking in a way that is threatening...but—"

"It's waiting for something," Remnant said grimly.

I nodded with a low growl. "Or someone."

"Look! The pookah!" Riella cried, dropping her dragon fruit in shock the moment a black bunny appeared before her with glowing red eyes.

Reflexively, I kicked out at the rodent while Remnant pulled Riella away, but it was faster than even my shifter speed, disappearing and then reappearing on top of my daughter's shoulders.

"Hey!" Riella exclaimed as the pookah ripped the crown from her head, and launched itself into the sand, turning to hiss at us through its large front teeth, its ears twitching. "That's mine! Give it back!"

I growled, stalking the edge of the silver path. "Listen you little shit, give my daughter back her crown or I'll be roasting you for dinner tonight."

But the damn pest only hissed back again, before it turned to run away, heading straight for the crystal blue eyes that continued to watch from afar.

"Give it back now!" Riella raged before her raven haired head shot past me in a blurring speed straight into the white sands of the Eithne—*off* the silver path.

"Riella no!" Remnant cried, running after her.

Roaring, I tore off after them both, surpassing Remnant quickly. Despite her speed and prowess, my soulmate wasn't equipped for speed like I was and I loved a fucking chase...and roasted rabbit.

But this time the stakes were different. My daughter was involved and currently was goddess damn racing straight into the danger—at a speed that was not normal for a mere faeling.

Riella was *fast*.

Faster than she should be. Frowning, I blurred across the white sands to stop her, no crown was worth her being delivered into the hands of whatever was stalking us, and it was clear this pookah pest was setting the trap.

I roared into the night for Riella to stop, even pulled on our bond, but she shoved it aside, moving faster as I scented her hot fury and indignation towards the creature that dared take her crown. "Riella stop now!"

At last she listened, but it was too fucking late. The pookah spat the sparkling crown out upon the sand, then vanished. Snatching it up with a snarl, Riella looked up only to gasp at the large snow leopard grinning lethally down at her, its crystal blue eyes twinkling in the twilight.

Roaring again, I slid to my daughter, wrenching her away from the creature and easily tossing her yards behind me where I knew Remnant would be following to catch her. My momentum didn't slow as I continued forward, attacking the great cat head on, but it simply leapt away, leaving me to slide on my hands and knees, sand rippling upwards around me. Spitting out the grit and shaking it off my body, I rose to slowly stalk around the creature that gazed patiently back at me. The pookah reappeared again between the snow leopard's great spotted paws and hissed.

The warm sun and forest scent was strong now, and even in my rage it was soothing, calming me when I did not fucking want to be calm, and it was way to fucking familiar. "Who the fuck are you," my voice rattled, straining against the calm inducing feeling and my raging snarls.

The snow leopard chuckled and I stilled at the familiarity of the sound and the voice that came after it.

"Language my cub...I know I raised you better than that."

I swallowed hard, slumping to my knees, and sinking into the sand. "Fuck...Jar?"

CHAPTER 20

THE SNOW LEOPARD'S GRIN widened, the crystal blue eyes calculating, its long tail curled up around him. "I see that my unicorn fashion has taken off since I have been gone." The master healer's deep soothing voice emanated from the majestic cat.

"Jar," I croaked, not able to tear my eyes away, hardly believing what I was seeing.

The feline predator chuckled. "Yes, your majesty, it is I."

"*Emon?*" Remnant's hesitant voice sounded in my mind. "*Is that...?*"

"*Yes,*" I choked back to her, realizing this was the master healer's shifted form, I had never seen it before but had always known him to be formidable.

His crystal blue eyes zeroed in over my shoulder where footsteps of my daughter and soulmate could be heard slowly approaching. "Well met *forta*, and our newest shadow shifter cub. Greetings, little Riella."

"Jar?" Remnant whispered, the three moons suddenly peeking over the sandy dunes bathing us all in moonlight.

The cat shook its head exasperatedly and arched his brow, looking down at the pookah that started to roll in the sand. "This is not going as I expected. It's almost as if they thought I'd be wandering the Vagari in my death rather than the Eithne. Any suggestions, friend?"

The pookah stopped its rolling and hissed, disappearing into the twilight.

"Spirit guides," Jarquinn's cat sighed and rolled his eyes. "You can never fully trust them."

Riella giggled behind me.

Jarquinn's tail twitched before curling it further around him, turning his sight on my daughter. "Little cub, I must say I am terribly sorry for the way we last met and I will apologize for Zaki. He is an eager and somewhat tactless spirit guide. Until you came he preferred setting my tail on fire rather than helping me."

"Will he come back?" Riella asked shyly.

Jar's regal spotted head dipped, narrowing his gaze on her. "I do believe he will, little cub." Rising back to his full height in sitting, he hissed. "Before you two become complete numpties, staring at me with drool hanging out of your mouths," his eyes shifted between Remnant and I before rolling again, "Let us move on. We have some things we need to discuss...these lands, while beautiful, cannot always be trusted." He eyed the sand wearily.

I glanced back at my soulmate, neither one of us moving, having been solidly frozen in shock, still unable to comprehend what was happening before us.

But our daughter did not hesitate, delicately placing her crown back on top of her head she marched forward with eager determination.

My hand shot out, stopping her, and she looked at me with confusion. "Not without us Riella. It is dangerous for you to go off alone."

My reprimand only served to deliver an adorable pout from her.

Snickering, I rose from the sand, brushing it off from my leathers and feeling its coarse granules scraping beneath my shirt. Reason number forty one not to wear a fucking shirt.

Remnant stepped next to us, reaching for Riella's other hand. "Your father is right, that crown was not worth your life, little one.

You must think about what you are doing before you chase after something again."

"But I did think," she sulked, looking between us. "There is a silver path beneath us and grandmother said the path is safe." As if her words commanded it, the sands parted to reveal the glittering walkway under our feet.

The snow leopard chuckled and his eyes twinkled at our daughter. "Clever, little shadow shifter." Rising smoothly, he began to stalk away, indicating us to follow.

I barely repressed my laughter when Remnant shot an arched brow at me.

"How did you know this, my cub?" I peered down at the top of her head where her crown glinted in the dusky twilight.

She swung our hands, happy once again, pulling us forward to follow the snow leopard. "I asked the lands for a path and it told me yes."

"The land speaks to you?" Remnant gasped softly, shooting a concerned look towards me.

"Yep!" Riella hummed.

"What else do the lands say?" I said carefully, watching the sauntering snow leopard ignore our conversation, leading us casually over the next dune.

She tilted her head to the side and then nodded once. "They say to follow Master Healer Jarquinn and that they love your shirt father."

Barking out a short laugh, I squeezed her hand. "It is not for them, it is for my beautiful daughter—" and something else entirely.

The pathway shifted beneath my feet and I stumbled into a curved divot that was not there before. Cursing, I growled down at the lands.

Riella giggled. "They did not like you saying that but say they also agree. I am beautiful."

Smiling, ruffling her hair fondly. Amazed at the child before me. "Little fiend."

"We are here," Jarquinn's voice rang out and the three of us stopped to see a beautiful soft light flickering above the sand no bigger than my hand. Its warm glow illuminated the elegant spotted coat of Jar's cat and it hummed, singing a voice of longing and promise.

"Can you feel that?" Remnant asked through our bond, *"it's the same feeling I had earlier, this light wants us to come to it."*

I grunted, the song pulling me inward just a Remnant said. It was...peaceful, the same feeling I had always felt when I entered the healing quarters. Like a warm blanket, soothing the storms that raged within us all.

"Jar," I began.

The snow leopard shook his head. "We talk when we are inside."

I peered around us, seeing nothing but sand and the dead end of the silver path we stood upon. "Inside?"

Jarquinn rolled his crystal blue cat eyes again. "Sometimes I do worry about you, Daemon."

My soulmate stepped forward and tilted her head at the warm light. "It's a gateway," she breathed.

Jar nodded. "More or less." Turning towards the light he looked over his shoulder, poised just inches before it. "It is the doorway to my promised peace. You will see them scattered throughout the Eithne should someone want you to visit them."

Pouncing through, he was immediately absorbed by the enchanting glow.

"Ooooo, I wanna go!" Riella cried, yanking on both our hands and dragging us stumbling through the gateway with surprising strength.

"Her shifter powers are manifesting already. The strength, her speed," I sent to my soulmate before we touched the light.

"We must teach her how to use it to her benefit then, and soon," Remnant said firmly.

"She will know how to use them when the time is needed. It is not the faeling's powers I would be worried about. It is yours," Jarquinn interrupted our internal thoughts, reading the worry easily on our faces.

Snapping my head up, I stared at my friend, now in his fae form—a fae who I had just seen beheaded by my soulmate only days ago.

He was every bit the ancient fae I remembered. Sky blue robes, blonde hair shining, slanted bright blue eyes staring with so much depth to them that I could get lost trying to understand it.

My gaze shifted to the world surrounding him, surrounding us, and reached out tentatively to a purple wisp that floated right in front of me. It fluttered at my touch, and then rose away into great towering trees full of thick glittering foliage. From their wispy leaves, heavy rain drops were frozen in time, reflecting soft beams of light from the warm sun, casting millions of rainbow prisms all around us.

The master healer shook his head exasperatedly and walked forward through the towering oaks that hummed, their branches moving to softly touch the healer in greeting as he walked by. Flowers bloomed from each step Jar took, a trail to follow in the most wondrous of ways.

Riella tugged on my hand, her eyes wide. "I want to be able to do that," she whispered before skipping off in front of me to follow, her little hands trailing over the fragrant petals.

Shaking my head, I carefully stepped through the vibrant green moss of the forest floor, avoiding the blooming flowers, not trusting any of them not to bite my balls off.

Remnant snickered next to me, reading my mind and likely hearing the same distant snores of gnomes just as I did. Another thing that would likely bite my balls off if I allowed them to get too close.

Jar paused, stooping to pluck an odd looking yellow bloom sprouting from the ground.

"Ah. Yes this will do." He muttered to himself and held the odd looking plant outwards into the sunlight. The forest around us hummed like it agreed and was pleased.

"It's so beautiful," Riella whispered beside us.

Jarquinn smiled softly at our cub. "It is, isn't it?"

Frustrated, I ran my hand through my hair. "Why did you bring us here Jar? You must know why we are in Sheol. Why is it that you are standing here acting like you didn't almost kill my soulmate then beg her to end you."

Remnant flinched, the pain this had caused her evident on her face, the guilt burning brightly in her eyes.

I swept her hair back. "Let the guilt go, little umbra. Jar knew it was his time." I bent to hoist Riella in my arms. Tucking her close into my chest, feeling suddenly protective of my family, I glared at the master healer accusingly. "You knew, didn't you? That you would die."

Jar raised a singular blonde brow at me, dropping his hand that still held the plant. "I am an ancient fae, Daemon. My days have always been numbered," he sighed. "But even more so when I broke the wards on Riella. The Sanguine is not easily destroyed, in order to save her I had to take pieces of it into myself. I am sorry to say, I was foolish enough to think that the small amount I did absorb would not affect me."

I growled low. "That still doesn't explain why we are here."

Remnant rested her hand on my upper arm and I ceased my low growling. She gazed at the healer expectantly, "Why *are* we here Master Riss? Why have you sought us out?"

Tilting his head, he smiled calmly back at us. "You are here, *forta*, to heal." Catching my gaze he smiled softly, "It is time to heal all the scars, even the ones hidden." Then he turned in a swirl of blue robes to walk further into the forest and the humming began anew. "Follow me."

Looking down at Riella, I let my gaze go cross and my tongue hang out. She smothered her laughter with her hands. "What do you say, my cub. Do we follow master crazy pants over there?"

"I heard that Daemon, and for the record, I don't wear pants...I like to feel the breeze," called out the healer.

I scrunched my nose up with utter disgust which released more laughter from my cub, erasing the worry that I had seen there moments before.

My soulmate slapped my shoulder playfully, rolling her eyes. "Come on, let's follow, I don't sense any danger from this place."

When I looked up, Jar had paused and was smiling at me. "Fatherhood suits you, as I knew it would. There is nothing better." He looked away wistfully and started walking again.

I swallowed, holding Riella closer to me and I gingerly walked around the gardens, specifically avoiding a pod of vicious looking blue dragon plants, not surprised to see them slither up towards me. "Jar. It's about Quinn, I don't know—-"

The master healer held up his hand. "I may not be in the world of Faerie anymore but I am still able to check in on my son. Let me settle your worries, your majesty. Asher was successful in subduing him before the death god stole him away. Eshe has since taken over, both in the care of my son and of Finlandia. Repairs have begun for the city and as well as my son's heart—they have soul bonded."

I glanced at Remnant, watching her expression but she did not seem surprised by this fact, as if she knew the two were meant to be paired.

Tension eased from my shoulders, Quinn and Finlandia would be okay. I had been a shit king, an absent king...but at least the fae I loved would be in safe hands. "Soulmated," I whistled. "How did Eshe take it?"

Jar gave me a wide grin. "About as well as your own soulmate."

I chuckled, grinning at my mate. "Denial and death threats. There's nothing a shifter loves more than a hard earned challenge."

Remnant's cheeks flushed but her eyes narrowed on mine. "How can you say that? I'd say losing his father, friends, and king while falling into bloodlust was challenging enough. He has paid his due."

"Fate has a funny way of showing its hand, *forta*. Those trials were exactly what my son needed in order for their bond to finally show. Only in darkness can the light be seen, and that light was Eshe." Jar shook his head. "That does not stop me from wishing it had been different but it will not help to dwell on these things. Right now, we must ensure that there is a world for all the people we care about to continue to live in, which means—pardon my language, that you two need to get your shit sorted."

I grunted, but was quickly distracted when Riella gasped in my arms. Stepping out of the grove, we were met with a stunning field that stretched for leagues on end with the same bright yellow buds Jar held in his hand. My rebuttal to Jar's cryptic words failed to form as together we watched the entire valley ripple in greeting to us, releasing the sweet smell of honey blooming on the air.

"It is a field of dying kisses." Jar held up the sapling. "You see the petals form a shape of lips and once every summer solstice they release their petals high into the air and when they fall down upon you it is said to give you the memory of your lover's last kiss." He stared at them fondly, lost in a memory. "I met my own soulmate in a field such as this. They were rare, but if you knew where to look, you could find them, and with just a single petal, one could prevent the end of any death." His head bowed, the blonde locks falling around his face, shielding him, but it did nothing to hide the sadness when he spoke again. "I could have used just a single flower to save my Lova...but the blood fae had found the fields early on in the war and burned them all to ash."

I swallowed hard, Jar had never shared with me the details of his wife's death. All I knew was that she was lost in the wars, leaving behind her infant son and her soulmate who vowed afterwards to never lift a sword in bloodshed again. That was how I had known my father had gone too far in his bloodlust...the moment he ordered Jar to fight was the moment I challenged him to the bloodlust rites.

I frowned, looking around me searching. If this was his promised peace then his mate should be with him. "Jar...where is Lova?"

Remnant inhaled sharply next to me, her eyes glittering with unshed tears, while Riella remained intelligently quiet in my arms. The incessant need to draw Remnant closer to me and hold onto her forever was stronger now than ever before.

Sighing, the healer looked out over the yellow plains. "Not here." Turning back towards us he smiled, the sadness diminishing just as quickly as it came. Holding the yellow flower up he blew it from his hand. The sapling fluttered in front of us, dipping and swirling until it landed perfectly in my daughter's hair, tucked over her ear.

Awed, Riella reached up to touch the seemingly gentle flower and then beamed at the healer. "Thank you," she whispered excitedly.

His smile grew. "You are welcome my little shadow shifter, it is enchanted so it will never die or tarnish, keep it close to you."

He winked at her and my eyes narrowed...what was he fucking not saying?

Then he smoothed out his robes, glaring at the two of us before piercing my soulmate with his calculating gaze. "Now, let's talk about your powers—both of yours. I thought you had learned your lesson, accepting who you are, *forta*."

My chest rumbled a warning, not liking his chastisement of Remnant, seeing and smelling the way shame coated her.

Jar rolled his eyes. "I cannot take your threats seriously in that pink shirt Daemon."

I pointed a finger at him, barely keeping the smile from my face. "Now you know how I felt all those years with you and those damn unicorn slippers."

He smiled, folding his arms within his robes. "That was on purpose to see if you could keep your head on straight as a king, your majesty...and they kept my feet wonderfully warm."

Riella giggled.

CHAPTER 21

Remnant

"Come, come," Jar called towards us, leading us back into the grove. I felt the rush of a gentle wind pushing us forward, eager for us to follow. I breathed in Jar's sweet haven, loving the smell of the fresh woods, sunshine, and the sweet honey smell still radiating from the dying kiss flower in my daughter's hair.

My heart still pounded fiercely seeing the ancient healer standing before me, whole and well. I had to blink several times to escape the vision of him from before, his face had been so contorted in pain, his eyes begging me for death. Now those same crystal blue eyes sparkled at me with warmth and clarity, forgiveness and love.

Two things I never felt as if I deserved.

Riella's hand reached out from Emon's arms, pulling me back to the now. "It's so beautiful here," she whispered.

I smiled at the way the golden sunbeams highlighted her innocent beauty while the large oak trees hummed again at our return. Encouraged, wisps swirled around her enchantingly, drawn by her soft innocent voice.

Jar smiled back at her. "Thank you child. It is where I grew up. As an ancient fae we emerged from the grove, it taught us about the world, the trees whispering its secrets until we were ready to leave to live as part of your world."

Riella's little brow puckered and then her jaw dropped. "The trees say they were sad to see you leave."

Jar nodded, not an ounce of shock or surprise in his features. "You hear them too. I am not surprised, my little cub. Your powers are manifesting as we speak." He waved her over and placed her tiny hand on the smooth silver wood. "What else does it say?"

Emon shot me another look of concern, how many was that today already? My hands twitched at my sides, aching for the comfort my shadows brought me during times of uncertainty. That was something that was always clear. Their power.

She smiled again, looking between Emon and I with wonderment swirling in her gold and green eyes, drawing out a chuckle from her father. He was irrevocably smitten by our daughter and I loved him all the more for it. "They say they are happy to meet me."

Jar nodded. "Faerie honors its miracles. Yes, your power will be full soon." Then his eyes narrowed on Emon and I with full disappointment. "Unlike your own powers. Both of you. Your manipura's are blocked, the source of all fae's power and strength."

Emon smirked, sheathing his claws. "I'll have you know healer I am shifting just fine."

Jar raised his brows. "Is that so, your majesty? Show me your beast then?"

Emon narrowed his golden gaze. "I fail to see how this is your concern healer."

Jar snorted then. "Don't be daft, boy. I am a goddess damn healer."

My brow furrowed, anger and realization dawning on me. "Emon..."

He turned to me, raking his hand through his hair with a guilty expression. "You said you never doubted my power. Don't start now. My beast does not define me and nor does your shadows."

I breathed heavily, then hissed through my teeth. "So you what...purposefully distracted me from the full truth?"

Emon stepped toward me growling low, his hand cupping my face. "No, little umbra. I took your fears and loved you, honored you, worshiped you for them and ensured your mind got the rest it needed."

I pulled his hand from my face and snarled. "You cannot keep doing this, Emon. Using this uncontrollable need for each other to not face the truth." I glared at his pink shirt for emphasis. "We are not whole and that puts our daughter in danger. Pretty words and soft kisses don't change that!"

Emon snarled, turning away from me to prowl the grove. Raking his hand through his hair over and over again, shaking out his claws and retracting them. Snarling and hissing at the wisps that attempted to reassure him.

He had every right to be frustrated...but so was I—and hurt. I had confessed my fears to him and expected that in return. He could not possibly think that just because he had no beast that I did not see him as powerful? Was he that worried I lacked so little confidence in him?

Jar sighed, shaking his head. "I suggest you both reflect before you leave here. What you find will assist you with the journey ahead." He bent down to gaze at Riella. "While your mother and father work, would you like to see more of the grove?"

Riella's eyes swirled, the gold in them shining more brightly. Emon paused, his hand dropping from his face, seeing it as well. "Oh yes," she said, turning towards us and I inhaled, her eyes almost pure gold now. "May I?"

I nodded dumbly. "Yes of course."

Jar gave us both a knowing look. "Sort this out and do it quickly, you don't have much time." Then he glanced over at Emon. "Try not to hurt any more Prime trees here." The woods hummed and then shuddered. "They know what you did to their kin and won't take kindly to your outburst a second time."

Emon's fangs flashed with frustration. "I also apologized."

Jar chuckled, his eyes sparkling before a flash of light shifted him into a powerful snow leopard. He was a beautiful beast, especially when the golden light shined down upon him.

Bowing to Riella she scrambled upon his back, grinning madly at us with her golden gaze and waving goodbye as the snow leopard stalked through the trees.

"Her eyes turned full gold," Emon said softly, breaking the silence between us.

I turned towards him, fisting my hands at my sides, my teeth bared. "I swear to the goddess Emon," I hissed, "if I had a sword right now it would be laid across your throat until you spilled every truth you have been holding back from me."

Emon narrowed his eyes, anger and excitement flashing in them. "If you could even get close enough to me in the first place that is."

I held his gaze and exhaled slowly, "Is that a challenge shifter?"

Emon chuckled darkly, shifting our bag on his back. "Perhaps, it is little umbra."

I grinned, there was no happiness or pleasure in it—there was only dark intent, "You've made a grave mistake."

Emon returned my smile with a feral one of his own. "See if you can come at me then, soulmate. First touch on me, no matter how light, and I'll confess all my fears for you to hold in your already tortured heart. Since that is what you fucking want so badly."

Fury, pure fury had me lunging for him but I knew my shifter, knew he was faster than any other I had come across. I could see it in every coiled ounce of his muscle as he spun away from me, a dark chuckle teasing me as he went. But I was pissed enough to make it happen.

This challenge would be a difficult one.

"Too slow, my love."

Baring my teeth, I moved again, faking my advance and spinning towards the direction I knew he favored. His eyes widened with surprise for a brief second before twirling from me. My hands grabbing onto the pack he wore on his back instead of his body, and ripping it towards me.

With stealth, he allowed it to be pulled off of him and I threw it down with mild irritation. The sound of its contents spilling and the knowing slide of steel drew both our attention.

Chests heaving we stared at the pair of black swords before lunging at the same time. Emon slid and I flipped, grasping one of the pommels before I launched over his head.

Spinning without pause, I faced him, our swords ringing loudly in the grove and the trees around us shuddered. Emon was still on his knees, the sword held high above him and his golden gaze was like being pierced by pure fire.

A slow smile curled up on the edges of his lips before he rose, pushing my blade upward with his great strength and towering height. "Shall we change this game?"

Raising a brow, I swung my sword down and around to dance back from him. "First blood?"

"Would that satisfy my savage soulmate then?"

I inhaled deeply, feeling my mind calm with the weight of the sword in my hand. "Perhaps."

His teeth flashed the sunlight peeking through the trees. "So be it."

Without preamble or flourish, Emon attacked me head on, his brutal force ringing through each deflection. But I shifted and moved with him, not against him, letting my body flow with his attack. His size and speed were his advantage, his reach was great but I was small and the closer I could get to his physical self the less ability he had to use his weapon. If I continued to play defense he would tire me quickly and win this charade.

For that was what it was.

Ducking beneath a deadly arc of his blade, I stepped into him, leveling my sword to slice low at his feet where he could not deflect. I could practically feel my victory, his blood would be mine and so would all his damned secrets.

Until his hand slammed heavily down on my wrist and the hilt of his sword punched heavily into my back, shoving me into his chest. Dropping my blade, I launched my knee straight into him, slamming it hard into his upper thigh. I was too close to him for my true target but it still felt fucking good.

He hissed, and in a move I had never seen before, I found myself with a blade across my throat and a shifter pressed against my back. The delicious scent of him falling around me in a thick cloud.

I sucked in a deep breath. Sweet goddess.

CHAPTER 22

Remnant

"**D**O I REALLY NEED to draw blood, little umbra or do you yield?"

"Screw you shifter."

Emon inhaled, his nose trailing along the outer curve of my ear. "You know my response to those words, Remnant. Care to try again?"

I huffed, the fury that was once there slowly dissipating into hurt. "Why did you not tell me?" I whispered, staring out at the beautiful grove, full of sunlight and warmth. The opposite of what I felt inside.

Growling, Emon threw the sword across my neck away, hugging me closer into him. His face buried in my hair and his chest rumbled against my back before he spoke. "Little umbra, in a span of just a few days, you gained a daughter, a soulmate, were forced to kill a fae you had just gained as a friend, you were reunited with your family who happens to reside in Sheol with towers full of soulless fae including our own friends, and then learned that I also will succumb to this in a few short days." His arms tightened around me more. "And here you are, sacrificing a piece of yourself for others...again. Goddess, Remnant, if holding back my inability to shift gave you one fucking moment of peace in the chaos of your long list of worries then I'd do it again in a heartbeat."

Defeated, I closed my eyes and let my head fall against his chest, my hands reaching up to hold onto his strong arms.

My chest rattled when I let out a long sigh. A sound drawn straight from the warring agony inside of me.

He was right, goddess damn it, I didn't want to admit it but he was right.

The trees shook softly and hummed in agreement, blowing my dark hair across my face, and, whispering the secret music of life upon the wind.

Unfolding his arms he trailed his fingertips along my own before threading his fingers through my hands, and spanned them over my abdomen. "Dance with me," Emon purred huskily, his hot breath sending pleasurable shivers through my entire body.

The grove seemed to answer for me. The sunlight sparkled and the wind increased to gently push us with the sway of the trees.

I simply nodded, not wanting to whisper a word that would break the sudden enchanting moment we found ourselves in.

"Breathe," he whispered against my skin and I exhaled. "Move with me, little umbra."

I nodded, moving with Emon, our bodies swaying together, following the shift of the wind within the grove—its warm air guiding us in a series of steps, twirling and cutting to music that only it knew the sound of.

Soon I was lost in the moment and began to glide along without the support of the breeze, Emon falling in step with my rhythm without hesitation. My hips rolled and his followed, my arms drifted low and his engulfed me, hovering his gigantic body just inches over mine. And when we arched backwards, the movement was so fluid that together we opened our hearts up to the sky, to the world, and to the universe.

Enthralled by the feel of him, our bodies twirled and swooped, curved and bowed, the flow of the wind following us this time, the trees dancing inward drawn by our grace, and the glade whispered its joy while our soulmate bond burst into life. Emon's breath was my breath, his heartbeat was my heartbeat, and when his hands trailed over my body...pushing and pulling us as one, I dared not open my eyes, wanting to be lost fully in this moment.

Never returning.

Stepping into me, Emon spun my body to face his, his leg pressing between my own. Rolling my hips, he dipped me to the ground, his nose trailing up from my stomach to my chest, his other hand sliding up my leg, gliding over my calf, burning deliciously over my heated skin. His hand moved higher, teasing over the hem of my shorts and moving upwards to lovingly spread wide over my womb, pausing there longer than any other place, as if he was willing his golden light to heal the scars and the emptiness from what had been taken from me—from us.

Tears prickled behind my closed eyes and I felt Emon's warm shaky exhale against my cheek before his hand moved upward again, grazing over my breast, and settling between them over our joined beating hearts.

This was love...this was *power*.

My eyes snapped open, seeing my same realization reflecting in Emon's golden stare.

"Do it," Emon bowed his head, whispering against my heated skin, his chocolate spiced scent dominating my senses. "Command the shadows just as you command my heart."

Breathing deep, I reached out to the darkness. I beckoned to their cool, simple existence, letting them come to me through the flow of my body, gentle and peaceful waves of shadow that embraced me in their purity.

Sighing, I released them, blanketing the grove in complete darkness, the only light shining was from Emon's and I's burning gazes.

"Fucking beautiful..." he purred. Pulling me upward, taking my hands in his, his body slowly twirling and spinning me through the darkness. "The way you steal my air." He whispered in the dark, pushing my upper body away from him but keeping his lower half pressed tightly into me where I could still feel our energies connected. "The way you seize my heart." He circled me low, so that my hair grazed the forest floor before pulling me back up. Our noses brushing, my breath gasping, "the way you dominate my soul." His eyes bore into mine. "All of you is so fucking beautiful." Growling, his eyes gleamed, spinning me away from him before pulling back slamming me into his chest with a breathless gasp. "Move them," he commanded. "Make them dance with us."

I smiled widely and twirled my fingers still captured by his hands. The darkness began to shift and glide, following Emon's shifter grace as he waltzed us around the grove, and when they spun around us, he picked me up, pirouetting me in the air with them. I laughed, stretching my arms out wide, dipping my fingertips into their cool abyss, sighing as I weaved them up over my arms.

Bringing me back down, Emon nuzzled my cheek, inhaling deeply.

I cupped his face, feeling rather than seeing the rough stubble of his beard. "Your turn, shifter," I said breathlessly.

"Close your eyes then, little umbra and feel me."

My breath caught and my eyelashes fluttered closed, a slow victorious smile spreading across my face when a flash of bright light sparked beneath my eyelids.

When I felt the large brush of an animal rub against my hip, the flickering of soft furred tail wrap around my bare leg, the low purr circling around my still form, and a long warm lick on my tattoo brands, I grinned wider.

"Drop your shadows, little umbra, and open your eyes."

Reaching out with my hands I drew them up towards the sky and my eyes followed, opening to unveil the darkness. Blinking into the sunshine filled grove, I stared in awe at Emon's majestic beast sitting patiently in the middle of it.

His shifted form was gorgeous and it was his. A large *black* panther bowed its head down at me. Golden eyes, I loved with every fiber of my being watched me with the same reflective emotion.

"Amor vincit omnia. Love conquers all," Emon purred in my head in ancient fae, bowing to me as if bestowing gratitude. *"You did it, my love, my soulmate, my little umbra."*

Stepping towards Emon's bowed form, I pulled his great panther head to me, and ran my hands through his midnight black fur. "No Emon. *We* did it."

CHAPTER 23

I WOULD HAVE NEVER believed I shifted except for the fact every single one of my senses was vibrant and more intensified than ever.

The grove was awash with colors of scents that were vibrant and potent, and I quickly categorized them in various groups of potential threats. Tilting my head, I could hear the soft flutter of the wisps, the tiniest insect crawling on the blade of grass beneath me, the brush of my soulmate's hair along her firm back, and then there was the power. Raw and feral, the strength that coiled inside of me was *wired*, every muscle poised and alert.

A sudden joy that I had never felt before filled me. This was what it was like to be your own beast—I felt *everything*. None of it was processed and filtered by another, including the lovely sight of my soulmate standing in front of me.

And when she touched me...goddess. Through my panther senses her touch felt like the most exquisite torture, one that ripped a deep purr from my massive chest. Pure ecstasy clouding all my heightened senses.

"Ah, you have finally done it. Well done you two." Jar's smiling ancient eyes stepped through the trees with our daughter holding his hand. Remnant attempted to step away from me but I wrapped my long tail around her waist to keep her close.

I gave the healer a lethal grin full of sharp white teeth.

Riella gasped, "Father! Will I look like you when I shift one day?"

Inhaling deeply, I shifted back to my fae form and crouched low, opening my arms wide.

Riella grinned and her tiny body blurred, her image shimmering into a cloud of darkness before slamming solidly into my chest.

I smoothed back her hair, marveling at the beautiful creature that was my cub. "Whatever you shift into, be it a panther or something else entirely, you will be glorious. Right, little umbra?"

Peering up at my soulmate, Remnant smiled with the same light in her eyes, pulling her hair back and tying it off. My mouth watering when her body arched deliciously while performing the task.

"More than glorious, little one," she responded back, arching her brow at my hungry stare. "There will be no one like you, ever in this entire universe."

Weaving shadow, Remnant morphed her darkness around us—jumping dolphins, galloping unicorns, and dancing pixies danced around our daughter. Eyes alight with possibilities, Riella watched entranced by the darkness.

I looked over at the master healer who was watching us with tears in his eyes before connecting with my own. "Thank you, Jar."

"You are most welcome Daemon," he smiled softly at me, plucking at his robes

I tilted my head watching the action, the familiarity not lost on me...it was the same behavior he had when he first told me about Riella.

"What else is there Jar? I sense there is something you are not quite telling us," I said gently, watching his tears turn from ones of joy to ones of sorrow.

"It is about Lova." Another pluck at his sleeve with his long tapered fingers.

Remnant and I drew in together, bringing Riella close to us. "What has happened to her?" I said, tugging on my pink sweater, loathing the renewed feel of it back on my body after shifting. "Why is she not with you here?"

Jar hesitated and the trees hummed around us in encouragement. I did not miss the way Riella's head tilted, studying their humming sound with keen interest.

My soulmate's hand rested on my shoulder and squared herself to the healer, her voice stern. "You have loved us all like family master healer, and family takes care of their own. What do you need from us?"

Folding his hands in his robes, he sighed. "My soulmate has always been a fierce defender of the weak, her greatest strength and greatest weakness was pursuing justice in this world. My Lova was more warrior than I ever was and the call of it tempted her many nights."

Remnant gave a soft inhale. "She did not seek eternal peace when she died."

Jar shook his head. "I should have known. My Lova would never forgive herself for leaving behind our cub and myself. She would have sought a way to avenge what was taken from her and so many others."

My lips thinned.

Well fuck.

"She is lilin," Remnant breathed, saying the exact words I had been thinking.

The healer gave us both an imploring look. "I have searched these lands, scoured every doorway, made friends with the pookah who reside here just to hear even a whisper of her. Even Shea could not find her within the Eithne but he assured me he did not banish her to the Vagari. She must be within The Well, waiting for her time of justice to come, following that strong beat of battle in her heart."

Remnant's gaze met mine, a new line of worry lining her brow. I growled inwardly at the sight of it. The only lines I wanted to see on her gorgeous face were the ones that were created when she smiled, when she laughed, and I was losing that battle.

Turning back to Jar, I moved to envelop him in my arms. "We will seek her soul along with the others in The Well," I said for my soulmate, despite the doubt I felt along our bond.

Jar wrapped his warm arms around me and I felt his wash of healing power rejuvenate my entire being. "That is all I ask. If my Lova must avenge the life stolen from us, then I will honor her need to stay lilin and will continue to wait for her return here in our grove."

A sharp stab in my leg had me pulling away from the healer's embrace with a loud curse making everyone jump. "What the fuck?" I spun, looking for the source of the pain, seeing a sharp needle thin piece of wood implanted in my lower leg just above the lacings of my boot.

Jar chuckled. "Oh that's Henry."

"Who in the Faerie fuck is Henry?" I snapped.

Remnant gasped then, dropping to her knees. "Henry," she whispered to a rodent sized bearded creature stepping out from the coverage of a massive tree trunk—goddess help me, Henry was a damned gnome?

The arrogant garden guardian was dressed in thatches of stitched leaves with the exact same sharp twig weapons as the one currently embedded in my leg, sheathed at his back. His blue floppy hat tipped to the side as he waddled forward towards us, his long white beard dragging on the forest ground while he bared his needled teeth.

"It is you!" Remnant cried. Her hand reached out to the untamable creature.

"Of course it is *forta*. Your father made sure your gnomes were also granted the Eithne. The others are here as well, Anthony, Donald, and Raymond stay more in the herb gardens I tend. They like the butterflies there, I really wish they'd stop tearing their wings off though, the glitter gets everywhere."

Remnant laughed. "Yes, they do make quite a mess. Hi Henry." She turned her attention to the creature, cradling the gnome to bring him up to her face, nuzzling her nose against its belly as I wrinkled my own at its grubby hand patting her skin affectionately back.

Dragoon was right. My soulmate did love her gnomes.

"Oooo, he is so cute!" Riella squealed.

Growling, I yanked the gnome's sharp weapon out of my leg. "Little flower pissing Henry made your soulmate bleed, little umbra. Do you not care for my well-being?"

The gnome turned then, his jaw widening with his needled teeth, hissing.

I hissed back. This was why no fae fucked with gnomes.

Remnant laughed. "It's his way of saying hello."

"And to stay away from maedere, he says." Riella interpreted for us all as the gnome beamed at her, frowning innocently, she asked, "What does maedere mean?"

Remnant froze and I could hear her slight intake of breath. I pulled her into me, ignoring the hissing Henry in her hand. I could sense that a part of her heart craved that title without realizing she wished it to be so...because mine did too.

Perhaps someday...

Jar gave our daughter a wide smile, blue eyes twinkling. "It means mother in ancient fae, little cub."

"Oh." Riella's head tilted in thought.

I broke the terse silence with a playful growl down at Henry. "Mother or not, Remnant is still mine you glitter addicted bastard." I raised my soulmate's other hand up to my lips to kiss it softly, loving the soft laugh escaping her. Smiling, I dropped it and leaned towards the glaring gnome she held, "But I can make a promise to you to always take care of her, forever." I handed him back his tiny dagger, the most painful splinter I had ever had. "Those better not have been poisonous, Henry."

The gnome yanked his weapon from me and scowled. I stared back, meeting his challenge, unblinking. There was a long moment of silence before Henry grunted and nodded.

It wasn't until I heard a small steady splashing on my boots that I looked down to see another gnome bastard pissing on them. I snarled harshly, shaking its glittered urine off my boot with irritation.

It grinned back, shaking its tiny pindick before stuffing it back into its pants.

"Donald!" Remnant admonished, but she could not keep the snorting laughter from escaping her as the gnomes cackled with glee. Jar and Riella were not much further behind in joining them.

Henry jumped from my soulmate's hand and with one final hiss at me and a tip of his hat to Remnant, he scampered off with his companion.

I pointed an accusing finger at my soulmate. "My vow will be paid now. Surely, those flower pissing rodents have been avenged as well as their own personal vengeance upon my person."

Remnant arched into me, placing her hand on my chest, plucking at the pink sweater I knew she hated...I fucking did too but it was necessary. Standing up on her tiptoes, she planted a soft kiss on my lips. Happiness glittered in her emerald depths and I knew then that all the pee pollinating gnomes in Faerie could piss on my boots if it put that look in her eyes. "They are shifter pissing rodents now, my love."

Jar chuckled deeply behind us.

I huffed but I could not stop the smile from spreading across my face, tucking her hair back. "As long as I don't start sprouting flowers and urinating glitter, I am okay with that term if only to have that smile on your face permanently."

With good added measure, I pecked a kiss on her cheek where the little bastard Henry had touched her, erasing its scent with mine.

Pulling back, I winked, seeing Jar stoop low to our beckoning daughter at his side. Her mouth and voice were obstructed by her small hand as if she imparted an unknowing secret to him. When Jar's eyes widened, he glanced towards me with a large smile before turning back to my daughter nodding.

Remnant quirked a brow at me, shaking her head, drawing my attention back to her. "Is the big bad shifter king really worried about a few little gnomes claiming me?"

"I don't underestimate anything when it comes to you, little umbra...it's always the least suspected entity that has the most power."

Feeling Riella suddenly tugging on my arm, I looked down at her. "What is it, my cub?"

"Father, what about him?"

I pulled her to me, resenting the panic in me as I searched for more gnomes. Remnant and Jar exchanged amused looks at my frantic movement.

Riella tugged harder, yanking me forward. "See father, it's the pookah again!"

She pointed to the sudden appearance of a black morphing mass, the familiar shape of a black rabbit taking hold, the same creature that stole Riella's crown.

It's red beady eyes staring at my cub with a deep yearning.

I bared my fangs at it, not liking that look one damned bit, but happy it wasn't the last two remaining gnomes, Anthony and Raymond. "What of it, my cub?" I hissed through my teeth.

Red beady eyes fell in my direction to glare at me and the reminded me far too much of Cronin's kraken. "He says his name is Zaki and he is coming with us," she giggled. "He says he is mine and I am his."

My claws lengthened and I stepped in front of my daughter with a vicious snarl. "Like fucking Sheol he is."

First gnomes and now this goddess damn shit.

The rabbit's ears drooped but its red eyes flared, still staring up at me.

Jar hummed a warning. "It is considered a bad omen to deny the assistance of the pookah Daemon. If this one is claiming to be Riella's then that means he is her spirit guide. They are meant to be, just as—"

My hand sliced through the air, my eyes slashing towards the healer angrily. "I'd be very careful with the next words you speak, Jar."

My soulmate's touch lowered my threatening claws, her lip curled back with irritation and her glare just as strongly directed at the pookah. "I don't like this either, shifter, but if this pookah can provide Riella with even more protection, then I am willing to have the creature tag along."

The pookah's eyes shifted slowly to my soulmate before he morphed into a small black gnome, bowing low.

I bared my fangs and hissed, watching its gnome body startle and then mock me, snapping into the damned rabbit again, teeth bared.

Riella hugged my leg and then looked up at me pleadingly, her eyes back to the even swirl of green and gold. "Please, faedere?"

My eyes widened and Remnant's filled with tears. Faedere meant father in ancient fae, its use one of love and trust. "Where did you learn that word?"

Her lip stuck out and she hesitated, glancing at Jar who nodded to her encouragingly, "The grove, they call Master Jar faedere and I wanted—I..."

"Your clever little cub asked me if it meant father and if she could call you this too." Jar said softly.

I dropped to my knees in front of her, trying to choke back the burn of emotions leaving me speechless. Since the moment I knew Riella to be mine I had been overcome by my failure to protect her, the fear that I could never amount to be the father that she deserved and yet—here she was, with big unsure eyes, taking me in as her own, claiming me as her family...her *faedere*.

Remnant's hand squeezed my shoulder and I placed mine overtop of it, reaching out to my daughter with my other and sweeping back her hair. Hair so much like her mother's. "Of course you may call me this, my little cub. As long as you choose to, never because you feel as if you must," I choked.

Her face instantly switched from weariness to full joy. Throwing herself into me, her small arms barely wrapped around my wide frame as she rubbed her face into my chest. Happily, I held her tightly, inhaling her sunlit meadow scent that reminded me too damn much of home and of how quickly things could change.

Looking up, I scowled over my cub's shoulder at the pookah, "I will allow you to join us but I will not tolerate secrets..." I started saying, but then Riella cheered, jumping out of my arms, and reaching out to the spirit guide with needy fingers. Its lithe bunny frame hopping up to her shoulder.

"Thank you, thank you!"

Rising, I held up my hand and her cheers disappeared but her wide smile did not. Suddenly, I knew I had another weakness—her smile undoing me just like her mother's in a much different way. Goddess help me the day my daughter learned *that*. "On one condition. I want to know what that damned thing is whispering to you and *we* will determine if it is safe or not." Looking up at Remnant, she nodded, before I shot our daughter a stern look. "Understood?"

Petting the red eyed glaring rodent, Riella looked up at me smiling even harder, hugging my leg tightly to her. "I understand, faedere. Thank you!" She nuzzled her sweet innocent face into my hip once more and I chuckled, patting her head affectionately. My hand stilling when the pookah's paws also embraced my leg.

I glared down at it and held back my growl at the utter possession in its eyes. A claim on my daughter I wanted to snuff out of its tiny body *"Game on you bastard."*

I thought I'd have at least a few thousand years before I had to worry about sharing my daughter with another being...no matter what the goddess fuck it was—it seemed I was wrong.

Jar chuckled softly, and I looked up to see his soft blue eyes observing me, full of pride, and twinkling with a mixture of amusement and sadness.

It was time to leave—and I couldn't help but think he had mastered this whole thing, sending me off whole and healed again, along with a well placed gnome attack that still fucking throbbed, a new beat of my heart claimed by my daughter, and the gift of a feral spirit guide as our final goodbye. All that was missing...

Jar winked, tilting his head downward and I followed, snorting.

There they were...the exact thing that was missing from this perfect moment.

Unicorn slippers.

CHAPTER 24

Remnant

Our goodbyes were short.

Emon held on to the master healer longer than the rest of us, knowing that it was likely the last time we would ever see him again. Both had tears in their eyes when they pulled away and when Emon turned to leave he never looked back—but I did.

When Jar's crystal blue eyes met mine for the last time, I felt the horrible images of his death wash away, leaving me with the beautiful sight of him standing in his loving grove of yellow dying kisses floating around him, his smile as bright as the sun peeking through the trees, and then he was gone.

The moment we stepped back through the light we were on the main silver path where the cù-sìth still rested peacefully, snoring loudly under the star-filled twilight, completely unaware that we had been gone.

But there was one obvious new addition to our little party and it was in the form of a demon eyed black bunny sitting smugly upon my daughter's shoulders. While Emon's distaste for the spirit guide was obvious, mine was much more subtle.

I called to a small shadow upon an embankment of a dune and watched as it rose up to trail over my knuckles, swirling around my arm before morphing into a spear that my daughter recognized immediately.

"Is that for me?!" She jumped with excitement, forcing the pookah to struggle and hold its purchase on her shoulder.

I nodded. "Yes. Your shadow spear from The Under." I patted Sadhbh awake. The great death hound yawned and shook her head, licking gently at her cub to wake as well. "I will teach you more on how to use it."

Emon snorted, giving the pookah a disgusted look. "Or at the very least teach her how to stab vermin."

Riella's pookah hissed at my soulmate and I snapped my fingers in its face. "None of that Zaki. Our journey is perilous, our world is at its end, and Riella is our daughter. We will protect her with everything we have and you have not earned our trust to deserve any indignant attitude."

The spirit guide's ear dropped but it still glared with contempt.

Riella spoke softly, petting its drooped ears. "Zaki says he understands."

My brows rows and Emon huffed next to me.

"Good." I handed my daughter her spear before stopping to quickly braid back her hair to the side. Smiling down at the way she looked like a dark fairy princess warrior dressed in black leather, with her glittering star crown, a shadow spear, an iridescent indigo dragon scale looped around her neck, a yellow flower tucked in her hair, and a spirit guide sitting proudly on her shoulder. "Why don't you get settled with Blaithin?"

Riella nodded eagerly and then skipped happily over to the cù-sìth pup that was more than excited to meet a new friend in the pookah. Launching itself from Riella's shoulder it hopped between the prancing feet of the pup, playing along.

Emon pulled me back into his embrace and I allowed his scent of chocolate spice to wash over me as we stood witness of the young innocently playing without a worry in their hearts.

"From the healer's instructions, it will only be a few more hours before we reach Vagari," I said quietly, Sadhbh turned her red eyes on us and huffed in agreement.

Emon grunted, sweeping my hair to the side to drop a kiss on my shoulder. "I am with you. Every fucking step of the way."

I turned in his arms, searching his eyes. "How have you been feeling?"

Emon's gold eyes twinkled down at me. "I just danced with my soulmate in an ancient grove and shifted for the first time on my own...I feel pretty fucking fantastic, little umbra."

I gave him a reproachful look and shoved him away. "You know what I mean, shifter. Shea said you would start to weaken. You will tell me if you do start to have symptoms. We must be prepared for everything and anything when we enter the Vagari. Don't hold it back to spare me, I will feel better knowing."

Raking his hand through his hair, he growled. "I have not felt anything since the first occurrence. I will not put you or our daughter in danger, Remnant."

I shot him a glare. "You know that is not what I mean, Emon."

His stormy golden gaze softened. "Fuck, Remnant. I know but I sometimes wish you would goddess damn trust me. Have a little faith that I know what I am doing."

I stepped towards him, my hand shaking as I raised it to the thundering heart in his chest, a deep sigh of irritation escaping him. "This isn't about me not trusting you Emon. This is me not trusting that I deserve you and that at any moment's notice fate will wake up and realize she has made a horrible mistake and take you from me."

Emon reached up and pressed my hand harder into his chest, the pink sweater soft under my fingertips, and his eyes flashed brightly. "Fate can go fuck herself, little umbra. I am here and I am not going anywhere. I promise. You don't need to draw first blood for me to spill that from my soul."

I shivered at his dark tone. Leaning heavily into him, I inhaled his scent once more, letting it calm me while the lingering doubt still slithered through my thoughts. I stared at the dancing unicorns stitched on the fabric before I answered. "Okay," I breathed, then pulled away. "Let's move then."

Emon's hand fell from mine and I could feel his calculating golden gaze on my back. There was a weariness radiating off of him that I recognized from before...before when he kept secrets from me.

My hands fisted at my sides. He was asking me to trust him while keeping me in the dark.

What was I missing?

Watching Riella clamber up on the cù-sìth pup, my lips pressed into a grim line. There was only one logical reason why Emon would do that—our lives were at stake.

CHAPTER 25

IF I EVER THOUGHT traveling through Sheol would be dangerous, then I was a fool. Nothing was more dangerous than the silence and quiet simmering anger of my soulmate for the past *two* hours.

I licked at my bottom lip with a soft snarl. I hated fucking silence.

Discreetly, tucking another folded piece of parchment I had written on into the pack, I glanced down at my daughter and then glared at the rodent settled in her lap. Even that damn pookah slept peacefully, silently, no longer hissing in my direction.

All I had for the past two hours were the haunting undulations of the white sands and the panting breaths of the cù-sìth keeping me company. Goddess, I even missed Ethereal's arrogant voice. I was sure he would have had a comment or two about what a fairy boy mess I had made of things.

Running my hand through my hair, I sighed. There was no explanation I could give to calm the growing irritation inside my soulmate, but this damn silence was a fucking waste of the time we had left together and I could not change what was to come.

Finally, the cù-sìth slowed to a halt and I unwrapped my arm from my soulmate's waist, thankful, at least, that she still allowed my touch even if she hadn't spoken one word to me.

Dropping to the silver path, without any flourish this time, I held my hands out to her, a peace offering. She quirked a brow at me. I couldn't help but grin back—she wasn't going to take it.

Instead, she called out to our daughter with a sweet voice that I knew meant fucking trouble. "Riella, watch carefully, let this be your first lesson in shadows."

Throwing out discs in succession she stepped down from the death hound beast, her eyes glaring down at me. But I did not care, this gave me an excellent front row view of her gorgeous form and my eyes stayed glued on her powerful legs, clad in thigh high boots and skimpy black shorts that hugged her ass in a delicious way that made my hands flex hungrily. The shadows gathered behind her after each step, trailing like a cloak before she placed a graceful booted foot down on the silver path.

"With the shadows, you are reliant on no one and nothing." Her eyes were twin emerald blades cutting into my heart. Turning away, she crouched in front of Riella and tapped her nose. "They can build you a home, weapons, clothes, and even a companion. You can fly, surf, and tunnel through lands and air...*all by yourself.*"

I chuckled, challenging my soulmate with a smug grin and crossing my arms in front of my chest, the pink shirt straining against my bulk. "Your mother is correct, my cub but also know that you cannot eat shadows, they cannot love you with their last dying breath, they cannot fight for you when you no longer can."

Remnant looked up and scowled.

I knelt beside them both, brushing back the loose strands of hair that had escaped Riella's braid. "What your mother is trying to say is that you need never feel indebted to another no matter how strong they are but should you choose to *share* that strength with someone," my eyes met Remnant's, "you will have more than anything this life could ever offer you."

"Like you and mother?" Riella gnawed on her lip while her pookah hopped down from her shoulders to the silver path, uninterested in our conversation.

I turned towards Remnant who had her lips pressed thinly together before she blew out a hard breath, rolling her eyes.

Smiling, happy at least the silence was broken, I gathered Riella into my arms to stand, and then pulled my soulmate along with me. "Exactly like your mother and I."

A short bark had us turn to Sadhbh, her black shaggy head pointed towards where the sands rose upwards into a giant ascending wall. I could already sense the unrest, the pain, and the loss behind the wall of white sand, the decaying stench of death and bitterness of betrayal seeping from the waves.

"The Vagari," I growled, the realm of Sheol's banished and wandering souls.

"I believe this is where your journey ends, my dear friend," Remnant whispered and the cù-sìth mother bowed her head. Remnant dropped her forehead upon the death hound, her face etched with another painful goodbye.

I understood. The memory of the bitter grief I felt saying goodbye to Jar was still strong. Every part of me had screamed to find a way for him to come with us. One last adventure. It only took a singular look at his peaceful eternal grove and I knew I had no right to ask it of him. He was where his soul was the happiest and it was my turn to do everything I could to protect that.

Just like he had for me all those years.

Riella whimpered in my arms. "I don't want them to go."

Seeing the tears form in her beautiful swirling eyes was enough for me to forget all about my own grief. "Do not be sad, my little cub. You love your new friends, do you not?"

Riella sniffed and wiped her eyes with the back of her hand. "Yes."

I gave her a sad smile. "When you love someone, you protect them. The Vagari is not a safe place for Blaithin and her mother. You would not want them to be harmed would you?"

My daughter's lip quivered. "No. I would not." Then she buried her face into my chest. "You aren't going to leave me behind are you faedere?"

Shocked, I hugged her tightly and my voice shook. "What makes you think such a thing?"

She cried quietly, her tears wetting my shirt. "Because you love *me* and you always protect me."

My hand stroked her hair. "Shhh, my cub. Do not upset yourself any further. Of course we are not leaving you behind," I reassured her.

Then I looked up hopelessly for support from Remnant. *"How do I fix this?"*

Remnant went to open her mouth, but a sudden bark from Blaithin had us all turning to look down at the pouncing pup.

Riella hiccuped, her voice still quivering when she spoke. "Blaithin says she has something for me."

I nodded and gently lowered her to the path. Clumsily, the cù-sìth pup bumped into her with her own excitement. Snapping my hand out, I steadied Riella before she went sprawling to the ground.

"She says to hold my hands out." Standing upright, Riella looked between the two of us.

Remnant gave her an encouraging smile. "Go ahead then, little one."

With the determined expression crossing our daughter's face, that was an exact replica of her mothers when she faced impossible odds, Riella nodded.

Feeling a sudden weight on my booted foot, I looked down to see the pookah's rabbit ass perched just so. Its ears twitched, feeling my narrowed gaze, it turned its soft black bunny nose up at me and hissed.

Resisting the need to drop kick the little shit, I prayed for the hundredth time today that whoever would steal my daughter's heart, it wasn't going to be this fucking vermin.

"Eww," Riella laughed with a sudden look of disgust on her face as Blaithin coughed buckets of drool onto her outstretched hands. But instead of it splattering to the ground it moved and shifted until becoming one solid object the length of my daughter's arm balancing delicately in her grasp.

Remnant inhaled sharply. "A bás fang." Shadows swirled instantly around Riella's hand to cover it in a coat of darkness, a protection from the lethal weapon—a soul destroyer.

I knelt next to my bewildered daughter. "Riella. This is a rare gift. But it is also very dangerous. One scratch from this fang will end not only the life of another but also completely destroy their entire existence...it will end their soul." Looking up at the cub and her mother, I nodded. "You honor us. I thank you for your gift in keeping my cub safe."

"Yes thank you, Sadhbh," Remnant whispered, beckoning Riella to her, "Bring it here my little chickadee, I think I have the perfect solution for your gift."

Riella moved with careful steps holding the sharp glinting white fang like a sacrifice in her hands—now weary of its presence.

"She's learning," I sent to Remnant.

"Perhaps." She answered back, shadows swirling up from the ground, forming a long slender pole. With inky like tendrils it extended out to the bás fang, plucking it from my cub's hands and braiding around it so that it anchored at the very top.

"It's like my spear!" Riella clapped her hands together.

Remnant nodded, tying off the shadows. "A perfect tip for your lethal spear."

Glittering gold and green eyes blazed up at my soulmate, "Thank you."

Chuckling darkly, I stood to my full height and danced around our daughter whirling her new weapon like a magic wand, her crown sparkling with each movement. Even the cù-sìth cautiously backed away from her excitable waving.

I tilted my head, a small smirk playing across my lips. "Goddess help me, I have one female in my life that prefers dangerous beasts over flowers, and another that has taken to enjoying dangerous weapons that can destroy souls over toys."

Remnant snorted next to me. "Would you have it any other way?"

I was in front of her in seconds, my hand threaded in her hair, tilting her head back ever so slowly so that she could meet the ferocity in my gaze. "Never," I purred, kissing her lips softly, loving the sexy little inhale she made when my lips touched hers.

Low growling and barking drew our attention back to the giant sand barricade. Shaking her head, I released my hand from my soulmate's hair just in time for us to watch as the sands parted and the silver path extended into an oblivion of light, what-ever was beyond this barrier was too blinding to be seen from here.

The death hound turned to us, whimpering softly.

"I think she is telling us it is time to go." I said grimly, the stench of the Vagari stronger now than ever, the smell of cinder and ash adding to the death decay. The hairs on the back of my neck rose and I growled darkly towards whatever impending doom we would face next. "We need to be prepared."

Riella stilled her movement, tapping the spear down loudly on the silver path, her face comically serious as she faced the wall. "I am ready, with this spear I shall protect what I love." Turning toward us, her eyes swirled like fireworks bursting in the sky. "All that I love."

Nodding to my soulmate, I roared. Shifting into my panther and snarling into the blazing abyss, I raced towards my daughter who laughed as shadows plucked her from the path and settled her onto my back. Her tiny body immediately wrapped around me warmly, her spear lowering like a jabbing lance in front. All those years of her riding a water dragon in The Under assisting her with our charge.

Beside us, Remnant ran, jumping onto her shadows, and racing them against my powerful sprint, straight for the opening to the Vagari.

Behind us the cù-sìth mother and her pup howled. Not a death omen but a warning for all those who dared to fuck with our little family.

We were coming.

CHAPTER 26

T HE LIGHT WASN'T LIGHT at all.

It was fire. Pure uncontrolled fire and it was raining down from the sky in a torrential storm. In front of us, hundreds of grotesque yellow eyed beasts that seemed to be drawn from a faeling's goddess damn nightmare screamed, skewered, and fucked each other in a chaotic swarm.

"Hang on tight, my cub!" Praying to the goddess and her worthless hide that Riella could hear me along our bond. A bond that all shifters had with their cubs. She had astonishingly bonded with me while in healing sleep the very day Jar told me she was mine and ever since that day, she filled a piece of my heart that I never knew was missing.

Unable to avoid our path colliding with the monsters bathing in a deadly foray of fire and blood, I roared right before we were submerged into the chaos. Riella screamed and flattened her body along my sleek bounding frame, whether she heard me or not, it did not matter, her hold was locked tight. Small hands dug tightly into my hide and her bitty booted heels dug straight into the space between my ribs. Darkness descended, coating us in shadow to shield our daughter from the spitting fire above.

Wherever my soulmate was she at least had control of the shadows to battle against this cluster fuck. Racing and weaving, I easily dodged the large clumsy beasts, their smell assaulting my amplified predator senses drowning me in the stench of shit, blood, and the distinct smell of sex that had my stomach fucking roiling. My claws ripped through the ashes and carnage, seeing every move before they made it, my shifter side hitting me stronger than it ever had and it was...fucking glorious.

This—this was what it was like to be a *true* shifter. No other beast controlled me, I was no longer a passenger in another's body.

I was just me.

My panther's smell was mine, my vision was mine, my fucking choices were mine, and I chuckled inwardly at the euphoria that burned through every fiber of my being, finally at peace with my shifter side.

And although running through a blood soaked battlefield with bloodthirsty monsters, and my young club plastered to my back would send most into a goddess damn panic, my focus only sharpened more.

But as much as I was enjoying this newfound freedom in my beast, I still needed to get the Sheol out of here with my family intact, which meant the hunt for my soulmate would begin—my favorite kind of hunt.

I grinned. Remnant could and would never be lost to me. One way or another I would always find her...always come for her. It didn't matter if it was in this realm, in another world, or in death. My soul was hers and it would always call to me.

Roaring, I leapt sideways, claws outstretched to rip through a charging beast. Riella's hands dug deeper into me as we slid along the blood soaked grasses, my muscles coiling to launch us outward before crashing into another bumbling sex crazed beast.

Cut, weave, slash, lunge, then inhale...my soulmate's scent was like a guiding beacon in a stormy frenzied sea. Instinct had me racing toward her with a mad focus, protecting my daughter along the way, tearing through beasts with my teeth and claws.

Soon it wasn't just the grass that was soaked in blood and I licked at it hungrily feeling an even larger desire to kill that was beyond just my own panther senses. The pull to tear down and rip out every throat that surrounded me was immense and instead of dodging the next beast I met it head on, my teeth ripping into its throat before the monster hit the ground.

Throwing my head back I roared my triumph, immediately seeking my next prey, I needed more.

A small whimper at my back stalled my prowl.

Riella.

I blinked seeing the chaos in slow motion, a bloodbath of creatures, and I was no different than them in my thirst for more. What was fucking wrong with me? Where had that hunger come from? It felt like Ethereal's rage when he lost control but much much worse. The need to simply devour without any intent sent a foreboding chill down my spine.

As if I didn't already have enough to goddess damn worry about.

Fuck me.

Shaking my head, the world snapped back into place at an accelerated rate and I quickly dodged fire that razed down the beasts, forcing the others to combine to either fight or rut each other.

My eyes widened. The fire was controlling them, corralling them together! Like the herding of sheep which meant one thing—another predator was masterminding this furor.

Sharpening my gaze, my head immediately snapped upwards towards an unknown horizon of red skies, sensing a power akin to mine, where a regimented army of winged lifeforms watched serenely from above.

"Faedere!" My daughter's scream reignited my instincts and we barely avoided sharp horns and hooved feet ready to trample us into fertilizer.

"Apologies my cub!" I sent through our bond. I was still unsure if she could hear me but I did not waste time wondering before I set off again, the floral scent of my soulmate overpowering the putrid stench around us.

Lilies after a fresh night rain. The vision and smell I fell asleep to every night for the past one hundred years.

"There you are, little umbra," I growled to her from across the field.

"Hunting me shifter?" she snarked back, feeling the same euphoric adrenaline along our bond just as I experienced in battle.

I grinned, as if I couldn't fall in love with her even more. My vision of her finally connecting with her scent.

The blue in her hair glinted in the firelight, her shadows swirling and lashing out around her in a deadly choreographed dance. Her clever emerald eyes flashed mockingly at her foe, a grim smile pulling across her kissable lips while she wielded darkness like an extension of her own body.

The distance was still too great for her to see us, but I could see her well enough. I saw Remnant Ezra Solaire Dark in ways no one else ever could, in more ways than even she could and there was no fucking way I was leaving this goddess damned place without her.

CHAPTER 27

Remnant

I COULD SENSE MY soulmate drawing near and felt a sense of relief despite the chaos of beasts, blood, and fire separating us—I was going to kill Shea.

Raising the shadows around me, I fell into the familiar dance I had been trained to do my entire life. Adrenaline pumping through my body as I faced the most grotesque creatures I had ever seen, a grim smile on my face. Using shadow like a blade, I cut down the monsters with ease. They were simple minded creatures acting purely on instinct, too large to move quickly, too stupid to recognize my shadows as a threat.

And so I fought—a new foe on a battlefield that was not mine in the making but it seemed I was to participate just the same.

My brow raised when one of the beasts deflected my shadows with its heavy ax, showing a bit more fortitude, learning from its slain kin.

Tilting my head, I studied the creature towering over me, its focus so intent that I could see its nostrils flare with sickening desire.

I wrinkled my nose. *Gross.*

Half man, half bull, it stared at me like a prized possession. Triumph flickered in its yellow eyes while curling horns tilted in my direction, as if it had already won this fight, and I would play that to my advantage.

"Get Riella out of here," I commanded Emon through our bond, the monster bowing its head and charging me. Summoning my shadows, I gathered them into a sharpened blade, fitting perfectly in my hand for a kill.

"Not without you, little umbra," Emon snarled in my mind. *"Incoming!"*

Grinning, I spun away from the charging creature, leaping upwards, throwing my leg over my speeding soulmate who raced his way through the frenzied battle. Sliding quickly over the top of his powerful panther body, the momentum caused me to slip over to the other side, heading face first into thick black grasses seeping with blood.

"Mother!" screamed Riella, catching me with a shadow arm that looped around my waist and hauled me back up behind her.

I blinked at my sudden upright position while Riella stared down at her arm that was whole again. "I became shadow!" her tiny voice was full of disbelief.

"Yes you did, well done, my beautiful brave little girl!" I gasped into her hair, hugging her close, shielding her with my body from the violence and chaos we were surrounded by. "We will have to discuss it more later," I breathed, kissing her cheek before I sent an explosion of shadows outward, opening a path for Emon to race through.

"Above!" I screamed just before a blaze of fire poured down from the skies. Emon's powerful panther form cut to the side, the blaze just inches from us and searing hot against our skin.

Riella whimpered and I grit my teeth, glaring at the inferno that continued to pour down, its fire rippling beneath Emon's massive paws, lighting up the entire valley.

"The fire is coraling them but I cannot distinguish its source," Emon snarled in my mind.

My head snapped up and I smiled with realization—clever shifter. *"We need to get into the skies."*

"Plan on doing a bit of sightseeing?" he chuckled through our bond, sliding along the grass to slice out with his claws taking down several monsters along the way and forcing Riella and I to hang on even tighter.

I smiled tightly, rising up over Riella, and carving my hand upwards. The shadows splitting through the creatures like a guillotine of darkness. *"I plan on making a new friend of course."*

"Little umbra," he grumbled along our bond, *"we are not bringing home one of these disgusting creatures. Your attraction to beasts is unhealthy if these are your interests. Even your gnomes are pushing the line."* Lunging, he released a roar, teeth tearing out the side of one of the monsters to fully emphasize his protest.

I snickered, drawing large masses of shadow to me and breathing deeply, I squeezed Riella. "Hold tightly, little one. We are going to get out of here."

Her head bobbed against my chest and pulled her hand up where her spear was still held tightly in her tiny fisted grip.

"Keep it ready," I whispered, kissing the top of her head. *"It's time to ascend, shifter."*

Emon purred along our bond, *"I will follow any path you take me down, Remnant Dark. Besides, a sky that breathes fire is still better than being submerged in The Under."*

I grinned, throwing out the shadows like discs in front of us. *"Then let us see if you can fly, shifter king,"* I teased and held my breath as Emon launched himself onto the platform, mere feet above the wild frenzy below. Then he leapt to another and another, following the shadows ascending into the deep red sky with trust and confident agility.

I inhaled. He was spectacular.

"So are you, little umbra," he purred, hearing my inward thoughts as we rose from the ashes and blood.

I smiled, breathing in fresh air untainted by the rotting carnage below and brushed back my hair when I heard the large swoop of wings and sensed a massive shadow hovering above us.

"Remnant...please tell me the sun just went behind the clouds, and that is not the smell of what I think it is," Emon growled.

"There is no sun here, Emon. Get ready to dodge, shifter," I called back to him.

"Fuck," he snarled, just as flames shot out in front of us, burning the next shadow step. Instinct had Emon veering sideways

in a powerful blind leap without a shadow in place and my heart skipped at the incredible sense of trust he had in me as we all momentarily flew across the Vagari skies. Right when he started to fall—I laid down more shadow, his feet silent as they hit our new path.

A burst of laughter exploded from our daughter. "That was so much fun faedere! Do it again."

Incredulous, I looked down at the wild excitement blazing in our daughter's eyes, the fear minimal as the winds blew her hair from her braid, tangling itself on her glittering crown.

"If you enjoyed that, then look over to your left, little chickadee." I said, smiling down at her with motherly pride and just the same amount of excitement even while guiding the shadows to race alongside the winged beast.

"Is that—a sky dragon?" Riella gasped. The awe in her voice was one of reverence.

"It is. Rather, a smaller version of the true ones. This one is a firedrake." I said with just as much breathlessness. Taking in the sparkling hues of its red scales, its fearsome powerful wings and the bright orange orbs of its eyes, I watched as the beautiful creature glared with irritation and curiosity at us right before it burst into flame.

"I seriously hope you have a goddess damn plan, little umbra," Emon growled again, still leaping from one shadow to the next.

I squeezed our daughter, leaning down towards her, concentrating on the horizon so we did not plummet from the sky, I raised my voice against the rushing winds, "Riella, you have been able to communicate with any living creature. I want you to try to communicate with the firedrake. Say these words exactly. *Natrix Drakaina.*"

"Dragon Queen," Emon grinned in my mind, not surprised at all.

I narrowed my eyes on him, *"You knew?"*

Before he could answer, Riella assaulted me with big eyes over her petite shoulder. "But that is what Shen Shen called you!"

I pressed my lips together, that scheming braggart of a water dragon. "Yes, it is. Hurry now, before it decides to turn its fire upon us again."

Reilla nodded quickly, turning back to the firedrake that was now indistinguishable from the flames pouring off of him. The stench of smoke swirling thickly, choking the air from our lungs.

"How did you know?" I whispered fearfully to Emon, if he knew then that meant the dragons were at risk.

Emon purred reassuringly, *"Your secret is safe with me, little umbra. Although one day I do want to hear the story of how you became the ruler of the sky dragons instead of eliminating them as requested by your own queen. As always your strength and power captivates me. You are fucking incredible, Remnant Ezra Solaire Dark."*

I hummed inwardly. *"A tenuous rule based solely on giving them free reign of the Southern Mountains separate from the crown. A decision that cost me dearly."*

"Would you do it again? If given the choice?" The seriousness in his question made me feel like there was a possible wrong answer.

I licked at my lips nervously, what did Emon actually know? *"I would have found a way to save them...without the cost,"* I replied with sincere honesty.

Emon grunted, launching himself onto the next shadows.

Within the seconds it took Emon to expose my truths, Riella had already conveyed my message and the firedrake answered. Flames died off its body, leaving behind nothing but a smokey trail and two giant orbs swerving to meet mine. Instant love and loyalty shining within them.

This was why I loved dragons. It didn't matter who I was or what I had done in the past. The dragons were all connected spiritually and once you were a part of their family there was no escaping their infinite devotion.

I would have never slain the majestic beasts even under orders of the former queen but it had cost me and put everything I had worked hard to preserve in jeopardy including my own family.

"The ridge," Emon growled in my mind.

Looking outward, I could finally see the large looming cliff I had noticed when we first entered. At first I thought it had been the Red Caps but those gracefully extended into a lavender blue sky. Elegant in their presence. These lands conquered each other, unwantedly the earth split and separated in a rough manner that wasn't at all elegant...it was *violent*.

I frowned at the sound of drums and the presence of dark and red skinned beings that lined the cliffs ridgeline. I could just barely make out their massive wings tucked regimentally behind their backs, spiked with sharp talons, and their heads adorned with savage horns. Their entire demeanor was different from the creatures we were fighting below. Calmer, more organized, superior, these were not beasts...but something different altogether.

The firedrake roared, calling out, and arcing over our bodies, sweeping to the other side of us. Its low rumbling continued. Clouds of smoke puffing from its scaled nostrils.

"He wants us to ride him down to the cliffs. He is bound to return and they want to meet us," Riella called out to me, pointing down to the beings I had just been assessing.

I threw another sequence of shadow out for Emon to run along, pressing my lips together.

"Can we maedere? You did say we would fly on a dragon one day." She practically bounced begging me, waving her spear, and I quickly wove shadow around the fang to prevent us from losing any of our souls today.

My heart, however, was stuttering. *Maedere.* She had called me mother in the ancient fae language, the first time she had ever done so.

Her pookah appeared on her shoulder, its ears twitching at me, red eyes laughing at my moment of happiness.

Emon snickered in my mind, *"That spirit guide is a right bastard, an excellent manipulator but I need you to focus, my soulmate. Either give me more shadow before we meet our deaths with rutting monsters or we fly a firedrake that could incinerate us in seconds and will likely deliver us into another goddess damn mess."*

I jerked, snapping shadows out in front of us just as Emon's paws left the last shadow I had provided and glanced back at the firedrake. "Tell him to drop below us." Riella squealed with excitement as I sent silently to Emon, *"Stay in your panther form. I am going to mask Riella in the shadows and then she will blend in with your own body."*

Emon grunted, *"A panther riding a fucking dragon. Tyr is going to be laughing his ass off when he hears about this."*

The firedrake's great wings stretched widely and he bowed his elegant head downward before swiftly cutting through the air below us, hovering for Emon to land.

Dropping the last shadow, Emon landed, claws scraping to find purchase against the ruby hues of the firedrakes scales before finally finding his footing. Crouched low, almost flattening his body along the spine of the dragon, I couldn't help but laugh at the timid way Emon's panther ears were pulled back, his entire body vibrating with irritation and caution.

The firedrake roared, spitting flames that made Riella clap happily before descending effortlessly down to the cliffs.

"Riella ask him his name for me please," I called, slipping off Emon carefully, standing on the firedrake's back, the winds doing nothing to cool the thick atmosphere of the Vagari.

"He calls himself Ignaz," she said, looking down at me from her perch atop Emon, studying me with interest. "Can I do that too?"

I shook my head, watching disappointment morph across her face. "Not today, little one. You must stay hidden, please ask Ignaz if he told the one summoning us about you."

Riella tilted her head, her crown slipping slightly over her brow as she nodded while listening. Shaking it, she grinned, "He says he has said nothing, they only know a female is riding a panther."

"*Thank fuck*," Emon growled along our bond, his body tensing when the firedrake's wings flapped lazily.

I sighed with relief and then crouched low, sliding my way up to the long neck of the firedrake, dropping my legs with my knees bent on either side. I patted its scales soothingly. "We are seeking The Well of Souls my friend. It is imperative that we get there and that my daughter stays safe. Keep her a secret for as long as you are able. I will be hiding her when we land."

The great fire beast rumbled back and I did not need Riella to interpret to know he agreed with my task.

"Thank you Ignaz."

The firedrake warbled and I scratched its scaly head, listening to its deep purr. My many years of fighting then taming the dragons on the Southern Mountains of Faerie were paying off. I did not speak of my time there...ever. The fate of many lives depended on my silence, including the dragons that lived there, but maybe one day I could share the story for Emon's book, *The Unaccounted Life of the Last Shadow Fae*.

I smiled at that.

"*I have to admit, I don't like riding dragons but the view makes up for it.*"

Feeling Emon's predator eyes heating up my backside, I laughed, "Yes the view is spectacular," I teased, nodding to the deep red skies and then down to the regiment of beasts that were drawing closer. "Riella, it is time to hide now. The shadows will mask you but you must stay brave and silent for me."

I did not wait for her answer when I shifted to my aura sight searching for the light that shined brightest amongst them…the true leaders. Standing out within the dimming auras, a brilliant red glowed, its bold power almost tangible from such a distance.

Reaching out and I patted the dragon's flared head, smoke curling up around my fingertips, "Bring us down now Ignaz."

The dragon huffed its assent before he dipped into a deep dive, plummeting towards the cliff and the army waiting there. Emon's hiss of distaste could be heard over the rushing wind along with his claws scraping sharply against the dragon's back to keep his seat.

Grimly, I cloaked Riella in more darkness from the firedrake's very own shadow racing below us and then sent a prayer to the goddess to keep her safe. Rearing with the great beast, his wings beating to slow his ascent, we landed with a loud thunderous boom that shook the stoney earth beneath its four legs.

Before it could even raise its head in a flame filled roar, Emon and I launched ourselves off the beast in an ostentatious display of power that would have my brother laughing his ass off at the sight of it. But it was enough to send their stoic regiment reeling back, scampering away from the fire and the shadows rolling off of me in waves of darkness. Behind me, Emon bared his teeth and hissed, his great head hovering above mine menacingly.

I patted his side, my eyes never leaving the red aura when I turned off my sight to reveal the hard violet eyes of a tall beautiful female with pure olive skin. If I didn't know any better I would have thought her to be human but she was far from it.

And flanking her sides, stood two dominant males. One with great black leather wings, curling horns, and a red skinned body and the other, a glaringly beautiful being with auburn hair, bright blue eyes, and even brighter white feathered wings.

It seemed that none of us were ready to break the silent stand off between us.

I tilted my head. *"Are you thinking what I am thinking, shifter?"*

"That that feathered bastard looks like a goddess damn angel in the middle of the Vagari?"

I hummed back to him, *"Yes that is exactly what I am thinking, but why would an angel be in the equivalent of hell?"*

Stepping forward from the protection of her males, all arrogance and insolence in her demeanor, the violet eyed female broke the silence, "Who the fuck are you and why are you trespassing on my lands?" She said in a silky smooth tone despite her condescension.

A common trait of a young ruler...a very young ruler if I were to guess correctly, especially compared to my two thousand year old status. Her claim on this realm did not go unrealized however and my lips curled into a tight smile.

"Trespassing? I think not, *cousin*."

CHAPTER 28

Remnant

THE WOMAN'S BROWS ROSE high on her head, ignoring the fact that I commanded a very fiery, irritated dragon behind me, along with a monstrous black panther that was clearly checking out my ass.

"I have no kin," she simply stated.

Shadows licked up my arms. "Consider our fathers...distant relatives." It was a hunch but the death god did say to trust my instincts...

Fire lit in her eyes and she stepped another foot forward threateningly, stopping when a golden hand from her angel companion fell on her shoulder.

I kept my reaction neutral, but I immediately took a dislike to him, how in the goddess was an angel in the Vagari anyway? My eyes subtly shifted to the other male whose jaw was clenching hard, flanking her opposite side.

Despite his red skin and great horns, he was remarkably handsome. Shoulder length black hair was pulled halfway back from his scowling face and his great wings were far more impressive than the irritatingly bright feathers of his companion.

A companion that he obviously loathed, the darkened expression on his face growing with every whispered breath the angel made when he leaned into his leader.

When the fire in her eyes died out, she responded back to him, muttering under her breath

"She asks if he has ever seen creatures like me before," Emon translated smugly.

I grinned inwardly, *"Sometimes it pays off to have a shifter soulmate."*

"Sometimes..." he growled back.

"Have I told you that I love you today?" I added facetiously.

I could hear Emon's panther chuff quietly, still watching the female and her companion whisper conspiringly towards each other. *"If I could lie, I'd tell you no, so that you'd be forced to say it over and over again, like you were last night,"* he growled low and I shivered. *"The last few hours of silence was the worst kind of torture. You know I love to have anything spill from those delectable lips...anger, love, the cry of my name...anything but that fucking silence,"* he paused. *"The angel cannot be trusted. He is suggesting we are a danger and that she should kill us."*

Wings snapped outward before tucking back in, startling all of us. "For fucks sake, my queen do not listen to that feather brained *idiot*," the one with fierce horns and deep red skinned growled. "They are fae. Powerful ones. I can fucking smell it on them." Something swished fiercely behind him in his outburst.

My eyes widened. It was a tail! One that was tapered black at the end, same color as his curling horns, and it was flicking back and forth like a sharp whip on his very large muscular body.

Realization dawned on me and I cursed my father to the darkest depths of Sheol. *"Demons. They are demons,"* I called to Emon.

He hissed. *"And one angel, fucking goddess, Shea did say this realm was shared, which means the Vagari is also—"*

"Hell," I finished for him. *"And this must be Lucifer's—"*

"Offspring. Fuck," Emon spat and I nodded, fully agreeing with his sentiment.

The female's hand shot up to stop the irritated demon towering over her. "Calm yourself Zazion." She frowned at us and her voice was laced with condescension. "*Fae*...as in tiny little winged creatures with fairy dust flitting around getting humans trapped in dancing rings."

I twirled the shadows around me, before curling them over my hand and arm. Bowing mockingly, I smiled. "A common misconception...the fae don't flit."

Emon's panther snorted.

"Fae." She tapped her finger to her red lips, deep in thought before a slow sultry smile spread across her face. "Ah yes, I remember now." Snapping her fingers, instant fire circled around us and from it, heavy chains sprouted, snapping outwards like poisonous snakes.

The fire drake roared, his instinct to protect me, his *queen*, strong as he breathed his own vicious fire down upon the unsuspecting army. Demons cried out, breaking their lines and sending them into chaos.

Dodging the chains whipping around us, one grazed the bare skin of my leg and I felt a familiar searing pain that caused my stomach to seize.

"*Iron!*" I hissed at Emon who leapt away only to hiss as the fire closed in on him. Charging the shadows, I doused the flames, blanketing them in darkness and opening a path for him to bolt through. "*Go!*" I roared inwardly to him.

My soulmate did not hesitate, escaping right before another iron chain wrapped itself around my leg, sending me crashing to the ground.

I hissed through the goddess forsaken metal burrowing into my flesh and the sudden immense void of my shadow power being gone...again.

"*Remnant!*" Emon roared in my head, I could just make out his gold eyes flashing back at me even as he ran at full pace far from here. The shadows masking my daughter on top of him unraveling, her eyes locking with mine, clutching her pookah tightly to her chest with one arm, and her spear with the other.

Subtly, I shook my head towards her. "*Don't stop. Don't come back. I'll find you,*" I commanded.

"*Little umbra—*" Emon's voice felt strained, our connection quieting the further he went, the more the iron bore into me.

"*Trust me shifter.*"

"Lucifer's cock!" the female cried and slashed her hand down. "I don't have time for this! Zazion. Hunt down that monster of a cat, send the hell hounds after him if you have to. I can't have the realm of Wrath gaining the upper hand with power like that!"

Hesitating, the handsome red demon gave me one final thoughtful look before stretching out his leathered wings, monstrous compared to his frame before he snapped his tail down and thrusted up into the air. I watched as he banked immediately towards the blurring panther in the distance. I narrowed my eyes on him, the way he just looked at me...

I snapped up when a sharp wail cut off the firedrake's inferno that was still raging upon the demon army and watched with veiled horror as it thudded to the ground, huffing out its final breath in a smokey plume. A singular orange eye locked onto mine, his final thoughts so easy to see.

Remorse for not being able to protect me.

Slowly my eyes trailed up from the fallen firedrake and stared coldly at the angel who yanked his spear from the beast's heart, swiping back his auburn hair with an air of annoyance and arrogance.

Despite the sickening nausea from the irons and the rising panic the searing metal created, I rose against them and held the male's gaze while my flesh burned. "You just made a very grave mistake."

Angry violet eyes suddenly bored into mine, shielding her gloating companion. "I don't respond well to threats, fae. Especially ones made to my angel," she sneered.

I stepped forward against the chains and didn't flinch when it burned so hot my leg split open, the trail of my blood trickling down my thigh cooling compared to continuous burns. "Nor do I, demon."

She snarled holding my gaze a moment longer before the most gorgeous wings unfurled from her back. Red feathers covered the tops and crest while they slowly faded into black leathered wings on the bottom. "I don't have time for this. The centurion mating frenzy is now out of control thanks to you."

My brows rose. A mating frenzy?

Snapping her fingers, several fierce demons with varying degrees of horns, tails, and wings circled around me. "Place her in more irons and drag her back to our camp," she commanded before swooping her wings downward and launching into the sky with her angel following after her.

I turned to watch them but was forcibly yanked back by more chains lashing across my wrists. Snarling, I rounded on the new group of demons, rolling towards one that had a rather pretty and *sharp* sword on his hip. Wrenching it from his side, I stood again, holding it high over my head, slowly turning in a circle studying every single one that moved in closer.

My hair whipped across my face and I breathed in deep, feeling the deadly calm the weight of a sword in my hand brought me. Cocking a brow at the stunned demons, I grinned darkly. "Who wants to play first?"

CHAPTER 29

ANGUISH.

My heart stuttering to a mewling stop in its sorrow.

My feet dragged with each racing stride, screaming at me to turn back.

My soul raged, tearing me to shreds in its fury to reconnect to its better half—especially when that bond went dead.

From the moment I smelled my soulmate's flesh burning with the sting of iron, everything in me fought to go back—to kill the very beings that dared to even look at her, let alone chain her in blood and fire.

Except Riella was our priority, I knew Remnant would have it no other way and so I would suffocate on this pain to ensure our daughter was safe before I prowled back to the demon army to bathe in their blood—because *I would* have it no other way too.

I purred at the thought. I could destroy them all, slaughter them until there was nothing left but their rotting demon carcasses and then I would hunt—eliminating their kind from the fucking pits of hell where they came from. Their blood would be delicious, their deaths sweet, none would survive—

Riella's body trembled against me, still riding low on my racing panther frame bringing my attention back to her.

I blinked slowly. What in the actual goddess fuck was I thinking? My vendetta was against Deirdre, not these pawns...of course I was going to kill whoever dared to touch Remnant but to want to eliminate an entire race, that was dark shit that I frankly didn't have the time for—except *something* inside of me felt very different about that.

"I must warn you..." Eve's words whispered from the dark recesses of my mind.

Snarling, I focused on shoving my bleak thoughts away and picked up my pace. *"All will be well my cub."* I would goddess damn make sure it was, the soulless sleep and this madness could go fuck itself.

I had once confessed to Jar that first day I knew she was mine that I had no idea how to be a father—but I knew now. It could not have been more clear than in this very moment.

I would sacrifice *everything* to make sure she was loved and safe, even with the last beats of my dying heart and for that—I continued to run...further and further away from the very air that gave breath to my lungs.

Spurring on harder, I ran across the dense black grass, knowing that this worked to my own advantage in masking me from the skies, aside from the sparkling star crown my daughter now wore which likely gave us away for a hundred yard radius. Still I would not risk removing it. No matter how much Shea was an insufferable ass, there were no lies in his tone when he said the crown would protect our daughter.

Spotting heavy dense black trees ahead and the crisp scent of fresh running water, I bolted quickly for the ominous forest backlit by deep red skies.

Crossing into its cool dark canopy, the hairs on my nape rose and a low growl escaped me. There was just as much danger in these woods as there was behind me. Narrowing my eyes on a low hanging branch of a thickly needled tree, I leapt onto it, climbing stealthily upwards. Riella's small hands clenched tightly in my fur and the thick foliage clawed my sides while I stalked its branches until I found one that would hold us both with room to spare.

Shifting quickly, Riella cried out as I gripped her tightly in my arms, our hearts thudding fiercely in tandem. The pack on my back was like an anchor holding us steady to the wide tree limb as I rocked her to me.

"Shhh my cub. Shhh, are you hurt?" I whispered, purring softly to ease her terrified soul.

Her face rubbed into the fibers of my shirt as she shook her head no, soot and ash, staining the pink fabric to gray. Her tiny hand still gripped the bás fang in a white knuckled hold even though the shadow spear shaft was long gone along with her damn spirit guide.

Goddess good riddance. I didn't want to have to deal with that rodent anyway.

Letting out a sigh, I unraveled her tiny stiff fingers from the death hound's fang. "Let's keep this in a safe place for now," I murmured, handling it with care and storing it safely and securely in the pack, making sure no unwanted soul-ending scratches would occur.

Summoning for the water canteen, I poured the crisp cool essence into my hands before I brought them to Riella's heated cheeks. Still dirtied by demon blood and soot, I gently wiped away the grime from her bronze face where streaks of tears stained her skin. Splashing more water, I rubbed it on the back of her neck, pressing softly to ease the tremors.

"Breathe with me, little cub." I inhaled and exhaled for her, watching her tiny chest rise and fall, listening to the thundering of her heart slow and ease. "Good Riella, good," I purred again, sweeping her hair back next, running my fingers through the tangled raven blue strands. Having years of practice with my own hair, I deftly redid her braid, smoothing it over her petite shoulder before adjusting her crown that lit up the gorgeous glow to her eyes—eyes still wide with shock and fear.

Leaning forward, I placed a gentle kiss on her forehead and felt her entire body slump. Exhaustion quickly replaced her state of terror.

"There, now you look the proper princess again. Here, drink." I held out the canteen full of self replenishing water and looked out into the darkened canopy, keeping my worries hidden from my face. I didn't know what else lurked in this forest but there was a faint stench of death and decay that seemed all too familiar. Something was in Hell from our world that shouldn't be.

Her hands shook in the dim light as she took the canteen. The water sloshed as she hiccuped a soft sob before sipping at it.

"That's it, my cub. Take a long drink."

"Mother..." her voice whispered.

"Hush now," I soothed. "Do not dwell. She will be okay." I swallowed against the fierce ache where my soul continued to battle against my better judgment. Remnant was strong, intelligent, and clever. All things I loved her for. This would be child's play for her and she would never forgive me, nor would I forgive myself if I didn't take care of Riella first.

"But father, her shadows disappeared." She gnawed on her lip, intently staring at her hand, flexing her stiff fingers where the cù-sìth tooth had been. "My spear is gone."

Taking the canteen from her, I sighed, placing it back into the bag and lacing it closed. "There are very few things that weaken a fae Riella, but iron is one of them. Once it touches us, it burns, weakens, and snuffs out our power. It is when we are at our most mortal selves."

Her lip quivered. "It burned mother. I saw it."

I grunted and pulled her closer to me, stroking her hair. "Your mother is so very strong, my cub, do you think a little burn will stop her?"

"No," she sniffed and then raised her head. I blinked at the sudden regal vision she made with her crown and fierce tilt of her chin. "I can be brave like mother."

"You already are brave, my cub. I know you used your shadows to help during that battle." If one could even call it that, the scent of sex had been strong but the violence and bloodshed...my nose twitched.

Why was it I was always finding myself in the middle of goddess damn orgies? First The Under, now Hell.

"But I don't know how I did it." Big swirling eyes pooled with large crystal tears, a quivering lip pouted up towards me.

"Your powers will manifest in the time you will need them to. Just like Jar said." I nuzzled her nose with mine. "We must keep moving." I sniffed at the air, a new threatening scent joining the other. "There is water nearby and there is something following us." I eyed the massive black trees where streaks of red sky peeked through their canopy, ominous whispers of something coming.

"If I shift we can travel through the woods with ease, follow the water...it's likely the demons would have camped near its source and we can then track your mother from there."

Sighing shakily, Riella nodded. "That's what those creatures were?"

"Yes," I snarled softly. "We are no longer in your grandfather's realm...there are no rules here, my cub, none that the fae understand. We will have to be vigilant, and above all cunning, if we are to take on the beasts of Hell."

She sniffed, wiping her eyes with the back of her hand, trailing more ash across her face. "I could hear you out there.."

I paused, raising my brow, "Hear what, my cub?"

"Your voice inside my head."

I gave her a reassuring smile. "Your powers are growing, this will be helpful for us to communicate when I shift. Are you ready?"

She nodded.

Kissing her forehead one more time, I brushed off the fresh smudge of dirt she had smeared across her face and shouldered the pack before crouching to shift back into my panther form.

Turning my glowing gaze on my daughter, I bowed low and waited for her to scramble up on me, grunting as her tiny booted foot dug into my ribs and her hands ripped at my throat to find purchase. Her petite size and my large frame made the task difficult but she was a determined little cub, with more than her fair share of her mother's fierce ambition.

"Stay strong, little umbra," I whispered through the soul-mate bond towards Remnant, ignoring that cavernous feeling the distance had created between us. Not knowing if she could hear me but attempting anyway. It was a painful reminder of all those nights I had spent without her, wide awake, unable to sleep from the ghosts that haunted my memories and the even louder thoughts of all the things I would have changed to just spare her even a few seconds of the horrible fate she endured.

Then when those thoughts were too much, I'd talk with no ears to listen but for the unwilling beast inside of me. I'd paint tales of new adventures I'd take her on, the beasts I'd impress her with, the nights I would lovingly cherish every ounce of her darkness, and the beautiful vision of her ruling my court alongside me...the Finlandia sun highlighting her beauty down to her very soul—a soul I knew was just as searing as the heat of the lands we ruled.

"I am ready, faedere," Riella whispered, my ears twitching at the soft lilting sound of her voice.

"Can you hear me, my cub?"

"I can hear you, just like the last time, " she whispered, her small arms wrapped barely a quarter around my neck as she leaned low, her heart starting to beat wildly in her chest again as her hands embedded into my sleek black fur. "I can hear all things that wish to speak to me."

I purred, proud of the fae she was becoming. *"Keep low and hang tight. I do not know what lurks in this forest and the needles on these trees are rough."*

I rumbled when she pressed even tighter into me and then stalked the branch gathering my strength to leap across the next wide limb, hearing Riella gasp as I landed softly upon roughened bark, the black foliage brushing against us with yearning. *"It is a true gift you know. Your secondary power to hear all living things,"* I spoke to distract her, feeling her heart rate pound against my body. *"A fae is lucky if they are given one. Only the most powerful are able to evolve this way."*

I could practically hear her mind whirling with questions. "What is mother's?" her warm breath whispered along my fur.

"Hold on," I growled low, sliding down a massive trunk only to spring sideways towards another large needled tree. Something rustled in the brush. Lunging, my teeth sunk into the feathered neck of a large bird, a small tiny squawk the only sound it was able to make before its neck made a sickening crack and the strong metallic taste of blood filled my mouth.

The hunger roared to life inside of me but I was ready for it this time, shoving it back beyond the deep mental barriers I trained myself to build for Ethereal.

Riella stiffened on top of me.

"Apologies, my cub but I cannot have it revealing us, we are still being followed." Slowly, I lowered the feathered creature to the wide branch, praying that it would at least feed whatever else that lurked in here that may be hankering for a snack instead of us.

"I understand," her voice quivered.

My body rumbled with a purr to soothe her, feeling her sadness like a sharp stab in my gut. Unlike all the fae I had ever known, Riella expressed her emotions outwardly. Both joy and sadness were always so innocently naked on her face, a trait worth honoring and protecting...even if our courts saw it as a weakness.

"Your mother has aura sight," I said, hoping to change her current sadness as my senses constantly analyzed and cataloged the world around me at a heightened speed, carefully dictating my route.

Something slithered and hissed above. The black imposing trees we traveled seemed much too conscious of our presence and brushed against us when I knew there had been more clearance just moments before. It forced me to alter my direction often, and I just barely avoided a strange looking group of spiny flowers that grew on thick vines. Their petals mouthed the air, reminding me too much of the ball biting dragon plants of Faerie.

"Faedere...what is my aura?"

I paused. My clawed paw suspended in the air while I searched my memories. *"I...I do not know."*

Her body wilted against my back and I realized then, that Remnant had never actually told me mine either. *"Aura power is not always reliable, like the sight it has its limitations. What I do know is that your mother has never read another's aura for them and spoke of it. They are like peering into the essence of one's soul and revealing the truths that could very well change someone's fate if they knew."* I shot her a toothy grin over my shoulder. *"But we can still ask your mother when we see her again. Deal?"*

Riella nodded against me. "Deal." Her mind was loudly racing again. "What is your secondary power, faedere?"

I hummed, avoiding dark drips from above that smelled of blood. *"This is a secret I have not told anyone before, not even your mother knows. Do you think you can keep it for me?"*

Riella nodded eagerly and I chuffed, launching higher up into a cluster of dense trees to avoid the drip of whatever poor creature was bleeding out from above us.

"Iron does not affect me the way it does most," I confessed. *"Yes, it prevents me from shifting but the longer I am chained to it...the stronger my shifter strength becomes. My power feeds on it."*

"Iron does not weaken you?"

I chuckled bitterly. *"Oh it weakens me plenty...initially but over time I can overcome it as long as I am not injured."*

After that, Riella grew silent and so did I. The stark crisp scent of water hit me before the sound did...sniffing at the air I quickly realized while the waterway gave us guidance, it also drowned out the scent of our stalkers.

My hackles rose.

"Keep quiet and duck low," I hissed in my daughter's mind before I clawed us quietly into the deeper coverage of another heavily needled branch. Its brush raked against us and my underbelly scraped against its rough bark. Pausing, I lowered my head, my shoulders rising where Riella gripped me tightly. Her breath increased quietly against my neck as we both peered down through the thick trees.

If the forest was ominously quiet before, it stopped breathing the moment the massive red demon, the same one that had identified us as fae, appeared along the river's bank. Bare from the chest up, his heavily muscular body rippled with agitation, as did his sharp whip of a tail, and wide thick leathered wings. Growling, he ran his clawed hands over his curling black horns and flowing dark hair before snapping his wings wide and shooting himself back up into the deep red sky. Disappearing into it.

Riella's heart raced against my back.

"I am going to descend. He is looking for us from the air now," I called to her and then sniffed again. *"I can sense a demon camp nearby..."* And that wasn't the only thing...clenching my jaw, I held back the snarl of frustration. We were quickly becoming surrounded by enemies, the opposite of what I had hoped for my cub.

Quietly, without a single sound, I dropped us from branch to branch in rapid descent. Registering the demon's scent deep in my memory, a unique smell of firewood, ash, and marshmallow...I quirked a brow at that. Surely a threatening demon wouldn't smell like a baking campfire?

Landing softly on the forest floor, I felt the dry needles prick the underside of my rough paws before I started to slink my way along the dense trees. Keeping to their main trunks that blended perfectly with my coat and far enough from the water's edge to not be exposed from the sky.

I grinned when we started to lose the demon, but I should have known destiny was a bitch that had it out for me.

Stumbling, an abrupt wave of weakness blurred my vision and my front legs caved—the sound of my head crashing into the forest floor was practically deafening as it echoed through the woods. Panting, the rest of my feline body involuntarily followed, slumping down as my mind warred to get back up. Slipping from me, Riella cried out, her hands frantically attempting to pull me back to my feet. When she failed to do that, she cradled my head begging me to get back up.

Unable to move, my eyes frantically searched up towards the sky, squinting through my blurred vision, my breath labored, but my scent—my scent worked just fine and the smell was one I knew all too well. Terror froze my blood.

Fearfully, I swung my gaze to my daughter, her swirling green and gold eyes a blur, my head heavy in her shaking hands. I could feel her tears dripping on my fur as she continued to plead with me.

"Run," I managed to growl inwardly, before another wave of weakness took me, a painful lurch hit my chest, and I felt my consciousness leave me briefly, hovering outside of my body like a spectator before slamming back inside of myself.

Fucking goddess, this was the effects of the soulless sleep. My time was running out.

"King Daemon...you will be mine soon..." Whispers and sadistic laughter filled my senses but so did that smell, the overwhelming stench of death and decay, of disease and rot...blood wraiths.

"No!" I roared, clawing my way back, blinking hard to clear my sight from the looming darkness only to stare up at a dark hood and blood dripping rags.

Snarling, I shoved Riella behind me with my last remaining strength, right before a blue blaze of fire from the blood wraith rained down where she once sat. Its heat seared the edges of my fur while numerous shrieks suddenly filled the forest...where there was one abomination there were hundreds more.

Hissing and spitting like a cornered beast, I dragged myself to shield Riella as the wraiths filled in through the gaps of the trees, the lush black needles upon the forest floor curling up and graying with the unnatural mist that snuffed out life itself.

"Run," I whispered to her again, feeling the blood wraiths descend, their horrid decaying stench filling the last of my senses.

Suddenly, a ferocious roar filled the air, sending wraiths scattering as the ground thundered from the landing of a great beast. Squinting through my tired vision, I stared at the back of the demon that had been tracking us, his wings spread wide, shielding us from the blood wraiths as fire ignited in his hands, lighting up the woods that I now realized was more than black. It was an array of deeply saturated color, just as vibrant as the fluorescent life of The Under but in the opposite way.

"You're trespassing on the Prince of Greed's territory and I don't take kindly to uninvited guests." The demon's voice whispered promises of death and violence as he faced the wraiths single handedly. Then with one powerful blast, a fire unlike anything I had seen wielded before, roared around him like the breath of a dragon, incinerating every single wraith within seconds. The remains of their rags floating to the ground like black snowy ash, blending in with the dark saturated colors of Hell's forest.

It was as if they had never existed at all.

When he turned on us, his black demon eyes settled on mine. His fangs dipped over lips that were thinning with displeasure, and his wings snapped behind his back again, tight and rigid. A long lethal tipped tail curled around the black silk of his trousers like an irritated hand on a hip.

My head raised weakly in the challenge and I held his *who the fuck are you really* stare for a solid five seconds before my head hit the ground with a heavy thud. Riella's tiny voice frantic in the darkness of my subconscious.

"Faedere!"

CHAPTER 30

Remnant

*R*EMI DARLING...YOU WILL COME *to me...*

I hissed, jerking awake at the distant cooing voice of my for-mer lover and blinked back the final visages of her manipulation. I knew it was only a matter of time before she grew stronger, using the spirit realm against me—before she became my nightmares.

Licking at the blood coating my face, I hung from a thick wooden post in a large yurt of a war camp where my wrists seared against the irons wrapped around me. Tilting my head, I listened to the howling and beastly grunting outside my sheltered prison, the stench of sex and hedonistic gluttony thick on the warm night air.

The demons were celebrating.

When the flap of the thick canvas of the yurt was drawn aside, moonlight poured in accenting a full figure too sensual to be male.

"Fifty seven," the silky voice said from the entrance, dropping the heavy flap and enshrining us both in darkness once again. "You killed fifty seven of my demons before they were able to subdue you."

I withheld the wince when my grin reopened the split in my lip. "Not my personal best but not too bad either, considering..." I jerked my head up to the irons still searing my skin.

A blast of fire lit a wooded pit to the right of us, sending a wash of light into the large yurt, the sudden brightness blinding, and I squinted through it to keep eyes on my newfound cousin—or enemy. It entirely depended on the choices she made from here on out.

Bright violet eyes regarded me for a brief moment before she sniffed and strolled past me towards several trunks lining the back side of the enclosure. Unlacing her linen top coated in ash and blood, she let it drop from her shoulders to the ground, revealing small pert breasts and smooth olive skin before stooping to open a chest. Donning a clean white shirt, similar to the one she just was wearing, she glanced up at me as she tied the laces. "And if there had been no irons?"

I sucked at my lip, tasting the sharp bite of my own blood on my tongue. Releasing it with a soft pop, my gaze bore into hers. "You would no longer have an army."

Her violet eyes sparkled, her soft red lips forming into a small smile before turning back around and stripping off her soiled pants and boots, a supple ass greeting me as she bent yet again to rummage through her trunk. "What is your name?"

Admittedly enjoying the view and her feminine curves, I answered simply. "Remnant."

"And how exactly do our dads know each other?" she called, her ass wiggling as she shifted through her clothing.

My brow rose, did she really think she could interrogate me by distracting me with her naked sex? "And your name is...?"

She snorted, rising up to hold up a pair of faded blue pants, sniffing at them, before turning them side to side. "I am called Avalon."

I nodded. "Our fathers...both deal in death. Shea is a the death god of Faerie. He sorts souls for the afterlife. Yours is a fallen angel that tortures souls that have been sent to Hell. It would seem their lands overlap each other."

Her long blonde hair fell over her shoulder as she half turned to look at me, shoving a foot into her clean pants. "Lucifer never bothered to torture souls, they torture themselves just fine enough, there's a realm for everyone here." Her grin flashed in the firelight. "Hell will do that to you if you're here long enough. Half those beasts you and your pet cat plowed through earlier today were once humans, powerful ones, whose souls were so warped they became what we call centurion demons." Shoving another leg into her pants, she turned back to me, shimmying her hips into the tight fitting clothing.

Emon would love that she called him a pet...but at least that told me she was still ignorant of shifters—and my daughter.

"Where is the dark angel now? Your father?"

Avalon's eyes bored into mine, brief pain passing in them as she fastened her pants. "Dead."

I tilted my head. "My condolences. I do hope he was a better father to you than mine to me."

Her expression grew wistful for a moment before she frowned. Waving her hand, a large cushioned chair suddenly appeared with a glass of a strong smelling spirit in her other. Settling into the chair, she crossed her legs, her bare feet with brightly painted red toes bounced as she regarded me, sipping her drink. "He was the best father actually...and then he was betrayed by his own inner circle. All because I begged him to protect a strange being I had never seen before. I wasn't even eight summers, my birthday was the next day."

My mind raced, piecing her story together, my eyes widening slightly, "Your angel?"

Brows raising, "Yes," she hissed. Taking another drink, she swallowed, licking her lips. "So you see, I don't like it when strangers come to my lands uninvited because then I must decide what to do with them...and if I release you from those irons, just as Lucifer released my angel from its cage, what price will I pay this time?"

Suddenly, Riella was in the forefront of my mind—vulnerable and alone. My stomach clenched and my heart twisted in my chest, seeing Lucifer's daughter for what she really was. A child that had to grow up too soon, a young ruler that was bound to play the games of court, rules she was still learning so that she could one day break them and finally be free.

"I am sorry," I said sincerely. "Sorry that you were left alone. And so very sorry that you cannot trust without fear."

She tilted her head for a moment, a lock of her blonde hair falling across her flawless face, showing the angel innocence that she hid well enough in the world outside this tent. "Those irons look like they hurt."

I shrugged, the hateful metal clinking. "You get used to them, but the smell of your flesh burning never truly leaves you."

She leaned forward, biting at her wet lip, considering me. "I believe we got off on the wrong foot."

I arched a brow, amused by her play at seduction. "Is that what you call this?"

It was her turn to shrug, leaning back in her chair. "Like you said, I have trust issues."

I snorted and twirled my wrist in the chains, my flesh sizzling for dramatic effect while the young queen's eyes widened slightly. "Clearly. Speak then, make your deals demon, state what you want of me."

Recovering quickly, she took a sip from her glass, then swirled the contents thoughtfully. "You're not the first trespassers to come through here recently."

"Sounds like a *you* problem and I still did not hear a question," I said dryly.

She hummed and picked up a piece of her long blonde hair, studying the ends. "I want to know why you are in Hell and how the fuck you just appeared in the middle of a controlled centurion mating frenzy?"

My brows raised. "That was controlled. I hate to see what uncontrolled is."

"You would, they'd destroy half this realm." Her violet eyes looked at me pointedly.

I sighed. "This realm is called the Vagari in my world. It means to—"

"Wander," she finished for me with a frown. A shadow slowly edged across the olive skin of her high cheek bones and my fingers twitched, aching to summon it to me. When the small casted darkness shifted unnaturally, my eyes widened—.

Lucifer's daughter snorted, reading my shock for the completely wrong reason. "No point in looking surprised fae, I am not so uneducated."

Recovering, I schooled my expression. "Apologies. But yes, the wandering lands are for souls that are banished with no gift of an afterlife, and like I said before it seems to overlap with Hell," I said, waving my hand subtly and watching the shadows shift slightly again. My heart began to quicken, they were responsive to me, I glanced subtly down at the irons that were also wrapped around my thighs, realizing their burn was not as severe and my raw flesh was beginning to heal.

"Which means you have come here looking for someone. A soul perhaps?" she said calculatingly and I picked up the sudden fear in her eyes, the way she glanced towards the entrance of the yurt where sensual demon howls and screams were still at full peak. But it wasn't them she was worried about and I would bet my life that it had everything to do with the arrogant white feathered angel that slayed my firedrake—her response when I had threatened him was strong, lover strong...even if it was misplaced.

"Not someone..." I reassured her and saw the slight release in tension of her wide shoulders. "Something. The Well of Souls."

Her entire body stilled. "You will not find The Well of Souls in Greed territory, although no one has heard from that damned recluse demon for years, you think that ass would at least show himself...he is greed for fuck's sake, he should be attempting to take everything around him, a public swindler."

Raising my brows, I waited for her sudden rant to end.

When she noted my wry expression she waved me off, sighing deeply. "Yes I digress, what I mean to say is that The Well of Souls is in *Wrath* territory." Slugging her drink back in one gulp, she slammed it down on the arm of the chair, the glass cracking ominously in her grip, her lips pressed into a firm line. "And it is the one place in Hell, I cannot allow you to go. That bastard betrayed my father and if what you boast is true, then allowing you to leave would be trusting that you are not his ally. You are far too powerful to deliver into his hands anyway. I have worked way to fucking hard to control this kingdom. Cousin or not, I will not risk it. Not ever again."

I laughed dryly. "Then you are making a foolish mistake, demon queen. What is your plan then exactly? Keep me your prisoner till the end of days?"

She pursed her lips, standing to wave away her chair and glass, sauntering towards me in her bare feet. My fingertips twitched slightly and the shadows moved along the ground behind her.

"Honestly, I do not know what the fuck to do with you now, hopefully my demons will drag your pet cat here soon and then I will meet with my council to discuss your fate." She turned to walk away.

"He cannot be trusted."

"Zazion has been with me since the beginning," she said dismissively, her blonde hair swaying along with her confident stride.

"Not your demon, oh mighty queen of Hell. He will be loyal to you indefinitely." I said sweetly at her back and grinned when her violet gaze turned back to me startled.

"Who then do you mean?" she snapped and I could see fire burn in her eyes. It reminded me much of the emerald flames in my father's eyes...perhaps it really was a family trait.

"Your angel lover, his aura is wrong. I'd be very careful if I were you."

Her face darkened and I could feel the power inside her lashing out, wanting to be released. "You know nothing about Shaniel and I care not for your warning that sounds more like a fucking threat. Be very careful with your next words, fae."

My irons clanked loudly, flesh scorching just like my smile leaning in towards her. "If I am wrong then you have nothing to worry about, cousin, but if I am right...it won't be just your father you lose."

Her eyes flashed with real fire then. "I'd start worrying more about your own fucking future," she hissed before reaching out to snuff out the fire, her violet eyes glowing murderously at me. "Any hope of you leaving this place alive is growing slimmer and slimmer, little fae. And yes, that is my own threat, *cousin*." Exiting, she left me in the deep warm darkness, the demons outside roaring in greeting to their leader.

I grinned into the pitch black night of the yurt, feeling its peace wash over me. "Hello friends," I whispered to the shadows, pulling them from around the room and twirling them to dance to the heavy hedonistic drumming outside. "It's now our turn to play."

CHAPTER 31

"WAKE UP, PLEASE WAKE up." Riella's desperate call to me was the lifeline I needed to claw my way back to her.

The soulless sleep was not going to fucking have me today.

"No Zaki!" Riella cried out suddenly.

I pried my eyelids open, blinking hard at a fluffy black tailed ass of my cub's spirit guide. Shrieking at the imposing demon, it guarded us both from him, unafraid that the demon had just taken out a score of wraiths with one fiery blast only seconds prior.

The hilarity of my goddess damn situation wasn't lost on me as I forced myself to rise upon the trembling legs of my panther form.

"Faedere!" Riella gasped, throwing her arms around me.

I winced at the effort it took to keep my head up as she squeezed half my returning energy from my healing body. Watching us, the threatening demon frowned in confusion—his eyes darted between the three of us before resting on my daughter.

She trembled under his dark gaze and I narrowed my eyes on the bastard. No one made my daughter tremble in fear without paying for it.

Noticing my reaction, the demon cursed. "Lucifer's cock, look fae, I really don't want any more bullshit today."

"Riella, climb up and get ready to run," I snarled in her mind, keeping my gaze trained on the demon's rigid frame.

When my daughter shifted, he narrowed his black eyes but it was the slithering dark voice of the pookah that startled us both. "No one goes," it hissed.

Riella and I stiffened, staring idiotically at the spirit guide when it began to morph. Growing, it rose in height, changing into a black upright figure with long tapered fingers, piercing fangs, and the same beady eyes.

He looked like a cross between a human, demon, and fae and I didn't fucking like it one bit. No way was that thing hanging around my cub.

"Figures. Here comes more bullshit," the demon sighed, rubbing at his eyes and blinking at the pookah in front of us. "What the fuck is this thing?"

"She is mine, demon!" the pookah wailed, turning its piercing red eyes on him.

I growled, glancing worriedly down at my daughter, and scented her shocked wonder. She actually liked his claim on her, the excitement filtering on her beautiful scent. A scent that was manifesting with her powers. A cross between the salty ocean air and sunlit meadows.

Fucking goddess, I wish Remnant was here, I was not cut out for anything claiming my cub and letting them walk away from it alive. Perhaps, Ethereal would have offered to eat him for me. It certainly seemed like a better option than keeping it around.

But neither my beast nor my soulmate were here which meant I had to work extra hard not to snap his little bunny ears right off his head or in this case the tapered arms dragging on the forest floor.

The demon huffed in response and his sharp pointed tail started to twitch agitatedly, his eyes darting between all of us. "I may have been the one sent to hunt you down but I am not here to hurt you. I would have thought that to be obvious by now," his black eyes shifted onto me, "I'll ask again. What *exactly* is this grotesque thing? It reminds me of an imp."

I chuffed in my beast form before shifting, pulling my daughter behind me, relieved to feel that my body had fully healed from the threatening soulless sleep. The demon not at all surprised at my fae form, simply stared back. "It is a pookah...my daughter's self appointed spirit guide." I wrinkled my nose with disgust.

The pookah creature turned, his fangs bared, an endless void for a mouth. "Zaki."

Tilting my head, I narrowed my eyes at the bastard. "Apologies rodent." Looking up at the demon and shrugging, I added the obvious, "His name is Zaki."

The demon watched me carefully, lingering longer on my somewhat pink unicorn shirt before looking down towards Riella. "She is your daughter? That little thing that is wearing a crown of stars and a dragon's scale around her neck, she is yours, yes?"

Suspiciously, I snarled, "She is."

"What is her name?" he growled back.

Stepping out from behind my leg, my cub's chin tilted high, her swirling eyes glaring at the demon over Zaki's hunched fae-like form. "My name is Riella and I demand you take us to my mother to free her before we answer any of your questions." On cue, the pookah shifted, appearing on her shoulder in his *regular* bunny form, glaring in the same manner.

The demon's black eyes widened at her bold declaration before shooting back towards me with a quirked brow.

I grinned lethally, crossing my arms in front of my chest, and jerked my head towards my fierce offspring. "What she said."

The demon inhaled sharply and then cursed. His rigid frame melting into a pacing beast, muttering to himself about manipulating witches and cursed oaths. His tail flicked fiercely back and forth, his wings opening and closing as he ran a hand over one of the curling horns surrounding his head. Spinning back towards us his eyes glowed with fire.

Instinct had my claws unsheathing and I stepped alongside my daughter. Giving her the space to be brave but also the protection she needed.

The fire in his eyes died when he looked at her courageous stance again, and his voice was solemn when he spoke. "You remind me much of a little girl I once knew," he said wistfully, then shook his head, his wings snapping rigidly behind him. "I will help you free your mother."

My cub grinned and then blurred towards the demon, hugging his fierce leg before I could even react. "Thank you!" she breathed.

Fucking goddess, she was faster than me. "Riella!" I barked, lunging towards her with my heart seizing in my chest, terror I had never known before piercing through it.

Startled, the demon's wings flung outward as he peered down at my cub, eyes wide with shock.

Growling, I slowly approached them, watching the pookah who still sat on my daughter's shoulder, entirely calm throughout the whole situation. In fact the fucking thing was falling asleep.

The demon was cautious as he gently patted my daughters head, grunting. "Go back to your father, little fae."

Riella's swirling green and gold eyes turned back towards me seeing the anger and fear as I prowled closer. Then she raced back toward me, a blur of shadow before she clung to my leg. "I am sorry, faedere. I did something wrong, didn't I?"

Blowing out the breath I didn't realize I had been holding, I pulled her tightly to my side. "You are incredibly fast, my cub. Your shifter strengths are in full effect, I assume you do not smell a threat from the demon?"

She nodded, beaming up at me, happy that I understood she had at least given some thought towards her rash decision making. "Yes!"

I nodded and then bent low to her, nuzzling her nose with mine. "You are smart and you are cunning, but you must exercise caution. Just because you do not scent a threat does not mean it will never be there. Powerful beings are very good at masking their emotions and needs. I know you can sense the demon's power along with having seen it for yourself."

Riella's eyes widened and she peered back at the demon, sniffing. "I can." Turning back to me with a crestfallen expression and slumping shoulders, she added, "I understand now, faedere."

I kissed her forehead softly. "I am proud of you," I whispered, watching her face beam and her shoulders pull back once more before rising and adjusting the pack over my shoulder. I narrowed my gaze on the demon. "What is the toll for helping us?"

He grinned at me, his white teeth flashing brightly against his red skin. "You don't believe I do this out of the goodness of my heart."

I snorted. "You are a demon, I am fae, neither of us assist strangers out of our own free will. So I ask again, what is your price?"

His tail whipped to the side and his grin vanished. "It is not you who owes me, but rather the opposite."

My mind raced, had I fucking made a deal with a demon in my past? "Explain yourself."

The demon grinned. "I made a deal with a fae witch many years ago, and in return for her help, there was a price. An oath that bound me to assist a fae family once the time came—that family is you. And—I am called Zazion, not demon." Waving his hand at me he added blandly, "It is how I know what you are but also who you are, it was foretold by one of your kind that you would come here. You are Emon, king of the shifter fae, she is your daughter, heir to the Faerie throne, and your mate is Remnant, Goddess of the Well of Souls."

The blood drained from my face and my fucking heart stopped again. "What?" I snarled, pulling Riella behind me.

"Faedere?" Riella's small voice quivered—she had heard it too.

Heir to the Faerie throne...

Heir to the Faerie throne...

Heir to the Faerie throne—

Ah fuck.

What was it that Deirdre had said when she possessed Jar?

What I want is what was stolen from me! What I want is what should have been mine! And I will take it back!"

The demon regarded us with confusion before he shrugged, starting to repeat himself. "I am called Zazion—"

"Shut the fuck up demon," I snapped. "Take me to my soul-mate now!" I snarled.

CHAPTER 32

I EYED THE CAVE I just left half of my heart in with trepidation but I wasn't about to bring my daughter into a fucking demon infested camp and that was exactly where I was going. At the very least she had the pookah to stay with her even if I despised the bastard.

Riella was the future queen of Faerie...it had been *foretold*. I'd love to hunt down the fucking witch who even dared to utter those words from her mouth because just the thought terrified me and I wasn't a fae to succumb to fear.

I frowned...Zazion had said it was one of our *own*.

My fear continued to brew, bubbling just beneath the surface threatening to spill over and drown me. The last attack of the soulless sleep sent me closer to my goddess damn grave and I didn't even want to fucking think about the hunger...every kill had me craving more, needing more. A disturbing force that wanted to consume. It was far past self preservation, far past the need to fucking protect, even more hungry than Ethereal's power, the world destroyer. I had locked it down enough after years of mental shielding against the cat but I could feel it inside of me too, clawing through the deep recesses of my mind.

"You are worried about her. Don't be, this land is bound to me and my commands. Nothing can get in or out of that cave for now. She will be safe."

My attention snapped back to the demon named Zazion and I snarled. Moving quickly enough that before he could fucking blink my claws were at his throat and another just seconds away from puncturing his wing. "You don't get to tell me how I should feel about leaving cub in the middle of goddess damn Hell alone, demon," I hissed.

Zazion crossed his arms in front of his chest, glancing down at my claws. "Do you really want to go here all for the simple fact of paternal guilt? I'm your fucking way in and way out fae."

I grinned, my teeth flashing in the night. "I love it when beings underestimate me. Trust me when I say this, your help is *convenient* only and we both know it. You need me more than I need you. Fucking oaths are a pain in the ass aren't they? You'd think a demon would know how to make a more favorable deal for themselves."

Zazion growled and knocked my hand away from his throat. I let him.

Chuckling, I nodded to the blazing pillars of fire piercing the deep red night. "You think you can pull this off?"

The demon wings shifted behind me and I could feel his black eyes boring into the back of my head with loathing. "Taking great pleasure in dragging you in chains through the camp? Of course."

Snickering, I cracked my neck side to side, "Should be fun."

Snapping his fingers, heavy chains landed at my feet and I could not restrain the visceral growl, nor the instinctual step back I took at the fucking metal that made me weaker than a newborn pixie. I did not relish the feel of my newfound power being sapped out of my body and the instant hollow feeling that came along with it, the same feeling Remnant was experiencing right now.

"You act like a human with arachnophobia," Zazion said dryly, stepping next to me.

"Fuck off, I'm not hyperventilating demon." But I feared that Remnant would be, her panic attacks had been less since we officially accepted our bond but that did not mean the scars suddenly healed. Flashbacks of my chained soulmate still haunted my own memory.

I clenched my fist still feeling the way my hand broke, pummeling the unforgiving metal over and over again until it cracked. Our soulmate bond was supposed to be a glorious moment but for me it was tainted by my heart breaking for the beautiful fae that begged for her life to end.

At least, I had been able to give her that moment. A moment to heal and a moment to choose. Goddess what I wouldn't give to hear her laugh in the Cave of Lovers again.

Zazion cleared his throat, arching his brow at me. "This was your idea, remember?"

"Just give me a goddess damn moment," I growled.

The demon's horned head snapped up to the skies, his nostrils flaring at a new scent besides campfire ash. I smelled it too, like sour grapes baking in the sun, the same scent of the arrogant feathered companion to the demon queen—the one who killed Remnant's firedrake.

"What the fuck is he doing out here?" the demon muttered, a spark of flames lighting up in his eyes.

My brow arched, "I take it you two are not fond of one another." I crossed my arms growling. "This isn't some sort of lovers quarrel is it?"

Zazion's tale swished out and he snorted, "I'd rather fuck an imp but our Queen feels differently."

I snickered, I was starting to like this demon, and instincts told me that even after this journey, I'd be seeing him again. So naturally, curiosity had me pushing further...my cat personality peeking through, oh the irony. I could practically feel Ethereal rolling his eyes, muttering about death wishes. "So what then? You pine on the sidelines hoping she one day sees you and wakes up to what the angel truly is?"

The demon tilted his head, "Demons do not pine, that is meant for the tortured souls here and it matters not how I feel. My queen is happy with her angel and I will always ensure her happiness. Even if it means I must be on the proverbial side of the angels." Then he growled, pointing at me. "I don't even know why we are speaking of this, we have no time for it."

Grinning, I gave him a wink, "I have that effect on others..." I shrugged, holding my arms out wide, "You sure you don't just want to kill him now? I'll help you." I narrowed my eyes on the demon, my look lethal, "He's a dead angel boy anyway. You know that right? Either I help you kill him, solve all your problems, help you get the girl or I hunt that bastard down on another day for killing my soulmate's firedrake. I will take great pleasure handing her the knife to gut him just like he did that dragon."

Black eyes bored into mine, a wide grin too bright against his deep red skin spread across his face revealing sharp fangs. "Times up fae," Zazion purred, snapping his fingers.

I snarled at the iron chains that suddenly cinched around my entire torso, the hideous sound of the clanking metal and the immediate loss of my power heavy on my solid frame and my mind.

This was the only time to be fucking grateful for wearing a goddess damn shirt. Although it had lost much of its brightness, something I hoped Riella would not be too upset about. I glanced back at the cave and then snarled.

"Get me further away from here. I don't want that bastard anywhere near my daughter."

Zazion snickered with no sense of urgency in his demeanor, "Unusual for one to trust a demon over an angel. What kind of fucked up world do you live in?"

"One where pretty things are true monsters inside. Your angel is rotten, I know you smell it."

"He's not my angel and all things stink here, its fucking Hell. Speaking of pretty—"

I saw his fist coming, I could even make out his sharp black tipped claws but my shifter side was drained from the iron and there was no way I could avoid the contact that sent me careening to the side.

My nose shattered on impact, the force of the demon's hit even fracturing the other bones in my face right before I hit the ground with a loud thud.

Blood poured down my throat and I growled, rolling onto my back and ignoring the way the irons into it, I glared at the smug demon.

"Did that make you feel better, demon?"

"Shut the fuck up fae and play your part," he hissed, waving his hand. I growled low when a gag dug painfully into my mouth, shooting sharp pain through my fractured face.

I didn't have to pretend at being pissed the fuck off when the asshole demon's foot kicked me over onto my stomach, his heel digging into my spine with enough pressure that with just one more press he would fucking sever it.

I snickered through the gag, my eyes flashing up at him in knowing, meeting the brightness of his own. Oh this bastard was enjoying this.

Fucking demons.

Growling loudly, I squirmed a bit pathetically. This would be the time Ethereal would tell me my acting was abysmal but again...audience.

I heard the soft landing of the angel just feet away from us instead of smelling him, my nose obliterated from Zazion's strike. No matter, I didn't want to smell his spoiled rot anyway.

I fake roared through my gag, thrashing a little bit against the chains, then stilled when a sharpened object dug into the back of my neck, threatening to puncture the vulnerable flesh. "I'd stop squirming like a fucking worm before I slice open your spinal cord, fae," Zazion growled.

"This doesn't look much like the panther you went hunting for, Zazion."

I stilled, pretending to breathe heavily through my gag, low rumbling growls emitting from my chest.

The demon chuckled. "That's because hes a fucking shifter, Shaniel. Honestly, did heaven not educate you enough on the other beings of this world, or is your brain truly full of feathers too?"

The grinding of the angel's teeth was audible to my sensitive hearing. "You know that I did not receive such an education, demon. I was just a cherub when I was taken. Your queen would be displeased to hear you mention it...*again*," he drawled.

Zazion chuckled and I trembled to hold back my own laughter.

What a fucking prat.

I grunted when the demon's booted foot kicked me in the side breaking a rib, forcing a real growl from me this time. Asshole must have sensed my mirth and effectively changed it with his vicious assault.

"Oh dear..." Zazion drawled, "Did I hurt your virtuous feelings again, Shaniel? Apologies, my delicate feather." His mockery was not helping...and I bit on the gag just to stop from chuckling, focusing on the pain instead. "Now, are you actually here for something or was it that you were concerned for my well being?"

Shaniel huffed and I fucking wished I could turn my head to see his face but the damned demon's talon was still sharply digging into the back of my neck. "If it wasn't for our Queen, I would not put up with your insolence."

My brows rose.

"I will return back to camp to let your queen know you have captured the beast. She will be pleased you have not failed."

Zazion chuckled darkly, "You seem disappointed, feather."

The sharp whoosh of wings disturbed the air around us, breezing over my body. "Return to camp immediately, demon. Once you deposit the prisoner then we will have your full report. Do not leave her waiting."

I renewed my squirming, fighting the chains and hissing through the gag, pretending I did not want to go into that camp.

But they both ignored my best acting yet.

"It's so cute that you think you can give me orders, Shaniel, like a baby imp cutting its horns thinking it is a fully fledged demon." Stooping, he hauled me to my feet with ease, surprising considering my bulk. Instantly, I felt the blood drip down my face, finally getting a good glimpse at halo boy. "Now piss off, feather. I'm fucking busy."

I growled and thrashed in his hold but my eyes stayed locked on the pompous face of the angel, his heavenly features pulled back into a sneer that did not do well for his flawless complexion. I wanted him to know his death was coming and when it did, these were the eyes he was going to see.

Zazion shook me hard, rattling my teeth. "Stop your growling, fae. Your fight is futile now."

Looking between us, Shaniel spat, "Disgusting," before he launched into the night, banking back towards the demon camp where the looming fires turned his bright white feathers into a hue of orange.

"Prick," Zazion spat, watching him go, sharp fangs extending from his mouth when he set me down on my feet.

I chuckled against my gag, wiggling my eyebrows at him since I could no longer speak.

"Shut up, fae," Zazion snapped, his black gaze dragging over my fractured face with his tail swishing behind him in irritation. "Lucifer's cock, your acting is atrocious. You're going to fucking get us killed the way you are going."

I grinned widely from behind the muzzle and shrugged.

The demon grinned back, seemingly taking sadistic pleasure in the thought of our deaths...or maybe it was just mine. "Very well."

CHAPTER 33

Remnant

"C URIOUS," I MUTTERED, FORCING the shadows to dance with the debauched drumming outside the yurt, flexing powers that should not have been possible while in irons. Slowly they were growing in strength, and so was I. Soon I would be able to control them enough to release me from my restraints.

My head jerked up when victorious roars rose even louder outside, shaking the very cloth that shrouded me in captivity. I sighed heavily, there could only be one answer for the demons to sound even more triumphant—my damn shifter of a soulmate was playing catch and release again.

Bait.

Swallowing my own scream of frustration, I forced the chains deeper into my skin, making them burn my flesh to hide the sudden healing that had occurred. Angry red imprints was all I could manage, my resistance to the irons more resilient.

Pressing my head back with another deep sigh, I released the dancing shadows moments before bright firelight spilled into the darkened yurt. Forcing an expression of boredom, I studied the tall red skinned demon ripped with heavy muscle and soul stealing black gaze. With a thin grimace of displeasure he muttered before hauling my shifter soulmate through the entrance, tossing Emon inside with a simple grunt.

Relieved that it wasn't the queen of Hell, I settled further against the wooden post, hiding my impressed musings. It was no mean feat throwing the king of shifters. Not risking a look towards my snarling, foolish soulmate even though my heart soared to have him near again, I tilted my head to hold the demon's dark glare.

His eyes shifted to the chains and then back to me. "You are unhurt."

A statement, deathly and dark in its tone.

I shrugged, "Child's play by a child queen."

His dark eyes burned suddenly with flames, his tail slashing through the air as he dropped the heavy flap. "Perhaps."

Snorting, I finally turned to observe my soulmate, who had been studying every inch of me. I could feel his anger at the blemishes on my skin, the disgust he felt for the irons snaking around my body, and the palpable relief being together brought him. The feeling was mutual and when our eyes met those golden depths burned. So fierce was his love in them that there wasn't a single dark piece of me that wasn't touched by it.

Even in my fury.

"Your nose is broken again," I said, the blood staining his face prominent.

Lush brown hair fell over his brow when he spat out the gag around his mouth, "I missed you too, little umbra. You are even more gorgeous than the last time I saw you." He licked the blood off his bottom lip, smirking up at the chains. "I can work with this." Then his growling voice penetrated my mind, weak but there. *"Can you hear me, my beautiful mate?"*

My heart, that had deadened the moment our bond went silent, started beating true again. "I'll never tire seeing you at my feet shifter king," I purred back, playing his game, while snarling harshly through our bond. *"I told you to trust me. Where is our daughter?"*

Emon's face split into a wide predator smile. "Time to leave demon, my soulmate is hungry in a way only I can satisfy her in."

Then his serious tone cut through my fury and fearfulness. *"She is safe."*

"Emon...how exactly is our daughter safe while we both were here?"

"Much has happened, Remnant. I will explain later," he said softly, gently, as if I was on the edge of exploding...perhaps I was.

The demon growled at Emon, striding forward during our exchange and yanking him upward with a singular arm. Again, I marveled at his strength, before I assessed the iron chains wrapping around my soulmate, noticing that they had been carefully placed over his clothing—that goddess damn unicorn shirt preventing any burns on his smooth bronze flesh. "You will do as we discussed, fae." The demon shook him with emphasis, "Your female will just have to wait for her pleasure." Throwing him disgustedly towards the ground, the demon snapped his fingers to direct the chains to wrap around a secondary post across from me, pulling Emon tightly to it. "Stay put until I am ready, understood?"

My shifter deep chuckle filled the darkened space and caressed over my heated skin. "Haven't got laid in a long while have you demon?

I snorted softly, realizing neither one of us played the role of captive well. Predators and monsters never did.

Looking between us, the demon snarled, spinning away with his wings snapping tightly against his wide muscular back before he paused at the tent flap. Black eyes glared at me over the ridge of his wing. "My oath will be fulfilled after this..."

I tilted my head and studied the demon more closely. *"Do I want to know?"* I shot through our bond still watching the curious demon in front of me.

Emon shook his head, his voice still faint. *"No."*

"And by the way," the demon hissed, "your acting is atrocious." Exiting, his tail whipped the flap of the yurt closed before snaking back to its owner.

The howls and cheers started anew as their second in command returned to the revelry.

My whisper was harsh, the chains rattling against the post. *"What* agreement, Emon?"

Shifting in his chains he wrinkled his broken nose, wincing slightly, "As I said before, some things have changed and become more problematic."

"Clearly," I quirked a brow, waiting for him to explain more.

Emon's gaze trailed up my body, fixated on the chains wrapped around my thighs, anger and lust swirling in its depths. "Especially more problematic with those chains, they will have to go" he licked his lips again, adding smugly, "but we could keep the top ones, since you are healing now."

My stomach clenched and I shifted again in my restraints. "You don't seem at all surprised, shifter. Something you need to tell me?"

He looked up at me frowning. "It's a theory, but if I'm correct—" His focus seemed to drift inward, then widened as he sharply inhaled. "Sweet goddess above, your aura...Remnant—your soul is just as breathtaking as I imagined it to be and so much more."

I leaned in, watching the wonderment wash over him. "Emon..." I said slowly, although I had already come to the answer, "how is it that you can see auras?"

"Did you know?" he whispered reverently. "Did you know that your aura is just as stunning as you are? I always knew the depths of you exceeded even the unparalleled beauty on the outside. I see you, Remnant Dark," Looking at me dazed, he shook his head, "I see all of you, even the parts you hide in your darkness."

My chest rose and fell with each quickened breath, with each loving word escaping his sensual lips. "Emon." His name a whispered prayer escaping my mouth.

Blinking, he moved against his chains, his own sight returning. "Im sorry little umbra...it's just, you never cease to take my breath hostage, not just your beauty but all of you, and I never fucking want it back if it's you keeping it."

Tears threatened to spill. In Emon's eyes I was the reflection I had always desperately dreamed to be but somehow I could never find...until him, until now. "I love you, shifter."

If he had access to shift, I swear his fangs would have lengthened salaciously at this moment. "Tell me, soulmate, does your aura brighten if I were to show you exactly how I love you?"

My stomach clenched and my thighs pressed together. "I'd say that's an abusive use of our shared powers." Regarding him sharply, I added, "That's what this is isn't it? We are connected from our soulmate bond...you're immune to iron."

The fabric of his blood stained pink shirt stretched when his chest puffed with pride. "Clever little soulmate. Not at first though...the longer I am in irons...the more resistant I become, as long as I am not weakened physically. For example," With a deep guttural growl he pushed his arms out from his sides, thick muscle straining tightly against the chains around him before a loud crack echoed sharply in the yurt. It was quickly followed by the clinking sound of the irons falling from his body.

I bit at my lip, watching him slowly rise from his bonds and the more severe crookedness of his nose straighten slightly, healing to its original perfectly imperfect form. His predator presence sucking every ounce of air from my lungs while he slowly stalked towards me with an intensity that was feral.

Waving my fingers at him with a smile, I summoned the shadows, halting his slow stalking. His head jerked down in surprise to stare at my darkness anchoring him to the rug covered earth.

"Remnant," he said in a slow deep warning.

I gave him a wink. "While I appreciate your bad alpha hero saving the princess act, you should have learned by now that I am no damsel." With calculated precision, the strengthened shadows slashed my restraints with two dark blades, slinking away from me.

I sagged with relief but it was a short reprieve, memories flooding back with such violence that I clutched my chest with a sharp gasp. My breathing erratic, my body trembling at the sight of the monstrous metal that I had thought I had escaped from—I was so wrong. The trauma of my past still haunting me, branding me for life.

Chocolate spice enveloped me like a warm blanket and Emon's large gentle hands cradled me into his wide muscular chest. The scent and feel of him chasing away the panic.

His hand softly gripped my chin, tilting me head to look into his golden eyes, Emon breathed deep, his nostrils flaring. "I love you and you are safe." Then he bent his head towards mine, trailing his tongue across my bloodied lips with a groan.

Hungrily, his mouth moved quickly over my cheek, the top of my shoulder, my collar bone—my breath quickened. He bowed, studying the scratches across my torso, licking through the torn leather at the wounds beneath. I gasped when his head ducked to my thighs where the irons had first come in contact with me during his and Riella's escape. Delicately he licked at that skin too, healing the invisible scars, and groaning loudly again as if he had just sampled the sweetest most delicious morsel in all his years.

Heat licked its way from my head to my toes and back to where the hot breath of my soulmate still tickled my upper thigh.

"I love you too," I whispered and reached down to pull his mouth back to mine. Swiping with my tongue at the blood covering his roughed face, returning the favor he had graced me, Emon released a predatorial purr of satisfaction followed by an explosion of our bodies crashing into each other like violent seas.

I gasped against his mouth when my back slammed into the large wooden post, instinctively wrapping my legs around him to close the distance, wanting to feel every inch of his hardened body against me.

"I need to be so far inside of you that I'll stay there permanently. I'll never be without you again," he growled low, biting and sucking at my lips like a starved beast while ripping my shorts down past my knees and thrusting his fingers deep inside of me.

He swallowed down my passionate cries while the loud drums of the demon celebration outside drowned out any noise escaping from us in the darkened yurt.

His thrusting joined the quick rhythm of the heathen drums and my stomach clenched hard as his thumb brushed against my clit. "Cum for me, little umbra." He shoved deeper, snarling against my lips while I clawed at his arms. "You may not have needed me to save you and you may not be the damsel in distress, but I'm sure as goddess going to fuck you like one."

I screamed, my cries of pleasure muffled by Emon's talented tongue, riding out my release in bursting spasms. Emon's chest vibrating with his own dark sensual purr of satisfaction.

Too quickly for me to comprehend, I gasped when Emon's cock pushed fully inside me. Wrenching my hands from him, he forced them up over my head, his grip enveloping both my wrists as he pinned me to the post. "I told you I would work with this," he growled, his fangs biting at the sensitive skin between my shoulder and neck—his cock continuing to plunge rhythmically deep inside me.

"Yes!" I hissed, meeting him just as hard, wanting to feel him just the way he described, so deep that he could never leave me again.

We would be one forever.

A clawed hand dug into my ass, tilting me in a different way that sent me gasping and writhing against his grip above.

Jerking his golden gaze up to meet my own, his thrusting slowed, concern for my well being so obvious that I snarled, biting at his lip and tasting his sweet chocolate spiced blood on my tongue.

"Don't you fucking stop and don't you dare slow down."

That was all the consent he needed. Snarling harshly, he kissed me again, feeding me more of his blood from his nicked lip, furiously pounding into me. All his fears, frustrations, and worries were being relinquished onto my body and I goddess damn loved every minute of it.

My release shot through me like Hell's fire and I felt Emon's hand rip from my ass to cover my mouth while his own buried into the crook of my neck, sinking his teeth into my skin and sending me crashing towards another release that blinded me with an explosion of stars. My mind numb, I was only half aware of his own muffled roar as he came with deep irregular jerks, spilling his essence so far inside me that I fully believed he had indeed accomplished what he set out to do.

There would be no separating Emon from me. Not on any level of this universe's existence.

Not ever.

CHAPTER 34

MY SOULMATE WAS A fucking gorgeous mess, staring at me utterly dazed and satiated as I approached her with a clean dampened cloth I had dug from the trunks nearby. Slumped against the wooden post I had just taken her against, I couldn't help but purr with pride at the way I could fucking undo her—just like the way she undid me.

Even now my heart still thundered in my chest, my body still roared with the aftershocks of pleasure, my mind still screamed to never stop touching her, and my soul still craved to claim every inch of her.

She watched me through hooded eyes when I tenderly wiped away the blood I hadn't managed to lick and kiss from her. She was right, she was no damsel, she was a stunning savage that wielded death to perfection—the very death that always sought her.

A fact that had me trembling with rage.

Those demons had taken her blood. I could scent every single one on her body and they were now my new prey. The need to kill the ones she hadn't killed herself, radiated through every fiber of my being—and I would do it too...someday. Growling softly, I controlled my fury, kissing her healed wounds where I knew hidden beneath her pale skin, new scars had formed.

"The demon's name is Zazion. Turns out he owes someone a huge favor," I whispered to her, kissing her lips softly and moving that cloth over her shoulders to wash the grime and blood from her arms.

My grin flashed in the darkness when she only hummed back to me. I goddess damn loved this part of her. When I fucked the words right out of her, destroying her mind to a puddle of satisfied mush...barely able to make just one comprehensive word.

"Someone," I continued, wiping her gently between her legs, our mingling scents lighting up my desire for her all over again—I was a fucking beast after all and she....she was an addiction of the best kind, obliterating all my other senses so that there was just her and the darkness that claimed my light. A light that would never shine for anyone else, so consuming was her grip on my heart and soul. "Someone...that has powerful sight. Someone, with the ability to see things happen before they occur. Someone. that is fae."

Remnant's hand snapped out to my wrist, gripping it tightly and stopping me. My eyes rose to those gorgeous emerald depths that I could drown in, seeing keen understanding shining within.

I smirked. My soulmate's mind was fully back to its cunning functional status.

"Penina." She released my wrist and stepped away, making quick work of returning her clothing to its proper state. I eyed her shorts...were they even clothing?

"Likely," I grunted.

Tearing off a piece of leather that had ripped from her vest, she pulled her hair back with a ragged sigh and wrapped the strap at the crown of her head. The long length of her ponytail swinging, her blue highlights flashing in the dim darkness. "What else aren't you telling me, shifter? That cannot be the reason you decided to play bait...*again.*"

Tossing the cloth to the side, my lips thinning with irritation, I braided my own hair back roughly. "That fucking demon called our daughter the heir to the Faerie throne."

The flush from our lovemaking rushed quickly from my soul-mate's skin, her hair whipping across her face as she turned to look at me. "No. Absolutely not. Not ever. Faerie can not have her...she is ours. The fae..." Her voice broke and instinctively I was in front of her, pulling her into my arms. "That's why Deirdre wants her. Riella is a threat to Deirdre's plans...but why give her up then? Why place her in The Under for me to find?" she whispered into my chest.

I ran my fingertips up and down her spine. "There have to be players hidden in these games we have not identified yet...someone else may be playing Deirdre's strings—and it seems, it might be in our favor this time."

My hands fell away as Remnant began to pace the darkened room. Unaware, she summoned the shadows to her, their darkness swirled around her fingertips like sparks ready to ignite. "Falcon is not discreet enough to be able to deceive Deirdre. She called herself a goddess the last time...a blood goddess."

Crossing my arms, I enjoyed the sight of her magnificent mind at work.

"That could mean the Blood God must be a part of all this...how could he not be? The origin of the Sanguine, only he would have the power to grant her such a status. If that's the case then—"

"Faerie," I spat. Our goddess had a lot of explaining to do, especially why she gifted me with her son's soul and power but how exactly was this blood god still at large. She was supposed to have destroy him.

Remnant paused and spun towards me, her eyes wide. "The Goddess, what if...what if she never abandoned us, Emon? What if she has been trapped all this time...in the Sanguine?"

And there it was, the way my soulmate could cut through all the mess and chaos, puzzling out the world in a whole new light that no one even considered.

I fucking loved her for it but her realization only served to facilitate the fear I had for our cub. "My mother once said that only Faerie had the right to declare and designate the true ruler of our world. It is why the shifter kingdom never agreed to Deirdre's rule."

Remnant's clever light quickly flashed back to panic. "Faerie," she gasped. "If I am right and if the demon Zazion is to be believed, then Riella really is the true queen of Faerie. The goddess must have bestowed this upon her within the Sanguine at her birth." Remnant shook her head and exhaled shakily, "Emon, our daughter...if she is the true Faerie queen," she shivered, pulling her arms across her body, "Deirdre doesn't just want her back because Riella replaces the child she lost from the Blood Wars, she wants her back to destroy her. If she does not, then her true claim on this world will always be threatened. Even if she is a blood goddess now. Deirdre will see her as a flaw in her own rule—a queen blessed by Faerie, something Deirdre never had."

My response was cut short when the sound outside the yurt changed. The distinct sound of scuffling and grunting could be heard just on the other side of the heavy fabric of the enclosure.

Instinctively I moved, pulling Remnant with me into the darkness on the far side of the wall, away from the heavy thuds of bodies dropping to the ground—I knew that sound all too well for it not to be.

"We will keep Riella safe, little umbra, our family will keep her safe. Deirdre will never come close to ever touching a single hair on her head." I whispered reassuringly inside her mind even though my own raced. My fear for my cub just as fucking palpable as Remnant's and it stirred the hunger I had locked away.

My soulmate's lips thinned in the darkness and she nodded once before curling horns and stern black eyes ducked inside the tent. The demon had returned, and I smirked as his nostrils flared, peering into the darkness with his tail thrashing with aggravation.

"Lucifer's cock, fae. Did I not tell you to fuck your female at a later time?"

My soulmate stepped out of the shadows she had masked us under, her teeth bared. "What makes you think it was him doing the fucking, demon?"

I snickered, stepping beside her with smug arrogance.

Black eyes assessed my soulmate warily before he growled back at me. "There is no time for these pointless fae games. The entire demon army is conveniently pissed or rutting their balls off and I finally convinced that feathered bastard to join the celebrations and service our queen for her victory." His face wrinkled with disgust, mine did too.

That angel gave off rotten fucking vibes and this poor bastard had it bad for his queen. Like a lap dog not getting a bone, he had to obediently watch the whole charade, loyalty and love his perpetual suffering. I knew the feeling, it was easy to recognize.

"Another herd of centurions are also on the move...with reports of those abominations heading north into Wrath territories. It seems one of our enemies has joined forces with yours. This complicates things." His eyes narrowed on my soulmate. "You didn't happen to tell the queen that your destination is The Well, did you?"

Remnant ignored him and glared at me. "You did not mention the blood wraiths shifter."

I grinned, shrugging. "I got distracted."

Remnant snorted and the demon glared at the both of us, his tail tapping, waiting for his answer. She pursed her lips at him. "I was attempting to appeal to her...*good side*."

Cursing, the demon ran his hand over his curling horns. "Avalon has no good side, fae. It died when her father was murdered at her feet, just seven years old." He glared harder, flames in his eyes. "She will send her entire army to hunt you down, including me, and she will not stop. If I help you now, my side of the bargain will be fulfilled. So I must warn you, I will no longer be bound by my debts and my loyalty to my queen is infinite. If she orders your death, I will be the hand that delivers it."

Remnant frowned. "Then why even cash your debt? Why not kill us now? You are a demon, you have no respect for the honor of bargains."

The demon grinned and this time I could see the dangerous power behind him, a power he had been holding back...perhaps even from his beloved queen. "You are right, I certainly do not. Except this was the price I accepted to *keep* her safe...if I do not, it will be stripped away, and so...I will betray my queen at the same time as I strengthen her rule."

Fucking goddess above and below. This poor bastard was fucked five ways in his own Hell, and the sharp way he looked at me now...he knew I understood him too well. There was a fire raging inside us, the dark urge to incinerate the world to ash, building a throne from its deadly cinders for the females we loved—then admiring our work from our venerated knees amongst the bones of their enemies.

I grunted, nodding back to him with acknowledgement and respect.

Remnant glanced between us both and I could hear her teeth grinding with displeasure. "Then I accept. Get us the goddess out of here, far enough to give us a good head start, safely, with our daughter, and I will call your debt paid." The shadows darkened around her, "But know this demon, should you hunt us, I will not hesitate to cut you down and your little child queen too. I have a talent for bringing thrones to their crumbling end, and your beloved Hell? It will be no different should you force my hand."

The demon looked back at me and I rubbed at my lips not able to hide my smile. That formidable strength...I goddess damn *loved* it and I loved that it had passed down to our daughter. I tilted my head towards my soulmate, "What she said, demon."

The demon's white teeth gleamed as his grin spread across his face. "I see where your daughter gets it from, fae."

This time there was no hiding my wicked smile, pride glowing inside me when Remnant and I's gazes met. "Indeed, there is no power greater than when one knows their own worth and is not afraid to *unleash* it." I said more to my soulmate than to him.

The demon grunted, "agreed," turning back to Remnant, the shadows swirling menacing around her. "So be it, Goddess of the Wells."

CHAPTER 35

Remnant

"S HROUD YOURSELF BACK INTO the shadows and step in," the demon commanded harshly, widening his wings, indicating we step into either side of the leathery membrane.

"You're going to cover us with your wings." I placed a hand on my hip and pursed my lips. "As if no one is going to notice how they suddenly sprouted legs?"

The demon hissed, swiftly gathering me in his wing and sandwiching my body to his back like a bedroll. With one powerful thrust, he hoisted me off the ground without so much as a grunt, then peered down over his shoulder at my shocked expression. "Yes," he simply stated.

"No." Emon growled loudly, his claws slashing downward. "Unhand my soulmate."

Peeking over the dark ridge of the demon's wing like a mischievous child, I snickered at the furious expression on Emon's. "I am perfectly fine, shifter, it is rather cozy here." I shot him a wink. "I think you should join me."

He snarled at the demon, "he did not ask for permission to touch you, little umbra."

I goddess damn loved this shifter. He saw my scars, my trauma, and instead of trying to erase them, he protected them. "I am giving it now, Emon."

His fury lightened slightly and I could see the slightest twitch at the corner of his mouth as he studied me in the demon's wing.

"This is fucking ridiculous," he growled through our bond.

"We don't have time for this," the demon snarled, "that feathered head only lasts a heavenly seven minutes if we are lucky, we need to move."

Emon turned on him, fangs lengthening, "That's not my problem, demon, it's yours. I'll hide within the confines of the shadows. Your kin are too fucking pissed outside to take notice of me."

The demon's body vibrated before he released a dark laugh, the wing holding me not even straining. Stretching his opposite wing out wider, he grinned. "You may have blood coating your hands shifter but you're not a completely immoral depraved beast without a soul...to them you smell like a sweet fucking virgin and they will be like flies on honey the moment you step out of this place. Only my cum would stop them from finding you in your shadows at this point."

I guffawed at the matter-of-fact way the demon rationalized his stance and the darkening features of Emon's face, likely thinking about being marked by the essence of another male.

Emon purred in my head, *"You like that idea, don't you?"*

I licked my lips, it did seem intriguing. *"Perhaps."*

The demon looked between us, watching our exchange with gleaming eyes. "Sorry to disappoint you little goddess but I'm in no mood to fuck a fae tonight. Your beastly lover wouldn't be able to handle me anyway."

Amused, I cooed at Emon, *"You hear that shifter, he thinks you cannot handle him."*

My soulmate's eyes glowed even brighter. *"I always love it when beings underestimate us."*

I laughed, the sound carrying within the yurt, but still not loud enough to be heard over the drums. Emon was good at playing the underestimated bait. Not many would play that card but he did, a patient predator, striking when you least expected it. His cunning was my equal in every way.

Again, the demon huffed and stretched his opposite wing out wider, fixing Emon with a hard expecting look. "Cut the shit, fae. Now hurry along shifter king and let us be done with this."

Emon cursed, smoothing his hand over his braided hair, his claws sheathing and unsheathing. With a harsh sigh, he pulled his shoulders back and stepped towards the large expanded wing.

Zazion shuddered, with what I could only assume was disgust as he quickly wrapped Emon tightly within, like he was scum he had to suffer touching. The slight stiffening was the only indication the additional weight from my shifter caused him any strain within his enclosed hold.

"We speak of this to no one," Zazion added, before turning toward the entrance.

Emon chuckled softly. "Oh I don't know about that...sharing that demon's cuddle is a great start to a story over a stiff drink."

I hummed in agreement. "Yes and with their treasured wings no less. I am told wings are quite sensitive."

"Shall we test that theory, little umbra," Emon teased.

"You may try, fae, but it will be the last breath you take," the demon snarled softly before wrenching aside the heavy fabric of the yurt.

Swaying with each heavy step the demon took, I blinked over the ridge of his wing at the sudden bright light of roaring towers of fire, quickly using the demon's shadows to hide my peering eyes while watching the debauched spectacle. My curiosity of beasts had always been my greatest weakness and that's what these beings were in their raw form.

From my minimal view I could see demons of all shapes and sizes dancing and fucking around the multiple fires. Their screeching and roars echoed along with the thundering drumbeats and steady slapping of sodomizing flesh.

A beautiful naked human woman was suddenly thrown in the wake of Zazion's steady prowl, her deep blue eyes raised up towards mine through the mess of long blonde hair—pleading, but there was no way she could actually see me.

I stiffened in Zazion's wing, the pull to help her consuming all my senses, especially when another grotesque demon landed directly behind her, raising her hips up and impaling her with one swift thrust straight into her ass and rutting her into the ground.

Seeing the wings of the powerful Zazion she clawed at the ground reaching for them. Her efforts were thwarted however when the lusting savage behind her yanked her hair back, raking open her skin with his claws as his other hand pawed at her breast, never stopping his vicious thrusting.

With fury I reached towards the shadows. I would stuff them down this demon's throat and suffocate him without anyone ever knowing I was here.

"Don't," growled Zazion, turning his head down towards me, whispering quietly, not even bothering to acknowledge the vicious assault. "That is not a human woman, Goddess of The Well. They are called Rakshasa. Evil entities that change their form to manipulate others. They are like sirens relying on your soft morality to draw you in and then they eat your soul. Perhaps at one time they were once human and deserved mercy but then again they have been judged by the Redeemer on earth and sent here." The demon shuddered at that, as if he feared this *redeemer.* "Demons do actually have a job here in Hell, fae. We are to make sure their suffering has no end."

After a brief pause, he faced forward recognizing that I would not do anything foolish for now. Unfortunately, I couldn't stop watching. A second demon had joined his comrade with a club in hand, kicking them over and he squatted, impaling the Rakshasa with his spiked weapon, thrusting it in and out of the creature's body while taking his long cock in hand, pumping it fiercely to the drums. The demon beneath them roared, his thrusting following his brethren's rhythm.

"Fortunately for demons we do not hold the same moral guidelines as other species might, and have no problem with their manipulative screams...we find pleasure in it." Zazion added as the violent assault escalated.

Opening my aura sight, I grimaced. Zazion was right, there was nothing redeemable about the Rakshasa. I had seen many auras in my lifetime but nothing equated to this...it was putrid and sinister, a patchwork of other auras surrounding it, grieving souls it had consumed.

Realizing it could not be manipulated as Zazion continued to walk away, the beautiful woman shifted into a grotesque mutilated animal. Howling, the other two demons called forth more of their friends. My view of it was quickly hidden as demons swarmed with whips and chains, not caring if they were lashed as well as they continued to sodomize the creature.

Shuddering I averted my eyes, only catching the outer surface of the demon Zazion's aura. The blazing hot red surrounding him was intense and gorgeous. It was the exact replica of his queen.

Thoughts racing, I reached out to my soulmate's mind. *"Emon, when you looked at my aura, what color was it?"*

"White...a golden glow so bright it was almost white," he said, the mystified awe in his voice the same as when he first looked upon me with my own powers.

I breathed in deep. *"I have not looked upon my own aura since we bonded. It is difficult to do on oneself but it was never that color before, shifter."*

It was a moment before Emon spoke again. His tone low and calculating. *"It has changed since you accepted the soulmate bond."*

I flinched at the sudden loud shriek ending quickly on the other side of us—-*Emon's side.*

"Witches fucking cunts," Zazion cursed softly and the drumbeats faltered, "did you really just fucking kill one of my demons with my own knife, shifter?" he whispered sinisterly, low enough for only our ears. Then he looked up at the sudden pause in the revelry, multiple pairs of demon eyes gazing at him warily and with confusion as to why their leader just killed one of their own. "Burn the imp! He displeased me, unable to handle a single fucking fae while I was gone. Hell take him and Lucifer curse his shameful line!" The demon bellowed, covering up what-ever the goddess my soulmate had done.

"Emon, what-ever possessed you?"

My shifter snarled. *"I could smell your blood on that demon and there is no being in this world that I will allow to live with your blood staining their hands."*

My lips twitched. *"What about being a patient predator, shifter?"*

I could hear Emon's smile. *"Zazion's knife has been right here the whole time, I took it as an invitation to play."*

Grunting and making sure the demon's got lost in their new disgusting task, Zazion began to stride forward. Anger emphasized in every powerful step he took, our sway increasing like rocking a babe that stubbornly refused to sleep. "Try that shit again shifter king and I'll break our agreement and leave your daughter stranded in hell without her parents."

Fury had me latching onto the shadows in the darkness but I paused when the demon stiffened and Emon's low purr reached me over the demons' celebrations. "Not before I rip out your spinal cord and tear these wings from your back like fucking twigs leaving your poor little queen left with an invalid to protect her."

The demon grunted and I realized Emon's claws were slicing into his side.

"Go ahead demon, threaten my mate and my daughter's future one more time," Emon added with a hiss. "That kill was clean and just, more than a demon deserves and you know it."

Zazion chuckled darkly. "Cease your prattling, fae. Before we are both found out and cannot make good on our promised threats to each other." His powerful wings shook us slightly in retribution before the three of us fell quiet again.

I bit at my lip, our previous discussion before Zazion interrupted with his vicious vengeance on my behalf nagging at me. *"Emon?"* I whispered in his mind.

I could practically see his grin. *"Hmm, little umbra?"*

"About our auras, if what you say is true, then my aura is the exact replica of yours. I should know because the beauty of it nearly dropped me to my knees the first time I saw you."

Emon chuckled in my head. *"Well we can't have that, little umbra. It is my job to fall to my knees in reverence of you, not the other way around. I will fight you for it if I have to. It is my new religion and I am determined to be devout."*

Flashes of Emon on his knees, in the glow of the moon, and falling stars reflected in his eyes were suddenly so vivid I could still feel the smooth slide of his mouth against my sensitive skin. I exhaled shakily. Had it truly only been a day since that night?

"The demon Zazion has the same aura as his queen," I whispered softly in Emon's thoughts.

Another brief pause. *"They are soulmates."*

"Yes. So it would seem."

Emon snorted in my head. *"Poor bastard. I wish him all the luck...that's a time I never want to relive again, but I would if it were the only way I could ever have you forever."*

I frowned. *"What do you mean shifter?"*

"The desperate lost feeling of having your soulmate right in front of you, looking into her eyes knowing that she is yours forever, to love and cherish and yet...she cannot see it."

Tears pricked at the corner of my eyes, this fae destroyed me in the best way. *"I see you now, shifter."*

"Do not fret, my little umbra. I was blessed in having to earn your love. It will always be one of the greatest accomplishments of my life."

"Only one of them?" I said teasingly, but I knew he could hear the catch in my tone, the way he could make my heart weep and soar at the same time.

"Yes, my love. One of...there are two others. The second greatest is our daughter."

I swallowed. *"And the third?"*

His voice was a soft caress in my mind, endearing, devotional, burning. *"The third is knowing that I have yet to let a single day pass without making sure you both know you are loved so wholly and irrevocably, forever and ever by me."*

A single tear fell down my cheek and wiped it away with shadow. *"I love you too. Emon."*

Slowly, the howls of the demons around us grew more silent, the fires were pinpricks in the distance and nothing but a dark maroon night surrounded us within a shadowy landscape.

Zazion grunted and unfurled his wings, setting us down gently.

I staggered when sharp needle-like pain stabbed into my legs, having gone numb while the demon carried us like babes to safety. A large, black tipped hand steadied me.

"The caves are up ahead," he said low, his black eyes even darker in the dim light as he released me. "Your daughter is hidden within, under my own power, but it will end the minute you step inside. Follow the caves and you will find passage through the rest of these lands into Wrath's territory."

I nodded, letting go of his hand, my legs already healed. "If we are headed into the territory of Wrath, what is this territory called?"

Black eyes gleamed as they turned down towards me. "Greed. These are the lands of greed and she does not give up what is hers so easily. Remember that, Goddess of The Well."

Snapping out his wings, he hesitated. "Be sure to tell your fierce little fae queen goodbye for me, she is brave to face down a full grown demon prince of Hell, and for that she will always be welcomed here."

Then he launched himself powerfully into the night, disappearing in its deep red canopy.

CHAPTER 36

Remnant

"MAEDERE!" RIELLA CALLED OUT from a small lit fire deep in the heart of the cave we entered.

I didn't hesitate, dropping to my knees much like my heart did at hearing her call me mother in ancient fae and when her tiny body came crashing into me, I held her in reverence. Gripping her tightly to my chest, my hand cradled her head, kissing the top of it where her starry crown still perched.

Behind her the pookah watched on from its curled position. It nodded at me once before closing its eyes, unmoved by our heartfelt greeting.

Looking away from the strange spirit guide, I held Riella's away from me, assessing every part of her from her clean face and smoothly plaited braid, down to her fresh clothing and tidied appearance. Out of place, I plucked thick black needles sticking out from her raven locks and straightened the slight tilt in her glowing crown before pulling her back into me again, sighing with relief.

Riella was a polished jewel in the middle of Hell's inferno and I knew exactly who was responsible for that.

"You did good, shifter," I sent him through our bond, goddess damn him for making me fall even more in love with him. Surely my heart would break from all the ways he filled me so completely with his own.

His chest puffed and strained the fabric of his shirt, unable to call it dirty anymore, while his eyes glittered with pride. *"We took care of each other, just as you would have wished for us, little umbra but please don't make a habit of leaving us again. Neither of us relished the time apart."*

I sent him a tight smile. Wishing I could vow such a thing would never happen, but knowing I could not. Emon's eyes narrowed, realizing this too.

Peering over my side, Riella searched the cave's entrance. "Where is Zaz?"

I arched a brow at her. "Zaz? The demon?"

Her eyes swirled and she nodded. "Yes. I like him. He is good. In here." She touched her small hand to her chest just above the thick dragon scale.

Smiling at her, I nodded. "I believe you are right about that, my chickadee." Shaking my head, I added. "He cannot come with us, little one. He is a leader among his kind but he did tell me to say goodbye to you, that you are very brave, and you are always welcome in his territory."

Riella nodded, her eyes flashing bright gold before the emerald green swirled back into them. "The beasts in the woods told me that he is called the Prince of Greed."

I glanced up at Emon, who simply shrugged, setting our pack down and rummaging through its contents.

"What else did the beasts tell you?" I asked.

Mimicking her father, she shrugged. "Just that they are going to keep me here. They like me."

"Mine!" hissed the pookah behind her, conveniently awake now with its ear twitching.

My lips thinned on the territorial creature that was now *talking?* But Emon merely grunted, occupied with laying bed rolls beside the fire. Rummaging in the pack again, he growled softly and then chuffed with happiness, holding up a canister and white box like a trophy, a wide smile on his face.

Riella and I both stared at his triumphant grin.

"Dinner," he cooed, crossing his legs over each other and cradling the white box in his lap like a babe, he opened the contents and tossed the canteen out on the bed roll. "I can't think on an empty stomach and these pastries won't last another day. Who is hungry?"

My mouth watered. "Those are the pastries you made in Eithne?"

Emon nodded, his eyes sparkling. "Yes. Your brother packed them for me." Then he winked, "admit it, you like my baking better than Drey's."

Scooping Riella up and savoring the way she giggled in my arms, I joined Emon on the padded bedding with her tucked neatly into my own lap, "I will do no such thing. We owe Drey our lives."

"Indeed we do. I will make sure he is honored for the sacrifices he has made once this is all over." Emon pushed the white box of baked goods towards my daughter. "The brave princesses of shadows first."

Riella rolled her eyes. "Warriors, we are the brave shadow warriors, faedere."

Emon barked out a laugh and plucked another hidden needle from her hair. "Apologies my cub, of course you are warriors. There are no damsels here, as your mother reminded me earlier." He gave me a salacious smirk before biting off a chunk of dried meat that he had also taken from the pack.

Riella, oblivious to Emon's heated stare, dove for the white box, picking out the biggest pastry, a flakey layered bun of cinnamon spices and sweet honey glaze. Biting into it with a happy hum, she chewed it eagerly before taking another large bite immediately after.

I snickered and left the box to her greedy little hands, choosing the dried meats, not even realizing how hungry I was until the flavor hit my tongue. Finishing it quickly, Emon handed me a canteen of water, watching me quietly.

"There's something else I need to tell you," he said softly in my mind. *"There was a moment where I weakened in the woods, the soulless sleep is starting to take a bigger hold but that is not the biggest concern."*

I slowly lowered the canteen and released a shaky breath. *"How is that not the biggest concern, shifter?"* Staring at him with beseeching eyes, *"How bad was it?"*

Emon shrugged and grabbed another piece of meat, handing it to me but I refused, my stomach churning. His lips thinned. *"I will tell you more when you eat more. You asked for me to be truthful. This is me following your wishes but I will not do so if that means I watch you waste away with worry."*

I growled at him before bending down and whispering in our daughter's ear, "Pick one out for me, little one. Whatever one you want me to try?"

Snatching a golden brown pastry, she held it out for me. "Faedere told me you like chocolate when I made this one for you. It's on the *inside*," she said secretly through her mouthful of masticated pastry.

I took the chocolate stuffed croissant from her. "I do love chocolate." Taking a bite, she watched me beaming, and I winked down at her.

"Did I bake it right, maedere?"

I kissed her, leaving a chocolatey smudge on her cheek. "You did an excellent job, Riella."

She hummed again and returned back to her own treat, bouncing in my lap to her own energetic rhythm.

Meeting Emon's eyes again, I took another big bite pointedly. *"Start talking."*

His eyes dilated as he watched me chew before he shook his head. *"I heard Deirdre again. She said she would take my soul."*

"Obviously, I won't let that happen. I am the goddess of souls here," I snapped haughtily, despite my racing heart. *"You are not the only one she has reached out to in this realm,"* I admitted with a soft whisper in his mind.

Gold eyes narrowed on me sharply. *"What?"* he barked.

"I was knocked unconscious for a short time fighting the demons. I woke up just as her voice whispered to me...saying that I would come for her."

Emon's jaw clenched and he raked a hand over his braided hair, before scrubbing over his beard. *"That's twice now she has attempted to use her spirit ability to manipulate us."*

Finishing the delicious chocolate bun, I chewed thoughtfully. *"Fear. To sow doubt. To push us into making rash decisions. To distract us from a bigger threat."*

Emon grimaced. *"There were wraiths in the woods. Her reach has extended now into Hell. If that demon hadn't been there while the sleep took me...I am a liability now, Remnant. You must realize that."*

My heart thundered and I knew he could hear it. *"I will not. Even as a soulless you could never be a liability to me Emon...you are my reason."*

He grunted. *"There you go saying shit I am supposed to say to you."*

I smiled softly. *"You have made me a poet, shifter."* He grinned back and I looked back at Riella, sweeping off the sugar glaze from her cheek, my smile faltering. *"I am scared for her, Emon. If Deirdre can reach us in the spirit realm..."*

Blood drained from Emon's bronze skin, his eyes falling on our daughter, watching the way she ferociously attacked another pastry. "My cub," he said slowly, cautiously, "I am going to ask you something and I need you to think seriously about this."

Riella looked up, flakes of pastry falling from her face where honey glaze shined on her skin from the firelight. "Okay faedere."

"Has anyone visited you in your dreams?"

I did not breathe, waiting for her answer, Emon's hand reached out to mine, his warm heat steadying my panic, his strength bolstering mine.

Riella shook her head smiling. "No one has visited me." Her shoulders slumped and her bottom lips stuck out. "Should they be?"

My entire body melted into her, I had not realized how rigid I had been sitting. Tilting her head back, I peered into her beautiful swirling eyes. "Do not be sad, Riella, it is good that no one has visited you. Remember the beautiful queen statue in Atlantis?"

Riella's eyes widened and I felt her body shrink into me. "Yes."

I kissed her forehead. "She is also known as the blood goddess and the blood witch, the one you feared, little chickadee. And she wants us...all of us."

"Mine!" hissed the pookah again and hopped into my daughter's lap.

Riella giggled and scooped up the black bunny, hugging him to her chest, feeding him tiny bites of her pastry. "Don't worry maedere, Zaki says he will protect us."

Emon shifted closer, pulling us all into him on the bed roll. "Yes, thank you Zaki."

I arched a brow at him. When had he started taking a liking to the spirit guide?

Riella paused, looking back at him. "Faedere, what did it mean when Zaz called me heir to the Faerie throne? You did not seem to like it very much."

Our eyes met briefly over the top of Riella's head before Emon answered her softly, "it means that should you choose it, you are the true ruler of our world little cub, the queen of the fae and all of Faerie's creatures."

Riella nodded, completely unfazed, "Ohhh *that*, yes, I knew that already." She said simply, tossing the last bit of her pastry in her mouth.

Only the sound of her chewing and the crackling fire could be heard as Emon and I sat in stunned silence meant for the complete moronic.

I cleared my throat, "Riella, what do you mean you already knew?"

She licked at her fingertips, "every living thing that speaks to me calls me Faerie Queen. I thought it was because of my crown." She shrugged and then yawned. "Sounds like fun to be a queen, maybe I can help fix the world too. I even know the first thing I will do as a ruler."

"What is that, little one?" I asked in a hush whisper. I was in both awe of her easy acceptance but also fearful of her innocence of the magnitude of what this role truly would mean. A constant struggle of power and intrigue—-a sacrifice of who you wanted to be versus who you needed to be.

"I am going to raise Atlantis back to the surface where it belongs, so we can all live there as a family together. I want it to be the bridge between our worlds again. Just like Shen Shen said it used to be...and then he can visit me there too." She tugged on the large iridescent dragon scale on her neck smiling, before a large yawn escaped her.

Emon laughed softly and his voice was rough when he spoke, "if anyone can do this, I know it will be you my cub. I look forward to living in the sunken city of Atlantis with you one day." Tapping her nose, he grinned widely when she yawned a second time. "Now how about a bedtime story? Maybe one that has nothing to do with broken worlds, watery castles, and queens?"

Riella grinned, her lashes fluttering upwards at Emon. "Oh yes please faedere!"

"Emon..." I began but Emon shook his head at me.

"Let her dream, little umbra, she will learn one day what it truly means to be a queen and we will be there to help her should she decide this but for now...let her be a little faeling that dreams of castles and dragons, of heroic deeds and having a family." He leaned in and brushed my lips with his chastely, snickering in my mind. *"Just as you once dreamed to become the servant of a weretree, seeking their bite to become a wolf. How old were you then?"*

I pursed my lips, tilting my head at him, *"Ten."*

Emon grinned back at me, *"a ten year old faeling, running feral for weeks on end in the Wildwoods, dodging her guards, hunting a werewood. Raising Atlantis from the depths of the ocean seems to be a much safer dream for our daughter to have compared to yours near that age. Tell me, Remnant, do you still wish to be a wolf, or is a cat more your preference these days."*

I inhaled. Emon was far too good at distracting me from my worries but goddess I loved him for it. Before I could answer him, Riella tapped my arm.

"Maedere?"

Looking down at her, I could see that her eyes were half lidded. I doubted she would make it through the first sentence of Emon's story. "Yes?"

She sighed, "You need to fix my spear. The shadows disappeared when you were captured. Faedere says it was because of the irons."

I nodded, "Yes, of course I will make you a new one. I am sorry, little one."

She grinned happily before another thought captured her attention. "Madere?"

I ran the back of my hand over her smooth cheek, smiling patiently down at her, attempting to set aside the worries and allow the dreams to stay bright in her eyes, just like Emon suggested. Clever shifter, always in tune with others needs even even the ones I didn't think I required. "Yes, little chickadee?"

"What does my aura look like?"

I blinked.

Realizing I had never checked her aura since the first day we met when the Sanguine masked her true nature. Peering into the swirling gold and emerald of her eyes, I switched my sight and was awed.

Tears welled as I basked in the glory of a brilliant halo of rainbows, sparkling like the exploding stars in the Eithne. A mark of veneration and glory, a mark of a *true* queen.

Riella was what I always knew her to be. What Penina had already foresaw. A miracle of hope...the balanced future that Faerie needed to survive.

The demon had been right, there was no doubting it now, no wishing it to be different.

"Riella...my sweet little chickadee, your aura is the most beautiful array of rainbow halos I have ever seen." I felt my tears trickle down my face, "A perfect aura to match our perfect little faeling."

Emon quietly pulled us all in even closer, his hold tightening, his silent strength unwavering.

"Once upon a time," he began, his deep timber voice filled the cave, but I could hear the shakiness beneath. He was just as terrified but he held us up against this new storm all the same, always spreading his golden warmth even when everything felt dead and cold. "There was a young faeling who dreamed of becoming a wolf..."

CHAPTER 37

THE LAST TIME I watched my soulmate and daughter sleep, I was awestruck by their very presence, but now—now it felt like I was desperately clinging onto each breath, each heartbeat, feeling the seconds stripping away our future.

My time was running out, that much I knew, but the rest was needed. Hell was not for the tame, and we did not know what The Well would bring.

I stared at the letters stacked and bound neatly by a leather cord before me, the firelight highlighting the fine script lovingly marked on each thick sheet by my cramped ink stained hands.

I had run out of paper.

There were over a hundred letters and it still wasn't enough...not even fucking close.

No letter, no poem, no fucking story could ever come close to what I felt for the shadow fae laying beside the warmth of a fire with our daughter wrapped protectively in her arms. My soulmate was a warrior, a protector of beasts, a fiercely loyal friend, a cunning strategist, a sensual lover, and now a doting mother ready to sacrifice herself to the world. I fucking loved every broken piece of her, honored to stand by her side, and yet I wrote letters...like a goddess damn coward.

Disgusted, I swiped up the stack, and growling at the perfectly folded pieces of paper, I placed them with great care back into the pack—knowing they would be safe until the time came.

Time.

Fuck whoever invented time. They were torturous bastards who must have savored its painfully slow passage and yet—relished accelerating its sadistic torment into having one beg for just a few more seconds of its cruel passing.

I did not enjoy falling prey to its ruthless schemes and I could feel the slightest changes in my body begin. The soulless sleep would not be much longer now.

Snarling silently, I rose and started to quietly pace, picking my way along the rocky interior of the cave. I was a fucking mess of emotions with the physical charged intensity of a beast...I needed to feel the same strain on my body that I now felt weighing heavily on every fabric of my soul.

Keeping enough distance to not wake my daughter and mate but close enough to still see them in the fire glow, I dropped into the shadows of the cave, and began to move. Silently, I shifted in and out of forms, physically exerting my body to erase the deep ache that was festering inside of me and then—releasing it. Finally able to breathe deeper, clearer, and calmer.

I could smell my soulmate's natural floral perfume steadying my heart, the cinnamon spices still left on my daughter's soft breath was the best air in my lungs, and the warmth from the scent of ash easing the knots in my body.

But there was also something else.

I sniffed again, noticing an odd underlying smell within the moment of tranquility.

The scent of waterlogged decaying meat.

Eyes snapping to the darkness, I dropped into a crouch, slowly backing towards the firelight, each step quiet and soft as I concentrated on the new unwelcome scent.

"Wake, little umbra," I jolted her with the sharp internal command.

Emerald eyes flew open instantly, the shadows snapping over our daughter and out in front of me as she sprang from the bed roll. Searching the cave, she went back towards the pack, slinging it over her shoulder, while at the same time drawing a blade from its depths.

"Friend or foe?" she whispered to me.

My claws lengthened, inhaling deeply, I shook my head, *"What is the difference in these lands?"* I whispered back to her, tilting my head as the scent grew closer.

"Time?" Her calmness a balm to the rising predator thrashing inside of me wanting to protect.

"None. It's already here. It watches and it waits." I scanned the darkness tracking its almost silent movement, and then I turned with it.

It was circling us.

Remnant crouched and I could see her waking Riella, pressing her hand softly over our daughter's mouth as she woke with a small squeak. Blinking up at her mother, confusion lined her perfect petite brow.

Suddenly the scent of putrid meat and salty water was everywhere—behind us, in front of us, above us.

"Run!" I bellowed to my soulmate and daughter as I lunged into the path of a gigantic fin framed head, mouth open wide and dripping with snake-like fangs. Its strike was aimed to devour my mate and child in one swallow. I grunted when my shoulder met its massive skull, pounding it straight into the unforgiving cave wall. Pinning it there, I roared over my shoulder to Remnant, "follow the caves into the deep!"

Jumping away from the fall of crumbling slate the massive creature shrieked, its cries bellowing loudly within the cave causing a cataclysmic rain of more rock and the snuffing out the fire's glow, draping us all in darkness.

Snarling, I shifted with ease and my panther eyes adjusting perfectly to the sudden depth of black and highlighting the color of smells, movements, and sounds. In the distance, I could hear the lightest footfalls of my soulmate and the whisper of shadow that could only be my daughter blurring alongside her.

I grinned inwardly. Jar had been right, her power was manifesting itself just when she needed it the most and it was growing stronger with each passing day, as was her scent.

Prowling back and forth, I assessed the beast thrashing its great finned head back and forth—a head attached to a long scaly snake-like body. Stunned, the massive creature shook off the momentary blow and turned back towards me. Mouth opened wide, it sent me a violent hiss, full of fangs that spat poisonous venom in my direction.

Sidestepping the spray, I watched the deathly liquid burn deep holes into our bedding and through the rock underneath it while serpentine white eyes glared with deadly retribution.

Dipping my head low, I bared my teeth in challenge, hissing ferally back, my tail flicking back and forth with each slow prowl. I just needed the damned thing to keep its attention on me—only on me.

Pleased that my daughter and soulmate's hearts were becoming fainter with the growing distance, I snarled again, watching the creature's serpentine body curl at the threat while my mind searched to categorize this new beast of Hell.

Sharp teeth, fanged venom, wide flaring fins upon its snake-like head, vertical white eyes, iridescent scales shifting in color, a long coiling body with a powerful finned tail meant to propel within something much different than dry land.

My eyes widened. An oilliphéist.

It had been a long time since I had come across the great worms of the water, natural enemy of the water dragons and much more primitive in their insatiable appetites, they once overtook the seas like parasites, breeding much quicker and faster than the dragons, and robbing the sea of its resources. When the time came for intervention the courts hunted them to the brink of extinction—the great solstice hunt of the lakes and seas.

My father once came home with the head of one. He dragged its bloody carcass inside and was nearly murdered himself by my mother for it.

I eyed the massive scaled body of the worm serpent in front of me. It had to be three times bigger than the one my father had proudly mounted on a wall in our home.

"I smell my youngs' blood on your hands, shifter fae," a feminine hiss caressed the inside of my skull.

I tilted my head with sudden understanding...this wasn't just *any* oilliphéist, it was *the* mother of them all. *"caoránach,"* I growled back.

A forked tongue flickered in the air. *"Smart little shifter king but not smart enough not to enter my lair. I will savor the taste of your young in payment of the ones I smell staining your claws,"* the demon mother of worms hissed.

Fuck Zazion, he wasn't lying when he said his protection would be lifted once we entered the cave but he certainly played his omission card well.

Feeling darkness brush against my fur, I glanced down to see the shadows shifting around me. I chuckled, slinking into them. *"We will pass on your midnight snack, mother of worms."* Fully camouflaged and hidden both in scent and sight, I watched its panicked forked tongue flicker frantically for my presence.

I grinned. The caoránach was blinded without her senses to rely on. It shrieked, lunging and snapping its jaws mindlessly into the darkness. Slowly, I backed away towards the deep recesses of the cave where I could feel the pulsing bond of my soulmate. My trust in the demon prince of greed was becoming less and less as I quickly picked across bones of recent and long dead demon remains.

"Emon?" Remnant whispered in my head and my gaze scanned the room quickly, frowning. *"Up here shifter."*

Narrowing my panther eyes, I looked up to see Remnant and my daughter perched on a rocky ledge.

Dropping low, every muscle of my body coiled before springing my massive cat body upwards, landing softly on top of the outcropping in a silent crouch.

Remnant's lips pursed as she looked up into my feline eyes. *"It's a dead end...unless."* She waved towards a deep pit at the center of the cave I had moved around in search of them.

I shifted back, holding back a grunt when our daughter silently jumped towards me, gripping my leg tightly. I patted her head affectionately and then sniffed at the air towards the pit. *"Water?"* I shivered, peering down at its never ending depths.

Remnant nodded.

I shook my head. *"Too risky. There has to be another way."*

There was a large snapping of bone and all three of us looked up suddenly. I flinched at the soft hiss that echoed off the cave walls stirring the decaying stench.

Remnants eyes widened. *"Please tell me that it is not what I think it is?"*

"A caoránach, mother of demon water worms? Sorry to disappoint."

Riella shivered next to us, backing away suddenly from the terrifying beast and tripping back against the rocky wall, setting off a waterfall of slated rock downwards. Reacting quickly, Remnant weaved her shadows, concentrating on muffling the sound so that not a single one clattered downward. The only proof was a plume of dust billowing around us, and then—Riella sneezed.

The three of us froze. The sound so horrifyingly loud in the silence of the cave that it seemed the entire world stopped to listen to it.

A cackling cross between a hiss and a roar followed quickly after and the large serpent crashed into the room. Her scaled body bouncing off the inner walls of the cave coiling higher and higher the more it infiltrated the space.

Riella's lip quivered at her innocent mistake, looking up at me with fear in her eyes. Quickly, I pulled her into my arms as Remnant weaved more shadow to mask us from the caoránach's senses.

Its finned head swiveled around the room, white eyes glowing brighter in the pure dark with only the disturbed water sloshing out of the pit echoing off the walls. "No where to hidesssss," it cooed into the dark, this time for all of us to hear.

I glanced down at the pit and then back to my soulmate, her lips thinning while she pulled out the cú sith fang, reweaving the shadow shaft for the deadly tooth before passing it to our daughter, bending to kiss the top of her head in solidarity. Looking back up at me, she nodded sharply, jerking the straps tightly across her petite frame, the muscles in her arms making her brands ripple.

I resisted the urge to rub at my own arms, instead I did the opposite and pulled the dirtied pink sleeves of my shirt further down, stooping to my crestfallen daughter, whispering into her mind. *"We are going to jump in for a swim, little warrior cub. Any part of that worm even comes close to you, you stab it with your weapon, understand?"*

My daughter's eyes lowered down to the exposed pit then back up to me, biting at her trembling lip, she nodded. *"I am afraid, faedere,"* her tiny voice whispered back.

I grunted softly, brushing back the strands of her hair that had escaped her braid. *"Fear is good Riella. I am afraid too. But it won't stop us, will it?"*

Her eyes flashed a solid gold while she listened. Her grip tightening. *"No."* Her voice strong once more.

Glancing over to Remnant, I nodded, *"We are ready, little umbra."*

Licking her lips she wove a halo of shadow around her head, forming it into a bubble around her before doing the same for Riella and I.

"We will have about thirty minutes of air, shifter. Swim swiftly and hard."

Hissing loudly the caoránach slammed its fangs into the wall only a few feet away, sending crumbling stones cascading around us. I lifted Riella into my arms. *"Count down for me, my cub."*

Riella's voice was but a whispered breath inside my mind. *"Three,"* I stepped us both towards the edge. *"Two,"* she breathed, peering down at the pit as I aimed our jump, her hand trembling around the spear and my shoulder. *"One."*

I jumped, the decaying stench of fish hitting my nostrils full force as I clutched my daughter tightly into my chest, looking up to see my soulmate watching grimly onward.

A shriek slammed into the cave walls and echoed around us in a chaotic symphony of the grotesque. The demon worm's coiled body unwound swiftly, blindly lashing outwards for our location, nearly catching us mid-fall but the shadows were there, punching it forcibly away, causing more wailing that sent my teeth clenching.

My eyes never left my mate when she jumped down from the ledge only to slide down the looped body of the caoránach. I watched in fucking awe as she launched herself off the demon worm, twisting in a head long dive away from a venomous strike and punching her shadows straight into its jaw.

"Savage little umbra, you aren't falling for me all over again are you?"

Breaking into the deep water, her hair swarmed around her in a dark halo like a fallen gorgeous angel of death, fitting for being in Hell.

"Whatever do you mean, shifter? I have never stopped."

CHAPTER 38

Remnant

A GODDESS FORSAKEN ICE plunge—that's what this water felt like as the bubbles foamed around us in the dark waters. Tickling along our bodies...downward?

I frowned. That was strange. And so was the immense pressure of the churning water...as if I had entered somehow into the deep ocean floor instead of just breaking its surface.

Warm smooth skin brushed against the pebbled chill of my own. Squinting, Emon's hand pointed down while still holding onto our daughter. Her spear still grasped tightly in her hands. *"Up is down, down is up. I have a feeling we are no longer in Greed territory, little umbra."*

Looking downward, my brows raised at the sudden flashes of light shooting through even heavier churning waves—the dark waters were lighter below us and a pitch black cavernous darkness above.

Blowing another bubble out from my shadow mask, I watched as it trailed downwards. My shifter soulmate was right, this realm was mirror layered.

Flipping over, Emon began to swim and I followed, watching with amusement as Riella flipped and twirled in the water, she was in her element—her first home having been the ocean.

My chest tightened. Did she miss it? Would she like the life Emon and I could provide her if we succeeded in saving Faerie? And where exactly would that be? The shifter fae court, the ruins of Faerie, the shadow fae court, perhaps back to my beloved cabin in the Wildwoods? Or would Riella do as she dreamed and raise Atlantis?

A tingling rush of foaming bubbles suddenly flew around us and with it the gaping mouth of the demon worm. *"Swim faster! The caoránach comes!"* I screamed at Emon, grasping for the shadows made by the flashing light below us...or was it above us, damn the goddess to Sheol, I had no idea anymore.

"You better be fucking right behind me, little umbra," Emon snarled in my mind. I didn't dare look up, keeping all my attention on the deadly and pissed off caoránach zig zagging in the churning waters with amazing speed, its ghostly white eyes boring into me, fins widening like a cobra head ready to strike.

"I am behind you," I sent back.

"Goddess damn it, Remnant," he snarled back at the same time as the worm serpent bellowed.

"You cannot escape me!"

Netting the shadows, I cast them outward, ensnaring the creature's snarling mouth and then constricting the darkness to slam it shut. A moaning wail shattered through the waters and I tightened the remaining shadows quickly around my wrist, saying a silent prayer before dodging out of the Caoránach's careening path. Holding tight to the shadows I had entangled the beast in, I twirled violently around it before slamming hard into its thick scaled back. Gasping, the air was punched from my body with the extra weight of our bag smothering me.

Gritting my teeth and struggling to inhale, I tightened my legs around the mother demon worm's thick body squinting through the rushing water. Hanging on desperately, it bucked and altered its course, propelling straight for my soulmate and daughter.

Loosening the tension in my body, adjusting to the extra weight at my back, my thighs tightened on my stolen ride, and

I conformed to its movements. Focusing all my energy on the massive amount of shadows I was wielding, I allowed calm to settle over me. This was a matter of life or death for my family now and I could not fuck this up.

Encasing them in shadows, I portled them, a trick my brother and mother used often, while the caoránach charged through empty seas. Within seconds my family was delivered in the shadows behind me, directly onto the back of the deadly worm.

"Hold tight!" I screamed into Emon's mind, instantly feeling his strong arms wrapping around my torso, sandwiching our daughter between us, her spear tilted forward over my shoulder.

"I thought we had agreed that I'd be the only beast you'd be riding from now on," Emon griped, but he could not fully hide the laughter smothered beneath his sullenness.

I smiled despite the strain. *"I would be foolish to make such an agreement, shifter but I can vow that yours is the only ride that can thoroughly satisfy me so transcendently."*

Together the three of us spiraled into a vast vortex of water and Emon's hold tightened, keeping Riella locked between us. The caoránach wailed through its shadow bonds with furious frustration. Its hisses sending raging bubbles around us while bright green venom leaked from her clamped mouth.

The dizzying spins continued and Riella screamed as we broke the surface of the raging waters, the serpent's propulsion sending us corkscrewing into a sudden blast of ice cold winds, and bright lightning. An angry ocean rose as we climbed above it, attempting to reclaim us back into its deep dark depths. Straining, my tenuous hold on the shadows broke and we became momentarily weightless.

Frantically, I reached for more shadows but was unable to grasp them as we began to fall, the gigantic worm wriggling in the stormy skies below us before a blur of shadow rushed by me. For the briefest of moments, my heart was overjoyed. My shadows had come, they freed themselves from Deirdre's clutches and came to save us.

Then Emon's roar, so loud it broke over the ferocious winds and thunderous cracking of lightning, shattered that small amount of hope I had, sending nothing but frozen fear straight down my spine.

"Riella!" he screamed, reaching for our daughter, but she was mere shadows now, blurring away from him with only a glinting cú sithe fang flashing through the pelting rain.

Seeing its oncoming death, the creature rotated, stretching its finned head upwards towards my shadow shifter daughter. I recognized this type of desperation. The demon worm mother knew her end was coming and she would take whatever she could with her—to be buried together in the dark graves of the ocean.

But I was *also* a mother and nothing would ever take my daughter from me.

No creature could ever take her from me.

No god could ever say I wouldn't sacrifice everything I had to keep her safe.

No death would I ever succumb to where I left her alone in this world.

Twisting hard, I weaved the last bit of shadow I could, snapping the caoránach mouth shut one final time. Its muffled screams carried on the harsh winds and white eyes turned towards me—full of loathing and outrage before Riella's bás fang spear pierced its thick skull. Splitting it into two, the entire sky rippled with a bright explosion of light, blasting outwards for miles as we fell through the sky, ending the demon mother of worms for good.

Diving steeply with rain pelting my face, I raced after my daughter, catching her and careful of the spear, I wrapped her in my arms. "Shhh, I got you, my little chickadee. I'm here." Inhaling, I cradled her dark entity into my chest, feeling her transform back to her faeling self, right before we plunged, returning to the ocean depths.

Together we kicked upwards, breaking the surface quickly as the sea tossed us in its violent storm. I smiled into the most beautiful solid emerald eyes of my daughter, her deadly spear still clutched in her hand as we both kicked hard, struggling to stay above water in the roaring crash of waves.

"You did it, Riella!" I cried out to her, kissing the ice cold bronze skin of her forehead, careful not to dunk her back into the ocean depths.

Spitting out the salty ocean, Emon broke the surface with a vicious growl, having followed us just moments after. "I fucking hate goddess damn water!" he growled, swiping at it. Retaliating, another dark wave crested and crashed, bombarding us back into its cold clutches.

Coughing and sputtering, all three of us broke the surface together this time.

"Maedere!" Riella pointed, smiling. "Look, it's Zaki!"

Bobbing in the water, I narrowed my gaze on the red eyes of the pookah upon the great bow of a very large metal ship. Fiery burning stacks lined its surface and billowed large puffs of smoke into torrential rain, suffocating the thunder clouds above.

A sudden force of water, similar to the powers of the water fae, swirled around us and tightened before it wrenched us straight out of the ocean's hold towards whatever fate had prepared for us next.

Splattering aboard on an unforgiving steel deck, I rolled into a crouch, water sluicing off of me as I rose, the shadows looming over the great metal ship in tall pillars around me. A bright light flashed and then a fierce growl hovered just above.

Glancing up, I took in the magnificent sight of Riella, sitting proudly astride her father's beast. Hair plastered to her face, her crown tilted and flashing from the bright lightning, a dragon scale waving in the hungry winds, and her spear rising fiercely above her head, she looked...like a Faerie queen.

Ignoring the fear I had for what this would mean for my daughter one day, I faced forward, and peered at a giant dark silhouette outlined by a roaring fire. A shovel, held by this massive figure, scraped against the deck of the ship, feeding coal into a hissing fire splattered by the rain.

"Who are you?" I demanded, drawing the shadows with a flourishing wave, swirling them to circle around us, framing the outline of a shield.

Lightning struck the deck of the ship in response, hot flashes of charged light shooting out across the metal surface racing towards us only to be replaced by bright silver eyes. Eyes that blinked against the harsh rain on a handsome blue face that was full of a matted beard, sparkling with tiny iridescent seashells braided within its white strands. Thick black scales lined his exposed neck and rose around the outline of his chiseled face. His thick frame growing larger and larger as he stepped closer to us, undisturbed by the violent rocking of the ship.

"Céad míle fáilte, a hundred thousand welcomes. Ye dinnae know how honored and humbled I am t' take ye t' The Well o' Souls, Goddess," he grinned with a mouth full of needled teeth that looked just like a water fae. "I am called Lir."

CHAPTER 39

Remnant

"Lir," I REPEATED, MY body tensing to keep in motion with the lurching of the ship. "The lost king of the water fae?"

His smile faltered. "Lost? Nay lass, I visit the seas for the sweet melody o' mi children's songs, I follow them in any direction I please. Mi cursed bonnie ex wife be the one ye ought tae thank for this raging storm. Dinnae know why she be such nippet wumman after all this time."

Fierce winds slammed into the giant fae, but he only grunted, smiling.

"Haud yer wheesht ye bloody hen. Ye cursed mi faelings and ye deserve ye fate, mi leannan!"

Emon chuckled in my mind. *Did he just tell the storm to shut up and that it deserved to be cursed while also tenderly referencing it as his love?*

I blinked at the crazed giant sea king. *Yes.* I shook my head, water running down my face in rivulets, my exposed body gone numb minutes ago. *"He'd be crazy to still love her. She literally turned his four children into the north, south, east, and west winds to taunt him with their voices but to never hold them again, all from jealousy."*

"If I remember correctly, Faerie was furious, and cursed his wife to the same fate, except her voice would never be heard."

I eyed the sea king who was still grinning into the face of the brutal gusts. *"I think she is making herself heard just fine."* Stepping forward, I anchored my feet with shadows to prevent myself from going overboard, the waves sloshing across the deck and over my already soaked boots. "Lir, you said you would take us to The Well of Souls? Does that mean we are in Wrath territory."

His needled smile turned back towards me, shaking out his matted beard. "Aye, dinnae ken where else ye see storms like this except for Wrath territory? Mi sweet wee Fi told mi you'd be here. Her wee song will guide us, take us t' The Well. She has taken to ye and I will do anything for mi faeling—" A fierce slap of wind and rain, shook the tied shells from his beard and his silver eyes glowed brightly. "Bite mi bawsack, ye radge wee shite!" he howled back and the seas suddenly lurched the ship harder.

I wavered with clenching teeth. Whatever this crazed sea king had just said, it seemed his ex wife did not appreciate it that much.

"Best ye be heading t' the cabin hull, lass!" Lir turned his back to us, stomping over to his shovel once more. "The seas of Wrath are raging t'nigh' and mi ex wife seems to be in fits."

The ship lurched again and I crouched, smirking when Emon's nails raked across the deck surface before he leapt towards the cabin hull with our daughter clutching at his hide.

The sea king chuckled, "Wee cat dinnae like water, aye? Unlike that beast there."

Swiping my plastered hair from my face, I turned to see the lightning highlight the sky where red eyes of the pookah glared at me through the gale winds as if it had something to prove.

Rolling my own eyes, I released the shadows. "Thank you for the shelter, Lir."

The sea king grunted once, turning his back to shovel in more coal. "Off with ye lass, get dry. It's gonna be a long nigh'."

I pursed my lips, effectively dismissed. Turning towards the cabin, I stumbled against the harsh rocking. It was the least graceful I had ever felt in my entire life, and I threw open the door like it was my lifeline, slamming it shut.

Best to leave the laughing crazed wind talking water fae to his own resources for now.

Warmth and tranquility embraced me and I sighed with relief when the rocking of the ship disappeared and the floor beneath my feet was level...unmoving. Thank the goddess this cabin was enchanted to provide all our needs, including a stable surface, much like the cabin of the Wildwoods.

Steaming warm fluffy white towels shimmered in front of me and I snatched one up with a sigh, rubbing my wet face raw, bringing back to it what the icy ocean and bitter winds had stolen.

Tossing the now damp towel aside I grabbed another, walking towards a roaring fire emanating from a large steel potbelly stove. Wood was neatly stacked from floor to ceiling against the walls surrounding it. Glinting in the firelight, Riella's bás fang spear hung nearby where Emon and Riella sat.

Our daughter's face stared vacantly into the fire and her body trembled harshly with chill. My soulmate was swiftly drying her off to bring warmth back to her cold petite frame but failed to see that it wasn't just her skin that was frozen.

My boots, full of water, squished noisily before I crouched low in front of my sweet little faeling. Her eyes were still solid in that beautiful vivid green but they stared past me, haunted and full of pain. My hand reached out to gentle Emon's aggressive drying and he paused confused, pulling away the third wet towel he had used. Taking the heated towel in my hands, I cloaked her in its warmth then cupped her sweet cherub face to look up at me.

"Riella?" I said gently.

A pair of emeralds turned outward, finally registering that I was there and large pools of tears began to fill her eyes.

"Oh Riella," I sighed, pulling her shocked towel clad body to mine, tucking her into me and turning towards the fire so that she could feel its blazing heat.

Emon watched us with worry furrowing his brow.

Our daughter's chest rattled then and a soft heaving cry broke the sound of the crackling fire. Turning her face into my wet leather, she began to sob. Her entire body trembling anew but this time not from the cold.

I breathed a sigh of relief that she was feeling again. A heart that was frozen would never heal and would fester. I would not want such a fate for my daughter. I wished that she'd never be harmed in the first place, but we were fae, and this was a cruel world.

"It's okay," I said, stroking the wet strands of her disheveled braid, rocking her to me. Emon shifted closer, draping another warm towel around me before wrapping his arms around us both.

"Little Umbra?" His worry penetrated my mind.

I looked up into his strong golden gaze, pecking his lips softly, *"All will be okay now."*

Riella choked, drawing our attention back to her. Using her arms to wipe her nose loudly, snot and tears smeared across her forearm. I grimaced. Tissues shimmered into our laps and we all stared at them blankly before Emon grunted and plucked one from the box, deftly wiping up the aftermath of her mess.

"Why do you cry, my little cub?" he rumbled from his chest.

More tears pooled in Riella's eyes before she buried her face back into me, shuddering with renewed grief.

Holding her tightly I hummed. "Oh, little chickadee. I think I know why...it is the caoránach, isn't it?"

Riella sniffed loudly, rubbing her face against me, her soft whispered yes barely audible.

I kissed the top of her head and allowed her tears to fall, rocking her steadily as she grieved the slain demon mother of worms. Emon plucked another tissue, his face stricken, holding it at ready but looking incredibly lost just the same.

Suddenly snatching it from his hand, Riella blew her nose loudly, like a bellowing horn inside the ship's cabin, and then returned to her crying. And so, the process continued as minutes passed by and tissues piled up beside us. When her body slumped against me and her breath evened on a slow exhale, Emon scooped up the mountain of snotty tissues and threw them into the fire, returning quickly back.

"I know she wanted to hurt us," Riella whispered, "but when I...when I—" Her lip quivered and more tears slid over her bronze cheeks, staining them in rivulet paths.

I tucked back her hair tenderly. "I was four when I first killed a fae," I confessed to her softly, staring out into the fire, feeling Emon's saddened gaze raking over my profile. "I was careless, fearless, playing beyond the boundaries of our home, on the outer crater edges of the Nocturnes." Riella's wide eyes peered up at me and I smiled remorsefully into the flames. "She was very beautiful, the blood fae that attacked me, I'll never forget her hair was just as red as my blood when she tore into me with her fanged teeth, right before the shadows pierced her heart."

Riella's small hand reached to gently cradle my face, drawing me back from the memory, and I tilted my head into her soft touch.

"My mother found me hours later clinging to the lifeless blood fae's body. I couldn't let her go, part of me felt that if I never did, I could bring her back. Find a different way." I sighed and turned to press my lips into her hand with a gentle kiss. "We will never know for sure but there was one thing my mother said to me that I have never forgotten."

A single tear fell down my daughter's face and she sniffed. "What did she say?"

I wiped her tears again. "The kindest death is the one followed by grief even if it be our enemy."

Riella frowned and then the emerald in her eyes swirled with her normal gold spilling back in. "I think I understand."

Taking her hand, I held it tight to my chest. "Take your time to grieve, my little chickadee." I leaned into Emon's damp heat, drawing on his strong quiet strength.

"We will be right here, my cub, loving and protecting you while you do," Emon added, his arms tightening again around us.

CHAPTER 40

E XHAUSTED, OUR DAUGHTER CRIED herself to sleep in her mother and I's arms. Tenderly, I cradled her sleeping body into me and rose. The cabin had shimmered moments before, providing a sleeping quarters complete with unicorn decor that was just her size and a large flower petal bed. Tucking the soft pink petals over her small frame, my vision blurred.

Fuck.

Gasping, I stumbled backwards, reaching the door frame and gritting my teeth against the sudden onslaught of weakness to quietly shut the door. My claws digging into the arched opening to keep myself upright even as my heart beat slowed.

I was out of time.

Squinting through my blurred vision, I peered across the cabin at the silhouette of my soulmate highlighted in the fire's glow. She was peeling off her wet clothing revealing the luminous pale skin of her back, the long waves of her wet hair falling sensually across it like a lover's caress. Blue highlights shimmered in the dim light and her toned muscles rippled as she dropped the wet leather with a splat.

Sensing me, her emerald eyes flashed over her tattooed shoulder, tucking her chin atop it coyly. My heart rate sped up and with it—the return of my strength. Evidently, I didn't need god blood in my veins to cure me...all I needed was my half goddess soulmate to entice me in a fucking strip tease.

I smirked inwardly, no wonder her asshole father hadn't mentioned this particular cure.

Hiding the claw marks on the doorframe by resting my shoulder against it, I folded my arms with a challenging smile. "By all means, don't let me stop you, my little umbra," I purred.

Her lips parted in a soft inhale before her delicate pink tongue swiped across her full lips making my pulse jump wildly. Hypnotized, she hooked her thumbs inside the hem of her skin tight shorts and shimmied them down over the delicious pale globes of her ass. I rumbled with an encouraging growl and she smirked back at me before peeling the wet clothing down her toned legs, kicking them to the side. Pivoting seductively, she faced me, naked, in only her waterlogged boots that laced to her mid thigh.

I fucking forgot to breath.

She was a goddess damn vision of my most depraved dreams and I was a young male fae caught with his dick in hand, not knowing how to proceed—a faerie fucking mess.

Panting, I followed her hand as it trailed down over her chest, running along the inner curve of her breast and then straight over the cut muscular lines of her stomach before dipping between her legs.

"Fuck," I croaked and I glanced briefly at the entrance of the cabin, where just outside the storm raged and a mad sea king laughed at the wind. Reading my wicked thoughts, the cabin responded with a soft click, locking both the outer door and our daughters.

I fucking loved these ship quarters.

Remnant's hand played with herself while she watched me salaciously, her eyes burning into the long sleeved pink unicorn shirt I still wore. It was a goddess damn miracle it made it this far...that I hid *it* this far. "Take those damp clothes off shifter, and come warm up your soulmate."

Licking at my descending fangs and feeling my dick press uncomfortably against the wet leathers I still wore, I shoved off the doorframe, praying to the goddess that I fucking had the strength to make it across the room—I'd crawl on my knees if I had to.

"My clothes are just about dry, my love. Perhaps I'll keep them on for a few moments longer, so that only you steal this show, just like you steal my breath..." Close enough to touch her, I took her hand from between her legs and lapped up the taste of her, "and my heart."

The soulless sleep had the worst fucking timing, I knew it wouldn't be much longer now, but I could not think of a better way to fall into a deathly sleep than for my waking dreams to put me there.

"How much, shifter?" Remnant whispered and I pulled my mouth from her fingers, staring down into her gorgeous eyes that implored me to share all my secrets—and I would have, the moment I had learned them, I would have confessed them all, on my knees *if* it wasn't the one thing I knew that was helping to keep her alive. "How much more do you think I'll tolerate your omitted truths before I break."

My brow arched and I smirked down at her. "I know for a fact that you can tolerate anything I deliver and when you break it's the sexiest thing I've ever seen."

Trailing her hands up her body she cupped her breasts, she was breathless with her next command. "Take off your shirt, shifter."

My chest rattled with my harsh inhale watching her touch herself only inches from me. "My shirt..." I murmured.

"Mmhmm," she purred at me, pinching her nipples between her fingertips. "I need you, Emon and I ache so bad...take off your shirt. Let me see you. Let me feel you."

My tongue licked at my fangs, fixated on her naughty hands. I took a hungry step forward but she countered, the same desperate space between us as before. Fire raged inside of me, my desirous need pulsing as my head snapped up, assessing her like she was prey. I tilted my head. "If you run, then I will hunt. I won't apologize if your game is to provoke the beast."

I watched as my deep husky purr made her body shiver, her heart beat wildly in her chest, her breath increase, a slow blush straining her pale skin. But instead of melting at my feet, she grinned.

"Awe, is my big bad kitten pouting?"

I took one step forward, she took one step back. My claws flexed at my sides. Desire and frustration thundering through me, I breathed deep, changing tactics. "Come to me, little umbra. If you ache, then allow me to soothe you."

Her thighs clenched together and the sweet smell of her sex clouded all my senses. "What I ache for Emon...is your body, I want it and I wish to see it, take off your shirt my shifter king."

My mouth watered, my soulmate was like falling into a pool of ambrosia when she stood before me like this, clouding my senses, my reason, my judgment. Snarling, I reached for my shirt, my claws hooking into the fabric, tearing it slightly with my desperation, peeking up at her through my lashes, I saw the flash of triumph glittering in her emerald green eyes.

My brows rose and I dropped my hands, exhaling shakily even when my body screamed at me to comply. "No."

Her eyes narrowed and her hands fell on the flare of her naked hips. "No?"

I grinned, growling through my teeth. "No."

"Take it off," she snapped, stepping forward. This time it was me stepping gracefully back.

I was a patient predator and I never did mind playing bait, especially if it meant my reward was her.

Shadows gathered around the room and my dick throbbed at this savage sight of her—fury and longing, wrath and yearning, it warred within her and it was fucking gorgeous.

"Emon..." she warned, raising the shadows. "Take. It. Off."

"Make. Me." I echoed her tone back.

Remnant snarled, her teeth bared, and my body burned to possess her this way, every instinct made me want to lunge for her, and I trembled with every second that I held back. "Just remember that I did give you a chance."

My smile brightened just before her shadows lunged for me. Despite my looming sleep, I still had one last reserve to play, one more memory to take with me. Tapping into my shifter speed, I blurred around the room, then back towards her, the loud smack of my hand on her bare ass echoed off the ship's hull, followed by the delicious sound of her loud gasp.

"Too slow, shadow fae," I purred into her ear, before blurring again. It was the last of my strength but it was worth it when her shadows surrounded me and I crouched low in the darkened corner of the room even as I felt my heartbeat slow once again, the slightest disturbance to my vision.

Fuck that. There was only one force that would ever bring me to my knees and I'd fight death itself to keep it that way. The sleep could wait a moment longer.

"Am I?" she snickered from the other side of the room as I watched the way her breasts and ass swayed with each seductive stride from my hiding place. "There is nowhere you can hide shifter...I am the darkness that resides in you, there is no place you can go where I won't be able to follow.

"There you go saying the shit I should be saying to you, my sexy little umbra. I have to admit, if you seek me every time in this way, I can guarantee you will always find me."

A sharp slap on my ass sent me sprawling from the darkness. Bellowing with laughter, I rolled over, surrendering to the shadow mischief in which she played—too weak to fight them and too turned on to care, I allowed myself to be dragged across the ship's floor until I was presented at her feet, staring up at her naked sex and the satisfaction in her emerald eyes.

"Fuck," I swallowed hard, my dick straining against my pants so much now that it was painful.

With a slight twitch of her fingertips, my arms were shoved above my head, the pink shirt riding up and exposing half my torso from the aggressive hold of her darkness.

"Fuck," I groaned again.

"It seems it is you who has been reduced to monosyllabic words this time shifter, and I am not even done with you yet." Remnant laughed above me before stepping over my body and lowering to straddle my hips, exposing her glorious naked sex for my eyes to hungrily devour. I grunted when the shadows yanked my arms up higher and my hips raised achingly upwards needing her touch in any way I could get it.

Shadows slammed my body forcibly back down again and a dark chuckle rumbled from me. "Savage," I whispered in worship.

She smiled lethally back, half kneeling over me, so that I could just barely feel her damp heat without her exquisite touch.

"You have refused to undress," she began, running her hand down her upper thigh, her hair tumbling in a dark mess over her pale naked skin and tickling the not so pink fabric of my shirt before she skimmed the laces of her boot to draw a sharp knife hidden within it. "And...I gave you my word not to use my powers to undress you." The knife flashed in the dim light when she twirled it along her knuckles. "You leave me no choice."

I was panting...drooling and aching like a slobbering mutt and when she teased the knife along the exposed skin of my abdomen where my shirt had been riding up from her forceful play, a guttural groan escaped me.

"Fucking goddess. Yes. Do it," I hissed. I was past caring anymore, my sheer need riding hard as the soulless sleep beckoned me. My eyes were hooded with exhaustion and desire—I could not tell the difference anymore. All I knew was that I surrendered to my beautiful dark haired goddess that owned my very soul.

Peering down at me with love and worry in her gorgeous eyes, she held my gaze as she forcibly gripped the collar of the unicorn shirt and started to slice through the fabric. My panting breath increased with each slow buttery slide of her blade.

Flipping the knife in her hand so that its deadly tip faced her now, she ran its hilt up my bare chest, opening up the two sides of my ruined shit, and tracing the hard edges of my muscle that twitched with every sensual caress she drew upon me.

I smiled when I felt a familiar trace of *I love you* upon my body. "I love you too, little umbra."

She exhaled shakily. "You are...*you.*"

I cocked my head to the side, grinning. "Did you expect something different, my vicious little soulmate or are you too afraid to admit that you just missed seeing me half naked?"

I watched with amusement and baited breath as she searched my exposed body once more. "Why the refusal then? And this shirt? Really Emon, we both know you are not a pink shirt with unicorns kind of fae, and of all the times to wear a shirt...a long sleeve—"

I swallowed hard.

Fuck.

Instantly, without the seduction of her slow cuts from before, she quickly sliced off the rest of the fabric, exposing my arms still pinned high above me and stared.

"*Quid fecisti...*" She breathed in ancient fae, barely above a whisper.

What have you done...

CHAPTER 41

Remnant

T HE KNIFE FELL FROM my hand onto the ship's floor with a loud clatter drawing a wince from my soulmate, but I did not care.

Shaking, I traced the beautiful bronze skin of his arms etched deeply with thick and elegant swirls of black *ink*. The art was sinful and exquisite and I followed a slow path from his tense shoulder down his bulging tricep, across the sensitive skin of the inner elbow, and down his thick muscular forearms, curling my hand around his wrist.

My vision blurred with bittersweet tears at the brands on his body...my brands on his body. They were *exact*.

A perfect match.

I pulled back quickly, my hands clutching at my naked chest and released the shadows that restrained my soulmate. My mind raced at the meaning of the brands, not believing the shocking conclusions that came with it.

"I don't understand," I whispered.

Emon's arms slowly lowered and I could not take my eyes away from the swirling tattoos and when he gritted his teeth to sit up, I continued to stare. His branded shoulder was now so close to me, I could kiss along the ink just like he always trailed kisses along mine.

"Remnant," his breath raspy, his thumb sliding up my neck where my pulse beat wildly, and then to grip my chin, tilting my face up. "Little umbra, look at me."

I tore my eyes away and stared into his loving golden blaze. "Please tell me this doesn't mean what I think it does, shifter?"

His brow furrowed before leaning in to kiss my lips softly, whispering his confession against them. "I told you, not even in death will I ever leave you. The soulless sleep can't have me Remnant Ezra Solaire Dark, only you can."

"But these vows, they are that of the shadow fae, vows of darkness," I said, feeling the powerful enchantment carved into his skin, tracing the scrolling lines. "Your kingdom..." I reared back, my eyes wide.

"Will survive without me—it already has survived without me." He tilted my head again so that I would see the sincerity in his face. "I knew taking these vows would break the ones I made as a shifter king, and I never hesitated, not for one goddess damn second. You are my home Remnant, you're my kingdom to worship and serve, I am in your fan club for all of time. The only difference is that now I have proof of it, etched into my skin like you have been etched into my very being."

I sighed heavily. "I would have never asked this of you, Emon."

He smiled sadly and kissed my lips again, his thumb sliding across my cheek, his breath enveloping me in his warm chocolate scent. "It was the only way to ensure our family's survival and for you to get to The Well—your mother, she had another vision."

"What?" I gasped, searching his eyes for the truth.

He nodded solemnly. "It was why I could not tell you, why I hid this from you. If you knew too soon we would fail, and just as she said if I did not stay by your side until the very end we would fail. So your mother and I found a way to avoid bartering my soul to Shea. By taking the vow of the shadow fae, I am tethered to you infinitely in your darkness, even in death we will still remain bound forever, you will never be alone."

Tears filled my eyes and I leaned to the side, placing a soft kiss on the top of his shoulder where his brands started, just like mine. "You leashed your soul to the darkness Emon, you belong in the light. You are my light."

His hand cupped the back of my head, running down my hair and naked skin, burning a hot path from my torso, to my bare hips, and then gripping my upper thigh, his claws prickling the sensitive skin. "Not just the darkness my love...it is *your* darkness. The only place where my light can shine."

I studied him, seeing the grimace of pain he had been hiding, the fatigue around his eyes, the slowing of his pulse at the base of his throat. I had known...of course I had known. I just didn't want to acknowledge it, like the slain blood fae of my childhood. I thought I could change his destiny if I just held him tighter to me.

The soulless sleep was upon him.

"How much longer?" I could not control the quivering in my voice.

He grunted softly and his hand brushed my hair over my shoulders, baring all of me to his burning gaze. "We are out of time," he rasped.

"No," I whispered, my hands reaching up to cup his face, his bearded scruff scraping across my hands. "You cannot leave me yet." My tears fell and through them I could see the strain it took for him to stay upright, the slight shake in his powerful frame, the panting breaths that I knew had not been only desire—I was a fool. Dropping my hand to the center of his chest, his strong heart was irregular and slow beneath my fingertips. "No," I said again, looking back up into his mournful eyes.

His forehead fell into mine and he blew out a shortened breath. "It's just my body—," he panted. "I will still—still be with you," he rasped and gave me a lopsided grin. It reminded me of the smirk he sent me when we first met in the Wildwoods, as he was bleeding out chained to a tree. "Need to—" He caught himself, eyes fluttering closed, his body pitching to the side. "Lay down."

I trembled and complied with his wishes, slowly lowering him down to the ship's hull, my hair cascading around us in a cloud of darkness, tears falling freely on his face.

"There are—," he huffed, eyes trained on my swaying breasts, "worse ways to go."

I snorted through my tears.

He smiled softly, his golden gaze glittering with amusement before a frown puckered between his brows when he met my watchful regard. "This pain, I'm sorry—" He reached for me, too weak to close the distance between us.

Taking his hand, I hugged it to my heart. "This isn't your fault Emon."

He chuckled weakly. "Not that. I'm sorry—," he gasped, his body lurching but he fought it with a feeble growl. "Sorry I can't finish what we started—hate wasted opportunities." A small flare lighting up the dimming in his beautiful gold eyes.

I couldn't stop the bitter laugh from escaping my lips. "Something to look forward to when I deliver you from this darkness." I leaned over and kissed his lips chastely...sweetly...to calm the devastation wrought on my heart, pieces breaking that only he kept together.

Emon smiled faintly, his eyes falling closed before he gasped one final breath, his voice barely audible against my lips. "Love you, little umbra—see you soon."

"I love you too, shifter." I dropped my head to his chest with a sob, still holding his hand while I pressed my ear against his smooth bronze skin, listening to his slowing heart.

Bum...bum...bum——.

He gasped.

Bum...bum——.

His grip on my hand went limp and I kissed the elegant ink around his wrist, shaking. I had wanted to be at The Well before this happened, so that I knew his soul would be safe but he had ensured my safety instead.

Bum—bu——-.

A slow exhale.

Silence.

My body shook hard, my agonizing sobs so visceral they had no sound. I knew then, that this would be the worst sound I would ever know. Even if we survived for that happily ever after—the sound of his beating heart ending was going to haunt me for the rest of my days.

Emon was gone...the soulless sleep had taken my soulmate from me.

I glared through my pain at the metal door where the storms raged.

The territory of Wrath may have been roaring its violence outside but it would never compare to the brutality of a grieving heart. The Well of Souls would answer to me and then Deirdre would too.

CHAPTER 42

Remnant

"WAKE UP, LITTLE UMBRA. Our daughter is rousing and as much as I love this view, I think it will lead to some questions we are not prepared to answer."

My eyes fluttered open to find my head still resting on the smooth plains of my soulmate's chest. I must have cried myself to sleep once his heart stopped. "Emon?"

"In the shadow so to speak," he chuckled, his voice behind me, no longer rumbling from his body.

My own protested as I pushed my still naked self into sitting, stiff from sleeping on the ship's metal floor and Emon's body. Slowly, I blinked at the black ghostly silhouette of my soulmate and then back down at his grayed body, then back up to him.

"You have become darkness," I sighed, pulling my knees to my chest and tucking my chin on top of them to assess him.

He looked like the same rugged, beautifully handsome, shifter fae I loved except that his form wavered in shades of black and grays and although his eyes were brighter than the rest of him, the pure golden light that always held my breath hostage was gone.

"For the time being." He tilted his head.

My lips pursed, not sure how to feel. "How long have I been asleep for?"

Emon's ghostly smile returned. "A few hours."

Shimmering between us, my dried clothes appeared and I mumbled a thanks to the enchanted ship's cabin and then quickly dressed. When the last bit of my clothing was straightened into place and my long hair pulled back, Emon sighed.

I couldn't hold back the small smile that twitched at my lips...his sigh heavy with reluctance of my clothed form.

"What have you been doing this entire time?"

He grinned. "Besides watching you sleep?" He shrugged. "I stalked the ship outside, checked to make sure that the sea king hadn't been murdered by the wind, and Riella's pookah hadn't fallen into the ocean—unfortunately that rodent bastard is still aboard."

My mouth opened to speak but was cut off by the tiny voice of our daughter, rubbing her eyes sleepily in the doorway of her room.

"Maedere? Why is father in two places?" She squinted, swiping back the ratted mess of her hair, sending her crown askew.

My mouth opened again but no words came out, how could I possibly begin to explain.

Her eyes widened at my pause and her bronze skin turned suddenly pale. "Is faedere dead?"

"No." The breath rushed out of me and I was quickly at her side, pressing her frightened body into me. "No Riella, he is not dead. This realm is not meant for the living without god blood and so they must fall asleep, remember?"

She attempted to push the crown back into place but it only served to slip further over her eyes. "Like Papa Asher and Penina," she sighed. "I miss them."

"I miss them too." I squeezed her and then guided her back in front of the fire, the shadow of Emon placing logs on it. So he could still interact with his environment...that was good to know. "Come let's eat something and I will explain more."

Riella glanced up at Emon's nervous shadow. "I'm happy you're not dead, faedere," she said before seating herself in front of the fire where a full spread of meat, cheeses, and fruits shimmered before us, complete with crisp juice and wine.

Emon grinned, his nerves at ease as he sat next to her. "Your strength will never cease to amaze me, my cub." Chuckling, she began stuffing her mouth voraciously with food, crumbs falling into her lap.

Brushing some from her face, I plucked the crown from her head and she stilled. "Eat, I am going to fix your hair while we talk."

Riella nodded happily and went back to her eating.

"Your father," I said, smoothing out her long raven hair, marveling at the silky texture so much like my own, and my heart skipped, knowing how blessed I was to have her, "tethered his soul to the darkness of the shadow fae so that he stayed with us to reach the Well."

She munched slowly on a slice of cheese looking at him thoughtfully. "What do we do with your body?"

Comically, we all turned to look at Emon's corpse-like form, grayed and lifeless. Realizing I had no goddess damn idea what to do with his body, I bit at my lip with my brows rising, looking for answers from my soulmate.

He just shrugged, shaking his head allowing a lock of his hair to fall between his eyes. "The Faerie if I know."

Riella tore off a piece of bread humming and watching the fire. "Just ask the cabin to keep you safe." Shoving cured meats into her mouth she chewed noisily, leaving both of us staring after her atrocious eating habits and quick wit.

"That is—" I began.

"An exceptional idea, my cub," Emon purred, fatherly pride shining in his eyes. Bright shades of gray instead of gold. My chest tightened with the sense of loss and I tried to ignore it.

Sensing my dismay, Emon reached out and brushed my hair back. *"It will all be alright, little umbra,"* he purred, infiltrating my mind.

A bright shimmer behind us drew our attention. The eavesdropping enchanted room anticipated our next needs, lifting Emon onto a golden platform, enclosing it in glass. Gold vines spread from its base, wrapping over it, sealing him in the glass coffin until the time came to return his soul.

I could feel laughter tickling along our soulmate bond.

"Don't even say it." Wry, wry words.

His shadowy brows wiggled, "What if one little kiss was all it took."

I narrowed my eyes on him but before I could respond Riella shoved a piece of bread into his smirking face. "Want some?"

Emon's face wrinkled at the bread just inches from his nose, wet from Riella's chewing with only the crust left behind. I could not hold back my snorting laughter.

"I don't really think I am in need of sustenance anymore, my cub," he said kindly.

Our daughter shrugged, and then stuffed the bread into her mouth. Grinning, I returned to her hair as she chewed thoughtfully, still watching her father. "So what can you do then?"

Emon's brows rose. "So far I have been just floating around waiting for the two most beautiful fae I know to wake up, but..." He cracked his neck to the side and then shifted into his panther...a shadow panther complete with black fangs.

Tying off her braid, Riella swallowed, her mouth falling open to stare at Emon's beast before he returned back to his fae form.

"I want to try!" she cried, jumping to stand, squeezing her eyes and fists tightly to force the shift. When it was clear nothing had changed she peeked one eye open, then the other, swirls of gold and green dimming with disappointment. "I can't do it."

I brushed her braid over her shoulder. "I'm sure you can do it, little one. Your shadow powers have just manifested, it will just take some time for them to become more consistent."

Her fists tightened and she stomped her foot. "We don't have any more time," she snarled. "Faedere is a shadow and Zaki just told me we are almost to The Well. You will need my help and you worry I am not strong enough, that you won't be able to protect me."

Emon and I shared a passing look, and I sighed, seeing the stubborn set of my daughter's jaw—she was too much like *me* and I *knew* what I would have done in her stead. Rising to my knees, I held up the crown of stars, its light casting sparkles around the room, and placed it on her head. It had kept her safe thus far, I was not taking any chances by tempting fate without it.

"You are very strong both here," I touched her brow and then the center of her chest. "and here. This has never been your weight to carry—but if you feel that it is, then allow your father and I to take the brunt of it."

Emon crouched low, shadows extended from his hands, sending them around her in a tickling fit. Pulling them back with a large grin at her, he kissed her forehead. "I agree with your mother. Your job is to laugh and smile daily, that is how you protect us. For then we shall not worry if we are failing you as parents."

Riella giggled again when Emon gave her one more tickle, then she sighed, her lip pouting. "I just really wish I could do it."

Sitting back on my heels, I sighed with her, a stabbing pain in my chest at her obvious disappointment. "Manipulating shadow," I started slowly, thoughtfully, "cannot be done by force, Riella. Shadows are darkness and like true darkness they have no beginning nor end." I called out to casted shadows made by the firelight and twirled them around her in a slow pirouette. "They are an extension of your wants and needs. That's how you were able to use them to fight the caoránach. You had a *need* to protect your family and you used what was around you."

I beckoned Emon to come closer. Raising his hand and then Riella's, I wrapped the shadows around their wrists.

Sliding back away from them, I whispered. "Do not force the shadow to be...use it to extend yourself into what you need."

My soulmate hummed, staring into her eyes, nodding encouragingly. "Feel what it is to be a shadow, my cub. This is what it means to shift as well."

Riella's swirling green and gold eyes brightened with concentration and my breath held when suddenly they stopped, glowing equally in the dim light. A sudden flash of light, forced me to blink, opening my eyes to see a mewling little panther cub with shadows flowing behind her like continuous flames of darkness.

Emon laughed proudly. "Well done, my cub." Grinning he shifted into his own shadow panther form, his massive body dropping low as he purred at the little cub of darkness. Pouncing, Riella's shadowed form dove on top of Emon's head, batting at him with her little shadow paws and biting at him playfully with tiny black fangs.

I laughed along with them.

Riella had done it! And it was a memory I would never forget. This...this was what it meant to have equal powers of shadow and shifter blood. The first of her kind, the hope of the future...a future that was now imperative, more so than ever before, for me to secure.

It was no longer a choice, it was a goddess damn fact.

CHAPTER 43

Remnant

A THUNDERING KNOCK RATTLED the metal door of the ship's cabin and the dual shadow panthers skidded to a halt.

Weaving shadows into my hands and curling them over my arms, I rose, indicating them to stay back. Breathing deeply, I slowly exhaled as I threw open the latch and shoved the heavy metal door open with my shadows poised.

I was met with a blast of icy rain and only half of the sea king's giant body in the doorway. Bowing down, he roared over the crashing thunder. "Trouble on the horizon!"

I grimaced when the water of his beard spattered upon my upturned face, frigid and icy, with the strong smell of fish and salt. Throwing a look over my shoulder at my soulmate and daughter, I narrowed my eyes, weaving shadow around me to block the storm and to wipe off the water. "Stay here."

Emon growled. "For now."

Riella nodded, her tiny features took on a deadly scowl, like a beautiful avenging baby angel. "For now," she growled, mimicking Emon's tone, stretching her arm out for her shadow spear that quickly responded to her summons. An impressive feat for a faeling who just learned to manipulate shadow.

Looking between them, my lips pressed into a thin line. They were two halves of my heart and just as stubborn as I was. Shaking my head, I faced the water drenched Lir and stepped out into the violent storm with the door slamming shut behind me.

Secretly, I wished it would lock, to keep what was my heart tucked safely inside beside a warm fire. I smiled softly, when the sound of a click could be heard over the bellowing winds. Sending the enchanted cabin my thanks and gratitude, I tilted my chin to Lir with calm resolve. "Show me."

Following him, rain and now...hail, pelted down upon us and I instantly thickened the shadows, not relishing the idea of being bruised by golf ball sized ice. Unfortunately, the shadows did not keep out the cold and my body began to freeze in the sleeting winds.

Lir's hand gripped my shoulder when the ship lurched harshly to one side, forcing me to slam into his solid frame. "There," he thundered, steering me and pointing north. "Mi daughter sings o' a red glow."

I tracked his pointed finger with dread knowing what I would see...and fate did not disappoint. Lightning lit the sky, revealing a deep burgundy haze oozing across the horizon, eating the storm.

The chill that was slowly freezing my body took no time to freeze my heart. My lost shadows, stolen from me by the Sanguine, had finally come. Twisted and perverse, they had been corrupted beyond recognition and there would be no mercy from their deadly intent.

My lips pressed into a grim line with Lir's strong hand still holding me steady. "So Deirdre finally makes her next move." My teeth clenched harder, hands fisting at my sides.

"Aye, that she has. Yer lead lass."

"How long do we have?"

Lir shrugged, "ye may have ten, fifteen minutes."

Feeling a sudden weight on my other shoulder, I looked to find Riella's spirit guide hissing into the howling wind. Reaching up, I smoothed down its twitching rabbit ears, scowling with him, my mind racing. "Any way we can avoid them?" I hollered back through the thick sleet.

Releasing me, Lir turned to pick up his large shovel, throwing coal into the hot furnace, steam rolling out as the flames sputtered from the pelting hail, clouding him in smoke. He shook his head at me. "Nay lass. One way in, one way out to The Well o' Souls."

Lightning cracked open the stormy night followed by the thick rattling boom of thunder. Still stroking Zaki, I assessed the narrow passage through the seas where the Sanguine shadows blocked our course.

"My dormant shadows won't be enough to take on the corrupted lilin," I cursed.

Zaki hissed at my confession, jumping down from my shoulder, his ear twitching towards the cabin.

Lir nodded at the spirit guide, "Ye be right." Looking at me thoughtfully, he added, "forgive me goddess, bit dinnae ye have a soul wraith?"

My head shot up. "A soul wraith?"

"Aye lass, yer soulmate lover. He is a soul wraith no? N' they have unlimited power. They're no longer bound by the laws o' the universe."

A soul wraith...they were legends only...myths. Made from broken oaths, sacrificial vows, and deep darkness. They had never been seen, never even existed—the cost to become one was too great. My mother *knew* that which meant—

"No cost is too great when your life and our daughter's hang in the balance," Emon whispered in my mind, his dark presence suddenly beside me.

I turned angrily, my hair whipping across my face, seeing Riella standing beside him using her spear to stay upright on the lurching ship. Quickly, I weaved shadow around her to shelter her from the harsh elements before glaring at my soulmate. "And what of your life—"

His chuckle was dark, lacking the warmth that normally followed his confident smile. "It is tied to yours now."

I inhaled sharply, taking a small step back, stumbling slightly on the rocking ship.

Seeing my retreat, he frowned, raking his hand through his shadow hair, "You know I will never leave you, my little umbra—"

"Oi! Ye might be wanting to save this bickerin' for another day," Lir thundered and we all turned towards where he nodded.

Riella gasped and I reached for her, pulling her to my side.

Gritting my teeth, I assessed the growing Sanguine shadows. Their reach was now massive. Meant for one thing—to engulf us all into its ravenous oblivion.

"Limitless or not Emon," I stared, clearing my mind, building my own shadows around me. "You cannot do this alone, Sanguine shadows are infinite with the lilin. We will need to weaken it enough to not risk you getting corrupted as well."

Riella whimpered and tugged on my arm. "Maedere?"

Bringing my attention to her, I noticed her body trembling. "What is wrong, chickadee, are you cold? It is probably best for you to go back to the cabin and—"

She shook her head violently. "No! It's not that...they hurt," she whispered looking back at the Sanguine shadows now quickly approaching us.

I dropped down in front of Riella, gripping her shoulders firmly and fixating on the torment swirling in her eyes that I didn't recognize before. "You hear them?" I breathed and glanced up at Emon.

He frowned, crouching next to us. "What do they say, my cub. It's okay, just tell us."

She looked over my shoulder, her face pinched with pain. "They are saying...*it takes and takes, hungry, draining,*" she let out a shaky exhale and looked back at me with tears, "*it kills, lost, forever. Release. Release us.*"

I stood, whirling around and gazing harshly up into the storm at the corrupted lilin.

"Lass, what be ye orders? We dinnae have much time."

The winds stung my face. "Emon?"

"Little umbra," he said wearily, his darkness rising to meet mine.

Shea's words from our last dinner together crept into my mind. There were two ways to defeat the lilin. One I did not have yet, and the other—he had said was a myth. A myth that was standing next to me, a rising growl rumbling in his shadowed chest.

A soul wraith.

"If they are in pain," I whispered, "then the Sanguine, it is draining them, killing their souls forever, and feeding its power. The blood crystal did the same in The Under, it devours any essence for power."

Emon spun me to him, gripping my shoulders tightly, "What are you asking me, Remnant?"

I closed my eyes, my chest splitting into two. There was no saving my lilin. "They are souls and they are in too much pain. End it."

He snarled. "No. The umbras...they are a part of you. To kill them, would be to kill a piece of you. We will simply defeat them, the Sanguine will retreat back to their master. Deirdre would not risk losing her new power."

"Better to be the hand of a merciful death," Lir joined the argument. "Ye lass be right, soul wraith."

Emon bared his teeth at him, the ship lurching at the same time. "There has to be an answer in The Well."

I shook my head, unable to meet his eyes, knowing my resolve would break if I did. "This is what Deirdre is expecting. She thinks I don't have it in me, that I will fail. Leading the Sanguine to The Well, where it can grow even more powerful. It is why they have not attacked outright, why they linger just beyond."

Riella cried next to me. "Maedere, they are begging."

Emon released me, snarling, "Fuck."

Barely able to inhale, my chest splitting into two, I spoke along our soulmate bond, feeling the vows of darkness etched on his skin, ordering them, "*I command you, Emon. Be my hand of merciful death, release my shadows to eternal peace.*"

A long pause, waves crashed over the sides of the ship and poured over our feet. Riella clutched harder to me.

"So be it," Emon snarled, then roared. A sound of defiance, of anguish, of fury, and of death.

I opened my eyes to see his soul wraith blur into shadow, rising high above us, unaffected by the elements. Lir raised his head with me, no longer jovial, grief etched even into the strands of his beard.

Sensing his powerful presence the Sanguine shadows turned towards Emon, hungry for the infinite power he held. I watched his darkness waver. Both of us sharing this loss, the heartache doubled along our bond.

Waving his hand, Lir wove a huge wave from the very depths of the ocean and Emon shifted. The bright flash revealing his massive panther, perfectly poised onto a platform of water. Regal and powerful, his tail curled around him and his fangs flashed brightly through the storm when his jaws opened wide.

He roared, a terrifying and horrible sound, quickly followed by a pure white light, the same light Ethereal used to destroy worlds. The goddess' power that he had been blessed with since birth. Without his weakened body, Emon's soul could access it easily, even without Ethereal's presence.

My breath held when his white light hit the Sanguine shadows, and I stumbled when I heard their screams, collapsed when their darkness was burned away, fell when inch by inch my beautiful darkness died.

Tiny hands reached for me, rolling me to my back with begging cries but I could not tear my eyes away, watching in agony as a piece of my soul died with every death of my loving shadows.

When Emon's second wave of light hit them, I threw my head back and howled. I felt my innate power call to me. Infinite shadows, from the seas and skies rose from their hiding, silently watching the exorcism of the Sanguine from their kin. Like attendees at a funeral, they hung suspended in the roaring winds of Wrath's territory to bear witness to the death of darkness—my most loyal friends.

"Goodbye, my loves," I whispered. "To the life given and the life taken too soon, the goddess take you with her golden light to live freely within our hearts where the devoted and young never die..." I gritted my teeth. "I *will* avenge you."

And when they burned from existence, it felt as if I did too. My eyes closing to the memories of their protective love, pure in their darkness, one last time.

CHAPTER 44

Remnant

I FELT DEIRDRE'S MONSTROUS *spirit before I registered that I was staring at her beautiful figure inside a mirror. Hair of silver that fell in straight glossy waves to the floor, skin that sparkled like water glittering in the sun, a voluptuous body draped in red that made others ache for her against their will.*

But all I saw now was a sick rotten soul, festering beneath the illusion of beauty.

Red eyes, Sanguine eyes, once two deep pools of turquoise, glittered back at me with malice from inside the mirror before her full figure stepped from its reflective surface.

"Hello Remi darling," she cooed.

Bile rose inside my mouth and I held back the urge to spit it in her face. Instead I folded my arms and glared. If only the death that whispered in my eyes was enough to end her forever.

Reading me easily, she laughed softly. "You had your chance to kill me, Remi darling." Stalking around me, heels clicking against a polished floor. "You failed then and you will fail now."

I said nothing. She was no longer even worth the breath it took to speak. Even so, it was amazing how effortlessly lies could spill from her lips because she actually believed them. Deceit and doubt was always her truth.

She sighed and waved her hands. "So dramatic. Honestly, your moods were always so exhausting. Why do you think I sent you away so often?"

A shrill scream echoed in the chambers around us and Deirdre narrowed her eyes when a small burgundy shadow drifted into the room falling down between us like paper from the sky.

She laughed at the suffering Sanguine shadow, the last remaining corrupted darkness that had escaped its death. "You have grown, Remi darling...attempting to kill your shadows, I would have never expected this of you, but again you failed."

Light flared in my hand, Emon's light. And with a quick flick, the shadow burst into flame between us. It burned hot and rapid, leaving behind the ashes of my cherished friends. My protectors since birth.

But upon the air, one final whisper brushed against my skin like a mother's gentle kiss goodbye. "Thank you."

My face was an indifferent mask and I could see every cold apathetic feature of me within the full length mirror Deirdre had stepped out of. Impassioned emerald eyes, relaxed stance void of tension, a steady slow beat of my pulse at the base of my neck, my hands loose at my sides. But on the inside, pain carved through my body like a butcher that enjoyed the slow agonizing cut of its quarry.

I was moments away from shattering but I'd be goddess damned if I'd ever give her that satisfaction ever again. "It is you that has failed. You failed being a queen, you failed your courts, you failed your dead family, you failed me, and you will fail as a blood goddess too. There is no ending for you but death and you know what the best part of being the daughter of a death god is?" I stepped forward, whispering just inches from her lips. "I have the power to annihilate your soul," I breathed, grinning coldly. "And when I do, you will even fail at existing."

The bright red glow of her eyes dimmed, even as they pinched to narrow slits. "You don't have the power to defeat a blood goddess, Remi darling," she smirked at the pile of ash. "Not anymore."

I tilted my head at the way her reflection wavered, this close to her I could see her mirage break. Her hair once shiny was coarse and brittle, her skin that was once glittering was dry and wrinkled, her body once ample, was sagging and haggard. Nodding to the mirror behind her, I said dryly. "looks like you will need to find a new source to feed your newfound power, blood goddess."

Panic lit in her eyes right before she spun, her long red train in her dress slapping against my legs.

"No," she hissed, touching her face, smoothing the frizz in her hair, blinking over and over again as if she could undo what her reflection showed her.

I crossed my arms. "You fed from my shadows, fierce vengeful souls. You drained them like beasts, like the blood fae of old, taking their powerful essence." This time it was me that circled her like prey, this time I was the predator—stealthy, patient, silent in my pursuit without the obnoxious clacking of pretentious heels.

"No," she hissed again when her aging continued. Hair turning gray, blemish appearing on her skin, her bones sticking out of her body from her flesh's flabby remains. Her dimming red eyes looked back up at me, where I stopped to stand silently behind her, watching as she transformed into the wretched creature she had always been on the inside.

"You should have known. The greater the power, the greater the need, the more you need to feed."

Silence stretched. The air still between us, holding its own breath to see who would break first.

Her shoulders started to shake and at first glance, it looked as if her aging body was shaking with rage, but then a coarse cackle struck the silence between us.

"Clever, Remi darling, and cute using the spirit realm to manipulate me," she purred, turning towards me with an evil smile, waving a hand over herself, returning the frightening beauty that was the former queen of Faerie. "It is also cute, that you think your shadows are the greatest source I have obtained." Reaching out she stroked my face. "I look forward to our next meeting, my love." Pulling away she kicked her dress back towards the mirror, stepping through it before turning to look at me over her shoulder, red eyes gleaming once more. "Oh and please enjoy your shifter king, Remi darling, one wouldn't want to waste time, you never know how much you truly have left," she said, blowing me a kiss.

Dread seeped into my already haggard soul but still I held my ground. "Do you know what the saddest thing about all this is, De?"

She paused, looking back at me again with her brow arched.

"All the power in this world couldn't even make you a being worth loving."

Then with another flick of my hand, I threw my silver blade, shattering the mirror with her in it.

Her mocking laughter filled the air. "Well played, Remi darling."

CHAPTER 45

Remnant

L IKE THE SHATTERING OF the mirror, so did the spirit realm
and I pried open my tired eyes one at a time, my salt crusted
lashes stickily peeling from each other.

Three faces hovered above me like mourners over a dead body.
"I am still alive right?" I lifted a sardonic brow, then noticed the
rains had ceased, the vicious lurching of the ship had settled, and
even though the clouds above were still thunderous, lighting up
the sky with consistent flashes and crackles of light, they seemed
content to not spread the vengeful wrath for now.

Thank the goddess.

Lir chuckled and rose, winking with a silver eye, banging his
metal shovel once more. "Nay lass, ye aren't dead yet. Cheers t' the
goddess for that."

I gave him a small smile and then huffed when Riella's tiny
body fell on top of mine, her face burrowing into my neck. Wrapping my arms around her, I pulled us both into sitting, kissing

her damp raven hair. "Hey, little chickadee." Hiding the hollowed feeling inside of me where Deirdre's final words echoed inside its cavernous hole.

Enjoy your shifter king...time...you never know how much you truly have left.

Over Riella's head, Emon's eyes met mine and even in their shades of gray they seethed, his nostrils flaring as if something disgusting had been shoved into his face, mouth thinning the longer we stared at one another.

Hiding my confusion, I kissed Riella one more time, tasting the ocean on my lips. "Riella, why don't you go see if Lir needs any assistance. I need to speak with your father for a moment."

Biting her lip, she nodded, reaching to touch my face tenderly. "I'm sorry, maedere."

"For what, little one?"

"For losing your shadows."

I swallowed the bitter pain and I cupped her hand with my own. "The hardest part about living isn't the burdens of our future, but the love we must leave behind. It is their time now to have peace, even if we must move on." Smiling softly, I tickled her, hearing the soft tinkling bells of her laughter, and then pushed her towards Lir, "go on now. See what stories that old sea king can tell you. I bet he knows a few secrets about Shen Shen. They did after all share an ocean once together."

Her eyes widened. "So he really is the lost King of Atlantis?"

My lips twitched and I hummed, "Why don't you ask him yourself?"

Her eyes suddenly became too large for her face, blazing with eagerness. My daughter most certainly shared her father's passion for storytelling. Unfortunately, Emon was in no such mood, his lips pressed together in barely restrained fury. When I looked up to meet his anger, his eyes narrowed before he titled his head behind him, indicating I follow him to the back of the ship.

Rising with a sigh, ice that had clung to me, fell off in glittering shards, crunching beneath my feet with each cautious step I took, trailing after a silent shifter.

When Lir and Riella disappeared out of sight, I took note that we were cruising slowly through a narrowed channel. Glinting in the continuous flashes of bright lightning, jagged rocks of deep blues and emerald greens contained us within the waterway we traveled. It seemed that one error within this rocky course could potentially be our last, and I found myself thankful for Lir's assistance. Who knew what kind of instincts would have eventually guided me to this place if I had followed my father's directions.

I gasped when my body was slammed harshly back into the ship's smoke stacks, my head cracking against the unforgiving metal, with Emon's wraith hand wrapped around my throat.

I blinked through my confusion before his ghostly lips crashed into mine, prying open my mouth with his fangs and tongue, delving deep, pouring out his anger with his violent kiss and despite my greater sensibilities, I kissed him back even harder.

His soul wraith form lacked the normal blazing inferno of his golden light yet despite that—he still made me burn, the flames of his passion licking up my body possessively. Whatever version of Emon I would get in this world, in this universe, it did not matter—he was mine and I would love this shifter with every fiber of my being, even if it burned me to ashes.

His other hand reached up into my hair, yanking my head back with a soft cry escaping my lips. Snarling and brushing his mouth against mine, his voice was brutal when he finally spoke. "You will *never*, and I mean, *never*, ask me to do that again."

My breathing was rapid, and I frowned up at the cascade of light splintering across the sky.

His lips kissed upwards along my jaw. "You're confused." He paused, then growled deeply at the shell of my ear. "Your shadows, little umbra...I felt what it did to you as I killed them. One by one. I felt it carve out a piece of you that you will never get back. I was the knife, slicing out pieces of your soul, and watching you fucking bleed."

"Emon—" I attempted to explain, licking my lips and tasting blood where his fangs had nicked me.

"No," he commanded, his hands releasing me only to grip my chin tightly, forcing me to look at the anguish etched into his beautifully savage face. "No, not this time little umbra. You think that sacrificing yourself in the stead of others is honorable...that you are expendable." His teeth bared. "But you're not fucking expendable to me, Remnant Dark. The sacrifices you make...giving away pieces of yourself, like they are worth fucking *nothing*—they are not yours to give anymore, they are *mine*. They belong to me, all of you belongs to me. Stop giving away what I own. They can't afford you and truthfully neither can I, but I at least know how to covet every beautiful dark piece of you and I'll never give it away."

Bright silver flashed next to my head, embedding a sharp metal object into the smoke stack I leaned against. Releasing it, his branded arms of ink rippled as he shoved away while his eyes trailing over every stunned inch of me.

I wasn't even fucking breathing.

"Never again," he whispered through gritted teeth. Scowling, he clenched his hands and turned back to where we came, following the giggling sound of our daughter's laughter, his large form disappearing around the corner.

I exhaled shakily, looking at the silver metal. Two green fiery pools of emerald looked back at me with my own whisperings from the past.

May you always accept who you are in your reflection.

Did I? Was that why I sacrificed myself always first? Could I live with the shadows' deaths on my hands?

Reaching up, I touched my lips where they still seared from Emon's passionate kiss. The cut from his fangs had healed but the swelling had not.

Something about it felt odd...and a tingling sense of dread overcame me. I did not like unknowns and even more so unknown feelings. It was unlike Emon to succumb to anger so quickly, even if he was goddess damn right.

Pressing my lips into a thin line, I looked back at myself again, as if my mirror image had the answers I sought, but there was nothing there—nothing but the pieces of me that Emon coveted.

Sighing, I shook my head. I was overthinking this.

Pulling the casted shadows dancing from the rolling stormy skies, I twirled them around the blade, and wrenched it out of the ship, slipping it back into my boot.

Emon watched me as I returned and the fire he had left coldly behind roared back to life under his gaze. I stared back, my chin tilted high, my body swaying to the gentle waves of the rocking ship with each stride, shadows dancing up my arms where they belonged, and a sudden wind blew the loose strands of my dark hair across my face.

Emon's eyes glittered in those grays, his nostrils flared, unable to stop himself, his hands flexed at his sides...I smirked.

Lir chuckled. "Aye Fi, she is the beauty o' death."

Startled, Emon and I looked at the crazed sea king but Riella seemed unperturbed, nodding as if she agreed with the insane words.

He grinned, "Mah daughter, that was her wind, she thinks ye make death bonnie."

I bit my lip, "Oh well, thank you Fi." The wind twirled around me and the shadows on my arms flickered upwards into its playful swirl, guiding them in a series of dancing pirouettes.

Riella giggled, her hand covering her mouth. "She says she's shadow fae now."

Lir smiled with a wistful sigh, tears glistening in his eyes while he twisted a piece of his beard. "Mah sweet Fi always did love t' dance." The shadows fell and wind swirled around the old sea king. He batted at it playfully, laughing again. "Ach lassie, be off with' ye now, pay no heed t' yer old da."

Watching him laugh lovingly at his daughter's singing winds, I glanced back at Emon, a deep seated fear suddenly spreading.

Reading my mind, he was in front of me before I could blink. Brushing back my hair with his cold wraith hand, like before, it left a searing heat that lingered on my skin. *I won't let anything happen to our daughter, little umbra."*

"Nothing is guaranteed when the world is at stake Emon."

"Faerie is only worth saving as long as you and Riella are in it. Ever since you dropped me to my knees, this has always been about you...never this world, and now it's about Riella too."

"How can you say that shifter? It was you who convinced me Faerie was worth saving in the first place."

His voice was low and breathy inside my mind. *"Because you love Faerie...all of her creatures, fae and beasts alike. To watch it die around us at the expense of our survival will never be in your nature, just as it is not in mine to watch you be torn apart at the expense of the world."*

"How do you do that?" I whisper through our bond.

His mouth twitched. *"Do what, my love?"*

"Cure me, love me, constantly taking my breath away," I breathed.

He chuckled and the sound of it washed over me, chasing away my fears and doubts. It was warm and rich and I clung to it, my lifeline for what was to come.

"I've learned by example, little umbra, for it is you that first took mine."

The sky flashed brightly, a deep vibrating thunder shook our bodies and rattled the ship. Riella jumped to our side with her spirit guide still attached to her shoulder, its rabbit ears twitching.

Tucking her into us simultaneously, our faces turned up to watch more lightning crackle against the tremulous skies.

Riella gasped as one white hot bolt thrust downwards into the waters ahead of us, breaking open the realm, splitting both skies and water into a dark cavernous hole, revealing secrets deep within.

The jagged onyx, emerald, and deep blue rocks that had surrounded us ever since we entered this channel suddenly rose from their rest. Like an intricate puzzle, the sharp rocks began to fit perfectly together, forming thick stone slabs that floated into place in front of us. I inhaled as they swirled into an ascending cylindrical stairway that surpassed even the thundering clouds above.

"Whoa," Riella whispered and I merely nodded in agreement.

"We are here," Lir said from behind us, his deep voice full of reverence. "Welcome mi goddess, t' The Well o' Souls."

The cool touch of Emon's large hand wrapped around mine, our fingers intertwining much like our bond. "Together?" His voice gruff, gone was the coldness from before.

I nodded, reaching down to our daughter and clasping her hand in mine.

She beamed back up as we both responded.

"Together."

CHAPTER 46

THE WELL OF SOULS.

It was beautiful in its simplicity, the glossy shine of each floating step, swirling with black, greens, and blues that were both welcoming and foreboding. Power was embedded here—I could feel its humming force and watched enthralled as Remnant's body shivered. I had no doubt every inch of this power caressed parts of her goddess soul.

She took a step forward as if entranced by the call, and I could see something take hold of her that was empty from before. Empty when I fucking murdered her shadows, cut them straight from her soul.

My hands clenched at my sides, the need for vengeance rolling inside my body along with the hunger I felt before. A hunger that was becoming difficult to control, that much was obvious when I savagely assaulted my sweet soulmate on the ship.

I did not regret what I said, but I did regret how I said it, causing her pain with my callous handling. That was not me...Remnant was meant to be cherished, worshiped, she was never meant to be cowered or bent.

Eve had warned me...

I choked back a snarl when a large hand settled on Remnant's shoulder, the mad sea king Lir, halting her. "Once ye step in t' the Well, I will nae be allowed t' stay, lass."

Crossing my arms over my chest I gave him a pointed look, "Where will you go?" I growled.

Silver eyes flashed over to me, dropping his large hand from my soulmate's shoulder who studied us both with pursed lips, "Fresh seas. The Well will lock me out but Fi will be able to fin' ye 'n' guide ye back to me." Turning to Remnant, he winked, "Keep yer wits about ye, Goddess, 'n' good luck." Kneeling he extended his large weathered palm to my daughter, a thick corded bracelet holding a silver conch shell lay daintily within. "Take this lassie, tis a whistle, call for me whenever yer in need. The winds will hear 'n' bring me to ye."

Riella wrapped her hand around the tiny shell whistle, "Thank you," her voice trembled.

He winked and stood gracefully despite his great height. "Now off wi' ye all. Ye have souls to conquer."

I blurred, gathering my life in my arms, Riella clutching atop my shoulder's grinning down at the soft gasp of my soulmate held tightly in my arms.

Behind us Lir chuckled and Remnant glared up at me, her hands wrapping around my neck, joining our daughter's strong hold. "What in the goddess are you doing, shifter?"

Watching the incredulous look spread across her face, I smirked. "Carrying my mate across the threshold." I winked and ignored the sharpness deep in my heart that I had not yet been able to give her all the celebrational customs my people had when a couple was newly soulmated. Saving the world and the future of our daughter had taken forefront but I could at least do this.

Her brow arched as I stepped with fluid ease upon the ledge of the ship, bracing to jump. "Are you afraid the big bad, evil souls will come to get me?" She teased.

I chuckled deeply, and then jumped, the air rushing by us as I sprung from the ship with Riella squealing and gripping me even tighter.

Landing perfectly on the smooth polished stone step without a sound, despite the weight I carried, I grinned down at her. "Of course not, I'm afraid they will come after me, I'll need their goddess close by if they do."

Riella nodded, patting my cheek fondly. "Oh yes, good thinking faedere!"

Remnant snorted and rolled her eyes. "Surely The Well would not attack its own goddess, shifter."

At that we looked around, it wasn't much of a fucking well. There was nothing here but air but I could feel the power in my soulmate slowly grow stronger. My soul wraith senses drawn to it, hungry again. A loud smack of Remnant's hand against my chest echoed with the soft water lapping around us.

"Let me go, shifter or I will make you," She commanded.

I growled low, my hands reflexively tightening around her, the hunger growing deep inside me. Fuck. "I think..." I said slowly, shoving the fierce power down and licking my fang, "I've proven that I am never letting you go, Remnant Dark and I never will."

Reaching out to me she ran a single finger along the new swirling ink of my devotion to her, branded by the darkness itself. I knew she could see my moods shifting like the damned sea winds around us and I could see the worry slowly bleed into her emerald eyes. My gripped tightened when her vulnerable voice whispered back.

"I know shifter and if I could stay in your arms like this forever I would, but no worlds were ever saved by being held in a lover's embrace."

Softening, I leaned forward and kissed her forehead, whispering against her skin. "But they *have* been saved by love, little umbra. If I cannot have you in my arms, then I shall hold onto that instead until you find your way back to where you belong." *And I did too*...I held that thought back, because I was not ready to admit that perhaps I was slowly losing myself to the price of being a soul wraith.

Lowering her, I let go and something visceral in me responded, not liking the sudden distance created by the loss of her in my arms. Instinct telling me to pull her back in, to take her and run from this place, and let this world devour itself instead of saving it.

But The Well had other plans because the moment her feet brushed the smooth polished stone, it suddenly sucked inward and the realm was still. My head jerked up, there was no sound, no rustling of air, no rumbling of thunder, no swirling of stormy clouds above, no breath, no heartbeats.

Then like a great geyser, the ocean burst from the deep depths and shot straight up into the sky between the spiraling steps, and beyond the clouds—its final destination.

I growled, holding Riella close on my shoulders.

"Look!" Riella cried, pointing towards Lir's ship rising quickly with the new flood of water, its crest growing higher and higher tilting the entire ship bow over stern.

Roaring, the great sea king jumped forth, his shovel turning to a glittering trident as he braced to command the tidal wave that threatened to destroy the only remaining physical thing he truly loved.

"Lir!" Remnant shouted out to him, as the wave began to descend.

His silver eyes flashed at her and his voice boomed. "Haud yer wheesht lass! I will be seeing ye again. No seas ever got the best o' mi."

I chuckled. The fucker was mad. My kind of water fae.

Roaring with laughter, he drove his trident down upon the metal deck and right before the great wave smashed his ship into nothing but scrap metal he was gone in sparkling silver dust.

The waves crashed downwards, destroying the powder that marked where Lir had once been, leaving only his deep crazed laughter on the winds and a soft mist.

I shook my head, my brows raised, "We do realize that that crazy fucker still has my body and our pack right?" I commented dryly, my hand squeezing our daughter's legs gently in my wryness.

Remnant blinked slowly up at my daughter who had inhaled sharply before laughter escaped them both.

It was a beautiful sound, one that I allowed to wash away the hungry darkness, then mockingly grumbled, "I fail to see how that is funny."

When Zaki appeared, hissing with Riella's lethal bás fang spear clattering towards me, I cursed jumping back from the soul ending spear, hearing Remnant laugh harder. Had we all fucking lost out minds? "Fucking goddess," I snarled dodging it deftly within the narrowed space upon the step and stomping on it before it slid into The Well's ocean. "Watch where you throw that thing, Zaki!"

"Oh thank you Zaki!" Riella cried out, scrambling down from my shoulder, causing me to grunt when her tiny knee slammed into the side of my neck. "You are the bestest friend evers," she cooed. Her face nuzzling into the soft black fur of the rabbit's body, its beady red eyes staring over her shoulder at us smugly.

"Bastard," I growled, stooping to sweep up Riella's spear and then paused, the hairs on the back of my neck standing on end.

Our daughter felt it too, and she turned with her eyes wide on Remnant. "Maedere?"

My lips thinned at the way her heart raced, my claws extending while I searched the area around us for the threat.

Dropping to her knee, Remnant studied our cub's sudden pale complexion. "What is it, little chickadee? Is it your father? He doesn't mean it, he likes Zaki."

I snorted, *like* was a strong word to use.

The spirit guide hissed at me from his regular perch, but Riella shook her head quickly, her tiny body trembling. "No," she whispered. "I hear...I hear them. They scream."

"Who—-" Remnant managed to get out before the rest of her words trailed off when the water rushing upwards stopped.

Instinctively, I shifted in front of my soulmate and cub, snarling right before sheer blinding rays of light exploded between the spiral steps.

"Remnant?" I shot back to her, watching the light through slitted eyes.

"It screams," she breathed painfully, *"Thousands upon thousands of voices—they are crying, screaming, roaring inside that light. I think...Riella must hear them too."*

"Fuck." I spat. What new goddess damn Sheol of a cunt had we stepped into now?

Riella keened against her and I turned, grinding my teeth to see Remnant covering her ears quickly, enveloping her body within her own.

There was anguish on my soulmate's face, a mixture of pain and death and I could feel it absorb into the power that she already radiated.

"This is...this is The Well of Souls," she breathed.

Snarling, I turned back when I felt the hum of power gather, using my soul wraith form to shield them both from the explosive bright beam that shot from the depths of Hell. The brightness surprisingly did not bother my shadowed form while the perfect beacon of light suddenly illuminated every daunting step that spiraled upwards where we were evidently meant to climb. My skin prickled and a low growl released when I felt the power within pulse and writhe, hearing Remnant and Riella whimper in unison. Then just as intensely as it came, it died down, the cylindrical confinement of light becoming duller, not as bright with its humming gentling to a soothing buzz.

Remnant stood with Riella in her arms, standing next to me, her awe palpable.

"It is alright, my cub, you can look now," I purred toward Riella who sniffed and rubbed her face into Remnant's chest. There was nothing malicious coming from The Well now, not yet anyway.

Our cub's hands fell away from her ears, before she lifted her head, her eyes just as full of awe as Remnant. "It's so pretty."

Remnant looked down at her glowing upturned face, the gold in her eyes highlighted even more by the glow, and then looked back again. "It is." Her voice soft and I shivered at the sound, goddess how she affected me. "Most souls are, in their purest form."

Glancing back at me, I saw her gaze shift inward. I smiled softly at her, knowing what she was searching for. *"Worried for me, little umbra?"* I wasn't about to admit I held my breath, something flickering her eyes, a slight frown pulling on her beautiful face.

"Remnant?" I said aloud this time, licking at my shadowed lips.

She blinked, "Hmm?"

I studied her briefly, my brows raised. "What's next?"

She tilted her head, looking high up into the sky, her emerald eyes catching on the staircase once again, she sighed, "We ascend."

Nodding, my brow still wrinkled with concern, I reached for our still stunned daughter, taking her into my arms, and placing her lovingly on my shoulders once more.

Her tiny legs immediately wrapped around my neck and I purred inside at the immediate trust she had in me.

"Ready?" Remnant breathed.

I grunted, "I am with you, Remnant. Always."

And I meant it, despite the war raging inside of me that wanted to take them both away from this place forever.

Riella's little voice sounded above me, "ready, maedere."

Sighing, she turned and her shadows cloaked around her, looping around her arms, and I watched with baited breath when her booted foot stepped softly to the first step.

A soft exhale escaped us both when her booted feet whispered across the second glossy stone step and nothing happened. Quickly, she took two more with the same response...nothing. I quickly followed her, my body vibrating with the tension, my eyes never leaving her, alert and ready.

Another exhale of relief escaped her as she watched us join, and another whole lot of—nothing.

Then I felt it, felt the hum of power wrap around her again and my claws extended, my heart racing, while her own body tensed like a bow drawn to the end of its range, quivering with tension before an arrow was released. Her shadows twirled with increased agitation around us and her eyes narrowed and I knew what she was thinking.

We were fae.

This was the realm of Hell deep within Sheol.

We were residing in Wrath territory.

She had full access to every soul in the universe.

This was...

"Too easy," I growled with warning inside her mind.

CHAPTER 47

Remnant

IT WAS A GODDESS damn bitch being right.

Especially when the swirling beacon of light from The Well flared, sparking a singular ember from its divinity. It sparkled over my head, shimmering in its descent to the stone step.

The three of us watched with bated breath as the small ember of light started to spin. Wider and taller its blurring light grew, a shadow slowly appearing with each pass. Then the light broke, scattering like dust around us, to reveal a tall fae female with long flowing silver hair that moved like a living entity around her. Slanted turquoise snapped open and bore straight into my being—so strong were its depths that they stripped me bare of all my secrets, knowing glittering in the tropical blues.

"Deirdre!" Emon snarled, lunging.

But my shadows snapped around him, a flaming wall of darkness rising between us, protecting my heart and soul from the replicated image of my former lover.

"Release me now," Emon roared in my mind, his hands banging against the dark wall of shadows, punching through them with ease, as they were weakened by the light.

"Calm your fears and your malice, Goddess of the Wells, Shifter King. I know I look much like my daughter but I am not her."

I shivered at the elegantly layered sound of the spirit's voice, deep and soft it flowed over us instantly with a sense of calm and forewarning. Everything about her was dangerous, from the proud way she stood embraced in light to the way her turquoise eyes stared through us all and beyond.

Tilting my head I studied the detail of her face. Slender nose, heart shaped lips, high cheekbones, dark lashes...her beauty was similar to Deirdre yes but it wasn't her. My gaze narrowed on the high slant of her ancient eyes.

"Talgira," I breathed, dropping the shadow shield already full of holes from Emon's vicious beating. His breath ragged, stepping behind me with an irritated snarl. I could not feel his heat, something I yearned for more than I realized, but I could still feel his powerful strength raging at my back.

A pearly white smile that did not meet her faraway gaze greeted me. "Yes. It is a pleasure to *finally* meet you, Remnant Dark. I know much about you."

My brows furrowed and I crossed my arms in front of me. "The sight may give you much knowledge but you know nothing about me."

She laughed but her smile lacked warmth. "I know that you have a heart of a mother but the soul of a monster. I know that you still do not believe you deserve love because it has betrayed you one too many times. I know that one time you had nothing to fear and suffered for it and now you have everything to fear but thrive because of it." Her gaze turned on my soulmate and daughter.

A shadow sword blurred into my hand. "You stay away from them."

Talgira turned back to me, her lips pinching in thought. "I know you cannot protect them from what is to come and save Faerie—"

My sword rose, the shadows sparking off of it responding to the lethal anger inside me. "I'd choose your next words very carefully, Talgira."

Emon's deep growl vibrated the long swaying hair at my back and a glint from the tip of Riella's bás fang spear tilted over my shoulder, the tiny voice of our daughter clear and strong. "Do what maedere says spirit, choose carefully."

Talgira's brow arched and for the first time they burned with warmth, seeing rather than looking at us. "That is...you cannot protect them from what is to come and save Faerie *if* you don't learn to trust." She shook her head sadly, looking at the three of us. "My daughter has clearly stolen that from you, all of you, but it was I that stole it from her first."

Emon stepped beside me with Riella still poised on his shoulders, their glares identical. "Perhaps one would trust easier if you made the reason for your presence known instead of provoking my soulmate," he snarled and Riella nodded snarling along with him, her eyes flashing bright gold.

Talgira ignored him but her eyes fixated on Riella. "Hello, little one," she said, this time her smile was full but also echoed a deep sadness. "You are even more beautiful than when I first saw you in my sight the night I drugged Asher."

My shadow sword lowered, she had foreseen Riella all that time ago?

"Papa Asher is sleeping, he is not drugged." Riella thrust her spear outwards with a flourish, unknowing of the past story. "Are you here to help us or to hurt maedere, because if you're here to harm her, then faedere and I will stop you."

Emon smirked, patting her knee affectionately, his fangs bared and his glare never leaving the ancient fae. "I couldn't have said it any better myself, my cub."

Tilting her head, Talgira stared for a moment longer at my daughter and I could see it then. That even in her spirit form, she still had the power of sight and new visions were swirling in her turquoise eyes.

"Look away," I hissed. My daughter's future would be her own, no one else's. Fate and destiny could shelve their gossip for now.

Talgira blinked and then turned her deep gaze on me knowingly. "We are not enemies, Remnant Ezra Solaire Dark. I am here to assist you...to retrieve the lilin."

My chin tilted high and I tapped my shadow sword against my thigh. "Tell me, how do I find them?"

Her eyes flashed brightly, and I could see it now. The painful life she lived and the death that ended it much too soon. The dark corruption of vengeance, devouring her bright spirit piece by piece.

I wasn't the only one with a monstrous soul. "You are one of them. You are lilin," I whispered.

"I am one of many," she replied flatly.

Despite her tone, I recoiled at the sharp shiver that ran up my spine. The Well hummed at my back, demanding, insistent, forceful. It tugged harshly, not asking but taking. "Nothing in this life is free," I murmured.

Her eyes glittered dangerously back at my words, she need not speak for me to see I had guessed right.

Emon's gaze turned on me. *"You owe her nothing,"* he growled in my mind. *"I thought we fucking agreed no more giving up yourself. You're mine and I say no."*

I warmed at his possessive tone but dared not take my eyes off Talgira. *"I agreed to nothing, shifter. You keep forgetting that I have already given you everything of me that matters the most in this world. Life can keep chipping away at what's left but my heart and soul are not in my possession, they are in yours. It is impossible for me to give away and even if I end up broken at your feet I know I can trust you to pick up the pieces."* This time I did look away, meeting the turmoil in his eyes. *"You're just going to have to trust me, shifter."*

His eyes flashed and I knew he was there—under the three moons, death surrounding us in the Balsam plains, dirt under our fingernails from digging a shallow grave where vows were made...they had become so much more than we ever realized.

"Using my own words against me again, little umbra?"

I smiled sadly at him. *"If need be, shifter."*

He grunted, his hand reaching out and softly cupping my face. *"Te amo."*

I nodded, inhaling deeply, wishing I could still soak in his spiced chocolate scent to strengthen me, but feeling the searing touch of his consuming love against my skin would have to be fortifying enough. *"Te amo, shifter."*

Emon nodded grimly and I exhaled slowly, looking up to meet the eyes of my daughter, her presence like a bright star, guiding me home. My hair blew across my face when I faced Talgira again. "Name it."

She shook her head, silver hair reaching out as if to coax me to agree with its glossy touch. "It cannot be named...but only experienced." Waving her hand at the step we stood upon, she spoke. "From here onward, each step has a name, a binding of an avenging soul. It is how we can exist outside the eternal peace of the Eithne but stay with The Well until we are summoned. You must break the binding to each step so that we can exist outside the Sheol but most importantly...so we can remember what our vengeance is for. It is a fine line between being a vigilante and villain, without our memories we are no more than evil souls threatening all that is good in this universe."

"Like how I bound my soul to you, little umbra..." Emon added, his purr soft in my mind.

"It's a miracle, you are the first male lilin then, shifter?" I teased back, ignoring my worries of the risk it had put Emon's soul in by binding it to me. My shadows also had taken that risk and the Sanguine consumed them.

Shaking my head, I swiped my hair back from my face, baring my teeth. "How does the binding work?"

Her aquamarine eyes darkened. "You must die."

Emon's claws were at her neck and Riella's spear was lowered dangerously at the center of her chest. "I don't know how well you are educated on soul wraiths but evidently I can kill anything I will myself to." His head tilted towards the spear in my daughter's hands. "And if I fail...well there is always my daughter's bás fang. You might also recognize its properties to completely destroy a soul. There will be no Well for you to return to."

Talgira laughed. A cold sound. "You are your father's son alright but with your mother's spirit." Shaking her head, she held up her hands, her silver hair flowing up around them. "There will be no need for such violence." Looking at me she continued. "You will die through the memories of my own death. You will relive every excruciating moment of it." Looking up at the thousands of steps that led into the skies her eyes gleamed. "All our deaths."

Then without warning she launched herself toward me, her spirit boring straight into my chest, the light of it searing as my mind flooded with darkness.

Emon roared out my name as I staggered, feeling Talgira's soul clawing inside my brain...then I heard her voice whisper. *"Ligare."*

CHAPTER 48

Remnant

I WAS NO LONGER me. My consciousness melded with Talgira's past, a past that was replaying in vivid reality—the last horrific moments of her life.

Her heart raced with such an intensity that I felt it would punch straight out of her chest, her strong legs carried us swiftly across a steep stoney terrain, and clutched protectively in her arms was a warm soft bundle, held with sweet reverence.

And with it, a desperate fear that I knew too well held us both in a chokehold. It was a mixture of panic and resolve, the knowing that one wrong move would result in the end of a cherished life.

"It wasn't supposed to be this way." I heard Talgira's voice inside my head.

She cried out at the brush of a hungry tainted power against her skin and I cried out with her. The sound echoing off the stoney cliffs she raced along.

A muffled whimper escaped the warm bundle and through her eyes, I gazed down at the perfectly round face turning upward. Thick black lashes fluttered before bright turquoise eyes blinked open with innocent trust through long curly black hair. Tiny pink rosebud lips quivered when tears splattered on the babes flushed cheeks—Talgira's tears, my tears.

"No," I said in horror and fought back against the mental binding. I knew this story from Jar, it was one I could not relive. "I cannot do this!"

My scream fell on deaf ears while her body spurred even faster, scraping against sharp jagged rocks, and sliding on loose gravel, instinctively shielding the babe from the harsh environment.

"We must," Talgira hissed inside my mind. "Or your life will truly be forfeit! Would you leave your daughter motherless all because you cannot face the truth of my own death, one that had already passed?"

Staring down at the child I felt a humming lullaby radiate from Talgira's memory, lulling the watchful turquoise eyes of the babe slowly back to sleep under the constant sway of her running body.

Distinct sounds of following footsteps sliding along the gravel behind her, propelled another burst of speed from her legs. Below Talgira, from the mountains summit, dark grassy plains waved in the distance, and a fierce grind of determination set in her jaw. Whatever the destination she was close and yet—the Sanguine closed in on her quicker than before.

I could feel the call of Sheol already gripping the thundering of her heart despite the rising hope it carried, skipping a beat at the sight of a stone circle set in the middle of the long grassy plains ahead. Jumping more than fifty feet, she slid down the rest of the stoney terrain, entering the grasses of the circle with gasping breaths and an aching body, cuts and bruises healing quickly as she slowed to a stop.

The ground was lush with soft moss speckled with tiny white flowers, and in the center was an ash tree sapling, its leaves waving softly in greeting by our distressed entrance. Suddenly sluggish with denial that I could not comprehend, her feet dragged across the mossy grounds to the sapling. Its long knife-like leaflets opposing each other, grew outward and then nestled together to form a diamond shaped cradle meant for an infant. Curling upwards, the ash tree hummed, a soothing safe sound that beckoned for her to bring the babe forward.

Her arms tightened. Holding the sweet faeling closer to her pounding heart for just one more second, one more moment for him to feel love.

"One marks the last beat of their heart as true death," Talgira whispered in my mind as we watched the faeling being laid within the cradle, the ash sapling covering the tiny bundle devotedly. "But that was not the case for me. My true death was the moment I laid little Ikelos within this circle, knowing that saving him would eventually cultivate the monster in my daughter, a monster that would fracture our world."

"Ikelos," I whispered back. I had never known Deirdre's son's name. I knew she held bitterness within her heart at the loss of him but she had never spoken his name nor what he looked like...who his father was. I had always assumed it was too painful.

Talgira's tears splattered on the long leaflets like the beginning of a great rainfall, reflected in the sorrow gripping her chest. A sorrow that I felt every painful inch of, the small scattered drops glowing like crystals under the bright moonbeam that suddenly descended upon the circle. Ikelos' face turned sleepily towards it, his beautiful innocence striking, just like my Riella.

Hastily Talgira started to mutter, an incantation that was foreign to my ears but laced heavily with the ancient fae language. Trembling hands pulled out from her pocket a polished peridot stone, the bright lime green color illuminating Ikelos' dark black curls. Woven around the glowing stone was a thick cord of leather and despite her shaking and the ritualistic murmurings whispering across her lips, she managed to tie it deftly around the babe's wrist, then secured one of the same onto her own.

"Vita et Mors." Life and Death.

Her words carried around the stone pillared circle, swirling, whispering, louder and louder—a bright flash and then the faeling disappeared, leaving behind an empty cradle of leaves.

Her anguish became my anguish.

The storm of Talgira's tears opened up and her body collapsed to her knees, deep dark clouds rolled over the three moons cutting out all light as she heaved with the deep darkness of grief, fists digging and twisting into her stomach if only to feel something physical to the gutting agony within.

"Vita et Mors." The whisper was wrenched again from her lips and I stared through her tears as the ash sapling unwrapped its

leaves, revealing another child, almost identical to little Ikelos but paler, a sickness wracking its body.

Rising she plucked the child from the ash tree, holding it just as dearly to her shattered heart.

"I am not proud of what I have done," Talgira confessed brokenly.

I stared at the sleeping child, a newfound horror filling the grief I was still choking on.

"You couldn't have...you didn't. A changeling enchantment! Jar said you were good, he said you were a kind generous fae."

"I was a mother! A grandmother!" Talgira cried back to me but I could hear her pain, the doubt of if she had done the right thing. "I searched the sight so many nights...too many nights to find another solution. Making Ikelos a changeling on Earth was the only way."

She smoothed back the child's curls before whispering to his soft pale cheek. "I am sorry little one. May the goddess guide you back to the light."

My own mind was sick, revolted by what I was seeing. "You sacrificed the human child instead, took him from his family."

"He was terminal," she attempted to explain, "this day was the babe's death day, he died in my arms before the blood fae ever got to us. In turn, his parents, in the human world, experienced a true miracle, an answer to their prayers. Their son would seem to suddenly be cured and my little Ikelos would live to dream on with those who would cherish his life."

True to her word, the soft rattling breath of the sweet babe left its tiny mouth and my internal self wept for his soul as the memory of Talgira's tired body stumbled from the circle, tears still streaming down our face, too tired to run, too stubborn to give up.

"What was his name?" I choked.

"Ezra," she whispered knowingly.

I reeled inside, wishing she would look back down at his pale face and dark curls, so that I could memorize his sweetness forever as was his due. His life helped save a future, and it would seem, made my daughter possible. "He was my name sake? But how?"

"Your father is more powerful than you give him credit for," Talgira said sadly. "He had already seen this poor soul's fate well before you were born. When he met with your mother he told her that if he were to ever have a child, boy or girl, they would bear the name Ezra, in honor of a soul that changed the world. I think he

knew even then...that this was the path you would be led to. That you would fight to honor the babe."

"He was right," I whispered, as she clutched the lifeless infant in her arms. "I will stop this cycle, once and for all."

Talgira screamed and I suddenly felt the horrid searing burn wrap around her ankle, a sickening hunger suctioning and pulling her downward into the tall grasses. Contorting, Talgira's ankle snapped to prevent the crushing fall on the sweet lifeless babe, and she groaned as the pain flared up her leg.

Pain I experienced every moment along with her.

Then they were there, dark hair, deep burning red eyes, dark brown skin swathed in white and black, layered upon their body. The perfect camouflage for a frozen tundra but blatant upon the soft greens of the grasslands, even as the dark continued to blanket the valley.

The blood fae were here and they circled her like a predator did with wounded prey, pulling down the cloth that covered their faces. Long sharp fangs hissed into the night, practically salivating at the call of her blood, the wild thumping of her pulse, the erratic thunder of her heart.

Breathing heavily, Talgira harnessed the wind from her gasping breath, sending more than one of them sprawling backwards from the gale forces that did not stop as she heaved the last of her energy into it. Talgira may have once been a powerful seer but she was an elemental fae first, an extremely talented air elemental.

Her power was immediately cut off when fangs pierced her through the leathers and I screamed internally at the sharp pain, just above where the Sanguine had wrapped around her ankle. Kicking out she snarled, her free foot smashing directly into the blood sucking leech, smashing his face in.

Free again, she clawed at the long grasses, their roots shearing from the earth and giving way, spraying her with dirt, its rich taste budding on my tongue from her open mouthed gasps as she crawled sideways on one arm, the still babe protected.

Then a sharp crack rented the night and she screamed through gritted teeth. The sound rattling my ears just as her upper thigh bone splintered under the force of a heavy booted foot slamming down on her—-pinning and immobilizing Talgira to the earth with one simple move.

A handsome face with sharp chiseled features, deep set red eyes, and shaggy hair cropped around his face crouched down in front of her.

At the sight of him, her loathing was my loathing, even though I had never seen this fae before.

Pulling back the sweaty matted silver hair stuck to the salted tears on Talgira's face, his fangs flashed brightly against his dark brown skin. "Hello Talgira." Thickly accented and dark, his eyes flashed as his nail scraped down the tear stained path of her cheeks.

The touch like a cut against my own flesh.

"Melor." Tagira's pain was unbearable and his name came out broken from her lips.

Running a black fingertip over them, he grinned, licking at his fang. "You remember me."

She glared, jerking away from him repulsively. "Even if I wanted to forget...there is no denying you are my grandson's father and my daughter's mate."

Melor ground his boot in harder, splintering the fractured bone more beneath his powerful strength. Talgira bit down hard on her cheek, the taste of her own metallic blood strong.

I was amazed at her strength, because despite the pain Talgira experienced, she still held her precious bundle lightly—protected.

A harsh grip reared her head closer to Melor's face, tongue licking at the saliva dripping from his fangs. "I forget how much you look like her," he purred silkily, his other hand running up the curve of her hip forming bile Talgira's mouth. "Perhaps we should play before I drain you dry." Wrenching back her head further, soft silver strands breaking in his rough grip, he leaned in, sniffing the smooth curve of her neck, his tongue flicking over the erratic beat of her pulse. "I can control your blood," he whispered and I could feel his cold lips smile on her skin when a throbbing started between her legs, "I can make you like it, cuming hard all over my cock while I fuck the life out of you."

Talgira laughed through bloodied lips where the skin had broken from holding back her cries of pain. The taste welcoming to the sour bile threatening to spew from her gut. "What a fae...no game of your own so you cheat to dip your prick."

He chuckled darkly, his fangs biting at her skin. "Perhaps, but never did for that sweet sweet cunt of your daughter's. She spread her legs anytime I told her to. I wonder..." The throbbing intensified as he controlled the blood flow straight to her core. "Do you scream like her?"

Biting her lip again to hold back her cry, she drove her fractured leg straight upwards, forcing him to shove her down even harder, the sweet pain flooding all her senses and driving away the sexual desire he manipulated through her blood.

Thank the goddess for that.

Pulling back, his red eyes flared with annoyance. "Clever," he cooed, then his eyes fell on the small bundle still wrapped in Talgira's arm.

"Give the child to me, and I will do as promised. Fuck you into your death while you give me that sweet vitalizing blood. No one else will touch you."

On cue the other blood fae she had dispelled with her air, formed another circle around her, smiling with delight.

Talgira held tighter to the little one. "No. You will never have him alive." Blood splattered outwards across his dark brown skin from the forceful vehemence in her tone. "Necare!"

The ancient fae command to kill.

Melor had been so wrapped up in his own selfish desires, he had failed to realize this whole time that the blood had stopped flowing in the tiny babe's body minutes ago.

"He wanted our little Ikelos for nothing but pure greed. A powerful seer blood fae hybrid to turn the war." Talgira whispered in my mind while Melor roared above her, backhanding her face into the ground.

I hissed internally at the blow.

Crying out in protest, he ripped the lifeless infant from her arms, unwrapping him in a vicious manner, ripping the soft blankets with snarls until he stilled, staring down at the pale cold form of the lifeless infant.

Snapping his eyes down at Talgira with pure malice, blood began to simmer hotly through her veins as he forced her to her feet like a puppet, her leg bent unnaturally sideways, her face only coming halfway to his chest.

If I had a voice to scream from, I would have been.

His nails pierced her skin when he snatched her head, forcing her to look deep into his burning red eyes. "You fucking cunt. You have ruined everything!"

Talgira smiled through the haze of pain laughing softly into the eyes of a true monster. "Fuck. You. Melor."

Snarling, his movement was quick when he backhanded her again, throwing her broken body to the ground. She whimpered, the pain of her blood boiling beneath the skin unbearable just like her battered body, her battered soul.

She succumbed to it. Death called her now. I could feel it just there, waiting to take her.

Kicking her over, she blinked through death's fog as Melor evilly grinned down at her. "You'll not die yet, bitch." Raising the small lifeless arm of the infant to his mouth, his fangs lengthened even further. "You think you have won, but I will make you watch. I will make you watch as I drink from your grandson's dead body and you will witness first hand what your shriveled carcass will look like when we are done with you."

"No!" I fought against the memory, screaming at her to fight harder. Little Ezra deserved more. So much more. But I could do nothing, and instead of being disgusted, she smiled amusingly when Melor's fangs sunk into the little boy's soft pale skin and he sucked hard. His cheeks hollowing, his eyes glittering hatefully down at her.

She coughed out a deep gurgling laugh the moment Melor's eyes went wide and he spat out the blood gasping.

"Sir?" One of his followers stepped forward with concern.

"Poison!" he bellowed, dropping the faeling to the ground.

Despite her crippled form and being on the verge of death, her air reached out with the last of her life force, catching little Ezra in mid air and bringing him safely back into her arms.

"How?" I whispered through the same pain she experienced, the last vestiges of life leaving her.

Melor frantically attempted to purge the blood he had consumed while raging at his followers. "Kill her! Kill that fucking bitch!"

Talgira's pleased voice answered me back "The little boy's illness, it is a deadly poison to the fae, much worse than any iron. It works quickly, the moment it is ingested."

She smiled into the thick black curls, breathed in the babe's sweet innocence when a dozen of pierced needles drew out her blood.

This time the pain I had been experiencing did not come. Talgira was already beyond, her soul already departing and before the last thready beat of her pulse ended, she stared into the unblinking red eyes of Melor, dead in the soft grasses beside us, his body shriveled just like his putrid soul, into an aged crippled male. It was what he would have looked like if he hadn't utilized blood to sustain him.

His immortality had been prolonged by taking others and now he met his end.

Tucking her head down to the sweet innocence she held, her voice whispered brokenly. "I will meet you one day on the other side little hero, sweet Ezra, protector of all fae."

She smiled when death came and I did too, long before the remaining blood fae drained the last drop of her blood.

CHAPTER 49

I BREATHED A SILENT sigh of relief when Remnant gasped loudly, lurching in my arms as a tiny shadow purged smokily from her mouth—its small form floating delicately above us, waiting patiently for her to open those beautiful eyes again.

My soulmate had done the impossible.

She faced death and *lived*.

I glanced upwards towards the thousands of steps she had left to travel upon, my lips thinning in a grim line. I had no doubt she could accomplish this over and over again but I had serious doubts if I could. Seeing how each one of these souls were ones seeking vengeance there was very little expectation that any of their deaths would be a peaceful one.

Watching the shocked expression of my soulmate, I listened for her heart to slowly regain its natural rhythm. "Remnant?"

Her eyes snapped open, glancing briefly up at me before our daughter barreled into her, face burrowing into her mother's chest, no doubt seeking the steady beat of Remnant's heart that had stopped for the most paralyzing seconds of my entire existence—I never wanted to hear that sound again, or rather the absence of that sound.

As always, silence could go fuck itself. Agreeing, the stormy skies of Wrath's territory lit up with blinding lightning and the ocean waters beneath us lapped softly, applauding the sky's violent display.

"Is that Talgira?" Riella asked, turning in her mother's arms to assess the little shadow still floating among us.

Extending her tiny hand outward, she laughed when the little flame of darkness danced a jig up her arm.

"I—I think so," Remnant answered hoarsely, touching her throat with surprise.

I tucked my face into the crook of her neck and then growled low through our mind connection so as not to alarm Riella. *"I thought—"* I squeezed my eyes hard. *"I thought I'd never have to hear you scream that way ever again. I can see that physically you are well, tell me you are unharmed,"* opening my eyes, I touched the center of her chest, *"in here."*

Pulling my head up, her hands brushed against the scruff of my beard. My soul wraith form hadn't done a single thing to the effect she had on me with her soft touch, if anything it made me feel more.

My emotions were volatile.

Fleetingly, I felt a flicker of something that wanted to just consume her with my need, swallow her whole in the darkness I now wielded. My stomach roiled with disgust, I did not have the heart to tell her this, she already suspected, already guessed that there was a cost. I prayed to the fucking goddess I didn't forget myself before I ensured she conquered The Well because there was something far more sinister hidden beneath my surface and for the briefest moments on that damn ship—I had forgotten who I was, what I was.

I had hurt her with this hungry anger...

"I am unharmed, Emon, nothing permanent although my heart and soul aches. I have learned much already."

I dropped my forehead to hers and breathed even though I had no need of air in this form, listening to the giggles of our daughter while picking up her hand to trace her palm with my fingertips. *"A better mate would tell you to stop this madness, to turn around, go back, and to find another way. A better mate would take your place."* My voice cracked. *"But then again that kind of mate would not be the one your soul needs, that mate would not be the one destined for only you. So while I cannot be this better mate, I sure as fuck can make sure I am the mate that puts you back together every fucking time you fall apart."*

I watched her eyes glitter with unshed tears while she gave me a wry smile. *"I cannot help but wonder if there are other things you can do in this wraith form, besides playing at rescuing the pieces of me."*

I smirked at her deflection, finding sweet innocence in her discomfort. Quickly, I spun us both to our feet, kissing the top of her head, I played along, *"If you're asking if I am still rock hard for you as I always am and thinking of all the ways I could fuck you around a sacred well full of souls, ask no further. The answer is yes."*

She snickered to cover the blush stealing across her face and I prayed that I would never lose the ability to spread that rosy hue across her cheeks.

Chuckling, I gave her one last playful kiss before placing my hands on her hips and lifting her up upon the next step with ease, my own heart, if I still had one, breaking for her. "Up you go, little umbra, time for you to die again."

Riella tucked her small body into my leg, holding tightly while lifting the small shadow up on the step as well. "Yes, good luck dying again, maedere."

I grinned down at her, ruffling her hair, and ignoring the shimmering script that appeared beneath Remnant's feet. "I do believe I am rubbing off on you too much, my cub."

"Emon..."

Glancing up at Remnant's wide emerald eyes, I frowned, scanning her from head to toe, my eyes catching the name on the next step, and I felt my heart drop in my stomach. Remnant reached out to me but it was too late, the next soul flashed brightly from The Well and I stared at the figure standing next to my soulmate.

"Mother," I whispered, feeling as if I would crash to my knees.

Standing tall and elegantly draped in the white golden glow of The Well, she smiled softly. Caramel eyes, the exact color of her hair, sparkled down at me, lightning electrifying them to a bright glow as Wrath's winds blew her hair gently over her beautiful bronze face.

"Daemon, my sweet cub." Her eyes scanned my person and her lips pursed with disapproval of my soul wraith form. "It seems neither of us expected to see each other in such a way."

I snorted. "More or less."

She grinned then. A full smile reached her eyes and suddenly I was that cub again, basking in his mother's warmth who felt pride and confidence in the fae she saw in front of her. Like my father could read the truth, my mother's gift was instilling our truths we could not accept ourselves, deep into our very hearts.

"Good thing your father is not here to see this," she added, reading my thoughts, although I did not miss the wistful longing in her tone. Her strong regard then fell down to my daughter who watched silently with wide eyes.

"Hello my little *nepta*. We meet again."

Hearing my mother call my cub granddaughter in ancient fae was almost too much for me to bear.

"*Emon?*" Remnant's voice whispered with concern in my mind.

"*I am fine, little umbra.*" I gave her a small smile but I knew it did nothing to ease her worries.

Riella beamed, tugging on my leg excitedly. "You are the pretty fae that came to me and told me to go find my mother in The Under!" She looked at Remnant. "That is how I found you by the dead seas. She told me where to go."

Glancing at Remnant, I crouched low to Riella and tucked back the strands of her hair behind her ear that escaped her braid.

"Riella, this is my mother, she died a very long time ago."

Riella frowned. "But I am telling the truth. She was there."

I looked up at my mother, who watched us with glowing love shining from her eyes, nodding. "In a dream, yes. We all have been watching over our sweet miracle."

My daughter grinned but then shifted uncomfortably. "You're not going to make my maedere hurt like Talgira did, are you?"

My mother's face saddened as she lowered herself to us. "I do not wish your mother any harm, my sweet *nepta*." She reached out and trailed a slender hand along my daughter's face. "In fact, I am here to help her." Riella nodded and my mother smiled, standing to turn and regard my silent soulmate for the first time.

Remnant spoke first, stepping forward, her face clouded with concern. "Queen Skyler, you do understand what you will become, what you will leave behind should Asher leave our world. He will be alone without you here waiting for him."

Skyler tilted her head, "I have often pondered what kind of fae my son would find himself tied heart and soul to. I never doubted he would find his soulmate in his lifetime and when I realized it was you..." she sighed, "I admit, I was not happy."

My eyes narrowed and I growled in warning, "Mother..."

Simultaneously, both fae turned to scowl at me.

"Hush, shifter."

"Hush, my cub."

My eyes darted between them both. Crossing my arms in front of me, I glared back. "Fine by all means, start off on the wrong foot. What do I know anyway?"

My mother snorted and Remnant rolled her eyes.

"As I was saying, I was not happy...my son deserved a love not tainted from *my death*." She frowned, shaking her head. "But you were exactly what he needed. Your beautiful darkness has complimented my son's blessed golden light so perfectly that there is no doubt the goddess has created you for one another and I want to be a part of that. Asher has come to peace with my death and he will understand my decision to join you as your lilin."

Remnant exhaled. "Thank you, Queen Skyler."

Her eyes twinkled looking over at me, lingering on the ink swirling around my arms. "Yes. It seems I have regained that title again, have I not? Since my son has forsaken his sworn vows to the throne."

I could feel Remnant's guilt snaking along our soulmate bond and I shook my head at her. "Don't," I growled. "If given the choice, I would choose this over and over again, little umbra. My place is with you, you are the only kingdom I wish to be bound to—there is no room for any other vow in my life but my commitment to you and you alone."

My soulmate gave me a small smile. "I know shifter, but you are a good king. Your court loves you."

Unable to resist, I reached up to her, our height level from the step she stood upon. "I love you. If there is one thing our kingdom knows, it is if a Strider falls in love there is nothing that will stop them to prove that everyday. My court will understand and rejoice."

My mother hummed. "That is very true." Clapping her hands she beamed at both of us. "Well then...I suppose we shall go die now."

I barked out a laugh and then in a flash, my mother's spirit crashed into Remnant's chest and I lunged to the step, catching my soulmate before she dropped into the sea.

CHAPTER 50

Remnant

*S*KYLER HUNG IN IRONS *and I with her, in mind and spirit. One body with two consciousnesses, she peered out of the sunlit window in front of her, the pain of the metal burning her wrists only for it to heal and then burn again.*

Emon's mother's voice echoed within my mind. "I will do my best to spare you the pain," she whispered.

Some of the sting of the iron burns eased.

"Thank you," I croaked. "I often wondered...how were you even captured?"

I could feel her bristle and then she sighed. "I was foolish and I trusted the wrong shifter. I had missed my homelands and Asher was so busy rebuilding our community that I needed time away. As much as I loved my people, I adored solitude. The quiet beach and soft lull of the waves against the shore of Inquus Islands where I grew up."

"Who accompanied you?" I asked, peering around us, noting that we were in one of the tower prisons. Despite its smooth white marble even smoother bones hung on the walls like trophies. Deirdre's enemies whose carcasses had long ago been picked clean from hanging on the city gates.

"Falcon," she whispered and I could feel the bitter regret. "Penina had warned me but I was convinced he could never betray us. He was always so eager to help, so loyal and charming. Asher and I raised him after the wars, both Penina and Falcon were like siblings to Daemon growing up. When Daemon found Tyr in those caves and their friendship bloomed, Falcon and Daemon's relationship grew apart. Little did we know, it was the beginning of a festering resentment and they quickly went from brothers to toxic enemies. It also did not help that Penina looked up to Daemon no matter how accomplished Falcon became."

I snorted and rolled my eyes. "Let me guess, he felt abandoned."

Skyler hummed, "Prepare yourself, she comes."

When the far wall shimmered to reveal Deirdre standing in a deep violet satin dress, Skyler remained stoic. Her reaction to the queen of Faerie's presence was only that of mere annoyance.

"Skyler..." Deirdre purred, her hips swaying with her long silver hair. "I don't think your king is coming to save you. I suppose I cannot fault him too much for failing my mother if he cannot even rescue his own soulmate. A shame really...all that raw power just to end up being worthless to the courts and also the love of his life."

Skyler's head rose, meeting the queen of faerie's feverish glare with a quiet acceptance. "Speaking of yourself, are you Deirdre Seelie?"

Raising a finger, I felt the air leave her body, choking and gasping as Deirdre stole it from her lungs.

"That's the look," Deirdre cooed, approaching closer and smiling viciously. "The look your face will have as your head is placed on a pike outside my city gates."

Skyler's body sagged, the smell of her flesh burning sickening, and I could feel my own panic rise. This was too close to what I had already suffered and I wished to fight, to claw my way back, but all I felt from Skyler was a gentle acceptance of the fate that would unfold.

"You gave up," I whispered in her mind.

"I knew I was not leaving the City of Light alive. She had requested my life in retribution long before this time, when her mother and son were found dead on Asher's watch."

Her body started to violently twitch, fighting for sweet air that would not come. The panic was almost unbearable—and then Deirdre's powers eased.

I sighed internally.

Coughing and sputtering fiercely, Skyler sucked in as much of the precious air as she could, tears falling with each wretched gasp.

Cold fingers with purple painted nails encircled our chin, their sharp tips cutting into our flesh as she jerked our head up. "You are pathetic. Not fit to be anyone's queen, unwilling to fight for your life and your court. I do hope your son has more fight in him."

I felt Skyler roar to life. "You will regret this day and every day after, especially if you come anywhere close to my son! I will make sure of it, even in my death you will not be free of my wrath if your eyes even turn his way."

The queen of Faerie snickered, her nails digging harder into Skyler's chin. I grimaced. "I hear he is quite handsome, your little Golden Prince—not so little anymore fortunately for me."

This time both Skyler and I's rage consumed us and she roared, her shifter side manifesting past the irons restricting her power just like my soulmate's—Emon must have inherited this unique gift from his mother.

It was enough for her to sink her sharp piercing teeth straight into the flesh of Deirde's hand, the queen of Faerie's royal blood filling her mouth and trailing over her chin while she shrieked loudly with pain.

I savored the taste, as did the queen of shifters.

A sharp sting of Deirdre's fire power seared the side of Skyler's exposed face and sent her head snapping sideways, but it was enough to rip a chunk of Deirdre's flesh with it.

Skyler turned her head slowly back to the queen with a feral smile. I watched with satisfaction through her eyes when Deirdre stumbled backwards, clutching her wounded hand to her chest—the dark stain of her blood blemishing the perfect silk dress she wore.

"You fucking rabid bitch," Deirdre, hissed.

Spitting out the chunk of the queen's flesh forcefully, it splattered against her flawless face, leaving behind bits of blood before it plopped sickeningly to the floor, marring its smooth white surface.

I could not stop my inner dark laughter. Oh I liked Emon's mother very much.

Skyler grinned, "I may be a rabid bitch but even I am not mad enough to ingest any piece of you. You are rancid to your very core, Deirdre Tatianna Maeve Seelie."

Deirdre reached up to wipe her face, staring at the blood smeared on her fingertips. The room fell silent, the very air poised for her next move before a deranged giggle escaped her red lips. Weaving water she cleaned her face, hand, and dress, wiping away all evidence of violence, her hand already healing quickly from the queen of shifter's attack.

"This will be even more enjoyable than I had already thought it would be." Her laughter simmered into a coo, before waving at the stone that anchored us. "Come shifter queen, your audience is waiting, and you are the headlining show." The marble stone above Skyler, from where she hung in chains, dislodged, and dragged her across the room, searing her flesh anew and sweeping her feet against the smooth white floor.

Blinking against the sun, a sudden roar rose up, cries of excitement and boos of despair drowning out the winds that forced Skyler's body to suddenly sway like a pendulum upon the balcony of the City of Light's tower. Finally able to adjust her vision, she peered out to see thousands of fae with their faces upturned towards us, like a swarm of pixies searching for their next fix.

Deirdre waved at the mob below, her voice low as she leaned into her. "Smile, Skyler, look how they adore us." Grinning with sickening sweetness, the queen of Faerie blew kisses, small blossoms of fire sparked from her lips and floated on the wind, sparkling all the way down towards the cheering crowd.

Disgusted, Skyler's eyes drifted beyond the nauseating display, towards the bay, towards the waves of the sea, towards the west, and a fierce ache tightened her chest. Even in facing her death, she was seeking the solace of her West Isle home, where her soulmate and son were safe...away from this tyranny and manipulation.

"My court, the City of Light, who shall you choose this day?" The queen of Faerie's voice was amplified by her air power and the crowd fell silent. "Executioners, step forward!"

The mob cheered wildly.

"Verdugo The Butcher!" Deirdre roared.

A tall fae, with veining muscle and pale skin, stepped up, his chest covered in blood with a cleaver in his hand. Long pink hair falling to his waist also stained with blood flew around him. Fire, water, air and earth shot into the sky around us while the court voted.

"Shahin The Slicer!"

Another fae, this time thin and lean, stepped forward. Covered in black flowing fabric with only their glowing yellow eyes showing, they raised up two long thin blades. More elemental power rose, possibly higher than the rest.

"Or Dragoon, Your Beloved General's Shadow Captain!"

"Riley," I breathed inside Skyler's mind, not surprised.

I knew this story.

He had confessed it all to me the moment I returned a few days later with the news the shifter queen had been murdered and we were going to war with The West Isles.

Searching, Skyler's gaze fell on the head full of green curly hair and calm hazel eyes, Riley's features too beautiful standing next to the others, his face a flawless mask of indifference in the rigid black leather he wore. A swirling silver pin, attached to his high collar. He did not bother to step forward to appease the crowd, he did not showboat, he did not even spare the queen a glance.

Deirdre turned the stone slab that Skyler hung from towards her. "It is clear who the people choose Skyler, but I like to consider myself a merciful ruler, so I shall leave the choice to you. Pick your executioner, queen of shifters."

Skyler's chin rose, defiance raging in her heart and in mine. "Use whatever hand you may, but my death is still by yours. Are you not Queen enough to claim your own work? I would have thought you'd want this claim for yourself."

Deirdre grinned, trailing her hand over Skyler's face, the touch cold and nauseating. "I was so hoping you would say that. And you are right, I do want this for myself. It is what I am owed after all and I am going to enjoy watching every suffering moment of your death, Skyler." Stepping outward upon the balcony, she raised her arms and immediately the court fell silent. Their fear palpable even this high up. "My fair dear court, the traitorous shifter queen has requested none of my favored executioners!"

A select few were brave enough to boo and Deirdre allowed it, nodding sadly. "Indeed she has asked for my merciful execution instead. I have accepted her request! Is not your queen generous?"

The fae below cheered and a small whisper of wind, grazed against her ear, a tender and sympathetic voice carried with it. "I am sorry I have failed you, Queen Skyler."

I did not need to look to know my former shadow captain's voice, and apparently neither did Emon's mother.

Skyler's response was barely a breath of air. "My son will be vulnerable, she will come for him one day."

There was a slight pause while Deirdre basked in the delighted cries of the fae below. "I vow I will do what I can to protect him."

Skyler hummed as her lips mouthed two words. "Thank you."

Deirdre turned with a wide manic grin on her face. "It is time now, dear shifter queen. Be at peace. I will make sure your family, especially your son gets everything he deserves in this life."

Skyler did not bother to look at her, instead she watched the waves, their white caps cresting in the bay, the water stirring angrily as if it rebelled against the treasonous acts being performed.

"Ignire!" Deirde roared.

White hot flames burst around her, crawling up Skyler and instantly blistering skin. I was no stranger to being burned by Deirdre's fire but even I could not hold back my scream until it died out in silent agony.

The fire seared slowly and hot, melting her clothes, her hair, the lashes from her eyes. Her sight went next, the smell nauseating, and she jerked in the chains she hung from, the need to vomit strong.

I whimpered, the taste of it filling my mouth.

"I am sorry, my daughter, I cannot hold back this pain from you." Skyler's voice echoed in my mind while I curled inwardly, attempting to block out the worst of what she felt.

"Hold tight Queen Skyler. I am not powerful enough to stop her but I can ease you into this death." Riley's whispered voice was full of sadness when it reached Skyler beyond the flames.

"To this day, I shall never forget the peace your shadow captain gave me and how he upheld his vow." Skyler whispered when not even tears of relief from Riley's words could fall. They simply evaporated just as quickly as they escaped before darkness took her.

With his merciful air, Riley had rendered her unconscious, sparing Skyler, and myself, the pain that was to come and the mocking laughter of Deirdre who claimed the shifter queen was so weak she fell before her torture even started. Those were the exact words she told me in her chambers, days later when I confronted her about Skyler's death.

I wept with uncontrollable sobs for the queen of shifters who could not have the horizon to look out upon. A horizon where her adoring soulmate and little golden prince would be waiting, watching for her return home—a return home that would never come.

346

CHAPTER 51

I WATCHED AS A second shadow exhaled from my soulmate's lips and morphed with Talgira's who had been playfully occupying Riella while I held Remnant's still form—waiting, waiting for her to come back to me alive.

It was nothing short of fucked up. While my soulmate experienced death over and over again, I was cursed to watch it—all my nightmares coming to life on repeat.

And this time fate thought it would be fucking funny for me to watch the reflection of my mother's death, to witness the tears and to hear the echoes of her painful screams when she was burned alive.

My wraith form trembled, not from sorrow but from rage, and I could feel the insatiable hunger start to rise again. The whisperings of Eve's worries scratched at the back of my mind. *"I feel that I must speak plainly about what it is you will be giving up, what you might become—"*

Remnant's eyes fluttered open and pulled me back from the dark thoughts. Tears quickly filled her emerald depths and I felt her body begin to shake. Panic spread through our bond like the fire that consumed my mother in the death she had just experienced.

Short breaths, a thin veil of sweat, her heart thundering so loudly it reverberated in my head, the flush to her pale skin absent and replaced with a sickened pallor that I understood too well. I had hoped our bond and our truths would have set her free of her paralyzing panic attacks, but hope...goddess hope was a fucking bitch that never did a single damn thing for me or any of us. And because of that...the past still stalked us, a cruel haunting that would never go away.

Wrapping my arms around her, my hands swirled circles down her spine, catching through the salted tangles of her hair. "Breathe, little umbra, breathe."

"Emon," she sobbed, gripping onto me while I could hear her heart race uncontrollably, she was doing the opposite of breathing. "I can't...oh goddess I can't."

"Shhh." I rocked her, the bond twisting and tightening in my chest, making every inhale difficult to draw while I fully comprehended the source of her panic—the knowledge that our grim future could one day leave our daughter parentless. Waiting to see us walk on a horizon that would never come, abandoned and alone in this cruel fucked up world. "I know, little umbra. I know..."

I couldn't tell her it wouldn't happen. Fae could not lie and I fucking hated that about us. There were no words I could say to soothe the future's grip on what was to come.

I stroked her hair and purred. This time letting her fall apart so that I could piece her back together, then put her back up on another fucking step only to watch her fall apart all over again. Fix and break, fix and break...it seemed that this would forever be our life's story but we would do it together and somewhere in those moments—love, joy, and laughter would be found.

No matter how fleeting.

Then on the whispering winds and the softly tossing seas, our daughter's voice rang, in the most beautiful singsong sound I had ever heard. Crouching low, she touched her mother's tear stained face.

"What do you do when the darkness comes?

Do you hide or do you run?
Nay neither!
What you need is the rising sun
Bringing forth the Shadow ones
Until the darkness comes undone.
Bearing a soul that has been won."

Remnant's heart slowed and her breathing eased while our daughter sang with her beautiful voice. If I had tears then, they would have fallen with pride. In this moment, I could easily see how she could be a queen. Beloved and cherished by all, with her cherub face and starlit crown, a deadly spear that eliminates souls clutched in her tiny hand, a pookah spirit guide resting on her shoulder, a powerful dragon scale swinging on her delicate neck, and somewhere on her person a conch shell whistle to summon an ancient sea king.

"Where did you learn that song?" I whispered, knowing it was one my mother sang to me many nights when she tucked me into bed as a boy.

She bit her lip. "The shadows told me to sing it to you." Looking at both of us, her tiny shoulders tensed with unease. Her bastard of a pookah hissed at us for causing her distress. "Did you not like it? Did I sing it wrong?"

Remnant shifted, sitting up, stretching her arms outwards for our daughter to climb into her lap. "No, my little chickadee. You sang it perfectly. You have a beautiful singing voice."

Dropping her spear on the step she lunged into Remnant's arms, forcing the spirit guide to flash from existence from her shoulder before it reappeared again on the stone step, sleeping in a curled ball. I glared at the snoring nuisance—I could easily toss it in the sea.

As if hearing my thoughts a single red eye opened, his ear lowering and twitching in my direction.

I bared my fangs silently and watched as the damn thing smiled before closing its eyes again.

Fucking asshole.

Remnant exhaled shakily, tucking Riella in closer, and watching as the shadows nestled in our daughter's lap like a slumbering kitten just like the umbras of old used to do with me.

Thunder rolled across the sky and Remnant watched it lost in thought, "Emon...there is something I need to tell you...about your mother's death."

I knew what she was about to say. "You need not relive this, little umbra. Riley has told me his version and while it had been difficult to hear and I wanted to rage at him for not saving her, his life would have been forfeit too. He gave her kindness and mercy and for that I will forever be in his debt."

My soulmate shook her head, resistance to my acceptance easy to see. "I knew Deirdre was unhinged...I knew she sent me away for a reason. I just wanted to believe..." Remnant scowled and shook her head, "no that's all an excuse. I knew Emon. Part of me knew that she was evil and I *allowed* it."

I tilted her chin up to me, our daughter's big eyes watching our exchange with quiet astuteness. "I have had much time to come to terms with my mother's death, little umbra. And there was a time where I wanted to blame you for it, using it as a reason to go to war against Faerie, especially when you rallied armies against us. I thought surely, the daughter of the shadow fae leader would follow in her mother's footsteps and honor the old alliance between our families once again. But you did not," I admitted softly, watching the winds pick up and the watery seas rise—Wrath's reprieve waning.

Remnant flinched, her eyes defeated.

"Maedere, is brave and good. You should have never been angry at her, faedere." Riella glared up at me.

I smiled down at my fierce daughter and tapped her nose. "You are so right, my cub. There is no fae more brave and good than she." I winked, "besides you that is."

Riella gave me one last narrowed look before nodding in a satisfied manner, turning back to the shadows to pet them.

I chuckled and then glanced back at the worried expression on my soulmate's face. Smoothing out the wrinkles between her brows, I planted a kiss between them. "Worry not, little umbra. My anger and resentment was short-lived."

"What changed your mind?"

"*Natrix Drakaina...*" I purred watching her expression, she gave nothing away.

"A silly title given by the dragons. You know this story already."

Gazing deep into her emerald green eyes, I whispered, "Now who is keeping secrets, little umbra."

She scowled and I laughed softly.

"I told you, that I knew you...all of you," I sighed, explaining, "Late one evening, just days before my departure, I received word from a fae I had thought had been slain in battle. He wrote to me saying that he could no longer live with the guilt anymore and that I had to know that he was alive...that so many of my people were living in Faerie's soil under your protection."

She inhaled, "He shouldn't have been able to. It was part of the vows they had to take."

"It was in an ancient language...one I had not recognized before and took me more than a day to decipher. It was in dragon tongue."

Remnant frowned, "Still impossible. He would have died from breaking that vow before it even got to you."

I grinned at her, "Not if it was written by a dragon."

Her eyes widened and then she cursed looking away. "Damned fae and their word games."

"I thought it was a trap at first honestly. Then Bane came to me. Asking me to investigate the rumors of you being a traitor to the throne and that you had disappeared. Then I told him about the strange note I received."

The rising wind blew her hair across her face. "Bane vouched for me."

I arched a brow at her, "Of course he did. He loves you. It's why I haven't killed him yet. After that I was captured and we both know how the story goes from there."

She shivered at the growing cold. "I stayed away after Morta, I feared what I would do, but I often wondered..."

"They are well and to this day, vow they owe you a life debt." Watching her eyes widen at my admission, I arched a brow at her and smirked, "I searched for you for almost one hundred years...you didn't honestly think I left a single blade of grass or grain of sand unsearched in Faerie during that time did you? Of course I checked on the shifter fae of the Southern Mountains."

She shook her head, "The dragons would have killed you on sight."

"My love...there is but one thing that holds more value to a dragon than even their treasure."

Riella held her hand up and exclaimed, "Their mates! Shen Shen told me that the mating bond is the most valuable of all treasures and should be protected at all costs."

I grinned proudly down at my daughter. "Yes. My cub. Their mates."

Riella turned her wide swirling emerald and gold eyes up at me. "Do you think I'll have a soulmate one day faedere? One like you and mother?"

The pookah's red eyes popped open again and glared at me, its ears twitching stiffly.

"There is no fae in this universe that deserves you...no beast either." I glared over at the damned rabbit and noted my daughter's lip forming into a tiny pout. "But I have no doubt you will be loved by many and perhaps one of them will be your soulmate," I choked out, the words distasteful on my tongue.

Remnant's eyes sparkled at me knowingly and I scowled.

Riella beamed. Her eyes already falling into a daydreaming space, and I prayed vehemently to the goddess that it would be a fucking millennia before such a truth became a reality.

CHAPTER 52

Remnant

T HE SKY BROKE OPEN and rain poured down upon my up-turned face, cleansing me of the death that had become one with me. Using the shadows, I shielded Riella from the downpour while Emon's wraith form repelled it completely, and then carefully stepped over the heavy water cascading off each step. The sight of it was magical, a clear fluid waterfall that poured over the smooth steps from the sky above, sparkling from the brilliant glow of The Well.

A flash of light shot through the heavy rain and I exhaled when the ethereal glow coming off a black scaled water fae with a matching set of electric blue hair and eyes peered back at me.

"Bay." My voice solemn, a part of me was not surprised to see her here, her big eyes widening as she took me in.

"My lady Solaire!" She waved her finned hands frantically, "Oh no, I apologize! My Goddess, Goddess of the Well, Remnant Dark!" She bowed low, her long blue hair sticking to her scales in the torrential downpour. Lightning cracked across the sky illuminating her gentle yet vibrant presence.

I smiled sadly, she had not changed in death, still vibrant and *talkative*. "Please do not bow to me, friends have no need to bow to one another and I had hoped you considered me a friend at one time." I opened my arms. "And I do believe friends embrace." I said gently, water sputtering from my lips.

Bay rose, her webbed hands cupping her face with pink tinged eyes—water fae tears. "Oh my goddess, yes of course! Always my lady, my goddess, my friend," she grinned, her sharp razor teeth flashing before she stepped into my arms.

I don't know how long we stood there, holding one another while Wrath's storm pelted us with its heavy rain. Grief weighed heavily on the bright soul that should have lived a full happy life with her artful paints and open heart. Turning inward to my sight, I basked in her bright blue aura, the one I would have seen the first day we met had not the Sanguine taken everything from her.

Pulling away, her webbed hands touched my face gently, careful of her sharp claws, the water dripping off of us in rivulets. "You are exactly what I thought you would look like in land fae form...although a bit wet still."

Waving her hand, she weaved the water, pulling it from around me and creating an invisible umbrella. Suddenly dry, I touched my wind blown hair with surprise.

She nodded eagerly to herself. "Yes, yes, that is exactly how I pictured your hair...so beautiful with those dark shades of blue and your eyes." She grinned, her sparkling gaze caught on the swirled ink of my arms and she traced her clawed nail along the markings. "You had these before we met, yes?" Glancing up, to see me nod she grinned even wider, if I didn't know her disposition well I would have said she looked almost sinister. "These are the markings I pictured when I painted your scales. It was as if I could see every one of these swirls...it was my favorite work I had ever done."

"As it was mine."

She smiled shyly then, pulling her hand away and shielding her eyes through the rain to look down at Riella. "The little fry," she breathed and stooped on the step. "I am sorry Mariella. I should have tried to protect you better. Had I questioned more..."

Riella tilted her head and bright lightning crashed around us, making her crown surge with its energy. Also staying dry from the shadows, her spirit guide mimicked her movement. "I know you.

You're Bay, the cousin of my..." she glanced up at me, "of Kira's guard."

Bay smiled gently. "Yes. I hope you will forgive me...and the water fae one day sweet little fry. We should have protected you, cherished you." Glancing up at me she smiled sadly, "found your true mother for you."

I watched as my daughter frowned, suddenly gripping the dragon scale tightly around her neck. "If I forgive you, will you help my mother?"

"Riella—" catching Emon's eye, he shook his head and my lips thinned.

Ignorant of our exchange, Bay nodded enthusiastically. "Oh yes of course! That is why I am here." Rising she turned back to me, her features turning dark and fierce. "My life was taken from me too soon...I want to see the blood witch pay for what she has done to me...and to my people. We will take long to recover from what the Sanguine has done. As your shadow, your lilin, I will assist you in painting the lands red with her blood."

Raising my chin, I honored the ferocity of her vow, "I accept."

Bay nodded, "I also warn you, the souls after me...they are eager to meet you but not in the way you hope."

I nodded, knowing deep in the depths of my soul what I would face. "They are the souls of Morta."

"What?" Emon snarled in my mind.

"Hush, shifter, it is only logical, their lives were taken too soon, of course some of them would want retribution."

Bay's eyes gleamed through the pouring rain. "They want you to hurt, my goddess, and they will try but know that there are rules that bind us all to The Well. If they break them, you have the right to forfeit their soul."

Emon growled low, not liking her words one bit, his claws slashed downward through the rain, glinting in the storm. "Promise me you will forfeit them if they harm you, Remnant."

My lips pursed and I ignored Emon's lack of control, his anger palpable and it seemed also *dangerous.* "Will they try to hurt my daughter and soulmate?"

"Remnant..." Emon growled, this time the warning inside my mind.

Bay's eyes widened as if she had not thought of this, her concern focused solely on me. "They may try." Her eyes flashed along with a bodily shaking crack of thunder. "I will not let them, never again."

My newly acquired shadows rose up between us and Bay tilted her head—listening? She nodded, drawing her wet hair around her, wringing out the long rivulet of tresses.

"We are in agreement. We will not let them hurt any of you should they step out of line but your lilin say you must appeal to their vengeful side to alter their focused hatred of you."

"If they don't behave, I will devour them myself," Emon snarled, flashing me a glare that said he was not happy about my ignoring him.

Bay grinned and her spirit form bounced happily at Emon's suggestion. "Yes, that threat may also force their allegiance should things go badly."

I sighed, eyeing my shifter with wariness, despite Bay's excitement. Emon was becoming more and more volatile and the shadows in his eyes were the same shifting darkness that distracted me when I peered into his aura. It had been there for just mere seconds but it was enough for my instincts to tell me something was wrong...severely wrong. Pursing my lips, I braided my dry loose hair back, grateful Bay's power had kept the rain from me for now, but once she became my shadow I would be exposed to the raging weather once more. This way, at least it would be manageable.

Flipping it back over my shoulder, I looked down at Riella, Zaki, and Emon. "Stay safe, please." Breathing deep, I rolled my shoulders and cracked my neck side to side. "I am ready Bay and I am honored to have you as my friend and shadow."

Bay's eyes tinged with pink again, washing away from the storm. "I am only sorry my death will cause you pain, my goddess and friend. *Ligare*."

Her bright electric blue soul sprung outward, straight into my chest. Kneeling with a gasp, I coughed before taking over her memories of her death, the last moments Kira, the former leader of the water fae, had robbed of her beautiful life.

CHAPTER 53

Emon

CATCHING REMNANT BEFORE SHE fell, I held her tightly to my chest, attempting to shield the heavy downpour of rain plummeting down upon her. The rain shield the water fae had created to keep her dry had disappeared the moment she crashed into my soulmate's body, drowning her once again in the torrential water.

Lightning cracked like shattered glass in the sky, a rolling thunder soon rattling our bodies, followed by a suddenly fierce blustering wind, kicking up the water from the step and with it—a rotten decaying stench of death.

Jerking, I bared my fangs into the sparkling rain soaked night.

"It's the north wind Fi," Riella called out to me, the shadows still keeping her somewhat dry as she used her spear to stay steady on the step.

Lowering my gaze, I ran my hand through my hair questioningly, "What news does she bring, my cub?"

Riella tilted her head, the winds swirling around her, whispering its secrets. "She says...a dark one comes, eyes of black, and he brings stones of red. Death, death is coming."

"When has it ever not come for us," I snarled, gently laying Remnant's body down on the step, already seeing the struggle start to claim her body.

Even my soulmate faced death in memories of another. It sunk its claws into her, shredding her to nothing but pain and grief, and I fucking *hated* it.

Hated every painful wrinkle on her face as she whimpered from the torture, hated every gasping breath she took as someone stole her life, hated every tear that fell down her cheek as she grieved for another soul she still believed she should have saved.

My hands fisted at my sides.

She owed them *nothing* and yet here she was again, giving everything. Down to the very final thud of her heart. I looked up at the waterfall of steps unable to even see past the rain where The Well speared the very clouds.

She had thousands to climb, thousands of deaths to suffer, lowering my gaze I felt my body swirl with darkness, felt the hunger consume me. There would be no more death weighing upon her, no more than that she already had taken on. Whatever came this way, it was mine to war with and it wasn't going to fucking win.

Both Riella and I tilted our heads when the winds began to howl with the thunder roaring above us, erratic screams calling out from the horizon.

"Faedere," Riella breathed, stepping closer to me with her spear. "They sound like the beings when we first entered Hell."

I growled low, placing a steady hand on her shoulder. "Demons," I glared in their direction, lightning illuminating the winged beings in the distance.

Riella sniffed and wrinkled her nose, "And blood wraiths."

I nodded, not taking my narrowed gaze off the hidden army heading for us. "Yes."

A faint steady beat of drums pulsed through the storm, streaks of fire bursting through the heavy downpour bringing with it the stench of decay mixing with the sharp bitterness of rage, resentment and a burning desire to destroy.

A burning desire I felt deep in my core as well, a fiery rampage that wanted to consume, the anger never being satisfied...the wrath always thirsting.

I crouched low, staring straight into my daughter's eyes, soaking up every golden swirl mixed with her mother's emerald green, imprinting the vision of her forever in my mind. "It seems the blood goddess has joined forces with the demons of Wrath, my cub."

Riella's lip trembled. "Is she coming for me again, will they take me away from you and maedere?"

Sweeping her up into my shadowy arms and feeling her small heart thundering fiercely against me, I soothed her with a rumbling purr, "I won't let that happen my cub, but I must go and meet them before they get closer to you or your mother."

Riella arms tightened. "I don't want you to go," she whimpered.

I squeezed her back. "I know my cub, I know."

Breathing in her sweet scent of sunlit meadow from her wet hair, I swallowed hard, peeling her fierce grip off my body like I was peeling off a piece of my soul.

Setting her on the step with eyes full of tears, I cupped her face, the storm raging around us, the drums growing louder, blue wraith fire lighting up the sky. "I will always find my way back to you and your mother, Riella Dark Strider."

Her breath rattled as she exhaled, nodding even with her lip still trembling, "I will protect mother while you go."

I gave her a soft kiss on the forehead, unable to meet the sadness in her eyes. "There's my brave warrior queen." Tapping her spear with a clawed finger, I growled, "This will kill any demon, wraith, or living creature with just a scratch. Do not hesitate to use it."

She bit at her bottom lip but nodded. "I will not hesitate. I am brave like mother...like you."

Just then Remnant's body bowed off the step as if she were possessed, the rain falling heavily on her supine form, her mouth open wide in a silent scream, the tension of her body echoing every ounce of pain of another fucking death I could not save her from.

I kissed Riella's forehead again, choking on a whisper, I had no more right words. "Yes you are." Pulling away at the sound of the drum beats and roars growing louder, I nodded towards Remnant. "If I am not back by the time your mother awakens..."

Riella placed her hand on my chest. "I will get mother to the next step faedere. We will do this together."

Picking up her hand from my chest I couldn't resist bowing over her tiny fingers and kissing it too. Anything to keep one more moment of her with me. "I love you, my cub."

"I love you too faedere."

Standing, I glanced over at the pookah watching me in the dark rain. "Zaki, protect my daughter."

The pookah's eyes glowed red and he hissed as if I had offended him by such a request.

I glared back. "Do it without the attitude spirit guide, or I will show you what it truly means to be feral." My fangs lengthened threateningly before turning towards the lingering shadows hovering above Riella.

"The umbras before you were loyal, self sacrificing, and loving towards my mate. She deserves nothing less and everything more. Do not disappoint me." Winking at them, I grinned, this one for my own kin. "Please don't fuck this up mother."

The shadows swirled around me agitatedly, whispering against my wraith skin and I grinned back. It was fucking good to have the umbras around again.

I missed their sass much like I missed the arrogant dry voice of the panther Ethereal.

Snarling against the tightening in my chest, I turned towards the faint outline of the winged beasts and heavy drums, and ran my hand through my hair—then gave way to the darkness.

Sharp painful hunger tore through my being, leaving me salivating at the destruction I could bring. All that I knew washed away as my first victim fell within my sight.

Spreading wide, I devoured the grotesque shrieks, absorbing souls and taking them within myself to burn in the shadows. Hissing with pleasure, I vibrated with more power, the beings' rage fueling more hunger—this was going to be a fucking feast.

I felt the fire and the sharp pokes of their weapons but none of it harmed me. I was aware of their talons and claws, horns and teeth, fire and death but none of it scratched me. And after each one, I wanted more.

Starved, insatiable.

More.

Needing, craving.

More.

I drank deep, falling into the darkness, spreading it out into the universe. Tendrils infinitely searching for all of life for me to consume.

I was the beginning and the end, there would be no need for anything else, no one else. Then I would wait with satisfied anticipation for when the fates decided to try again. Creating life in a universe of chaos to watch it struggle over and over only for me to end it once more.

The fates should fucking thank me for only I could end the pathetic turmoil life gave and bring them the peace of darkness they needed. An eternal sleep free of pain and sacrifice.

Echoed laughter and a mocking cry of a bird of prey drew me from my morbid reverie. The sound was familiar and an immediate distaste rose deep from the bowels of darkness I had created. Another ear piercing screech split my attention from the fire breathing demons and blood shrieking wraiths to lock on the agile winged creature floating on my immediate consciousness.

Recognition drew me back from the all consuming darkness as a bright flash landed on stone steps. Something about those steps was important but I could not remember exactly what. Then I saw him, manifesting like the darkness I carried, black beady eyes turned upwards and cut through the thick rain, a wide grin splitting across his face, rain splattering on the harsh whiteness of his teeth.

Friend.
Brother.
Betrayer.
Enemy.
Falcon.

CHAPTER 54

Remnant

I WOKE UP CLAWING at my throat attempting to breathe as another lilin joined my shadows. Kira hadn't just sucked the life out of Bay with the Sanguine. She slowly drowned my water fae friend with the very element that gave her empowerment. Bay had been chosen because she painted my scales to outshine even a queen—an act of treason Kira had called it. Even after her death, Kira's vanity knew no bounds nor did her cruelty, a life taken because of jealousy, a throne vied for because of vanity.

"Fucking bastards!"

My brows rose at the profanity sprouting from my daughter's mouth as she blurred over me, lunging with her spear through the rain. My lips twitched, the words comical with her small musical voice as she practiced her spear.

"Die demon ass scum!" she screamed and a wailing screech jarred my sensitive ears.

My eyes widened, that was no scream from a little faeling girl, which meant this was far from practicing forms.

"Riella!" Jumping upwards, choking on fear, I whirled around to see her wrenching her spear back as the demon in front of her slowly started to disintegrate into nothing. His dust drowned in the torrential rain.

Swiping the water from her face, she looked up at me, her eyes pure gold with sharp fangs bared. "Oh hello maedere."

My lips pressed into a thin line, a shadow blade morphing into my hand. With the other, I yanked down the dormant shadows being cast from the crackling lightning and booming thunder. Gathering together like curtains drawn, I gasped in horror at the sight of hundreds of demons and blood wraiths swirling above us within the storm.

Hollering through the heavy rains, I narrowed my eyes on my daughter, her eyes scanning the horizon. "What has happened? Where is your father?" Twirling my hand, shadows shot outward like a volley of arrows bringing down a few dozen hell spawn and wraiths alike to be swallowed up by the angry seas.

"Wrath demons and blood wraiths joined forces," she yelled back, water sputtering from her tiny lips as her crown slide over her brow, her eyes switching to an emerald green before she shadow jumped behind me, stabbing out into the storm, another demon cry piercing the night before being extinguished. Protecting me from its silent attack.

I stared, enamored with the tiny faeling warrior I was now in the presence of. Bás fang in hand, my new shadows, the lilin, faithfully hovering over her shoulder, and her pookah spirit guide poised on her other, its red beady eyes darting around her, searching for more prey.

"And that's faedere," Riella said, raising her spear upwards.

We both looked up when a fierce flash of fire streamed across the skies, gathered into an enormous fiery beam straight into a large consuming mass of darkness engulfing the swarm of demons on all sides.

My heart dropped. "Emon," I breathed his name, a painful worshiping sound.

Riella tapped her spear on the steps, tilting her head, listening to their cries. "They are afraid of him."

"It's his wraith," I said, recognizing the hunger. There was a reason why the soul needed a body and body needed a soul...without each other there could be no balance. This was the cost of a soul wraith. How long before he forgot everything but his taste to destroy life?

"So typical of him, isn't it? Jumping without assessing the consequences...how it could possibly affect others, all that matters is what he feels is right," drawled a high pitched voice straight from my nightmares.

Reeling, I pulled Riella quickly behind me. Shadows falling around us protectively while I manifested another sword in my hand.

Baring my teeth, I hissed at the fae standing on the step above us, barely able to discern through the downpour his black eyes from his dark skin. "Falcon."

"Remi darling, you have something that belongs to my goddess." Cocking his head he attempted to peer around me but my shadows rose higher blocking her.

Before I could answer, a roar shook the rain between us, Emon's large frame dropping in front of me, forcing us back on the edge of the stone step. His soul wraith transformed back into his fae form instead of the dark mass of shadow he just was in.

"Falcon," he growled with the thunder rolling above.

Falcon's too bright white grin turned on my soulmate. "Emon. You've looked better...more alive I would say." Teetering, he cocked his head to the side much like a bird searching from its high perch. "I don't know if I am flattered or surprised you can even remember who I am in this state."

"I'll be more alive than you will be, Falcon. Your death is going to taste the sweetest when I devour your deceitful soul."

Emon's cold and empty tone forced a dark shiver down my spine, instinct telling me this was not the same shifter anymore. Emon was a fierce protector, he was full of fiery hot passion whether it was rage or love but never void...never desolate.

The fae talking right now...it wasn't him. I eased Riella closer to the edge, watching them both with calculating assessment.

Again Falcon laughed. "Well I would be disappointed if you found my death disgusting, *brother* but I do know who would be disappointed if she saw you now. My poor sister always did look up to your pathetic ass."

"Penina will rejoice the moment you're dead."

I inhaled sharply as did my daughter but continued to side step us away.

Falcon's beady eyes glittered in the rain turning on our startled reactions. "Tsk tsk, my sister has been keeping secrets from you, has she Remi Darling? She is just as much as a deceiver as I am it seems...the family trait is uncanny, is it not? Although being the oldest by a few seconds, I'd say I am still better than her."

My mind whirled on our past interactions. Penina's eyes turned black with her anger, the same as her brother's now, the vehemence she had when learning Falcon was still alive, the secrets she held tight to her heart. *Did you know?* I shot along our bond to Emon but again, the words seemed blocked as if he had shut me out. Of course he knew...Skyler had alluded to just as much in her memory, I just hadn't given it time to puzzle out yet.

Emon snarled and stepped to shield us despite our side stepping retreat. "Your focus should be more on me, *foster brother*," he spat and lightning flashed brightly between them. Wrath's territory was enjoying this show.

Falcon's laughter joined the amused realm. "Oh I am not here for you...our time will be for another day, although it has been a pleasure watching you destroy yourself all in the name of some low grade shadow cunt."

I stepped beside Emon, shaking the water from my eyes. "Now, now Falcon, there is no need to be jealous. I can't help that the shifter king prefers my low grade shadow cunt over your pecking bird dick. But I can see how much you resent this...first Deirdre, then Emon. That must sting pretty bad. That no one wants you." Baring my teeth, I snarled, pointing my sword at him. "Now get the fuck off my step and out of my realm before I kill you where you stand, bird scum."

Falcon snickered but his eyes didn't hide the storm inside, even with the rain. Bowing low he grinned wretchedly. "Apologies, Remi darling, I have delayed you long enough. Enjoy my parting gift...I'll be waiting for you in the Sanguine." His eyes glittered before he shifted with a bright flash, his falcon wings spreading and flapping against the fierce winds and rain.

Emon roared, lunging forward and knocking Riella and I both to the side to shift into his swirling dark mass, pursuing the tawny wings and laughing black eyes that were disappearing into the storming clouds.

"Faedere!" Riella screamed from behind me, her spirit guide hissing and then disappearing completely when the sky lit up with thousands of winged beasts.

Then the storm above us started to glow...a red hue, a sinister light gathering above.
Blood crystals.

CHAPTER 55

T ORN, RENDERED.

I was floating in a haze of pain and anguish.

Who am I?

Darkness.

I was the darkness. A hungry void that desired nothing yet craved everything.

Faintly, I remember I was ravenous in my chase for the bird shifter's soul. His name mattered not—all I could recall was that he needed to be fucking wiped out from the universe for all of time. My need for it had been powerful, my hunger for him infinite. He had been mine to goddess damn devour until the time decided to make another foe to feed me once again.

There had also been fear and anguish, so much of it that I thought...perhaps it would be best if I consumed that too—an entire universe to gorge upon.

Then her voice screamed up towards me and I had hesitated.

Why did I hesitate? What was it about her sound that made me *feel* a shattered heart and remember a fragmented soul?

Torn, severed.

I was still floating, battered and wrecked.

That's what had happened. I paused and the red light burrowed deep, cutting through my all consuming darkness. There had been alarm, something inside me knowing a fear of this power that ripped through me. But in my ignorance, I did not listen and it had cost me.

Now that same power crawled through the holes of damaged darkness while I drifted through nothingness. Its presence fed off of my splintered soul, a deadly parasite that pulsed and writhed.

How had I gotten here?

What had I forgotten?

Fuck, who was I?

Torn, fractured.

"I'm not letting you go, shifter..."

Goddess that voice...it was light in darkness. Why did I want to hear more of it?

"You once said that one day you would get us right, and I would have nowhere to hide. Well you got us right Emon, and I will never let you go now."

Emon...my name was Emon.

I stilled.

Memories flickering in and out of existence.

The sweetest of laughter, fierce emerald eyes, a soft caress, shadows cool and soothing.

I grasped at them, untouchable.

But still I clawed towards them brutally.

Torn, shattered.

I was torn and shattered.

CHAPTER 56

Remnant

"E MON!" I SCREAMED, WATER sputtering from my lips as I roared my fear, sweeping my hands upwards, hoisting the shadows from the dark ocean, and blasting them into the sky.

But I was too late, thousands of bright red beams of light shot simultaneously outward, forming one horrifying blast straight into the heart of my soulmate's darkness.

"No!" Riella and I screamed, as the Sanguine burned holes through his shadow being, leaving him torn and tattered falling through the sky.

Using the waves of shadow, I sent them to cradle Emon as he fell. With only mere seconds to think, I desperately latched onto the remaining pieces of his soul. He was bound to me and he was mine, I was the fucking goddess here.

Emon resisted when I reeled him in but I had no time to ponder why as I glared at the looming demon army bright with Sanguine power, then over to the swirling smooth stone steps, thousands of them still cascading with the water that I had yet to traverse, and lastly over my shoulder at the pulsing Well of Souls. The bright well of light humming fiercely, calling to me once again.

"I'm not letting you go, shifter. You once said that one day you would get this right, and I would have nowhere to hide. Well you got it right Emon, and I will never let you go now," I whispered fiercely to him through our connection, not knowing if he heard me and then turned towards The Well. Running, I scooped up Riella in my arms, her spear tucked behind my back with shadow. "Hold tight, my little chickadee," I rasped, my booted feet splashing against rushing water and smooth stone.

"I am with you, maedere," Riella whispered.

I jumped.

Wrapping my body around her, I twisted in the air, shielding Riella from the first beams of light as we fell backwards into The Well, pulling Emon's tattered soul along with me.

Pressing my lips into her hair and calling on the lilin to wrap around us, I breathed a prayer whispering, "The end of your soul lives within Sheol."

CHAPTER 57

*"**A**BANDONED. THEY ABANDONED YOU. Everyone aban-doned you. She abandoned you."*

Whispers so many whispers inside this new darkness, I did not understand. A hungry pulsating thing that breathed against every fiber of my being.

"They abandoned you," purred a voice that drew me to it, one I knew forever. "Your parents left you alone as a boy to be raised by your people. Just a sweet innocent cub, all because of what?"

I shook my head and growled. "No. That wasn't what hap-pened. They kept me safe, they protected me."

"And when they found you in those caves, after you hadn't seen them in over a year, your father did not rejoice in seeing you."

"No, no. He was afraid. I scared him."

"Your friend didn't even try to save you when your father beat you with the lash. He let you take a punishment, never once saying it was his fault. He has been letting you take punishments your whole

life. You are his shield and he has never thanked you for it. Never once."

My mind screamed back. "Tyr struggles inside but he is strong, he has been loyal, he never asked me to be his shield. I chose that path," I snarled.

"He has never given you any other option to choose. Oh Emon, you are a bleeding heart."

The voices hummed, caressing against me as I frowned into the dark.

"Then your parents adopted the babies, Penina and Falcon. They replaced you as their dear golden prince. Then Falcon betrayed you, he who was supposed to be your trusted brother. He gave the queen your mother, then gave her your kingdom too."

"Stop!" I growled but I had no voice here. I was but a piece of the universe floating in oblivion. I felt hungry tendrils latch onto me, pulling on me with their spiteful words.

"The one you call sister holds secrets. Deep secrets. She sees and does not tell. She has let you feel this pain, the loss, the constant sorrow. She let you get captured."

The voices twisted the past and I gritted my teeth, blocking out the whispers but they were too loud. Too strong. I felt a suctioning pull and I groaned.

"Dragoon watched your mother burn, he did nothing to stop it, he was too afraid to lose his own life. He didn't do what was right to save her. He should have died that day too."

"No. No. No. I wouldn't have wanted that. She wouldn't have wanted that."

"Xi is only loyal to him. She cares not for what you have provided. Safety, freedom, choices. She will never repay her debts to you."

I curled in on myself, wishing I could block it out.

"Bane has loathed you forever. You are the product of what he wished he had, your mother. He despises you and wishes you dead."

I couldn't argue with that one but no. Bane would never, deep down I knew this. Our hate was not murderous deep, just the maiming kind.

"Your father loathes you too. He sees his soulmate in you every time he looks at you. He is disappointed that you gave the gateway away, that you let yourself be raped by a woman for months on end. You are not strong enough to even be called his son."

My father only knew truth. He said he did not feel this way. I shook my head, ripping away the thoughts but they continued to latch onto me. Boring into everything that I thought was true.

"The panther never cared for you either. He thinks you incompetent and unworthy. A disgusting parasite. He has told you this many times. It is why he has not returned, he hasn't even tried even though you pine after him. You disgust him."

Ethereal. He would know how to stop this. Did that really make me incompetent?

"Then there's me."

Me? My conscience piqued, I looked outward.

The darkness cleared and the most beautiful deadly creature leaned over me. She was a dark halo of blue black hair, large green eyes so brilliantly bright and gorgeous with flawless pale skin soft to touch. I would never forget the first time I saw her in this place. Lost in the depths of her eyes, I moaned when her perfect pale lips kissed mine softly, then followed her as she sat down beside the table I laid on. Strapped in with irons and shadows. A knife dripping with blood and darkness cut into my forearm pinned at the table.

The shadowy darkness swirled around the blade as it seared into my skin.

No this was not how it happened, I was...I could not recall but no the markings were my choice. Weren't they?

"You have always had a knack for beautiful storytelling, shifter. What a fantastical story you have weaved. Me being a lost hero, not the monster that you know I am, and the soulmate you wish I was. It's cute that you blame Deirdre for all this scheming without giving me credit for a single ounce of it. But you know you never left this place."

Confusion wracked me.

"No," I choked. "I love you. You love me."

She dipped the knife into my skin smiling, her green eyes glinting brilliantly. "Oh Emon. I don't need your pathetic simpering love. You gave me everything I ever wanted. Our daughter. And in due time, I will take her from this place, form my own army, and take over Faerie. Now with Riella to claim the shifter throne, your people will follow me to take out the Faerie queen. Her pathetic soul has fled, so cowardly afraid of me," she grinned, dragging the blade further down my skin with her dark brows furrowing in concentration. "But before I do, I will give you a piece of myself to remember me by because I do so enjoy your stories."

Leaning back, she sheathed her knife and blew a kiss to her shadows before lifting my arm to demonstrate the swirls of ink that were etched into my skin.

"See. They are exactly like mine, at least then I can make sure one part of your story has come true."

I shook my head, staring at the blood and ink. "No, you are Remnant Ezra Solaire Dark. You are my soulmate, our daughter, she calls you maedere. You dream of us being a family. We are to destroy the queen together. I know you. I know you. I know you," I say with hysteria.

She laughs. It's a cold sound but I still love it. Love how her face lights up, her back arches, her neck elongates. "Oh you are so broken, my shifter king." Rising she blew me a kiss. "Enjoy your daydreams shifter."

Tears fell from my eyes as she turned her back on me. "Little umbra."

She did not turn.

"Remnant!" I barked.

She paused then, pivoting slowly on her laced booted foot.

I narrowed my eyes on her, trying with all my might to see past this facade, but I could not. The illusion was too strong and I was too weak, the hunger of my soul wraith form destroying my resolve...my truth.

With my heart on the line, I growled, "Whether you are the monster of my dreams or the lover of my nightmares. You are mine and I will find you again. I will always find you."

She smiled at me then. "Perhaps you're not so broken after all." Turning back to the heavy iron door she called over her shoulder. "Can't wait for you to find your way back to me, King Daemon."

That name...Remnant never used my full name. But who had? Someone I could not remember, someone I knew I loathed.

Then she slammed the door, leaving me in darkness and with something else...deep dark red tendrils oozed upwards over the table and snaked around me. The Sanguine power hungrily latched onto my body, whispering its poisonous words anew while my mind weakened further.

"Abandoned. They abandoned you. Everyone abandoned you. She abandoned you."

My anguished roars rattled the walls but remained unheard for hours to come. If I had been in more of my right mind, I would have noticed the dark satisfied laughter coming from the former queen of Faerie, hidden within the shadows.

375

CHAPTER 58

Remnant

THE WELL ENGULFED US, my fate sealed with nothing but the sheer will that my little family would survive—I had no other choice.

Falling around us in a sparkling shimmer of white and gold dust, souls fluttered within the glow. Reaching out with a trembling hand, my brows raised at the sweet vibrancy of life's essence humming against my skin.

There was no malice here.

Looking down at Riella, I could see her face scrunched tightly as she breathed shallowly against my protective hold. Bringing my hand back down, I smoothed over the wrinkles of fear, whispering gently, "It is safe for now, my little chickadee."

Riella peeked one eye open and then the other, her eyes widening at the same splendor around us that I had just admired.

"We are flying," she said in awe, peering downward and then squinting up into the light that fell on her upturned face. It shimmered on her bronze skin, a dancing glow that fell away just as quickly as it descended leaving not a trace of its touch until another cascaded upon her.

Riella's nose wrinkled, "Can you hear them too?"

My lips thinned, wishing I had the ability to shield her from this innate power but I tilted my head to listen more intensely anyway. I shook my head, "I do not hear anything."

Riella squeezed her eyes shut. "So many voices, too many." Her tiny voice wavered. "I cannot understand them."

Alarmed by her fear, I weaved the lilin to form small black muffs over her ears, shielding her effectively from the noise.

Immediate relief spread across my daughter's face and she gave me an apologetic smile. "Thank you, maedere."

Nodding, I held her closer, whispering loudly against her cheek just as the lights began to speed up around us. "We are going faster. We must be prepared for what is to come."

Her body tensed and she looked quickly around. "But what about faedere?" Her voice held panic that she could not mask and I squeezed her reassuringly again.

Even though I felt anything but reassured.

"He is below, little one. Once we stop we will figure out how we can help him, okay?"

We both looked down simultaneously, seeing the tattered remains of Emon's shadow trailing behind us, like a defeated flag being dragged across the ground in retreat.

He had not returned to his fae form, and a small part of me cracked. But now was not the time to allow what ifs to control me, no matter how much the sight of the Sanguine ripping holes through his shadow being felt—like I had lost pieces of him that would never return.

I could just barely feel the whispers of our soulmate bond, the warmth of his love still glowing inside of me but it was wavering. Flickering in and out, dull and lost, then roaring back to life vibrant and strong, his soul was fighting more than just healing. It was clear he was fighting a battle much deeper, the presence of the Sanguine likely still sinking its hungry claws into him.

And—he was *losing*.

Swallowing hard, I cleared my anxious thoughts. They would do me no good. I needed to get us to safety first and I needed to figure out how to achieve the impossible goal ahead of us.

I had taken a gamble, a shortcut, one I was not entirely sure would work. Instincts telling me that traveling The Well not one step at a time but within its stream itself where all souls were harbored was the best route for our survival.

And if there was one thing that I was always able to achieve...it was my *survival.*

I just had to make sure the fae I loved and the world I was trying to save would survive with me this time...something I had failed at in the past. The whispers of doubt cast a dark shadow across my heart, doubt that Emon's light would normally chase away—but even while surrounded by the most transcendent light possible none of it compared to my shifter's and it never would.

Nothing ever would.

Peering upwards, I hid the tears forming in my eyes from Riella. A small black circle above us expanded the further we traveled. The inner sanctum of The Well revealing itself to us at last. This was its end...but only the beginning for what was to come next.

"Prepare yourself," I called out to Riella right before we burst through a thin layer of water and landed with a splash in ankle deep depths. It seeped deep into my boots, sending a dark icy chill through my body.

Standing, I shifted Riella around to my back, her spear glinting in my periphery. I did not trust these dark waters I now stood in...more than one thing lingered beneath and its vibe wasn't at all friendly.

"What is this place?" Riella whispered as we both watched the water ripple far beyond a never ending horizon. Above us stars shimmered in a pitch black midnight sky, its reflection a mirror image that if left undisturbed would show no difference on what was the sky or what was water.

Turning slowly, we both breathed shallowly looking at the endless nothingness, a complete void of darkness with just stars and water. There was no wind, no sound, no other being here. It was as if space and time paused.

"It is creation." I heard Emon's voice rumble next to me and my heart leapt into my chest at the sight of him, but my joy quickly turned to a frown. His fae form of his soul wraith was almost transparent.

"Shifter," I took a step towards him and then halted when he looked back at me confused. "Emon. What is happening?"

He growled and then shook his head. Muttering softly to himself before looking up at me with fear in his eyes. "I do not know...I am weak and I am forgetting." His eyes pleaded, "Are you real, please tell me you are real. This is not a dream I have been living in..."

Alarmed, I stepped forward, sloshing in the water, to touch his face but it only passed through him. My hand snatched back, my eyes wide with panic. Why could I not touch him? "Of course we are real. Emon, what is happening, is it from the Sanguine? Why are you fading away, why can I not touch you?"

He sighed heavily, "I think...I think. I have been compromised. I don't know...I don't know what is true anymore. It whispers. It whispers horrible things." His hands reached up cradling his head, his eyes closing in pain.

"Tell me what I need to do," I said brokenly.

His lips pressed into a grim line. "I'm sorry, Remnant. We tried. I tried. You know what you must do now."

"No." I stumbled back with Riella whimpering, clutching her arms around my shoulders. I knew she did not understand what Emon was asking of me but I did. Goddess, I did. He wanted me to take his soul just as Shea had taken my mother's, his eternal life would be no more...our eternal life would never exist.

I threw back my head and screamed. My rage and anguish shaking the very stars above us. Why? Why go through all this for the result to be the same?

When my voice trailed off into the echoes of space, a tiny hand touched my face. "It's okay, maedere. We are the bravest of warriors," Riella whispered softly into my hair, her own tears falling across the exposed skin of my neck, her body trembling.

I knew she could feel my pain and so I drew it back, shoved it down deep inside, icing it over as I had once done in the past. When my eyes opened, I stood struck by the sight of what it meant to see a soul cry.

Waving in and out of existence, Emon's face was twisted in torment and misery, his hands tightening and releasing, knowing he could not touch me but wanting to all the same while his broken promises laid shattered at my feet. It was up to me on whether I would keep the pieces to painfully cherish or leave them here in the dark cold waters.

With tears streaming down my face, I stepped forward towards my soulmate, the one love meant for me in this miserable

existence of life. The only one that could ever break me so thoroughly but also build me so high that I transcended into a world
beyond my understanding.

Holding my hand up and feeling like my chest was splitting
into two, I raised my chin high while Riella sniffled into my hair.
The words coming to me inherently, as if I had them all this time,
knowing full well it was The Well that conjured up the memory.
"Repeat after me."

Emon's chest heaved, his eyes closing with a rattling breath
he did not need. When he opened them again, they blazed as if
they were gold once more. Fierce determination and loyalty nearly
forcing me to stumble backward from its intensity while his hand
raised to hover in front of mine.

Looking over my shoulder at Riella, he gave her a nod. "I love
you, my cub."

"I love you too, faedere," she sniffed, her hand still giving me
strength and warmth along my cheek.

Emon looked back to me expectantly. He didn't need to say
the words, I could see it in his eyes and in our bond, and soon
enough, he wouldn't just be tethered to me anymore, he would be
a part of me. If I died, so would he, and our love would cease to
ever exist again. There would be no Eithne for us.

Exhaling slowly, the words trailed from my lips, unwavering.
There was no pause, no hesitation, I didn't need them—I would
love Emon in pieces, I would love him in death, and I would love
him even without an eternal life. I would be undying—our Eithne
would be what we make of it, not what was granted. *"Extremum
vitae spiritum edere, to death I give my last breath."*

*"Extremum vitae spiritum edere, to death I give my last
breath,"* he growled deeply, his eyes staring deep into my own.
Then with a lopsided grin of triumph, he whispered, "It wasn't
true. You are real, you are mine and I am yours, little umbra. *Amor
vincit omnia."*

Love conquers all.

CHAPTER 59

Remnant

I STOOD STRONG AS Emon's soul struck through my chest. I could feel him inside me, all of him and it was like the moment I had first seen his aura unfiltered. So pure, so glorious that time stopped.

But there was something else...and I knew then that Emon had been right. He had been compromised, tainted, the Sanguine burrowing deep within his golden glow. It was a slow poison, one that would consume us both if I allowed it.

My knees crumbled, Riella whispering words of encouragement that I could barely feel over the numbness of what I had actually done.

The cold dark waters enveloped my exposed thighs and I stared out over the glassy reflection of The Well of Souls.

"What now?" I heard Riella ask softly and I wasn't entirely sure if it was to the pookah who was now hanging on her shoulder or to me.

"I obtain the rest of the lilin." There is no warmth left in my voice, I could feel the ice in my heart return, despite holding the purest soul this universe would ever know inside of me. "I pull the rest of the souls from the source instead of each step, we wake up our family, and we obtain your father's body."

"But without the steps how will the souls be summoned?"

Dipping my hand in the waters, I peered at my blotchy tear stained expression in the dark reflection, the stars shimmering mockingly above it. "We make them come—all of them." Slicing my hand through the water to drive away my own pathetic reflection, I summoned shadows to form a platform and eased my daughter onto it.

She peered at me solemnly, still every bit the warrior queen, her hair that had escaped her braid curling delicately around her beautiful face. Her eyes swirled at me with sadness and determination. Using my wet fingertips, I wiped away the stained trail of tears from her bronze skin.

"No more tears now, my little chickadee." I gave her a grim smile. "We have work to do, daughter of mine." Peering up at the pookah, I reached for him, petting down his odd twitching ears. "Keep each other safe." Then I tapped the shadow spear, still in her hand. "Kill anything that comes for you. Lilin or not, no one touches my daughter."

Her chin tilted upwards. "No one touches you either, maedere. Father would expect it of me."

I gave her a small smile. "Do not worry, little one. No one will ever touch me without my permission. Never again."

Rising, the water sluiced off my skin, sending dark ripples of warning across the glassy surface.

Their goddess was coming.

Stepping forward, my shadows popped up beside me, swirling around my torso and up over my arms as I walked. "Ready to go to work, my loves," I said to them, feeling the pain of losing my previous shadows ease with their presence. It was their turn to avenge the life that was taken from them and in that, I would find my strength.

Sloshing through the water, I walked until instinct told me to stop. The hairs on the back of my neck rose, an ominous tingle rising up my spine, and the thrilling rush of anticipation punching me in the gut.

I bared my teeth at the glassy surface, they lurked beneath...all of them.

"You should have thought twice about who would come to honor your pledge of vengeance, souls of Morta. Now show yourselves and meet the one you wish you could kill but now must serve."

Plunging my hand into the water, I reached out for the shadows that lived and breathed just like the lilin I had already conquered, hovering nearby, ready to intervene if need be.

My power spread in the water like millions of veins flowing and splitting, latching onto every lilin soul floating inside these dark waters. I could feel their resistance but I knew it was fruitless. I was their goddess and their vows were unbreakable even in the depths. They were bound to obey, such was the deal they made.

"Come to me, souls of Morta," I purred to them. "Come to your goddess."

Standing I pulled them upwards with me. Their dark entities slowly rising from the cold waters. The closest were only a few feet away but where the rest of them ended, I could not see. The amount of them seemed endless and I was surrounded on all fronts by their wrathful souls. Energy that was dark and malicious, angry and fierce, and it all was directed at the monster that destroyed their lives, the one they were about to pledge themselves to.

Flicking my long braid over my shoulder and steadying my racing heart, I addressed them with a strong icy voice. "You blame me for your demise but it is I that has come to honor your vows. I shall bear your pain and deaths you suffered when the goddess's light was taken too soon from you. But know this...there is one who has much more to blame, one who gladly sacrificed you in order to flee with her own life. There is one who used you to fulfill her own dark purpose. One whom you once called your leader—Deirdre the queen of Faerie."

All at once the lilin rippled, their figures undulating like the water upon which they floated.

"Should you honor your vows...I, Remnant Ezra Solaire Dark, will be the hand that ends the tyrannous reign of Deirdre Tatianna Maeve Seelie, her life will be forfeit for the pestilence she has brought upon our world and for the deaths she has callously taken, her soul will be forfeit, an eternal life forsaken."

Inhaling deep, I laid down my final vow. "And for your assistance, I shall release you from your bindings to me and grant you a full eternal life in the Eithne."

A dreadful hushed silence surrounded me—even the stars stopped their shimmer above.

Then like dominos tipping into one another the souls began to swarm, swirling around me in a cataclysmic spiral, rising higher and higher.

Taking another deep inhale, I tilted my head, my eyes trailing up at the shadow cyclone that whipped my hair around me and threatened to send me stumbling. Exhaling, I watched its apex curve inward, and spread my arms wide.

"This I vow."

A dark comforting embrace fell over my tense shoulders and I smiled softly through my fear, feeling my resolve bolster from my own shadow's embrace right before the lilin pierced my chest.

My mouth tore wide in a silent scream as the floodgates opened and the first soul entered me, then another, and another. All at once, the pain, the suffering, the torment, the rage, the grief, and loss of thousands of lives stolen by death took my own life as well.

CHAPTER 60

Remnant

I DON'T KNOW HOW long I died nor the number of times I was brought back to life.

Over and over again, I was snuffed out, then reborn. The full circle of the travesty I had wrought during Morta, my well known legacy, was now coming to a head, and I told myself this was what I had deserved—but I did not fail to notice, that deep within the darkest recesses of each death was a gentle tenderness in which the shadows joined me, as if to say they did not fully blame me for their end.

By the time I gasped back to life with the last lilin, I was a shivering, weak, mess floating in a shallow pool of The Well, drowning in ankle deep water.

Coughing, I slowly rolled to my hands and knees, instantly feeling the need to purge the darkness I had absorbed. Exhaling deeply, I pulled the shadows from my body and watched weakly as they formed into the large inky clouds of darkness. Darkness I was so accustomed to.

I had done it.

I had obtained the lilin from The Well of Souls.

They were mine now and I was theirs.

I touched the one soul in my chest that mattered the most. Emon's golden glow was still bright despite the taint there. I ached to feel his arms around me, his breath purring against my lips, his voice rumbling saying how fucking proud he was of me.

I shoved that notion away. No tears would change what had already come to pass, now all that mattered was what I did with the future. Dragging my tired body from the water, I stumbled to stand. The effort reminded me of the last time I had pushed my body to the brink of exhaustion. When I had run the hills of The West Isles with Riella slung across my back.

My eyes widened. Goddess, Riella!

Turning quickly, I looked out over the glassy reflected surface of the waters to see my daughter standing vigilant in the distance with a contorted dark fae shaped figure standing in front of her.

I stumbled with alarm towards her, hearing her tiny voice growl at the being.

"I don't care what you think Zaki! I am going to help maedere! She needs me." Riella stamped her foot and I slowed my panicked stumbling, noting it was her spirit guide.

"Stay." I heard it hiss, then it added. "Mine."

My eyes narrowed and I could feel Emon's soul pulse angrily inside of me.

"I think we feel the same on this one, shifter," I whispered internally to him.

There was no answer, just the gentle caress of his essence against mine and I swallowed down the bitterness I felt at knowing we would never have an Eithne together.

Hearing my sloppy walking, Riella finally looked up from her angry glare and gasped when she saw me. Pointing her spear at the pookah, she hissed, "Move."

Zaki hissed back at her, then popped out of existence. Dropping her spear on the shadow platform she stood upon, Riella launched herself into The Well's waters. Its depth came to her knees but that did not stop her from shifting quickly into shadow and barreling straight into my chest.

"Maedere!"

Feeling her shadow morph into her fae form, I clutched at her tiny body. Our hearts thundered in unison while we held each other, my nose burying deep into her thick black hair inhaling her scent. Emon had told me once that she smelled like the most beautiful sunlit meadow. I couldn't agree more as I let it soothe all the bitterness and regret inside. The road to holding this sweet miracle in my arms was paved with crushing pain and soul wrenching tragedy but I would do it all over again just to feel her exactly this way.

Like Emon, she was a vital piece of me that had been so achingly missing...a hope I never thought I could ever believe in.

"I don't like The Well of Souls," Riella murmured into my chest.

Laughing brokenly, I peered down at her, nuzzling her nose with my own just like her father would do if he were here. "I do not like it much either, little chickadee, but there is one last thing we must do."

Peering into the inky darkness hovering nearby I nodded to the anticipating shadows, "Obtain the souls of the sleepers...all of them."

Their smooth dark tendrils paused and I held my breath with baited anticipation. This would be their first true test on how dependable they could be. We didn't have a few thousand years to grow together, we had a few days, and the quicker we both accepted that, the better off we would be.

I exhaled when they disappeared a moment later.

"They are different from the other shadows," Riella said softly.

Adjusting her crown, I assessed the worry on her face. "How so, little one?"

"They are more...vocal," she explained.

Shifting her to my side, I waved towards the shadow spear and released the island of darkness I had made for her back into the waters. "Anything I should be worried about?"

Riella shook her head, taking the spear I handed to her. "No. Bay is the loudest. She has taken charge as their leader."

I smiled sadly, picturing Bay's big electric blue eyes and soft voice commanding thousands of vengeful souls was the best way to envision my lost friend. "She would have made an excellent leader for the water fae," I murmured more to myself than to Riella.

"That she would have but then again, the lilin would not have her to lead them either. Fate is a fickle thing, *forta*."

Stiffening, I held Riella closer to me and turned, seeing a sleek spotted form of a black footed lynx gliding over the water. Yellow eyes glowed brightly over their depths, straight at us, before it spoke again.

"Greetings, Remnant Ezra Solaire Dark. I have been waiting my turn to meet you. Unlike those last souls, I am a patient predator and I have heard many great things about you, *forta*."

"I suppose that depends on where and who you have heard them from," I said to the lynx, assessing the way the tufts on its ears pulled back at my response.

The beautiful feline laughed softly, a warm and gentle sound that had my tired shoulders relaxing. "I suppose I heard it from your mother, she was a great friend of my soulmate and an even better dodging daggers partner. Although much has changed since the last we saw each other, if what the souls of The Well whisper is true."

I took a cautious step forward, tilting my head, my braid falling over my shoulder. "You are Lova."

The lynx purred, her sharp grin bright in the reflection of the glossy darkness. "Yes, *forta*."

I smiled. Hearing her say *forta*, like the master healer, a term meaning strong female, was like having Jar's presence envelope me again, chasing the cold and filling me with warmth I was desperately missing. Here before me, was Jarquinn's lost soulmate. "Why haven't you gone to Eithne? Your soulmate has been searching for you."

Lova's eyes fluttered wistfully, "My handsome beautiful soulmate, he has not forgotten me even after all this time." She smiled sadly at me, "When I died I was so angry. At myself for failing to protect my court, leaving my son behind, and for the heartache I had caused Jarquinn. He had never wanted any part of the war but he fought in it to be by my side and to save as many as he could with both his blades and talented healing. I heard your vow. The release of the lilin once the queen has been purged of this universe."

"A fae cannot lie," I said, reaching to Emon's glowing soul inside, feeling solace in the fact that when the end came, it wasn't the lilin that I needed but a future with Emon and Riella in it.

The spotted cat bowed her head, the tufts of her ears twitching again. "You are more than just a fae, *forta*. I can see why my Jar loves you." Raising her head, her yellow eyes peered into my own. "I know he is waiting for me, I can see it in your eyes and I have heard the whispers through the realms but I also know I have one last journey ahead of me before I rejoin him again in eternal life—if you will have me."

"If that is your wish," I said softly.

She nodded, peering at my daughter. "Once you get back, keep that dying kiss flower on you at all times, little shadow shifter."

Riella nodded and my brows rose but the cat ignored my silent question, instead she bared her fangs at me. "Brace yourself, *forta*. My death is not for the faint hearted and even the strongest may weep. *Ligare*."

CHAPTER 61

Remnant

Despite having fallen into thousands of death memories today, experiencing the physical pain of their last moments, the feeling was still utterly strange and disconcerting.

I felt a heartbeat that was not mine, breathed air into my lungs that were not mine, heard the thoughts and felt the actions that were not mine—and yet they were. I was the bystander, feeling everything and knowing nothing at the same time.

So when the icy cold air hit Lova, I gasped inwardly, all while her shifter lynx form puffed the frigid air with very little discomfort. This cold was different, it was a void, empty, and barren. It soaked through the bones and left a deathly chill that seemed to never end. But despite its bleakness, her world was still awash with color while she scented the air. I marveled at the way her predator saw it—more than transfixed by the blood splattering the frozen ground, barely crunching beneath her wide paws as she stalked the battle around her.

"Welcome to the Sanguine, a barren cold that leaves you feeling nothing but endless despair," Lova whispered in my mind dryly.

I snorted back my response, continuing to be enamored by the way she moved. She was small, unnoticeable in this climate until suddenly she was not.

Her attack was quick, swift, and the metallic taste of blood became strong on my palette as she pulled down target after target of the blood fae she stalked while a battle raged on around her. Her recent victim gurgled their last breath when Lova's fangs ripped her throat out without remorse.

"I enjoyed killing them with my own teeth, just like how they killed so many of my kin, my friends in kind," Lova commented, watching herself proudly.

Bodies became a blur around her, as she continued to utilize her shifter speed to take down more blood fae, but her tactics were soon noticed and Lova found herself encircled by powerful blood fae warriors, their eyes glowing red and their skin youthful from their most recent feed.

Hissing, Lova's head swiveled side to side, licking at the blood that stained her lips and fur, assessing their heartbeats to read who would attack first. Her claws crunched as they dug into the frozen earth when her body coiled, ready for the blood fae's first move.

But before a single one of them even shifted their feet from the ground, lightning blasted them all from above. Fierce bright blue and white, it sizzled hot, striking them all dead, leaving behind piles of ash.

I wrinkled my nose at the stench, as did Lova. Looking up, her yellow eyes narrowed on Bane "the bloodied" Steelhead sliding across the frozen tundra, coming to her rescue, blood pouring down his face and a grim look in his bright blue eyes.

"They captured Calliope!" he hollered over the sound of the battle that roared with growls, screeches, and screams. Weapons and claws clashing together, drowning out his words quickly even with him only a few paces away.

A bright light had Lova shifting into her fae form, instantly drawing her sword, she faced the fear wrought on the swordmaster's face. Bane never showed his fear but this was different...

"She was pregnant," Lova whispered to me. "She should have never been out here this day."

"Where is she?" Lova screamed at the swordmaster, punching him hard in the gut to shake the shock glazing over his eyes.

Bane grunted, glaring at her through his anger and despair. I watched as Lova breathed a sigh of relief, recognizing it for what it was. She needed Bane "the bloody" right now, not 'the friend" who was on the verge of panic.

Snapping his head over his shoulder, he glared out into the distance, his fist clenched as he directed fierce lightning across the tundra, striking down another dozen blood fae his comrades were struggling to defeat. "South, I have been tracking them south!"

Hissing, Lova turned, sniffing at the air and narrowing her eyes on the barely there tracks in the cold earth. "I hope you can run swordmaster."

Bane grunted, "Let us see who hunts the best, shifter."

Lova grinned, flashing back into her lynx form and taking off with a long leap across the snowy ground. The swordmaster huffed behind her, his feet surprisingly light for a fae his size, a version of him I knew well. I had, after all, trained with him during my early faeling years.

Easily beating Bane from the start, Lova spied the disgusting metallic trail of blood the arrogant sloppy blood fae left behind and with it, Calliope's scent, cedar, warm and trustworthy.

"Who is Calliope?" I whispered inside her mind, watching the world blur by her in an array of color again, her slight puff of breath in the extreme cold showing her incredible endurance at the speed at which she hunted.

"She was a fierce shifter fae, pregnant with twins during the wars," Lova answered me as we watched her hunt. "Like I said, she was not supposed to be here, her mate had just fallen in battle days before and she was wracked with grief. Revenge had clouded her judgment and instead of keeping her and her mate's legacy alive, she chose to make the blood fae pay."

Twins. My mind whirled hearing Penina's angry voice from the night we stayed at the summit of the Red Cap Mountains. "You always love to remind me of how old I am, you fucking fossil. But you know my very birth had everything to do with that goddess forbidden land since you were the one who cut me and my twin out of our mother's dead drained body."

"Calliope is Penina's mother."

Lova hummed, "Yes, but even more so, one of her unborn children had been prophesied by Talgira before her death as the next great seer of our time. Calliope was more than just Penina's mother, for us she held the hope of us all and perhaps that was our mistake.

You see, at this time, Eve had not returned yet from Sheol, and our goddess was fading quickly, her energy drained by keeping our lands flourishing but also fighting her brother, the blood God Ichor."

"Having another powerful seer born would have been a great threat to the blood fae," I whispered, seeing the scent growing more intense the further Lova ran, dark figures appearing on the bright icy horizon.

A distant high pitched cry that had to be Calliope had Lova bursting with additional speed, launching viciously at the first blood fae she saw. The sharp taste of blood this time was even more satisfying than her last kill but it also mingled with the strong scent of Calliope—her friend, and Lova's heart stuttered.

It was a deafening sound, one that had my chest tightening with grief. The same grief coursing through Lova.

She was too late. The blood fae had already started to feed.

Faster than her and now high on their nourishment of the shifter fae, they blurred, knocking her like a pinball from one to another, their cruel laughter rising as they taunted Lova with their strength while one took a turn feeding from her friend.

Her blood burned, and she dived, slashing out with her claws and severing the achilles of the blood fae nearby, sending him stumbling into his pack. She wasted no time then, attacking him as he fell and ripping out his throat, but again she was not fast enough.

Gasping and rearing back, a sharp blade plunged deep into Lova's side and I screamed, feeling it as if it sawed into my own torso.

Lova roared, dropping onto her back and using her weight to crush the blood fae's neck in a perfect twist. The plunging grip on the blade in her side released immediately just as the final sound of her enemy's spine snapping echoed.

Shifting back to her fae form, Lova stumbled, shuddering with pain, holding the knife firmly inside of her. To pull it out now would mean immediate death. She backed up towards Calliope, her shifter hearing sensing only two heartbeats left, not three.

Lova faltered whether from the numbness of grief or the damage of the knife, it was obvious it took her great effort to stay upright, my own legs trembling with her. "Stay back, blood whores," she hissed, guarding what remained of her friend.

Grinning with confidence, the blood fae licked at their fangs, stepping closer and twirling their own blades in either hand. "You're going to be our sweet treat, little ancient." His accent thick with the hissing sneer in which he spoke.

Lova snarled, baring her teeth. "You'll be tasting nothing when I rip out your fangs bloodsucker. Your kind are a disgrace to everything that is fae."

The remaining blood fae laughed and their leader narrowed his red eyes. My own narrowed on the blood crystal tied around his neck, knowing first hand what it felt like to be drained by the horrifying stone from Bay's death. "Typical shifter, overconfidence will not prevent your death this day."

She winked, seeing Bane run grimly towards her, "It's not confidence, it's a fact." Dropping low, Lova relished in the roaring sound of fire bursting into life just before it ignited several of the blood fae, killing them instantly. The heat of the blaze was searing and I attempted to rear away from it, but Lova simply stared deep into its infernal depths, full of smug triumph. There was nothing left behind, no bone, no metal, just scorched earth, the leader of the blood fae on the run, and a furious swordmaster who was closing the distance with more fire licking up and down his body.

Ignoring the blaze of heat the knife was ripping through her side, Lova rose slowly watching the deserters with Bane. "Leave them to me, swordmaster," she hissed and pointed towards where Calliope lay slain. "The babies, Bane. You must save the faelings."

Bane's blue eyes darted to the prone form of their fallen comrade, his fire snuffing out immediately, then back to us. "She is dead, you are alive," he argued, stepping closer to her, his eyes widening on the knife.

Lova shook her head, panting between her breaths. "There are two heartbeats, I can hear them."

Bane hesitated.

"Go!" Lova gritted her teeth, frustrated. "I'll take care of the rest of those blood cunts!"

Shifting back into her lynx form, Lova raced after the remaining fae, her adrenaline drowning out the fierce ache in her side, and I was suddenly overwhelmed with her thirst for vengeance—my mouth watering just as hers was, thinking about the feel of ripping their throats out with her own fangs.

Spotting a large rock jutting from the tundra, Lova launched herself from it, landing paces ahead of the blood fae's retreat. Turning with a lunge, her claws buried deep into the blood fae's leader, the shock in his eyes satisfying for the both of us as she landed on top of him.

Quickly, she slashed out, cutting out his throat before shifting back to her fae form, straddling the blood fae that writhed beneath her. "I told you I'd rip these fangs out blood whore." Holding his thrashing head, Lova pried open the blood fae's mouth, blood gurgling out the sides before she viciously ripped out the his teeth with her pure shifter strength. Dangling them in front of him, his light dimming, Lova smiled darkly, "You won't be needing these where you're going. May Sheol take you to its darkest depths where you will live this very moment for eternity."

He was dead before her last words cut through the frozen winds. Snapping her head up, Lova growled at the last two blood fae that stared in shock, fear shining in their eyes.

Throwing their leader's bloody teeth at their feet, she snarled, "Leave and never return or stay and suffer his fate. I care not which you choose."

They both blinked slowly, glancing between each other before spinning back around and blurring away straight towards the plains where the bruxa were waiting. The undead vampiric females never did like the blood fae, found them quite annoying mimicking their way of life.

Shoulders sagging, her adrenaline slowing, Lova climbed off the dead blood fae, holding the knife in her side like a lifeline, she squinted out in the distance—back towards Bane. The wind slapped against her face with its own stinging vengeance, and I shivered internally. It was more than the cold that chilled her body now.

With great effort Lova dragged herself over to the swordmaster elemental, and paused when she spied the tears falling from his crystal blue eyes.

"The babes," Lova gasped, "Are they—gone?"

Bane shook his head, "No. They are still alive..." his hands trembled over their slain friend, "I—I can't."

"Oh Bane," I whispered to Lova internally, understanding the swordmaster's plight much more now. "I always knew he suffered a terrible fate in the Blood Wars. When he came back from them, he was never the same."

"We all have different sides of ourselves, forta," Lova whispered back through our connection, "Sometimes life has a way of suppressing it, and sometimes life shows its hand without any remorse."

My throat burned, bitterness a sour taste in my mouth as Lova reached out to grip the solid fur covered shoulder of the swordmaster. "You must do this, my friend."

Bane's hands fisted, dropping on his kneeling legs, "I have no blades," he snorted through his tears. "What a pathetic swordmaster I have become, with not a single blade left for me to save these faelings." He jerked his head towards the scorched tundra, "I burned those fuckers too hot, there's not even a blade among their ashes." Shaking his head again, he reached out to palm Calliope's heavily pregnant stomach, unable to control his trembling once again. "I can feel them. If... if I use my fire, I may hurt them, especially if they move," he whispered.

I watched as Lova reached for his calloused hand that lay defeated on their friend and pulled it away to curl around the knife buried deep in her side. "My injury is fatal, Bane, but my life may still save another this day."

I inhaled sharply, tears burning my eyes.

Bane's head snapped up towards her, his eyes bloodshot from fatigue and grief. "No," he growled. "I can take you back to Jar. He can safely remove the blade and heal you."

Lova smiled weakly. "My soulmate is talented, but some damage he cannot undo. It has been too long, there is too much internal bleeding, and this blade runs deep. In the time it takes for all of us to trek back, you'll be delivering four dead bodies to my soulmate instead of two. Take the knife, my friend, save the faelings. Do not let my death be for nothing."

Bane cursed, his hand shaking harder around the blade as Lova's lips thinned. There was no time for his hesitation, not now.

With a sharp inhale and a final surge of strength, Lova curled her hand around Bane's and wrenched the long dagger out, blood spilling from her like a broken dam as she fell.

Bane stared horrified at the blade, and then back to Lova, watching as she dragged her bleeding body to curl alongside her fallen friend—deep brown eyes stared unseeing and vacant back at her.

"Your babies will live on, Calliope. This I vow," Lova choked on a whisper, a thin sheen of sweat beading on her brow, her lips twitching at the foul curses escaping the swordmaster's mouth as he made his first cut. Holding onto her dead friend Lova waited, growing colder in death alongside her.

When a high pitched cry of a newborn babe rent the frigid air, angry and fierce, Lova knew that he was the male foreseen in Talgira's vision which meant the female was next. Her breath slowing, the beat of her heart waning, she waited for the next cry, and when it came, a soft sweet whimper joined by the coo's of the hardened warrior that held her, the shifter smiled.

Through Lova's eyes, I stared in awe at Bane who was unsheathing his own fur, baring his body to the unforgiving cold, to wrap the twin faelings together in the heavy cloth.

"Penina," she gurgled and I choked on the blood filling her mouth. Bane's eyes drifted over to us, rocking the babe's in a subconscious paternal instinct. "Calliope wanted to name them Penina and Falcon."

Bane cleared his throat and it was then that I noticed through the haze of Lova's death that he had been crying again. "Goddess bless Penina and Falcon, children of the shifters Calliope and Maddox Ariti. Long may they live in the light."

"Long may they live in the light," Lova's lips moved but no sound left them.

Bane's shadow leaned over her, his soft heated touch chasing away the bleak coldness of the looming death. I could barely hear his final words. "Rest your warrior soul now, forta," he called to her. "You have fulfilled your vow, Lovisa Riss. May the goddess take you with her golden light to live freely within our hearts where the devoted and young never die."

Her breath rattled when she took her last—a harsh sound for a harsh end and I felt every vibration of it as I died with her.

CHAPTER 62

Remnant

I WAS GETTING TIRED of waking in a pool of water. This time Riella cradled my head, her tiny body submerged and shivering while keeping me afloat. I choked when the dark shadows of Lova's lilin poured out of me and I blinked up at the mocking stars.

"No more," I whispered, still feeling the weakness of death lingering, attempting to regain my own reality.

Riella was above me, smoothing my hair away from my face with her wet pruney hand. "No more, maedere. You did it."

Rising, I pulled her shivering body into me, rubbing my hands up and down her damp arms.

"Thank you, little chickadee." I kissed her forehead, seeing my haggard self within the reflective surface of her crown. "I fear you have taken better care of me than I have of you."

Riella curled into me. "Faedere would want us to take care of each other."

I tapped her nose lovingly, ignoring the deep set worry I had as Emon's soul fluttered inside. "That he would." Rising, the cold water dripped from my exposed legs and weighed down my boots. I grimaced, more than eager to feel dry lands beneath my feet and the hot sun on my face instead of the cold wet dampness of this realm. Adjusting Riella, not wanting her in these unknown waters a moment longer, I slung her across my back once again. Spying her shadow spear lying at my feet, I summoned it to my hand, carefully handing it back to her. "Let's get out of here," I whispered, walking towards where we had first entered.

Riella and I both gasped when the shadows popped up towards us, Lova's lilin joining them, becoming one in their agitated swirl. My steps faltered and my brow quirked, I had lived a long enough life with the previous shadows, I knew their urgency when I saw it.

"What is it now?" I sighed.

They furiously tumbled around us, shoving us forward.

Riella tilted her head, her eyes widening listening to their anxious swirling. "They say they have obtained the souls but the demons are still outside. They have captured Lir and lay in wait. A trap."

I ground my teeth, "We must free Lir, even if it is a trap—" my heart pounded, Emon's body was aboard that ship, vulnerable in the soulless sleep. "Take me to Lir and protect Riella at all costs when we get there."

They did not pause this time, in one quick swirl Riella and I were enveloped in darkness before we were sent stumbling onto a demon infested metal ship with the great fae sea king laughing with each blast of his glittering trident. Looking up into the sky, I inhaled sharply at the hundreds of demons above, illuminated in Wrath's skies by dark ruby red blood crystals.

"Lir!" I cried out, setting Riella down and watching the lilin cloak protectively over her. Nodding, Riella raised her spear in response, before I turned to run to Lir's side. Sliding across the deck, I sliced viciously at any demon in my way, my eyes trained on the sea king.

Lir fought valiantly, but their sheer numbers were vast and he was quickly buried beneath a heap of demon scum.

"No," I screamed, lunging forward only to be knocked to the side by a fierce wind. Its gusts barreled straight into the demon pile, sending more than several flying into the churning seas.

Whether it was Lir's jealous ex wife, his cursed north wind daughter Fi, or both, I would never know, but it was enough for the sea king to regain his footing. Reaching his side, together we blasted and skewered demons dropping from the sky, the glow above us increasing in its brightness—charging in strength.

My eyes widened, "They are sacrificing their own to build the strength of the blood crystals!"

Lir roared as he pierced two demons at once with his great trident, flinging them hundreds of feet over the sea with ease. "Dinnae know if I am happy t' see ye or not lass with such grave news!" Then he frowned, "Where is yer wraith?"

Gritting my teeth, I killed the last demon aboard and kicked him over the side. Riella anxiously joined me before the demon even hit the water, the lilin still cloaking her in a bubbled sphere of shadow. Turning, I gripped onto Lir's strong forearm, and shook my head, "There is no time to explain!" I pointed up at the demons gathering. "We must get out of here or we will all be destroyed!"

Shoving his huge body forward, I grabbed onto Riella's hand, a dark foreboding creeping up my spine, quickly followed by an echoed hum, so loud it vibrated the entire ship.

"Fuck!" I screamed, knowing that the Sanguine was about to blast us from the very hell in which we resided. Heaving shadow from the depths of the oceans and the skies, I arc'd it over us right before the first explosive blast hit the shield.

I fell to my knees, arms raised to hold the shadows, layering them just as I had to stop Ethereal in The West Isles, *a permanent weave* the death god called it. The Sanguine power crackled a brilliant red against the darkness, hungry to reach us.

"Get Riella out of here Lir! The lilin know what to do!" I roared over the charging hum.

"That won't be necessary, shadow fae," a sweet cultured voice from behind me sounded.

I stiffened before screaming, "For the love of the goddess and all of Faerie, you cannot be serious right now." Glancing over my shoulder, I glared at the queen of Hell, and her sidekick demon Zazion standing smugly with his arms crossed over his chest.

The glinting of the sea king's head caught my attention next as he bowed to Avalon and her demon, backing Riella closer to the cabin door, hiding her behind his massive body as he did.

I narrowed my eyes on Lir.

"Sorry lass, tis her realm and it's where mi children be," Lir whispered to me, seeing my reaction as he straightened.

My eyes fell on my own daughter wrapped in shadow, "Riella, come to me."

Her hand tightened on her weapon and she hedged away, but the queen of Hell moved quickly, stopping her progress with shocked curiosity.

"No." I growled, ready to summon the lilin to portal her from here but the command died on my lips when Riella hissed, her spear pointed towards the queen of Hell's heart.

"Get out of my way, before I take you from this very existence," my daughter growled.

Another battering of the Sanguine hit the shadow shield and I grunted, bracing it before the power destroyed us all. "I'd do as she says cousin, that is a bás fang she holds and she is my daughter after all...you know how many I took down even in the chains you bound me in."

But the demon queen did not answer. Her gaze stuck on the vicious snarl on Riella's face. She held up her hands and stepped back, stating softly. "How old are you, child?"

Riella growled, sidestepping around her with the spear staying on target, Zaki appearing on her shoulder hissing his own warning. "I am seven."

Avalon stilled and I knew why, she saw in my daughter the little girl she once was. Alone and having to fight for a kingdom that betrayed her family. "Seven," she whispered.

Riella took her opportunity to blur over towards me, becoming a shadow within lilin shadows, and when she reformed, she stood protectively in front of me.

Avalon spun, staring with wide violet eyes.

Riella pointed her spear again, "Either you help my mother and your own people," she nodded to the giant sea king Lir, "or you leave. What do you choose, demon?"

Red light lit up the sky and I braced for its impact, a shower of crimson pouring over us. A bead of sweat dripped down the back of my neck.

"My queen?" Zaz whispered, placing his hand on Avalon's shoulder. She was still frozen, watching my daughter, and with her face turned towards me now, I could see her trapped within phantoms of memories from long ago.

Zaz shook her this time, "Lonnie?" The endearment slipped from his lips and I had a distinct feeling we were never supposed to hear it.

Avalon blinked from the forceful shake, looking at the demon that was manhandling her. She snarled, swiping his hand from her shoulder before turning back to me. "She is truly your daughter?"

"Yes," I said, feeling the shield tremble. Turning my focus back to the shadows, I hissed. "I am a little busy right now demon queen, come back later if you wish to chat."

"That red power, what would happen if you released your shadows?"

I weaved more into the cracks after another blow of the Sanguine fizzled over the barrier. "It would destroy us all."

The demon queen hummed, watching me with agonizing silence before kneeling on one knee before Riella, "Lower your spear, fierce warrior, I have no desire to harm you or your mother, I have decided to help her."

Riella glanced back at me and I nodded, smiling as she sent the demon queen one more growl and dropped her spear to the hull of the ship with a loud thud.

I snickered. "You have decided to help me? It has nothing to do with the fact that we are all about to be blasted from Hell?"

"You still must return to my camp to hold trial for your crimes. My demons demand retribution," she drawled.

I laughed dryly and my daughter hissed. "Clearly I need help. I need my daughter off this fucking ship, my soulmate's body delivered to Sheol without dying myself, and if you want me that badly, of course I shall return."

Stepping beside me and giving the watchful Riella a respectful nod, she looked up at the power with a disappointed face, "I was at least expecting some sort of protest. You steal the fun out of everything."

I laughed coldly, "I've been playing these games much longer than you, *cousin.*"

She grunted, not sparing me a glance of her bright violet eyes. "This will mean declaring war on the territory of Wrath," she mused.

The demon growled behind us. "War has always been the fate of this territory, it was just a matter of time."

Avalon grunted, "So be it. Cover me if need be, Zaz." She spread her wings out wide, a beautiful array of both black leather-like skin and red feathers.

"Always my queen but you and I both know it will not be needed," the demon cooed smugly behind us.

Another explosive wave hit my shield and I panted against the power splintering more of the shadows under its massive force. My brows pulled inward, even a permanent weave could be destroyed by the Sanguine...could nothing stop it?

"Are you two done chatting now?"

Avalon bristled, studying the skies, "Right, be right back."

She launched herself sideways off the ship outside my shadow shield generating a rush of air that forced my hair to blow across my face, covering my look of disbelief. "I'm all for confidence but I am not entirely sure that was the best strategy."

The demon behind me chuckled, "Wait for it." Turning, he winked at my daughter, "Hey little fae queen."

"Hi Zaz!" Riella beamed at the demon, despite the gravity of the situation we were in.

"Little chickadee, go back to Lir," I commanded, seeing the Sanguine power recharge.

"Okay maedere!" Riella hummed, skipping over to the sea king and grabbing his hand. Lir laughed and then met my eyes, regret burning in them, understanding that it was not easy for me to trust him now that I knew where his allegiance lay.

"I am trusting you to keep her safe," I said to him as my eyes dropped to the lilin still surrounding her, *"You too, if we fail here, she must be brought back to Sheol with Emon,"* I called to them silently.

Zazion studied me curiously, a dark frown pulling on his features, "where is your shifter king, your mate?"

I stiffened. "He is not dead, so do not worry that your debt was not fulfilled properly." I seethed.

The demon grunted, "I can see why your thoughts would navigate to this fact, but this does not seem like a time where someone as devoted as your mate would leave behind his two most cherished possessions."

Startled, I looked up at him but a sudden blast stole my next words, the aftershock of the blow sending the entire boat lurching out from under the protection of the barrier, and slamming the demon and I both into its unforgiving sides.

I groaned with a curse and the demon's eyes lit with fire as he growled towards the dark sky, his hand outstretched to assist me to rise.

Only Lir and Riella had stayed put. Neither one had been affected by the impact.

Gripping the demon's hand, feeling his heat sear my skin like the fires of Hell, I stood, feeling the first splatter of hot viscous liquid on my upturned face. Then another and another until it rained heavily down upon us.

I grimaced at the smell, a mixture of putrid death and iron. Swiping at my face, I stared at the black and red essence that stained my fingertips.

"It's blood," I whispered, glancing over at Riella who was staring at my hands just as I had been, the lilin shadows protecting her from the carnage. I eyed the grinning demon, "She destroyed them all?"

Zazion's speared tail curled around his leg with pleasure, "Now you know how she has kept the throne since she was seven, fae. This power costs her much but I have a feeling, she felt inspired by a certain little faeling."

"She sees herself in Riella." I said knowingly.

The demon snarled, "She sees what she could have had if someone had protected her sooner."

Loud splashes and sharp pinging sounds drew our attention away from each other—my eyes widening as hundreds of blood crystals fell with the rain of blood. Several of them skidded to where we stood and I resisted the urge to shift away fearful of its dark power, still feeling their effects from Bay's death.

Zazion bent to examine them and I quickly pulled him back. "Do not touch them, demon. If you know what is good for you, you and your queen will bury these in whatever infernal pits of Hell you have to never be seen again."

Straightening, Zazion's wings twitched with agitation, but before he could speak a flurry of feathers and blond hair dropped beside him.

The demon queen crossed her arms in front of her chest, drenched in both wraith and demon blood. "I give the orders here, fae, these weapons are now mine to do with as I see fit."

I quirked a brow at her, "Fools are the ones who think they can harness blood crystals without repercussion. They will destroy you, cousin. What you should really be asking yourself is how this territory, under your rule, obtained them?" Swiftly, I kicked one over the edge of the ship, its splash barely heard over the churning waves.

Avalon's lip curled with uncertainty, "I'm starting to think the quicker you leave this place the better off Hell will be."

I grinned, knowing now that wasn't the true reason, keeping Riella safe was. Emon and I's prodigy was gaining allies just as fast as we ourselves made enemies. "I knew you would see it my way." Turning towards the sea king, I flippantly waved my hand down my blood soaked body. "If you please, Lir, while you all may love the feel of your enemies' death on your flesh, I do not."

He chuckled, "Aye lass, ye be a sight right now." Waving his hand, I gasped when I was drenched with salty water and then blasted by his north wind daughter Fi, drying instantly with her concentrated gale forces on my person.

"Thank you, Lir, thank you Fi," I said, smoothing back my wind blown hair, my eyes falling on my daughter, reaching out to her. Riella instantly jumped into my arms, exhaling slowly into my neck. I clutched her to my chest, exhaling slowly with her. "All will be well now, my chickadee. The demon queen is going to let us leave." My eyes lifted to bright violet ones that were staring at my daughter with the same flickering of haunted memories as before. "Isn't that right, Avalon?"

Her eyes tore away from Riella and refocused on me, blood still dripping down her face. "I thought fae could not lie?" she hissed.

A slow smile spread across my face but before I could reply, Lir's laughter boomed out across the seas.

"We cannot, your majesty, but we are masters of wording, while The Goddess o' The Well may have agreed t' return, the lass did not specify her time of return or if it was with ye." He winked, "With all due respect lassie, always be specific when making deals with the fae."

Black stained lips pulled back into a sneer, "The Goddess of The Well? As in The Well of Souls?"

The lilin fell off of Riella and draped around my shoulders with their comforting darkness while the queen of Hell tracked them with her scrutiny. "Yes."

"You could have told me you were its goddess."

My brow arched, "Would it have mattered?"

A small smile twitched at the corner of her mouth. "Not at all, fae. I would have still imprisoned you, *but* you would have become much more useful to me had I known what you were." But she could not stop her eyes from falling on Riella. The unspoken words were just there on the tip of her tongue.

She would not have made an exception for my status but she would have for my daughter. That was a weakness she could not expose, not even in front of her demon second who understood her more than she gave him credit for.

Swiping at the blood on her face, she stared at it, murmuring, "No matter, this blow against Wrath's territory has been....*satisfactory*." Curling her fingertips in a tight fist, she glared before stepping back with her wings spread wide but then hesitated, her eyes falling on Riella once again before she reached back to pluck a light red feather from her wing, holding it up in front of her. "Fi, if you would be so kind."

The wind picked up gently around us, snatching the small feather up in the sweet breeze and delivering it to us.

"For you, fierce warrior," Avalon nodded, smiling as Riella's eyes widened with awe. "Take it. It is a gift for you."

Riella's small hand reached outward and grasped the feather. A bright smile lit up her face. "It is beautiful! Thank you! It is so very soft," she said, running her hand along the edges.

Avalon smiled gently at her, her wings stretching before she tilted her head up to the sky. "Do me a favor, cousin. Don't bother returning, like ever. I shall inform the council you were lost in Wrath's seas."

I snickered before Avalon launched herself back into the night sky, twirling in her flight, her unique wings a wondrous display of power and beauty.

Zazion cleared his throat, and I glanced down at him. "Whatever happened to your shifter mate, I know that he will not allow his absence to be long. He will always find you, Goddess of the Wells."

I swallowed hard, not expecting a demon of Hell to care about my shifter soulmate. Their time together must of had an impact on him. "Thank you Zazion."

He nodded, his tail twitching, "I meant what I said before, Remnant Dark."

I sniffed. "Yes, I understand your loyalty to your queen demon, you guiding us into the den of the demon mother of snakes made that clear enough."

He chuckled darkly, "Yes, thank you for that, one less thing I need to take care of in my lands. Besides, her lair was the quickest way to The Well and I knew both you and your mate could handle it." Shaking his head, his horns glittering with blood, he regarded me seriously, "What I speak of is in regards to your daughter, Remnant Dark. The true queen of Faerie will always be welcomed in the realm of Greed. You have my word as a demon."

I pursed my lips, "What of your word as a *prince*?"

He grinned evilly then, sharp fangs shining brightly in the crackle of lightning spreading across the sky. "Princes covet shiny things, especially the prince of greed, and your daughter is a treasure I shall always keep safe should she seek it."

Riella lifted her head, still holding her feather tightly, and I winced when her crown caught in the windblown tangles of my hair. "Thank you Zaz."

He nodded and then pointed at the sleeping spirit guide who was not at all interested in our conversation. "Except that thing is not," he snickered. "It's a menace."

Peeking one eye open, Zaki hissed before nestling back into the crook of my daughter's neck, slumbering once again.

Laughing, his wings spread, his head tilting up to watch the acrobatic flight of his leader, dancing with lightning. "I trust you can take care of the blood crystals, sea king, and deliver them safely to the queen's palace."

"Aye, if that is what ye wish."

His black eyes never left the sky when he whispered, "It is. This territory has experienced a huge blow, but I would not linger here much longer, Lir. Fi will not hold it against you if you visit another territory for now."

The sea king grunted, a small tear falling from his eye and into his blood stained beard. "Thank ye, Zazion."

The demon grunted and then easily shoved his great body back up into the air, meeting the flight of his queen circling back for him.

The blood crystals slid across the deck when the ship rocked gently as if bidding them goodbye, their silhouettes disappearing into the dark ominous clouds.

CHAPTER 63

Remnant

L IR LOOKED BACK AT me. "Time ye be off too, lass."

I stepped towards the sea king, my eyes imploring him, intense worry for his safety pooling in my gut, "Come with us Lir. Dump these crystals far into the sea where no creature may find them, and join us to defeat Deirdre."

The giant water fae shook his blood soaked head, the scales on his face glittering like his silver eyes and the shells in his beard clinking softly together with his movement. "Thank ye goddess for inviting mi, but I have t' decline. I cannae leave my ship and the west winds of mi son Aodh calls mi now. I wish t' hear his strong baritone winds."

The north winds of his daughter swirled around us and I looked down at Riella who smiled when the breeze twirled her hair. Staring at the gentle smile of my own daughter, I nodded, my heart saddened for the sea king. "I understand." Exhaling, I placed a warning hand on his massive arm, "But Lir you must understand, these crystals, they destroyed Atlantis, they massacred half of the water fae people—I was there, I saw it with my own eyes. They are not to be treated trivially no matter how innocent they may look."

Together we both looked down at the several crystals still rolling across the ship.

"I had heard the tales but I never wanted t' believe it." Smothering his hand with my own, he smiled warmly at me, "I will take t' heart ye warning, lass."

I nodded and he patted my hand, shooing Riella and I towards the cabin door. "Now off with ye! I never be good at goodbyes so make it quick will ye."

With one hand on the door handle to the cabin, I turned back to the sea king, holding up my hand, *"Beannached leat,* Manannan Mac Lir." *Farewell.*

Riella mimicked me, repeating my words, "*Beannached leat,* Sea King of Atlantis. I still have my whistle you gave me." She held up the tiny seashell whistle that circled around her wrist.

He winked with more tears forming in his eyes, reaching over my shoulder and wrenching open the steel door, "Keep it with ye lass." Then he shoved us through, *"Beannached leat,* Remnant Dark, Goddess of The Well and Riella Dark Strider, true queen of Faerie." His normal booming voice whisper soft when the door clicked behind us.

I sighed heavily, Riella and I looking at each other with both fatigue and weariness. There were a hundred questions swirling in her green gold eyes but she kept them silent. Kissing her forehead softly, I set her down, and placed my hands on my hips surveying the cabin. It had stayed just the same as we had left it, except for one thing.

Emon's body was nowhere to be seen.

The shadows hovered above us, sensing my panic beginning. Had the demons gotten through? Did they take him? The heat from the nearby fire that still blazed was suddenly suffocating, the tightness in my chest beginning to form. Now wasn't the time to panic but my body wasn't going to listen to me, it never had since the attacks started plaguing me after Morta.

I reached for Emon's soul inside, and like always...even in this form, his presence eased my suffering, melting the surmounting fear from my heart and burning it out of my soul—but that wasn't the only thing there.

Leeching, like the hungry parasite it was the Sanguine was a dark taint staining the bright glory of my soulmate and its presence sickened me.

Pure frustration had me stomping my foot angrily and making Riella jump at my side. "Goddess, damn it, how can a gigantic shifter hide so easily?"

Riella tugged on my hand several times before I looked down at her earnest face. "But maedere, all you have to do is ask the cabin for him."

I stilled and the shadows shimmered beside me, laughing at my expense. What in the goddess was wrong with me? "Of course, I do. I am sorry, little one. What a clever clear mind you have after everything we have gone through today." I rubbed at my tired eyes, shaking my head in disbelief.

"I learned it from watching you maedere," she said sweetly, and I drew my hand away, stunned by her honesty and her love—something I never thought I was deserving of. But seeing her confidence in me now, I knew it was time I accepted this and *believed in it.*

Just like Emon had always done for me when I could not. "Please reveal Emon to us," I said gently, squeezing Riella's shoulder.

We both closed our eyes against the bright flash of light before opening them again to see Emon's body laying encased in the gold coffin, metal vines curling up over the glass keeping him safely locked inside.

I stared, my breath stolen from my lungs. Even with the ashen glow of his bronze skin, he was beautiful and I desperately ached to see the light peeking out from those golden eyes again, to hear his growling deep voice whisper the one name only he would ever be allowed to call me.

Little umbra.

It was a whisper in my heart and his soul flared gently inside me, despite the taint there. What would become of him, of us, of our family once I returned it to him? How much would the Sanguine change him and how in the goddess was I to save him from it? Even the past shadows, a power unlike this world had ever seen, could not truly fight its relentless hunger, succumbing to it.

I touched my chest still staring at Emon's soulless body. "I won't be able to restore him until we leave Sheol, if I do it now, we risk losing him to the sleep again," I murmured, seeing Riella's face etched with the same worry. Instinctually, I smoothed back the wrinkles from her furrowed brow, "We will leave, little one. The shadows will take him and us back to the Eithne."

"Wait!" Riella cried, running across the room to the fireplace, indicating our provision bag. "We have to bring this with us too. Faedere told me so. It also has Jar Jar's flower inside and Lova told me to keep it on me."

I blinked. I had almost forgotten. Striding towards her, I knelt, "Yes, of course." Rummaging through the pack, my hand fell on a stack of letters. Peering in, I could see that they were wrapped neatly with Emon's handwriting and my fingertips traced the name addressed on it, pausing on elegant script.

"What have you been up to, shifter?" my thoughts careening along our soulmate bond, but there was no answer back, just the steady pulse of Emon's soul still in my chest.

Exhaling, I set the stack aside and the flower fell into my hand. The small lip shaped yellow bloom Jar had gifted us still vibrantly alive despite being clipped and taken from its valley.

Raising it up in the fire light, I twirled the delicate petals, feeling a sense of dread for why my daughter would need a flower that could save any being from any form of death. Praying that it would never be her life in question.

Tucking it gently behind Riella's ear, the crown on top of Riella's dark hair flared in its presence, the dual yellow petals reaching towards it, happily seeking its shimmering glow. She was adorned from head to toe with mementos of our adventures, decorated and honored by priceless gifts that I knew could only be meant for one thing—her protection.

Feeling the dread ease, I smiled softly at her. "I love you, Riella."

She smiled and her small warm hand reached out to touch my cheek, her eyes turning a solid gold for a brief moment, her father's eyes, chasing away the rest of my worries, "I love you too, maedere."

Turning my head to kiss her hand, I stood throwing the pack over my shoulder, and tilted my head to my new lilin shadows hovering nearby. "Take us all back. Take us back to Sheol. Back to the Eithne, to Voltam, to the God of Death."

They swirled briefly before expanding, engulfing us and Emon's body in their dark shadowy embrace.

CHAPTER 64

Remnant

THE BREATH RUSHED OUT of us as we unceremoniously slid across the blurred silver path of the Eithne. Zaki struggled to hang onto my daughter's shoulder, his body flailing like a wind-blown flag before he simply gave up trying and disappeared from existence. Riella giggled as her slide sent her into a pile of white sand that rose to enfold her into its haunting waves, while my entire body slumped with exhaustion, stopping with a squeaky halt.

Flopping over, I breathed it in—the glory of the rainbow hues of Sheol's twilight. The three moons glow, the sparkling stardust, and the cosmos beyond. I let it all drape its peaceful presence over my tired body. Screeching its greeting high above us and setting the sky alight, an fire phoenix streamed across it, embers raining down before turning into rejuvenating ash that kissed my face.

Shadows encroached my view, twirling shamelessly as if they were asking for praise in getting us back here alive.

I arched a brow at them. "You're not serious are you, you dumped us on our asses, how is that deserving of praise?"

Riella giggled, clapping for them despite my admonishment. "I think the umbras did a great job and it was fun!" She frowned then, looking around her, "I don't think Zaki had fun through, he is gone again."

The shadows' antics intensified, banishing Riella's frown, and I watched with a smile of my own as they lifted Riella into the air, tossing her into the star-filled twilight. Their boastful pride knew no boundaries, so similar to the shadows before and yet young in their experience.

My amusement was short-lived when I sensed the death god slithering his way across the lands, stopping in front of me. Polished black shoes blocked my vision and I glanced upward, seeing the full powerful smile of Shea looking down. His silver and gold adorned hand reached outward, offering it to me.

I sighed. I wanted to rage at him, to scream, punch, and kick his arrogant smile right off his face. He sent us to literal Hell without a single word of the trials he knew we would face and it had cost us time we did not have. Perhaps if we had been sooner, maybe Emon's eternal soul could have been saved, maybe he would still have an afterlife.

Instead, I reached up and took it, blinking when I felt myself swiftly pulled to my feet as if I was his darkness to command with ease.

Still dressed in his well fitted black silk shirt and tailored pants, his bejeweled emerald eyes glowed intensely with admiration before I looked at the being gracing his arm.

"Tell me you didn't foresee this, mother." I summoned the shadows to bring forth Emon's body encased in gold and glass. The stars shimmered reflectively across the case almost as if honoring the incredible fae inside.

Silently asking the shadows to entertain Riella so that she did not become part of what came next, they rushed towards her in a flurry of dark waves. She laughed excitedly, shifting with them and flying through the air.

My mother smiled at my daughter and then looked back to me, sadness etched in her beautiful features. "Even if I had known, Remnant, you would not have wanted to listen, there was only one way for you both to survive this and the future to come."

"Why?" I said, angry tears sprouting in my eyes, "Why then have Emon become a soul wraith if bartering his soul was the end result."

She took a step towards me, her elegant hand outstretched to sooth my pain but I flinched back, my arms wrapping around myself and digging into my sides. Unable to stand looking at her, I turned away to focus on Riella playing with the shadows.

"I know you do not trust the sight, Remnant, but there has never been one more clear in my lifetime. Daemon knew this."

I shook my head, swallowing back the bitter tears.

"Daughter, I know you are worried but what matters most now is that you accomplished what you set out to do and now you have what you need to defeat Deirdre." Shea's voice echoed with fatherly pride but I felt anything but. I was beaten and battered, bereft, as if the trophy won held no meaning anymore.

This feeling—I recognized it, it was the same one Bane had the day he returned from the blood wars and like the swordmaster, I latched onto my anger to drive away the emptiness.

"You mean I now have the ability to save the Goddess, your sister. How long have you suspected that Faerie has been trapped in The Sanguine?" I seethed.

A cold smile formed on Shea's lips but his eyes lit even brighter with pride. I goddess damn hated it. If this was what it was like to be a god, scheming without a single pulse on the feelings of others then it could go to the pits of Avalon's Hell.

"Faerie has always done her own thing but to abandon her world...that is much unlike her," he drawled, "So how long have I known? Since the Blood Wars ended actually."

"And you have done nothing about it?" I snapped. "Instead you brought me here to go in your stead. That was your end game? Not the lilin, not the souls of our people, not the souls of my friends or my soulmate. None of that mattered to you. It has always been about your failure to save your own sister."

The death god's arms folded, stretching the silk shirt over broad shoulders, his green eyes turning to narrow slits. "You shouldn't be surprised, my daughter, that we share the same loathing for those who have wronged us." He gave me a pointed look and I scowled back, "My involvement in Faerie's conflict with our brother, Ichor, the God of Blood, cost me my family and a future life with your mother. For the first few hundred years after the wars, I simply didn't give two shits about what happened to my sister and before you go raising your judgmental head, a few hundred years is nothing for a God. It may as well be days for us and yes, Faerie is part of the end game. I know your healer explained this to you about the balance of your world. Ichor gifts life through his blood, Faerie nourishes it, and I—I have the power to take it. Without Faerie's powers, your world cannot be nourished...the lands will continue to die, lands my granddaughter will someday grow up in but—she is not the true end game. Deirdre crossed a fucking line when she chose *my family* to manipulate, *my family* to destroy, and I will relish the moment you stop her heart." The sky darkened threateningly, the death god's bejeweled eyes lighting up with fire, "And when at last, she arrives in Sheol," he continued, "I will personally torture her putrid soul for all the years she has been gifted living breath. My plans for her after that...well, even Hell would fucking squirm at it." He grinned, a pure evil smile, the sinister side of my father blatantly revealed behind his cultured poise. "So were my intentions of bringing you here selfish? Perhaps, daughter, if you choose to look at it this way. It still does not change the truth. Without your powers you would not have any chance to defeat Deirdre, and without Faerie, the world you think you are saving would still die. Bringing you here, ensured your survival, your family's survival, and the dreams you have of a hopeful future with them. I can see it in your eyes every time you look at your shifter, every time you hear your daughter's laughter, every time you dream at night...a future you never thought you could have but now want with every fiber of your being. I *know* what that feels like, and I will do everything I can to make sure you *never* have to live a second longer without that hope. You may not like all my choices, you may not agree with my approach but know this—I will do anything for you, my little chickadee."

My jaw clenched, our blazing gazes dueling with each other.

My mother stepped between us, her gaze just as hardened. "Remnant, there was a time where you implored me to trust you and I failed to understand—" my eyes cut to hers, seeing that moment clearly. Her, Kade and I standing on the palace balcony in the City of Light, where I had declared my vows to serve the queen as her general. "I am sorry I did not trust you and your decisions, I realized too late that you were protecting your court even while serving another," she reached out to me, but I flinched away. Her hand fell, "Do not make the same mistake I did Remnant, trust in our words even if you can no longer trust our motives."

I moved further away, my fingernails digging even deeper into my sides. I did not have the luxury to break now nor did I have Emon to put the pieces back into place. Instead, I willed my heart to turn to ice again, it was the glue I needed to keep it together for the sake of my daughter, to save my new family, to free Emon...

"So be it." My tone was cold and unfeeling but I could see that my mother understood while Shea's growling revealed that he did not. She stepped back into her mate and placed a soothing hand on his chest. He looked down at her hand, placing his own over hers, and I could see the painful look they shared between each other.

I did not have time to feel guilt for them, nor could I carry on this conversation further. Not without crumbling.

I searched the dim twilight, "Where is Kade?"

"I am here, sister," Kade's strong voice called out from behind me.

Pivoting on my heel, my eyes drifted over his tall athletic form, the formal leathers of the shadow forces covering the tattoos we shared, but that did not hide the rest of the similarities between us.

I wanted to run to him, to hold him, and tell him how much I loved him but I didn't. I released my sides, breathing deeply. "I have obtained the souls for our people as I promised, but I cannot release them in Sheol, the risk is too great. Our people must return to The City of Night, they must return home, and mother cannot leave this place, Kade. Her soul is tied to Shea. Our court will need a leader."

Kade frowned darkly, his green eyes glowing in the twilight. "What are you trying to say Rem Rem?"

"You are their true leader Kade. You always have been," I said softly.

His green eyes shifted over my shoulder to our mother. "You sister speaks truth, my beautiful boy. You have always been what our people needed Kade, and it is time for you to return home." I glanced over my shoulder at her, seeing her soft sorrowful smile. "Our court will flourish under your guidance."

Kade stumbled on his words, shaking his head. "The shadow fae look to your guidance mother. They trust you. They will only see me as a boy trying to fill his mother's shadow."

Eve snorted. "That may have been true at one time my son, but even in a soulless sleep, they will know who stood watch over them, who visited every member daily, speaking to them daily, these long years we have spent on death's doorstep it has been you that has been their true leader. It is you they need now, Kade Stellan Shea Dark, not me. My time in Faerie is done." She turned back to our father, his arms unfolding and wrapping around her, his own smile echoing her bittersweet sadness. Lost in him, she brushed back his hair, her eyes full of undying love, "It is also time for me to move on, I have done much in my lifetime for others...now is my time to choose myself."

The death god kissed her softly on the lips. "I will support whatever decision you make, my love."

Kade shook his head. "I—I don't—-"

I couldn't hold it back any longer and closed the gap, wrapping my arms around his solid frame. "You cannot live a life in death brother. It is time for you to..." I grinned at him, Emon's words echoed from a memory passed, "step out from the shadows."

His face contorted with disgust. "That was horrible." He arched a brow at me in our embrace, glancing over at my Emon's soulless body. "Did that really work on you?"

I released him then, stepping away to stare at the beautiful shifter and feeling his even more beautiful soul pulse inside me, tainted or not, there wasn't a any essence in this universe that compared to his. Even in The Well not a single one blazed as brightly as Emon's.

"Eventually, yes," I said, my voice breaking.

Kade's hand rested on my shoulder, I could feel the slight tremble in his body. "I'll always be here for you, Rem Rem."

I reached up to place my hand on his, my eyes still staying on Emon, our parents watching us all with quiet reservation. "Always," I whispered fiercely, "And it will be needed, Kade. Our court must be ready for battle in ten days time."

Kade choked on a dark laugh. "Are you seriously asking me to bring my court to war within days of my new rule with knowledge that the fate of our world rests upon it."

I turned towards him, "Ten days Kadey Kins, not a day longer. I will call upon you."

He folded his arms. "And how will I know where to find you?"

Holding my hand up, the lilin shadows rushed to swirl around it, bringing my daughter's shadow form with them. She shifted back at my side, smiling up at the both of us. "The shadows will come for you." I said gravely.

"Uncle Kade!" Riella beamed before turning into shadow and barreling into him. Stumbling, my brother cradled her shadow into his chest just as she shifted back into her fae form, wrapping her arms around his neck with a grin.

"Little bird," he laughed, looking down at her he grinned, "you have learned to fly."

Riella nodded excitedly, "And shift. Wanna to see?"

A small smile traced across my lips watching my daughter show off her new skills.

My mother sighed behind us, "I suppose this means goodbye, will you not stay to rest?"

I shook my head, feeling the sickening slither of the Sanguine slide along Emon's flickering light. "No. We have no more time to waste." My eyes shifted to my father, "Deirdre has extended her reach into the Valgari. Nice of you to tell me Hell shared its borders." I drawled.

My mother gasped. "Shea! You did not tell her?"

He grinned at her but spoke to me, "Would it have even helped if I had?"

I crossed my arms, "I think you need to visit your shared realm father because the Sanguine has spilled into your lands. Deirdre has recruited the demons of Wrath, supplying them with blood crystals. If what you say is true, that your main goal is to ensure my survival then they must be stopped."

Green fire rose in his eyes, "Surely Lucifer has it under control."

I shook my head, "Lucifer is dead. His daughter rules in his stead. She is strong but young and untried. She wants the Sanguine crystals for herself."

Shea's flaming glare died and he frowned, shaking his head of flowing black hair. "Dead? No that cannot be possible, I would have known."

I snorted and flipped my hair over my shoulder, "That's your problem to solve now, I cannot be fighting the demons in the Sanguine and Deirdre at the same time." One look at my mother gave me pause. The urge to still keep her safe and protected strong. "And you cannot allow the Eithne to be compromised," I added.

His head tilted, his eyes losing focus. "Noted daughter." A smile spread across his face, "I know you wish to be off, but you cannot leave just yet. You have a visitor and I must say, it's about fucking time."

My mouth opened but before I could ask who, a roar I knew well, shook the white sands into tremendous plumes, its height competing with the large onyx towers in the distance and from them, a great golden panther raced towards us.

Preservation would have had anyone stepping back from the blazing glow of a charging beast but that had never been my nature. Instead, our eyes locked and a small sob tore from my chest, then my feet were moving, then running, straight for the world destroyer...the one I called friend.

Rearing, his giant panther form slid across the silver path to stop our inevitable crash, but I did not care. Slamming into his front leg, I buried my face into his golden fur. "Ethereal." My tears fell and wetted his regal coat, soiling his perfection—I needed him.

His massive head bowed around me, hot breath stirring my hair like a summer wind. *"Princess of the shadows. What has our fairy boy done now?"*

CHAPTER 65

Remnant

I STARED UP INTO gold eyes that were so much like Emon's, blinking away the tears and swallowing down my heartache.

I would not break. I could not break. Not now.

"How are you here? How did you break free?" My hand stroked the golden panther's large head, the awe of his magnificence still just as strong as the first time I laid eyes on him that fateful day in front of The West Isle gates.

Not to have any attention stolen from him, Riella's spirit guide appeared, spitting like a rabid animal up at Ethereal, taking on a smaller feline form in front of a cat of giants.

"Zaki!" Riella cried, running towards her spirit guide with open arms. The pookah turned, its red eyes glittering with happiness, shifting back into a bunny before it launched himself into her arms. "Naughty pookah, where have you been?"

The spirit guide's ears tucked back as he hissed softly. "Free."

Looking between them, I arched a brow at Ethereal. "The pookah freed you?"

Ethereal's normally refined voice rumbled, speaking out loud for the first time. "I was already halfway free, rodent."

My brows raised. "You can speak outside our minds?"

Ethereal tore his narrowed glare back to me, "Only because we are within the Eithne. The realm of the dead allows all creatures to communicate like you do."

Ethereal huffed and my hair blew across my face. "Leave it to the fairy boy to collect more parasites," he said, disgusted and glaring at the pookah one more time before raising his massive regal head. "Death god. Lady of the Night Court, Lord of The Shadow Fae. Greetings."

Tucking Riella and her pookah into me, I watched my family's shock at Ethereal's presence, the only one not affected was Shea himself.

Kade looked at me with raised brows. "You got to be goddess damn kidding me, why do all the beasts end up loving you," he muttered towards me, playful jealousy in his tone.

I grinned smugly back.

The death god snorted, smirking at the panther. "Am I not uncle to you then, nephew?"

Ethereal's golden tail softly flicked side to side, and his nose wrinkled, "It takes more than blood to call you uncle, Shea."

My father chuckled, "So you do remember then."

He growled, "I remember some, not all, but I do remember what matters most." Turning back towards Riella and I, his gaze bored into mine. Sending blistering heat deep into my soul. "Where is Daemon? Tell me fairy boy is still alive," he inquired, fear lacing the deep dulcet tone.

Ethereal loved Emon. My shifter had a way of gathering lost souls, binding them to him with loyalty and love without ever realizing it. Emon had always swore they hated each other and perhaps their relationship was strained but that did not mean love did not tie them together.

"Just. He is in the soulless sleep," I whispered and the shadows shimmered, bringing Emon's body to us.

Ethereal bowed his head and whimpered, "His soul is not inside of him." Sad eyes turned on me, *"It is inside of you,"* his voice whispered inside my mind. *"And it is not well. the Sanguine taints him."*

I nodded, my lips pressed into a thin line, bitterness burning like acid in my throat. "Yes."

Ethereal sighed, "He will not be the same."

"You do not know that for sure nephew," Shea snapped behind us but I ignored him, knowing in my heart Ethereal was right.

Up until now, I had been denying my own fear...starting with Emon's demeanor as a soul wraith, the irrational uncontrolled anger, losing himself in rage, and then the Sanguine power ripping him to shreds. The last time we spoke, when I took his eternal life, he could barely believe I was real, something haunted him, a fae losing a battle within.

I could see my already pale face turn ghostly white in Ethereal's gold eyes. "What will happen to him?"

"There is no way of knowing, it could simply be parts of his memory will be lost or all of it, or it could be much much worse. His entire truth of who he is could change," his voice growled. *"Especially with the Sanguine corrupting him,"* he added in my mind, masking his thoughts from the others.

"Again there is no way of knowing this," Shea growled, "You worry my daughter unnecessarily."

I turned towards my mother, ignoring the death god, "Have you had any sight of this?"

She shook her head, her hair falling in waves like the shadows flowing over her, "My visions of Daemon ended the moment his soul left his body, but he knew the effects being a soul wraith could have on him—he prepared for it."

My heart raced. *The letters*...he knew something like this was going to happen. *"Shifter, when you are whole again, what happened to you in The Under will seem like a lovers caress compared to what I have in store for you."*

My thoughts fell away, my chest aching fiercely even while Emon's soul glowed within. If I were to be honest with myself, if Emon returned to me whole again, I would just as likely fall to my knees with pure relief rather than kick his balls through his throat.

Riella stepped around me without fear, her swirling gold and green eyes angry while she pointed at Ethereal, understanding fully what they were unwilling to say. "Faedere could never forget me, he would never forget us!" She turned towards me, confidence wavering in her eyes. "Right maedere. He will never forget us."

Sometimes being unable to tell a lie was a goddess damn curse. I knelt and adjusted her crown. "He promised he would always be with you. We will trust in that."

"Fairy boy is clever," Ethereal lowered his head, "Your father is almost too clever, I am sure he foresaw this as Eve has said, but to what extent I do not know, nor am I privy to his plans this time."

The heavy regret in his voice was audible. He blamed himself for not being here, for Emon, for us.

Ethereal turned his intense gaze on me and I shivered under the power he manifested. "I know I do not deserve another chance—"

The death god snorted behind us, "More like a third chance, nephew."

The cat snarled softly back at him before looking at me imploringly. "I know I do not deserve it, but let me help you, Remnant Dark. Allow me to accompany you and the others into the Sanguine."

I yanked back my hair, standing. "Even if I wanted to, you would be a giant beacon there, Ethereal. Besides, I unintentionally separated you from Emon. It was not purposeful."

"Undo it. Tie me back to him. You hold his soul inside of you, you will be able to do the same with me. You are the goddess of The Well of Souls, which means you can manipulate them as you need."

Shea barked, "With a cost. I do not wish that for my daughter, besides you will forget who you are again, nephew. You do realize that don't you?"

The panther did not even bother to spare him a glance, his eyes only watching me.

"I care not. I made a promise to the fairy boy, my memory means nothing to me now. My past and my future do not dictate my decision now. All that matters is making sure Daemon and his family survive what is to come." His eyes swiveled back to me, "Allow me to keep my promise to him and should I fail you, you may lock me away in shadows for the rest of my eternally damned life to remember all of what I have done," the great cat growled deeply and I shivered from his intensity.

In my hesitation, I felt the gentle touch of my mother's hand on my arm. Her eyes held mine, the sight a flickering ghostly whisper within. "It would be foolish to not have every resource at your disposal, my little chickadee."

Kade stepped behind her, his hands shoved deep in his pockets, blue curls falling over his brow, "I agree, Rem Rem. You are fucking facing a power that not even the goddess could defeat. For once in your life...accept you cannot do this alone. You're almost there sister, your soulmate helped you but now you must trust the help offered to you of your own free will."

Scowling, my hands clenched. "I—goddess damnit, I don't even know how to put his soul back."

Riella pressed her petite warm body into my side and my hand instinctively fell on her shoulder, soaking in her unconditional love shining up at me, "I believe in you, maedere," she whispered.

Shea sighed and then grumbled, "I will help you daughter."

Pursing my lips, I studied the reluctant death god glaring at Ethereal. He did not like this plan, did not want to admit that in all his scheming there was a possibility he could have been wrong...wrong that Emon and I would come out of this better than before. Reaching out to Ethereal, I marveled at his silky golden fur, letting it fall through my hands as I whispered, "Are you sure Ethereal?"

The beast nodded, "I have never been more sure of anything in my life, princess of the shadows. You, Daemon, and Riella are what matter to me now. Nothing else. You are my family."

My hand dropped, a heaviness falling on my shoulders, and Riella squeezed my leg again in moral support. "Tell me what I need to do, father," a sigh of reluctance escaping my lips.

Shea's eyes widened and I held his shocked expression without anger, resentment, or mockery. I could at least give him one memory of us, where I accepted our ties. This world was too goddess damn dangerous, the future too volatile to leave behind any more regrets.

"Thank you, little chickadee." His voice was gruff and he swallowed hard, clearing his throat before reaching for my hand. His many rings adorning it were cool against my palm as he placed it on the ever watchful golden panther. "Open your aura sight, daughter."

I breathed deep, following his instruction, blinded by the bright burning fire of Ethereal's soul, the world destroyer.

"The soul is nothing more than a shadow inside of a body," Shea said confidently, "Think of their aura as just that. Latch onto it like you would the shadows in the darkness and pull it into your body to hold. Just as you hold your shifter inside of you."

Pressing my lips together, I struggled to find anything to weave in the blinding blaze of the panther's soul—but each time I thought I had a hold on it, I lost it.

Sweat beaded on my brow, my hands clammy in his fur that continuously slipped from my grasp. Biting the inside of my cheek and tasting blood, I hissed my frustration.

"Don't force it, you know the shadows, they cannot be wrangled. They are coaxed, they are caressed, they are seduced by the very essence that is within you. It is what makes you a shadow fae and the daughter of the god of death." Shea's darkness flowed over my arm, following my brands as he pressed his hand harder into mine and continued, "Every aura has an outline, daughter, a shadow surrounding it. Use it, own it, you are the Goddess of the Well, that makes you The Goddess of Souls. This is your power by right and by blood."

My eyes watered staring back into the hot blaze of Ethereal's aura and I searched for what he described. My heart thudded widely when I finally found the faintest outline, a soft edge to the light, and then I called to it. Coaxing, caressing, seducing, just like my father described, pulling it into me, and I gasped loudly when Etheral's light suddenly set my whole body on fire within.

I held a world destroyer inside and he burned brightly along with Emon's soul.

Opening my eyes, I slowly lowered my hand from the empty space that was just occupied by the massive panther. A bright light flickered in the distance beyond and I took comfort in thinking perhaps it was Jar, his bright blue eyes smiling at me, saying well done *forta*.

I exhaled shakily, feeling unsteady before turning back towards my family. Kade's lips pressed firmly together but he nodded, my mother gave me her most encouraging smile, and Shea reached out, squeezing my shoulder with comfort.

My hand fell on Riella, stroking down her hair. "It is done," I said shakily. Ethereal's power inside me was slightly painful but it was easing. Even still I felt weak, exhaustion dragging on my weary body.

Shea squeezed again, "You did well, daughter."

I blinked back at him, more than relying on his firm grip to keep me from wavering on my feet. "Why do I feel so weak?"

My father's lips pressed together grimly as he held onto my shaking form. "Taking a soul within yourself should never be done lightly. There is a cost," he answered.

I shuddered, "Like the Sanguine."

Shea nodded, "Yes but worse for a god or goddess. You have learned that even we have universal rules we must follow and when they are broken, we suffer fates that no being truly deserves. I would not use this power unless you absolutely have to, my chickadee, even though it is uniquely from your family line," he winked at me before releasing his hand.

I pulled Riella in closer, "I understand." My eyes fell on Emon again, my voice trembled, "How do I release the souls of our people, how do I restore my soulmate's?"

Shea reached for my mother, settling her back into his side and even pulled my brother closer, squeezing his shoulder affectionately before turning his bejeweled green gaze back on me, lips twitching. "The lilin can easily lay their souls back into their bodies. They are souls too after all. But this will not be the case for your shifter, for him you must breathe it back into him while keeping it tied to your own. Your shared brands will help with that, it was not all for naught daughter. You did well."

I stilled, ignoring his last words focussing on the breathing Emon's soul back into his body, "You mean I have to...*kiss* him awake?"

Riella's hand fell over her mouth to smother a giggle and my brother's lips twitched watching her.

Grimacing, the death god nodded, "I suppose, if you wish to see it that way."

A snort escaped me, causing my daughter's giggles to burst loudly from behind her hands, the pookah who had been sleeping silently on her shoulder, scrambled to stay perched as her tiny body shook in fits.

But she was not the only one shaking, silent hysterical laughter was bubbling up from days of exhaustion and I had no resistance when it exploded out of me. The Eithne responded. Stars danced, sands vibrated with our echoed laughter, and far-away lights twinkled all around us, shimmering in the cosmic twilight.

"If he doesn't wake up, I'm not kissing him. I have no need for a prince."

Those were the words I had said to the shadows that first night I met Emon, when my darkness dragged his unconscious body through the Wildwoods.

I was still right though. I had no need for a prince.

No. I had a need for a king. The only king that would rule my heart and I was going to get him back.

Kiss and all.

CHAPTER 66

Remnant

I SHIVERED ON A frozen summit.

We were finally within the Sanguine lands, knocking on the former queen of Faerie's doorstep with six glass coffins laid before me.

The lilin had delivered us here before disappearing again to transport Kade and our people back to Faerie. The shadow fae had officially returned from the dead, no longer soulless, and the City of Night was no longer empty.

I was also no longer the last of my kind and my heart beat wildly with joy at just the thought of seeing my people again...someday.

Squeezing Riella's hand, I surveyed the frozen tundra that stretched for miles beyond the looming shadows of the Red Cap Mountains which stood regally behind us. The lands were still here, frozen in time just like the fae who slept under its frigid sky where a permanent eclipse covered the moons. If anything did hunt these summits they were not awake now, but that did not stop my vigilance.

Popping into a large inky cloud before me, I tilted my head at the shadows with a small smile on my face, "I take it it went well?"

The shadows swirled around us both excitedly, drawing a small giggle from Riella.

I reached out to them, running my hand through their darkness, sighing, "Are you ready for round two then?"

They shimmered over my hand and then gently tugged me forward to the first glass enclosure. My hand trailed over the cool transparent surface, staring down at the gorgeous mocha skin and petite frame of Penina. Her piercings still glittered and I could almost see her deep brown eyes laughing at my intense study of her.

I had missed her, more than I would have ever felt possible.

Lifting the lid carefully, I touched her brow and then looked up at the shadows, nodding to them. Diving into her chest, a sharp gasp left her pierced lips, her body bowing off the platform.

Another exhale released the shadows and Penina's lashes fluttered before her warm brown eyes blinked open.

A bright jovial smile crossed her face, "At least you aren't naked this time."

I laughed, and then threw my body over her, holding her tightly in my embrace. "I have missed you, my friend."

Her arms squeezed me tightly back, "I sense it has been a long few days for you," she teased but then hugged me tighter anyway.

I sniffed and then released her, pulling her into sitting, "As if you don't already know. You have a lot of explaining to do, shifter."

She grinned again, "Haven't the slightest idea of what you're talking about."

"Nina!" cried Riella who wasted no time crawling into the shifter assassin's lap. "These are for you," she smiled, shouldering up to her the heavy provision bag packed for each one of them.

Penina took it and arched her brow. "Please tell me there are at least some rainbow unicorn furs in here."

Riella giggled. "Don't be silly, Maedere says we must remain hidden from the queen. All our attire is gray and white." She waved down at her thick white hide snowsuit and gray boots. A trim fur lined her hooded cloak framing her bronze cherub face.

Penina wrinkled her nose, "White you say...I do like white." Opening the bag she rummaged through it with pursed lips. "I suppose I can work with this."

My lips twitched and I snickered, "Work quickly then if you can, I still need to wake the others and you are the one who knows the most about these lands. I don't particularly care for our exposure."

Penina's eyes glowed deep brown as she looked out into the tundra, "At least it is not night yet, there are caves along this summit that we can seek shelter in and then start in the morning. We have some time before the worst of the Sanguine comes out to play."

Setting Riella beside her, Penina quickly began to undress, muttering under her breath over Riella's rambling story about our recent adventures. "Honestly, it's a crime to be wearing the same outfit for three days in a row. *And* it's wrinkled of all things!" She gave my daughter a horrified look that caused her to giggle.

Shaking my head, I moved towards Riley.

"Wake Bane next," Penina called out, shoving a long sleeved shirt over her head.

I turned to arch a brow as she hopped off the platform and shimmied into a thick pair of white leather pants.

Feeling my questioning look, she added. "Bane is a fire elemental, he can keep us warm and his lightning may be needed to protect us. He will be our best defense against the beasts of this land, as much as I hate to admit it. He will also take the most time adjusting to the shock of returning here...not that I care but we cant have a frozen fire elemental fossil when it's colder than the goddesses tit out here," she growled, shoving an arm through a long gray coat. "At least whoever packed this had good taste."

I shivered again, not from the cold this time but from the image of Bane's broken look when he failed to save both Lova and Calliope.

The shadows rubbed against me softly and I patted their dark tendrils thankful for the comfort.

It was clear Penina knew very little detail of the circumstances surrounding her birth, and I was goddess damn sure the fool of a swordmaster would never tell her. All she had ever revealed was the brutal way she was born but she knew not of the tenderness of Bane carefully wrapping her in his own furs, covered in blood and ash, forgoing his own warmth to hold her in his arms, cooing and soothing her while grieving a great loss of two friends.

Riella's giggle pulled me back. "It was grandfather Shea and grandmama Eve that packed for you. They said maedere could not be trusted."

Penina nodded, "Yes, that makes sense, I heard Eve always did have excellent taste, it is only right that her mate would as well." She glanced over at the sleeping swordmaster with pursed lips, then back towards me with a wink, "Unfortunately, they are right, that talent did not pass down to your mother."

I snorted, shaking my head while I approached Bane's coffin. Waving towards the shadows, they wasted no time throwing open the glass and driving straight into his chest. Switching to my aura sight I watched as his soul returned. The deep navy color returning, the color of a troubled guardian, one who had lost much but could not stop himself from protecting others despite the pain it caused. Grimly, I released the sight, and stepped back, preparing myself for his awakening.

He did not disappoint. Where Penina was joyous, Bane was *reactive*. His eyes snapping open with fire igniting over his hands. Instinctually, he rolled from his platform onto the ground, shooting flames straight towards our heads.

Flicking my hand, I guided the shadows to intervene. They hissed their displeasure, snuffing out the blaze just seconds before it seared my furs clean off.

I sniffed. "Nice to see you too, swordmaster."

"What in the fucking goddess' hairy cunt have you gotten us into Dark!" he roared, popping back up into standing, his blue eyes cutting towards me and then widening as he surveyed the frozen tundra around us. "Fuck."

"Quiet down you old fossil before you get us all killed. We are in the Sanguine, you bloody fool," Penina hissed, standing fully dressed with her bag slung over her shoulder.

Bane's sharp blue eyes glared back but I did not miss the paleness to his face. "I know where we are girl, what I want to know is how and why?"

I sighed, "It's probably for the best that I wake you all first before I explain. I'd prefer not to tell the tale twice."

Bane's dark brows rose, "What do you mean wake the others?"

"You cannot be this daft Bane Steelhead. Isn't the number one rule of any training to take note of your damn surroundings?" Penina snapped, waving her hand at the five other glass enclosures that had the swordmaster's eyes widening in shock before she continued, "Have your eyes stopped working along with your brain? Did I truly make a mistake in requesting you to be woken second before the others...?"

Bane growled, "Enough girl—" he frowned, bright blue eyes honing in on her, "*You* requested for me to be woken?"

I stilled at the vulnerability in his tone.

Penina hissed, stamping her foot, "Of course you foolish fossil. You are a fire elemental, we are freezing our asses off in the cold and you wield lightning which will protect us from what lurks in the red haze of the eclipsed sky. I should not have to explain that to you," she waved her hand at his bare muscular arms and his thin flowing pants. "I mean look at you, you're barely shivering and it's well below freezing."

Bane's eyes flashed with fire before he crossed his arms. "Fine. I'll stand guard and wait."

Shifting into shadow, Riella reappeared and dropped a bag briefly in front of him. "Here is your bag, swordmaster Steelhead," she blinked her swirling gold green eyes up at him, her lashes fluttering on her innocent face. Bane's own softened, petting her head awkwardly, "Thank you, little cub."

Riella grinned widely up at him, "You are welcome." She waved her hand and her shadow spear appeared within it. Biting her lip she fluttered her lashes again from beneath her fur lined hood. "Maedere says you are the best weapons master around. Do you think you can teach me how to use my new spear?"

Penina snickered and leaned in whispering to me, "Oh she is good."

Bane's eyes widened before he shot me a death glare, "Dark are you aware your daughter is holding a bás fang weapon."

I grinned at him, "Very."

His eyes sparkled but his frown of disapproval was that of carved granite, even as he looked back down at Riella, "I suppose I have no choice but to teach you, lest you accidentally snuff someone from their entire existence before their time is truly up."

Riella jumped up and down excitedly, forcing Bane to step further away from her waving spear and I could not stop the small laugh escaping my lips.

A loving hand fell on my shoulder, Penina turning me towards her, "Allow me to help you, Rem. The quicker this is done the safer we will be." Her eyes flickered to my chest, "the safer Emon will be."

I studied her deep brown eyes for a moment, fearful of the answers that I would find in them, how much she already knew about Emon's fate. "Agreed."

Signaling the shadows to split between us, they obeyed without hesitation. "You wake Xi. I'll wake Riley."

Penina grinned as she opened up the glass and her eyes glowed happily with mischief. "Tyr will be so pissed he was not chosen to be awakened with them."

I shook my head, staring down at the wavy green hair of my best friend, brushing it off his brow. "Time to come back to me again, Ri," I whispered, dropping his soul into his body once more.

Hazel eyes blinked rapidly and shined brightly up at me. "Hey Rem," his deep voice croaked before groaning loudly as he rose up. My hand snapped out to ease his movement, feeling his body suddenly tense. Looking up, I smiled at the way he stared at Xi across from him, her posture mirroring his. "Hey *terella*," he rasped. *Little earth* in ancient fae, it was an endearment he only ever used in private with her. To witness it now spoke volumes of their bond.

Xi's hair fell over half her face when she leaned towards him. "Riley," she breathed before launching herself forward and wrapping her arms around him.

Catching her, Riley buried his face into her neck. "It's alright, Xi. We are alright. Our general saved the day evidently," he looked around him, brushing Xi's hair from her face, his lips smirking, "Although on second thought, I might retract that statement."

Xi sniffed and swatted at his chest, "Don't even joke about that Ri." Her gray eyes turned on me and then fell on the frozen lands. "Thank you for saving us, Rem. Is this...the Sanguine?"

The shadows dropped their provisions in front of them, making them both jump. "Yep!" I said with a bit of snark and winked, "Get dressed, I have three more shifters to wake and then we go to war."

Xi groaned, dropping her head back into Riley's chest, "Why is she always so happy about shit like this...that tone Ri, and you know it's never a good thing when it comes with a goddess damn wink."

Riley chuckled, squeezing her reassuringly, "Do not worry, I will endeavor to keep the blood from your hair this time."

Xi sniffed, her shoulders shaking with silent laughter.

Penina and my eyes met, nodding, we moved on. Quickly restoring Asher and Tyr, their souls settling with ease and their awakening smooth.

"Fucking goddess. My balls are already half frozen," Tyr growled once he got his bearings, swinging his legs down to the ground.

Penina chucked his bag at his head, laughing. "Then put a hat on them before the only brain cells you have freeze off of you."

Asher groaned, as I helped him to sit, his head shaking with disapproval at the two seemingly childish shifters. "I swear it on the goddess, Skyler and I did try to raise them the best we could...with manners and sensibility."

I laughed softly, "I know you did Asher."

Turning to me, he studied my face and then his gaze dropped to my chest, "You are almost as sorrowful as my son was when he brought you home to meet me." Cupping my face in his strong hands, he purred, "Tell me my daughter in law, where is my son's body and why are you so unhappy when his soul resides inside you."

Everyone grew quiet and suddenly, Riella shimmered to shadow, falling into my arms, wrapping around me, the fur of her hood tickling my face.

"Let us find shelter first," I rasped, "then I will tell you all what has happened."

CHAPTER 67

Remnant

T HE CAVE PENINA HAD found was large and accommodat-
ed the blazing fire Bane provided with ease. But despite
the added heat, the ice lining the walls barely melted, a shimmering glaze against the flames. The others gathered, stripping
off their outer layers and reaching for the warmth of the fire,
no one speaking, everyone waiting for my next words with
baited breath, quietly digesting what had transpired the past
two days.

"Where is he?" Asher asked softly, breaking the silence.

My lips thinned and stiffly I nodded to the shadows.
Everyone watched with avid interest as they swirled upon the
ground growing larger and then lifting away completely revealing Emon in all his sleeping glory.

Tyr crossed his arms with mock hurt, purple eyes studying
his best friend, "Of course the asshole got his first tattoo brands
without me."

My eyes trailed along Emon's markings as I traced the edges of my own just inside the fur cuff of my coat. "Do not worry my friend, he got them without me too."

Xi placed her arm around me and hugged me tightly.

"Rem?" Penina said softly. Tearing my eyes away from my shifter mate, I looked into her questioning eyes. "Where is Emon's bag? That he traveled with in Sheol? It might help him once he wakes to have something familiar."

My eyes narrowed on the innocent look in her warm brown eyes. Her piercings shimmering in the firelight.

Riella clapped her hands and more than one of us jumped. On edge in these new lands and after the story just told. "Oh, I'll get it! Zaki!" she cried.

When a long eared, red eyed bunny appeared hissing at everyone except for Riella and I, they reared back.

"Zaki," Riella sighed, "Be nice."

Tyr arched his pierced brow, the tattoos over his shaved head wrinkling, "Anyone want to explain why we are sharing a cave with a demon rabbit?"

Asher leaned in with a fascinated expression. "It's not a demon, it's a pookah."

"He is my spirit guide," Riella smiled at him and stroked his fur. "Zaki, we need faedere's bag."

The pookah nuzzled her hands before flashing away to return seconds later, dropping our bag in front of us with a loud thud that echoed off the walls of the cave. "Thank you Zaki," I said, shifting the bag over to Penina. "I am hoping having you all here once he wakes will also help."

"So how do we wake sleeping beauty?" Bane growled out from the entrance of the cave, his eyes never leaving the Sanguine night. It was only slightly dimmer than when we first came, the eclipse full and permanent in the sky.

I sighed rubbing at my temples. "His soul is inside of me, I must breathe it back into him with a kiss. "

Tyr's laughter roared, before twitches of smiles broke across all our faces. "Like a goddess damn princess?" he guffawed.

Penina smacked him. "Can't you tell this is hard enough on her?" But she could not stop the grin on her face from spreading. "I cannot wait to tease him for the rest of his life for this."

Asher winked back at her. "Aye, me too lass."

I sighed and rubbed my hands on my thighs before rising. "I cannot delay this any longer." Walking towards my soulmate, I waved my hand, the shadows making the glass disappear instantly. Staring down at Emon's strong jaw line, I trailed the scruff of his beard, before reaching up and brushing his hair off his brow. I was more than eager to see his golden eyes open, but also I was fearful to face what I might see in them when they did.

The others gave me my space, waiting patiently and supportively at my back.

Breathing deeply and closing my eyes to concentrate, I reached for Emon and Ethereal's souls. They flickered inside my chest just like the lights in Sheol. I felt for the shadow around their outlines, grasping onto them and pulling it upwards at the same time as my lips leaned over and touched Emon's.

They were soft and I savored the touch, feeling the loss of his soul acutely, leaving behind just the frozen chill of my heart that I prayed he could warm again.

Please, please, let this be enough, I pleaded, losing myself in the feel of his lips, breathing his soul back into his half dead body.

My weariness and grief was overwhelming, my mind foggy and slow with so much fatigue that I missed the warning growl rumbling from my soulmate's chest.

Rough hands gripped my upper arms and I practically sagged against the radiating warmth blasting from him, imagining that bronze glow of his sculpted frame coming back to life again, his power pulsing with it.

"Emon," I whispered against his mouth. My eyes fluttered open only to be ensnared by the blazing white gold of his—full of rage and *hatred*.

The vision of him blurred and I gasped when the snap of my spine echoed off the walls, my back hitting the floor in one violent assault. My skull quickly followed, cracking against the unforgiving stone. Sparkling spots danced in my vision as a new kind of beast leered above me.

Dazed, I felt my arms being pinned above my head and I gasped when claws pierced through their exposed flesh, anchoring me to the stone floor like a sacrifice. Another set of claws nicked at my exposed throat, where my pulse was beating wildly.

Blinking through the stars in my vision, I could see Emon rise above me, his fangs descending from his snarling mouth. His golden glare glittered with disgust and loathing.

"At last, Remnant Ezra Solaire Dark, the queen's dirty little whore, is all mine to play with. I told you I would find you again," he chuckled with satisfaction twisting his claws into my arms and relishing the tears springing from my eyes.

I knew he saw my tears as ones of pain, but they were far from it. They were tears of loss. I swore I would hold on, that I would not break—but I never promised I would not shatter—and I did, into thousands of pieces where there was no more light in the darkness. I had lost everything once but this was much much worse.

Leaning in he purred, licking at the tears falling from my eyes. "Such pretty tears. Give me one good reason why I shouldn't just fucking kill you for all that you have stolen from me, shadow bitch."

I tilted my head back, exposing my throat further to him, the words he once wielded against me when he first revealed who he was, whispered brokenly from my lips, "If you truly believe this, then fucking end me. I do not want to ever live in a world where you look at me the way you are now."

EPILOGUE

My Little Umbra, My Soulmate, My Love, My Queen, My Goddess, My Forever Eternal,

I vowed that I would never let a single day go by without my telling you just how much I fucking love you. If you're reading this then that means I could not stop what was to come and for that—goddess Remnant, I am so sorry but know that where ever I have gone...I love you and I will find my way back to you...

Acknowledgements

There is absolutely no way Shadows Ascend could have happened without my incredibly talented cousin, friend, and editor Sarah. From the title, to stubborn chapters, to my refusal to work on my formal sentence structures, she stuck through it all even while her life changed drastically in the process. I hope she knows just how much I am grateful and blessed to have her in my corner, making my dreams come true.

A secondary heartfelt thank you goes to my steady pillar in life, my husband, who even while I am writing this made sure our family was taken care of and that the house didn't explode. He spent many nights battling my imposter syndrome, drying my tears, reading my snippets, and helping me creatively with Shadows Ascend. The territory of wrath will forever be dedicated to him.

Lastly, I would be remiss not to shower every bit of gratitude and love I have to my Archiver Street Team: Lucy, Elisabetta, Megan, and Ali. I am not entirely sure I would have continued this dream of mine without their utter enthusiasm and love for my stories. I don't know if there is anyone that loves these characters more than they do...besides me of course! What they say is true. When you find your readers...goddess there is nothing like it.

ABOUT THE AUTHOR

B. K. Cavaleri is a dreamer living in Michigan with her husband and two rainbow baby boys. She works as a doctor of physical therapy by day and a writer by night...that's her moonlit vibe when the babies are sound asleep in their beds and hubby is entranced by The Office reruns. It's during that time she gets to dream amongst the stars and make it come to life on paper. It seemed a shame to keep it all to herself, and her characters are much too loud, so she

has decided to step out of the shadows and release her stories to the world. Thank you for joining her on this journey.
Want more?
You can visit here and subscribe to be an ARCHIVER for monthly newsletters!
https://www.bkcavaleri.com/
or on social, DM's are always open!
https://www.instagram.com/cavaleri.archive.author/

The Archive Universe

<u>Remnant Archives</u>

Shadows Lost
Shadows Ascend
Shadows of Air and Earth
Shadows Eternal (Coming Soon)

www.ingramcontent.com/pod-product-compliance
Lightning Source LLC
Chambersburg PA
CBHW022019300726
48970CB00003B/965